THE VERY BEST OF BARRY N. MALZBERG

Introduction by Joe Wrzos

Nonstop Press · New York

The Very Best of Barry N. Malzberg

Nonstop Press books may be purchased for educational, business, or sales promotional use. For information: nonstop@nonstoppress.com
114 John St., #981, New York, NY, USA 10272

Nonstop Press editor and book designer: Luis Ortiz • Production by Nonstop Ink

ISBN 978-1-933065-41-0 Trade Paper

PRINTED IN THE UNITED STATES OF AMERICA

www.nonstoppress.com

 Nonstop Press

Contents

Introduction

THE FIRST time I met Barry Malzberg was in New York City at the 1976 Lunacon, held that year to honor the 50th Anniversary of *Amazing Stories*, the world's first all-science fiction magazine, for which both of us had served as editors. And, like any one of the many bright-eyed fans milling about — the very first thing he did, after posing us politely, was to snap a memento photo (the pre-cellphone kind, of course) of my wife, my two sons, and myself. Tall, dark-haired, lean of build, even gracious, not only didn't he look like the enfant terrible then being critically excoriated for his iconoclastic novel *Beyond Apollo* (winner of the 1973 John W. Campbell Memorial Award) or "A Galaxy Called Rome," an ingenious exercise in "recursive" sf writing (science fiction about science fiction itself!), but he certainly didn't behave like one. Far from it. So much for the almost universal tendency to judge an author by the color of his writing.

Ironically enough, Malzberg never intended to be a science fiction writer in the first place. True, as an urchin growing up in Brooklyn, he had discovered some pretty good storytelling in both *Galaxy* and *Astounding*. But in that period, sniffy mainstream critics still tended to ignore the genre, as did most aloof academics as well. So, older and wiser, he cannily earned his B.A. at Syracuse University, supplementing it with a year as a Shubert Foundation Playwright Fellow. After which — now apparently fiercely ambitious — he set his literary sights higher than genre level, aiming his early plays and stories at loftier markets. The plays, hopefully, at Broadway (or at least Off-Broadway); the fiction, first at the literary quarterlies, and, then at the more upscale (and better-paying) slicks like *Esquire* and *The Atlantic*. He probably also tried some of the more prestigious book publishers like

Random House, but there too the results were not encouraging. Fittingly, though, in 1973, less than a decade later, after he had achieved a measure of success in the sf field, Random House itself came calling, now eager to publish Malzberg's prescient *Beyond Apollo*, his risky taboo-shattering challenge to the basic premise and gung ho spirit of NASA's military–industrial, manned space program. And this, at a time when most of us were still basking vicariously in the afterglow of those exhilarating 1969 TV transmissions showing a space-suited Neil Armstrong ever so tentatively planting his historic out-sized boot prints on the powdery surface of the Moon, the first Earthling to do so (and an American, too!).

But before *Beyond Apollo* stirred up all that critical dust, Malzberg had already begun to make a notable, if limited, impact on the science fiction field with "We're Coming Through the Window" (*Galaxy*, August 1967). The hilarious short-short about a hapless two-bit inventor, who concocts a homemade time machine but somehow manages (it's a question of faulty calibrators, you see) to inundate his cramped little apartment with hundreds of replicas of himself, each of whom, desperately striving to rectify the situation, only makes things worse! Malzberg followed this promising debut with "Final War" (*The Magazine of Fantasy & Science Fiction*, April, 1968), which he himself has capsulized as being "about an endless war in an ambiguous time fought for no reason." Exceedingly well written, exhibiting many of the skills he'd already honed before entering the sf field, this relentless indictment of all-out absurdist conflict could well have been snapped up — had they been given first look — by any of the top literary quarterlies or slicks of that period. But, fortunately, science fiction, as it sometimes does, got there first.

Oddly enough (perhaps due to some conflict of interest), Malzberg's early science fiction — including "Coming Through the Window" and "Final War" — wasn't written under his own name, but as by "K.M. O'Donnell" (a "cover" he later discarded). The pseudonym was Malzberg's oblique way of expressing fealty to pioneering sf writers Henry Kuttner and C.L. Moore ("Lawrence O'Donnell" being one of their many joint pen names), whose masterfully original, elegantly crafted stories (especially those published during the 1940s) were, and have continued to be, a major if only indirect influence on almost every important sf writer since that time. Including Malzberg himself, who has often acknowledged his debt to Kuttner-Moore's writings in general, and (I suspect) has also been deeply influenced, in particular, by their brilliantly revisionist novella, "Vintage Season" (*Astounding Science Fiction*, September, 1946), which with one masterly stroke changed the way "serious" sf writers (like Robert A. Heinlein, Jack Vance, and Robert Silverberg) would thenceforth handle the well-worn time travel theme.

With "Vintage Season," Kuttner-Moore stripped the apparently exhausted time travel theme of all its outdated baggage, changing the perspective, giving the story a dark and decadent tone, one that makes its impact indelible. For instead of time travelers from the future (whether near or far distant) dropping into the present for the usual reasons — a bit of research, to profit, escape future justice, and often to try, usually futilely, to tamper with the Time Line — the story's decadent party of tourists has made the journey solely for the thrill of being able to watch (up close and always at a safe distance) the utter destruction of a tranquil 1940s San

Francisco as it is being suddenly destroyed by a giant meteor strike snuffing out the life of every one of its sleeping inhabitants. As to what kind of perverted future society could have spawned such corrupt vacationers, the story's only clue is a subtle hint that in "their" stagnant culture, notions of a free society have long ago been displaced by some kind of corrupt monarchy sustained by super-technology, one indulging the depraved tastes of its privileged classes. And this is precisely the kind of unflinchingly dour viewpoint, with present-day civilization possibly heading for decline, which Malzberg himself (skeptical about our own chances) sometimes adopts (at least in his fiction), as, for example, he so pyrotechnically does in "The Lady Louisiana Toy" (1993), a riff on Alfred Bester's *The Stars My Destination* (1956), in the marvelous virtual crucifixion novella "Le Croix" (1980), and no doubt elsewhere.

The question of influences aside, in the science fiction field alone, ever since the 1960s (and at a consistently high level), Malzberg has been remarkably prolific, writing more than 200 stories, 30 novels, a plethora of essays, numerous articles, reviews, and introductions, besides somehow finding time to edit magazines like *Amazing Stories* and *Fantastic*, as well as almost a dozen genre anthologies. The range of his many subjects (in works both short and long) has also been richly diversified, including satiric scrutiny of the subtler perils of space travel, the insanity of warfare, the paradoxes of time travel, extrapolated urban nightmares, and a particularly ingenious series of "What if?" stories depicting what else might have happened at pivotal moments in the lives of famous poets, writers, composers, and heads of state. Like President John F. Kennedy, for instance, one of the author's favorite topics, whose bloody assassination in 1963 seems to have become almost an obsession with Malzberg.

But despite all the rich diversity of Malzberg's writings, his future status as an important literary figure (he long ago transcended the science fiction field, lifting the genre along with him as he did so) may not rest solely on his anti-manned-space flight warnings fiction. Most controversially on *Beyond Apollo* (whose initial impact, after subsequent limited vindication, has begun to fade), or on his unsettling recursive stories like *Herovit's World* (1973), exposing the often spirit-crushing cost of dedicating one's life to writing science fiction as a full-time career. Especially not advisable these days, at a time of low-circulation sf print magazines and the ever escalating digital ingestion not only of science fiction itself but of everything else into Singularity's all-consuming Internet.

Nevertheless, as is generally the case, time's weeding out forces — a consequence of changing critical standards, shifting popular tastes, and evolving cultural concerns — will inevitably determine "which" of Malzberg's sf and non-genre writings will survive. And though there are many candidates, I, for one, feel pretty certain that among them will be the choicest of his Alternate Writers & Co. series, the best of the Alternate Kennedy stories, and — they're too good to fade from sight! — his meldings (as, for example, in "Le Croix" and "Quartermain,") of dystopian, time travel, and religious ecstasy themes.

In the Alternate Writers & Co. category, first place should probably go to Malzberg's unjustly neglected major work, *The Remaking Of Sigmund Freud* (1985). In one of whose most delightful episodes, "Emily Dickinson Saved from

Drowning," the reclusive Belle of Amherst poetess is mischievously depicted as "selling out" to the masses, writing down for profit, and even touring the country for cash (stopping off in St. Louis, Missouri, for a brief but heated affair with a surprisingly "needy" Mark Twain). Only to end up perplexed and dismayed by a denunciatory letter she receives from Good Gray poet Walt Whitman, who, not deigning to mince words, roundly berates her for debasing her talent.

As for the very best in the Alternate Kennedy series, clearly one of the chief contenders would be "In the Stone House" (1992), Malzberg's unstinting portrait, etched in acid, of the decline of a flawed political dynasty. In this particular variant, young Joseph Kennedy, Jr., doesn't die in the war but returns safely, only to be forced by his father, Joseph, Sr., (and ahead of his younger brother Jack) to seek the Presidency. However, once in office, Joe, Jr. fails to measure up to his pater's cynically corrupt expectations, the latter then seeing to it that his recalcitrant son isn't reelected. In reprisal, and after Jack replaces him in the White House, the enraged ex-President (an excellent Veteran rifle marksman), secretes himself in the Dallas Texas Book Depository building and, waiting for his kid brother's glistening motorcade to come in range, gets all set to put a bloody end to the odious Camelot story for good!

For the third category of Malzberg science fiction likely to hang on, sf stories with a religious theme, I have a hunch that "Quartermain" (1985) has the best chance of besting the competition (few in number as they may be in this subgenre). Narrated by the titular character, it graphically recounts his daring attempt to "escape" from a hellish 22nd Century existence as a mere "cog" in a technologically advanced, dystopian society. One controlled by cynical Administrators craftily manipulating the restless populace with "escape outlets" like the Lotteries, the Slaughter Docks, and, for those potentially seditious, like Quartermain, "replication" tests (actually scams), the passing of which could presumably lead to social advancement. Hoping to become a cult religious leader (and benefit from all the perks), Quartermain undergoes a harrowing simulation as Christ, resisting all manner of temptation, but despite all his suffering, the duplicitous test givers callously welch on the terms of agreement. The ironic moral of the story? "In the twenty-second century you can't take anything seriously." And if one acceptable definition of a classic story (of any type) is that with each rereading, it somehow glows brighter in memory, and in apprehension, then I'd say that Malzberg's "Quartermain" fully qualifies.

A footnote. On how favorite writers, like Malzberg, can get under one's skin. Once, I had a dream — I can't seem to shake it — in which, inexplicably, I suddenly was reading a sleazy digest-sized magazine, a little fuzzy-looking in the dream, but I could still make out, quite clearly, that the contents page listed an "Alternate Malzberg" story, evidently the work of some envious rival. The burden of which seemed to be that early in his struggling career, the young Malzberg did go to grad school, did qualify and win that associate professorship at Extension U. (See Malzberg's "The Shores of Suitability" which is included in this collection.) However, as an unintended consequence, he never did get to write the wonderful and controversial stories for which (in another reality) he'd become famous, or, depending upon one's point of view, infamous. Stunned by this invidious "dream narrative," I angrily shook myself awake, discovered that I was in a cold sweat, and, a trifle vexed, realized that it had only been my old unpredictable Id toying with me again. But then I remembered that in "my" reality, Malzberg had never sold out for a college professor's subsistence level life, that he actually did get to write all those classic stories he dreamed of writing. And, calming down even more, I also, tangentially, recalled my first meeting with the author, at that 1976 Lunacon so long ago, where, happily he snapped pictures of selected celebrities and sundry. Which unfaded recollection, still green in memory, makes me wonder now: Whatever happened to those snapshots he took of me, my wife, and my kids?

Joe Wrzos
Saddle River, NJ

A Galaxy Called Rome

I

THIS IS NOT a novelette but a series of notes. The novelette cannot be truly written because it partakes of its time, which is distant and could be perceived only through the idiom and devices of that era.

Thus the piece, by virtue of these reasons and others too personal even for this variety of True Confession, is little more than a set of constructions toward something less substantial ... and, like the author, it cannot be completed.

II

The novelette would lean heavily upon two articles by the late John Campbell, for thirty-three years the editor of *Astounding/Analog*, which were written shortly before his untimely death on July 11, 1971, and appeared as editorials in his magazine later that year, the second being perhaps the last piece which will ever bear his byline. They imagine a black galaxy which would result from the implosion of a neutron star, an implosion so mighty that gravitational forces unleashed would contain not only light itself but space and time; and *A Galaxy Called Rome* is his title, not mine, since he envisions a spacecraft that might be trapped within such a black galaxy and be unable to get out ... because escape velocity would have to exceed the speed of light. All paths of travel would lead to this galaxy, then, none away. A galaxy called Rome.

III

Conceive then of a faster-than-light spaceship which would tumble into the black galaxy and would be unable to leave. Tumbling would be easy, or at least inevitable, since one of the characteristics of the black galaxy would be its *invisibility*, and there the ship would be. The story would then pivot on the efforts of the crew to get out. The ship is named *Skipstone*. It was completed in 3892. Five hundred people died so that it might fly, but in this age life is held even more cheaply than it is today.

Left to my own devices, I might be less interested in the escape problem than that of adjustment. Light housekeeping in an anterior sector of the universe; submission to the elements, a fine, ironic literary despair. This is not science fiction however. Science fiction was created by Hugo Gernsback to show us the ways out of technological impasse. So be it.

IV

As interesting as the material was, I quailed even at this series of notes, let alone a polished, completed work. My personal life is my black hole, I felt like pointing out (who would listen?); my daughters provide more correct and sticky implosion than any neutron star, and the sound of the pulsars is as nothing to the music of the paddock area at Aqueduct racetrack in Ozone Park, Queens, on a clear summer Tuesday. "Enough of these breathtaking concepts, infinite distances, quasar leaps, binding messages amidst the arms of the spiral nebula," I could have pointed out. "I know that there are those who find an ultimate truth there, but I am not one of them. I would rather dedicate the years of life remaining (my melodramatic streak) to an understanding of the agonies of this middle-class town in northern New Jersey; until I can deal with those, how can I comprehend Ridgefield Park, to say nothing of the extension of fission to include progressively, heavier gases?" Indeed, I almost abided to this until it occurred to me that Ridgefield Park would forever be as mysterious as the stars and that one could not deny infinity merely to pursue a particular that would be impenetrable until the day of one's death.

So I decided to try the novelette, at least as this series of notes, although with some trepidation, but trepidation did not unsettle me, nor did I grieve, for my life is merely a set of notes for a life, and Ridgefield Park merely a rough working model of Trenton, in which, nevertheless, several thousand people live who cannot discern their right hands from their left, and also much cattle.

V

It is 3895. The spacecraft *Skipstone*, on an exploratory flight through the major and minor galaxies surrounding the Milky Way, falls into the black galaxy of a neutron star and is lost forever.

The captain of this ship, the only living consciousness of it, is its commander, Lena Thomas. True, the hold of the ship carries five hundred and fifteen of the dead sealed in gelatinous fix who will absorb unshielded gamma rays. True, these rays will at some time in the future hasten their reconstitution. True, again, that another part of the hold contains the prosthesis of seven skilled engineers, male and female, who could be switched on at only slight inconvenience and would provide Lena not only with answers to any technical problems which would arise but with companionship to while away the long and grave hours of the *Skipstone's* flight.

Lena, however, does not use the prosthesis, nor does she feel the necessity to. She is highly skilled and competent, at least in relation to the routine tasks of this testing flight, and she feels that to call for outside help would only be an admission of weakness, would be reported back to the Bureau and lessen her potential for promotion. (She is right; the Bureau has monitored every cubicle of this ship, both visually and biologically; she can see or do nothing which does not trace to a printout; they would not think well of her if she was dependent upon outside assistance.) Toward the embalmed she feels somewhat more. Her condition rattling in the hold of the ship as it moves on tachyonic drive seems to approximate theirs; although they are deprived of consciousness, that quality seems to be almost irrelevant to the condition of hyperspace, and if there were any way that she could bridge their mystery, she might well address them. As it is, she must settle for imaginary dialogues and for long, quiescent periods when she will watch the monitors, watch the rainbow of hyperspace, the collision of the spectrum, and say nothing whatsoever.

Saying nothing will not do, however, and the fact is that Lena talks incessantly at times, if only to herself. This is good because the story should have much dialogue; dramatic incident is best impelled through straightforward characterization, and Lena's compulsive need, now and then, to state her condition and its relation to the spaces she occupies will satisfy this need.

In her conversation, of course, she often addresses the embalmed. "Consider," she says to them, some of them dead eight hundred years, others dead weeks, all of them stacked in the hold in relation to their status in life and their ability to hoard assets to pay for the process that will return them their lives, "Consider what's going on here," pointing through the hold, the colors gleaming through the portholes onto her wrist, colors dancing in the air, her eyes quite full and maddened in this light, which does not indicate that she is mad but only that the condition of hyperspace itself is insane, the Michelson–Morley effect having a psychological as well as physical reality here. "Why it could be *me* dead and in the hold and all of you here in the dock watching the colors spin, it's all the same, all the same faster than light," and indeed the twisting and sliding effects of the tachyonic drive are such that at the moment of speech what Lena says is true.

The dead live; the living are dead, all slide and become jumbled together as she has noted; and were it not that their objective poles of consciousness were fixed by years of training and discipline, just as hers are transfixed by a different kind of training and discipline, she would press the levers to eject the dead one-by-one into the larger coffin of space, something which is indicated only as an emergency procedure under the gravest of terms and which would result in her removal from the Bureau immediately upon her return. The dead are precious cargo; they are, in essence, paying for the experiments and must be handled with the greatest delicacy. "I will handle you with the greatest delicacy," Lena says in hyperspace, "and I will never let you go, little packages in my little prison," and so on, singing and chanting as the ship moves on somewhat in excess of one million miles per second, always accelerating; and yet, except for the colors, the nausea, the disorienting swing, her own mounting insanity, the terms of this story, she might be in the IRT Lenox Avenue local at rush hour, moving slowly uptown as circles of illness move through the fainting car in the bowels of summer.

VI

She is twenty-eight years old. Almost two hundred years in the future, when man has established colonies on forty planets in the Milky Way, has fully populated the solar system, is working in the faster-than-light experiments as quickly as he can to move through other galaxies, the medical science of that day is not notably superior to that of our own, and the human lifespan has not been significantly extended, nor have the diseases of mankind which are now known as congenital been eradicated. Most of the embalmed were in their eighties or nineties; a few of them, the more recent deaths, were nearly a hundred, but the average lifespan still hangs somewhat short of eighty, and most of these have died from cancer, heart attacks, renal failure, cerebral blowout, and the like. There is some irony in the fact that man can have at least established a toehold in his galaxy, can have solved the mysteries of the FTL drive, and yet finds the fact of his own biology as stupefying as he has throughout history, but every sociologist understands that those who live in a culture are least qualified to criticize it (because they have fully assimilated the codes of the culture, even as to criticism), and Lena does not see this irony any more than the reader will have to in order to appreciate the deeper and more metaphysical irony of the story, which is this: that greater speed, greater space, greater progress, greater sensation has not resulted in any definable expansion of the limits of consciousness and personality and all that the FTL drive is to Lena is an increasing entrapment.

It is important to understand that she is merely a technician; that although she is highly skilled and has been trained through the Bureau for many years for her job as pilot, she really does not need to possess the technical knowledge of any graduate scientists of our own time … that her job, which is essentially a probe-and-ferrying, could be done by an adolescent; and that all of her training has afforded her no protection against the boredom and depression of her, assignment.

When she is done with this latest probe, she will return to Uranus and be granted a six-month leave. She is looking forward to that. She appreciates the opportunity. She is only twenty-eight, and she is tired of being sent with the dead to tumble through the spectrum for weeks at a time, and what she would very much like to be, at least for a while, is a young woman. She would like to be at peace. She would like to be loved. She would like to have sex.

VII

Something must be made of the element of sex in this story, if only because it deals with a female protagonist (where asepsis will not work); and in the tradition of modern literary science fiction, where some credence is given to the whole range of human needs and behaviors, it would be clumsy and amateurish to ignore the issue. Certainly the easy scenes can be written and to great effect: Lena masturbating as she stares through the port at the colored levels of hyperspace; Lena dreaming thickly of intercourse as she unconsciously massages her nipples, the ship plunging deeper and deeper (as she does not yet know) toward the Black Galaxy; the Black Galaxy itself as some ultimate vaginal symbol of absorption whose Freudian overcast will not be ignored in the imagery of this story … indeed, one can envision Lena stumbling toward the Evictors at the depths of her panic in the Black Galaxy to bring out one of the embalmed, her grim and necrophiliac fantasies as the body is slowly moved upwards on its glistening slab, the way that her eyes will look as she comes to consciousness and realizes what she has become … oh, this would be a very powerful scene indeed, almost anything to do with sex in space is powerful (one must also conjure with the effects of hyperspace upon the orgasm; would it be the orgasm which all of us know and love so well or something entirely different, perhaps detumescence, perhaps exaltation!), and I would face the issue squarely, if only I could, and in line with the very real need of the story to have powerful and effective dialogue.

"For God's sake," Lena would say at the end, the music of her entrapment squeezing her, coming over her, blotting her toward extinction, "for God's sake, all we ever needed was a screw, that's all that sent us out into space, that's all that it ever meant to us, I've got to have it, got to have it, do you understand?" jamming her fingers in and out of her aqueous surfaces

—But of course this would not work, at least in the story which I am trying to conceptualize. Space is aseptic; that is the secret of science fiction for forty-five years; it is not deceit or its adolescent audience or the publication codes which have deprived most of the literature of the range of human sexuality but the fact that in the clean and abysmal spaces between the stars sex, that demonstration of our perverse and irreplaceable humanity, would have no role at all. Not for nothing did the astronauts return to tell us their vision of otherworldliness, not for nothing did they stagger in their thick landing gear as they walked toward the colonels' salute, not for nothing did all of those marriages, all of those wonderful kids undergo such terrible strains. There is simply no room for it. It does not fit. Lena would understand this. "I never thought of sex," she would say, "never thought of it once, not even at the end when everything was around me and I was dancing."

VIII

Therefore it will be necessary to characterize Lena in some other way, and that opportunity will only come through the moment of crisis, the moment at which the *Skipstone* is drawn into the Black Galaxy of the neutron star. This moment will occur fairly early into the story, perhaps five or six hundred words deep (her previous life on the ship and impressions of hyperspace will come in expository chunks interwoven between sections of ongoing action), and her only indication of what has happened will be when there is a deep, lurching shiver in the gut of the ship where the embalmed lay and then she feels herself falling.

To explain this sensation it is important to explain normal hyperspace, the skip-drive which is merely to draw the curtains and to be in a cubicle. There is no sensation of motion in hyperspace, there could not be, the drive taking the *Skipstone* past any concepts of sound or light and into an area where there is no language to encompass nor glands to register. Were she to draw the curtains (curiously similar in their frills and pastels to what we might see hanging today in lower-middle-class homes of the kind I inhabit), she would be deprived of any sensation, but of course she cannot; she must open them to the portholes, and through them she can see the song of the colors to which I have previously alluded. Inside, there is a deep and grievous wretchedness, a feeling of terrible loss (which may explain why Lena thinks of exhuming the dead) that may be ascribed to the effects of hyperspace upon the corpus; but these sensations can be shielded, are not visible from the outside, and can be completely controlled by the phlegmatic types who comprise most of the pilots of these experimental flights. (Lena is rather phlegmatic herself. She reacts more to stress than some of her counterparts but well within the normal range prescribed by the Bureau, which admittedly does a superficial check.)

The effects of falling into the Black Galaxy are entirely different, however, and it is here where Lena's emotional equipment becomes completely unstuck.

IX

At this point in the story great gobs of physics, astronomical and mathematical data would have to be incorporated, hopefully in a way which would furnish the hard-science basis of the story without repelling the reader.

Of course one should not worry so much about the repulsion of the reader; most who read science fiction do so in pursuit of exactly this kind of hard speculation (most often they are disappointed, but then most often they are after a time unable to tell the difference), and they would sit still much longer for a lecture than would, say, readers of the fictions of John Cheever, who could hardly bear sociological diatribes wedged into the everlasting vision of Gehenna which is Cheever's gift to his admirers. Thus it would be possible without awkwardness to make the following facts known, and these facts could indeed be set off from the body of the story and simply told like this: It is posited that in other galaxies there are neutron stars, stars of four or five hundred times the size of out own or "normal" suns, which in their continuing nuclear process, burning and burning to maintain their light, will collapse in a mere ten to fifteen thousand years of difficult existence, their hydrogen fusing to helium then nitrogen and then to even heavier elements until with an implosion of terrific force, hungering for power which is no longer there, they collapse upon one another and bring disaster. Disaster not only to themselves but possibly to the entire galaxy which they inhabit, for the gravitational force created by the implosion would be so vast as to literally seal in light. Not only light but sound and properties of all the stars in that great tube of force ... so that the galaxy itself would be sucked into the funnel of gravitation created by the collapse and be absorbed into the flickering and desperate heart of the extinguished star.

It is possible to make several extrapolations from the fact of the neutron stars—and of the neutron stars themselves we have no doubt; many nova and supernova are now known to have been created by exactly this effect, not *ex* — but *im*-plosion — and some of them are these:

(a) The gravitational forces created, like great spokes wheeling out from the star, would drag in all parts of the galaxy within their compass; and because of the force of that gravitation, the galaxy would be invisible ... these forces would, as has been said, literally contain light.

(b) The neutron star, functioning like a cosmic vacuum cleaner, might literally destroy the universe. Indeed, the universe may be in the slow process at this moment of being destroyed as hundreds of millions of its suns and planets are being inexorably drawn toward these great vortexes. The process would be slow, of course, but it is seemingly inexorable. One neutron star, theoretically, could absorb the universe. There are many more than one.

(c) The universe may have, obversely, been *created* by such an implosion, throwing out enormous cosmic filaments that, in a flickering instant of time which is as eons to us but an instant to the cosmologists, are now being drawn back in. The universe may be an accident.

(d) Cosmology aside, a ship trapped in such a vortex, such a "black," or invisible, galaxy, drawn toward the deadly source of the neutron star, would be unable to leave it through normal faster-than-light drive ... because the gravitation would absorb light, it would be impossible to build up any level of acceleration (which would at some point not exceed the speed of light) to permit escape. If it was possible to emerge from the field, it could only be done by an immediate switch to tachyonic drive without accelerative buildup ... a process which could drive the occupant insane and which would, in any case, have no clear destination. The black hole of the dead star is a literal vacuum in space ... one could fall through the hole, but where, then, would one go?

(e) The actual process of being in the field of the dead star might well drive one insane.

For all of these reasons Lena does not know that she has fallen into the Galaxy Called Rome until the ship simply does so.

And she would instantly and irreparably become insane.

X

The technological data having been stated, the crisis of the story—the collapse into the Galaxy—having occurred early on, it would now be the obligation of the writer to describe the actual sensations involved in falling into the Black

Galaxy. Since little or nothing is known of what these sensations would be other than that it is clear that the gravitation would suspend almost all physical laws and might well suspend time itself, time only being a function of physics it would be easy to lurch into a surrealistic mode here; Lena could see monsters slithering on the walls, two-dimensional monsters that is, little cut-outs of her past; she could re-enact her life *in full consciousness* from birth until death; she could literally be turned inside-out anatomically and perform in her imagination or in the flesh gross physical acts upon herself; she could live and die a thousand times in the lightless, timeless expanse of the pit … all of this could be done within the confines of the story, and it would doubtless lead to some very powerful material. One could do it picaresque fashion, one perversity or lunacy to a chapter—that is to say, the chapters spliced together with more data on the gravitational excesses and the fact that neutron stars (this is interesting) are probably the pulsars which we have identified, stars which can be detected through sound but not by sight from unimaginable distances. The author could do this kind of thing, and do it very well indeed; he has done it literally hundreds of times before, but this, perhaps, would be in disregard of Lena.

She has needs more imperative than those of the author, or even those of the editors. She is in terrible pain. She is suffering.

Falling, she sees the dead; falling, she hears the dead; the dead address her from the hold, and they are screaming, "Release us, release us, we are alive, we are in pain, we are in torment"; in their gelatinous flux, their distended limbs sutured finger and toe to the membranes which hold them, their decay has been reversed as the warp into which they have fallen has reversed time; and they are begging Lena from a torment which they cannot phrase, so profound is it; their voices are in her head, pealing and banging like oddly shaped bells. "Release us!" they scream, "we are no longer dead, the trumpet has sounded!" and so on and so forth, but Lena literally does not know what to do. She is merely the ferryman on this dread passage; she is not a medical specialist; she knows nothing of prophylaxis or restoration, and any movement she made to release them from the gelatin which holds them would surely destroy their biology, no matter what the state of their minds.

But even if this were not so, even if she could by releasing them give them peace, she cannot because she is succumbing to her own responses. In the black hole, if the dead are risen, then the risen are certainly the dead; she dies in this space, Lena does; she dies a thousand times over a period of seventy thousand years (because there is no objective time here, chronology is controlled only by the psyche, and Lena has a thousand full lives and a thousand full deaths), and it is terrible, of course, but it is also interesting because for *every* cycle of death there is a life, seventy years in which she can meditate upon her condition in solitude; and by the two hundredth year or more (or less, each of the lives is individual, some of them long, others short), Lena has come to an understanding of exactly where she is and what has happened to her. That it has taken her fourteen thousand years to reach this understanding is in one way incredible, and yet it is a land of miracle as well because in an infinite universe with infinite possibilities, all of them reconstituted for her, it is highly unlikely that even in fourteen thousand years she would stumble upon the answer, had it not been for the fact that she is unusually strong-willed and that some of the personalities through which she has lived are highly creative and controlled and have been able to do some serious thinking. Also there is a carry-over from life to life, even with the differing personalities, so that she is able to make use of preceding knowledge.

Most of the personalities are weak, of course, and not a few are insane, and almost all are cowardly, but there is a little residue; even in the worst of them there is enough residue to carry forth the knowledge, and so it is in the fourteen-thousandth year, when the truth of it has finally come upon her and she realizes what has happened to her and what is going on and what she must do to get out of there, and so it is [then] that she summons all of the strength and win which are left to her, and stumbling to the console (she is in her sixty-eighth year of this life and in the personality of an old, sniveling, whining man, an ex-ferryman himself), she summons one of the prostheses, the master engineer, the controller. All of this time the dead have been shrieking and clanging in her ears, fourteen thousand years of agony billowing from the hold and surrounding her in sheets like iron; and as the master engineer, exactly as he was when she last saw him fourteen thousand years and two weeks ago, emerges from the console, the machinery whirring slickly, she gasps in relief, too weak even to respond with pleasure to the fact that in this condition of antitime, antilight, anticausality the machinery still works. But then it would. The machinery always works, even in this final and most terrible of all the hard-science stories. It is not the machinery which fails but its operators or, in extreme cases, the cosmos.

"What's the matter?" the master engineer says.

The stupidity of this question, its naiveté and irrelevance in the midst of the hell she has occupied, stuns Lena, but she realizes even through the haze that the master engineer would, of course, come without memory of circumstances and would have to be apprised of background. This is inevitable. Whining and snivel-ing, she tells him in her old man's voice what has happened.

"Why that's terrible!" the master engineer says. "That's really terrible," and lumbering to a porthole, he looks out at the Black Galaxy, the Galaxy Called Rome, and one look at it causes him to lock into position and then disintegrate, not because the machinery has failed (the machinery never fails, not ultimately) but because it has merely recreated a human substance which could not possibly come to grips with what has been seen outside that porthole.

Lena is left alone again, then, with the shouts of the dead carrying forward.

Realizing instantly what has happened to her fourteen thousand years of perception can lead to a quicker reaction time, if nothing else — she addresses the console again, uses the switches and produces three more prostheses, all of them engineers barely subsidiary to the one she has already addressed. (Their resem-blance to the three comforters of Job will not be ignored here, and there will be an opportunity to squeeze in some quick religious allegory, which is always useful to give an ambitious story yet another level of meaning.) Although they are not quite as qualified or definitive in their opinions as the original engineer, they are bright enough by far to absorb her explanation, and, this time, her warnings not to go to the portholes, not to look upon the galaxy, are heeded. Instead, they stand there in rigid and curiously mortified postures, as if waiting for Lena to speak.

"So you see," she says finally, as if concluding a long and difficult conversation, which in fact she has, "as far as I can see, the only way to get out of this black galaxy is to go directly into tachyonic drive. Without any accelerative buildup at all."

The three comforters nod slowly, bleakly. They do not quite know what she is talking about, but then again, they have not had fourteen thousand years to ponder this point. "Unless you can see anything else," Lena says, "unless you can think of anything different. Otherwise, it's going to be infinity in here, and I can't take much more of this, really. Fourteen thousand years is enough."

"Perhaps," the first comforter suggests softly, "perhaps it is your fate and your destiny to spend infinity in this black hole. Perhaps in some way you are determining the fate of the universe. After all, it was you who said that it all might be a gigantic accident, eh? Perhaps your suffering gives it purpose."

"And then too," the second lisps, "you've got to consider the dead down there. This isn't very easy for them, you know, what with being jolted alive and all that, and an immediate vault into tachyonic would probably destroy them for good. The Bureau wouldn't like that, and you'd be liable for some pretty stiff damages. No, if I were you I'd stay with the dead," the second concludes, and a clamorous murmur seems to arise from the hold at this, although whether it is one of approval or of terrible pain is difficult to tell. The dead are not very expressive.

"Anyway," the third says, brushing a forelock out of his eyes, averting his glance from the omnipresent and dreadful portholes, "there's little enough to be done about this situation. You've fallen into a neutron star, a black funnel. It is utterly beyond the puny capacities and possibilities of man. I'd accept my fate if I were you." His model was a senior scientist working on quasar theory, but in reality he appears to be a metaphysician. "There are comers of experience into which man cannot stray without being severely penalized."

"That's very easy for you to say," Lena says bitterly, her whine breaking into clear glissando, "but you haven't suffered as I have. Also, there's at least a theoretical possibility that I'll get out of here if I do the build-up without acceleration."

"But where will you land?" The third says, waving a trembling forefinger. "And when? All rules of space and time have been destroyed here; only gravity persists. You can fall through the center of this sun, but you do not know where you will come out or at what period of time. It is inconceivable that you would emerge into normal space in the time you think of as contemporary."

"No," the second says, "I wouldn't do that. You and the dead are joined together now; it is truly your fate to remain with them. What is death? What is life? In the Galaxy Called Rome all roads lead to the same, you see; you have ample time to consider these questions, and I'm sure that you will come up with something truly viable, of much interest."

"Ah, well," the first says, looking at Lena, "if you must know, I think that it would be much nobler of you to remain here; for all we know, your condition gives substance and viability to the universe. Perhaps you *are* the universe. But you're not going to listen anyway, and so I won't argue the point. I really won't," he says rather petulantly and then makes a gesture to the other two; the three of them quite deliberately march to a porthole, push a curtain aside and look out upon it. Before Lena can stop them—not that she is sure she would, not that she is sure that this is not exactly what she has willed—they have been reduced to ash. And she is left alone with the screams of the dead.

XI

It can be seen that the satiric aspects of the scene above can be milked for great implication, and unless a very skillful controlling hand is kept upon the material, the piece could easily degenerate into farce at this moment. It is possible, as almost any comedian knows, to reduce (or elevate) the starkest and most terrible issues to scatology or farce simply by particularizing them; and it will be hard not to use this scene for a kind of needed comic relief in what is, after all, an extremely depressing tale, the more depressing because it has used the largest possible canvas on which to imprint its messages that man is irretrievably dwarfed by the cosmos. (At least, that is the message which it would be easiest to wring out of the material; actually I have other things in mind, but how many will be able to detect them?)

What will save the scene and the story itself, around this point will be the lush physical descriptions of the Black Galaxy, the neutron star, the altering effects they have had upon perceived reality. Every rhetorical trick, every typographical device, every nuance of language and memory which the writer has to call upon will be utilized in this section describing the appearance of the black hole and its effects upon Lena's (admittedly distorted) consciousness. It will be a bleak vision, of course, but not necessarily a hopeless one; it will demonstrate that our concepts of "beauty" or "ugliness" or "evil" or "good" or "love" or "death" are little more than metaphors, semantically limited, framed in by the poor receiving equipment in our heads; and it will be suggested that, rather than showing us a different or alternative reality, the black hole may only be showing us the only reality we know, but extended, infinitely extended so that the story may give us, as good science fiction often does, at this point some glimpse of possibilities beyond ourselves, possibilities not to be contained in word rates or the problems of editorial qualification. And also at this point of the story it might be worthwhile to characterize Lena in a "warmer" or more "sympathetic" fashion so that the reader can see her as a distinct and admirable human being, quite plucky in the face of all her disasters and fourteen thousand years, two hundred lives. This can be done through conventional fictional technique: individuation through defining idiosyncrasy, tricks of speech, habits, mannerisms, and so on. In common everyday fiction we could give her an affecting stutter, a dimple on her left breast, a love of policemen, fear of red convertibles, and leave it at that; in this story, because of its considerably extended theme, it will be necessary to do better than that, to find originalities of idiosyncrasy which will, in their wonder and suggestion of panoramic possibility, approximate the black hole ... but no matter. No matter. This can be done; the section interweaving Lena and her vision of the black hole will be the flashiest and most admired but in truth the easiest section of the story to write, and I am sure that I would have no trouble with it whatsoever if, as I said much earlier, this were a story instead of a series of notes for a story, the story itself being unutterably beyond our time and space and devices and to be glimpsed only in empty little flickers of light much as Lena can glimpse the black hole, much as she knows the gravity of the neutron star. These notes are as close to the vision of the story as Lena herself would ever get.

As this section ends, it is clear that Lena has made her decision to attempt to leave the Black Galaxy by automatic boost to tachyonic drive. She does not know where she will emerge or how, but she does know that she can bear this no longer.

She prepares to set the controls, but before this it is necessary to write the dialogue with the dead.

XII

One of them presumably will appoint himself as the spokesman of the many and will appear before Lena in this new space as if in a dream. "Listen here," this dead would say, one born in 3361, dead in 3401, waiting eight centuries for exhumation to a society that can rid his body of leukemia (he is bound to be disappointed), "you've got to face the facts of the situation here. We can't just leave in this way. Better the death we know than the death you will give us."

"The decision is made," Lena says, her fingers straight on the controls. "There will be no turning back."

"We are dead now," the leukemic says. "At least let this death continue. At least in the bowels of this galaxy where there is no time we have a kind of life or at least that nonexistence of which we have always dreamed. I could tell you many of the things we have learned during these fourteen thousand years, but they would make little sense to you, of course. We have learned resignation. We have had great insights, Of course all of this would go beyond you."

"Nothing goes beyond me. Nothing at all. But it does not matter. "

"Everything matters. Even here there is consequence, causality, a sense of humanness, one of responsibility. You can suspend physical laws, you can suspend life itself, but you cannot separate the moral imperatives of humanity. There are absolutes. It would be apostasy to try and leave."

"Man must leave," Lena says, "man must struggle, man must attempt to control his conditions. Even if he goes from worse to obliteration, that is still his destiny. " Perhaps the dialogue is a little florid here. Nevertheless, this will be the thrust of it. It is to be noted that putting this conventional viewpoint in the character of a woman will give another of those necessary levels of irony with which the story must abound if it is to be anything other than a freak show, a cascade of sleazy wonders shown shamefully behind a tent ... but irony will give it legitimacy. "I don't care about the dead," Lena says. "I only care about the living."

"Then care about the universe," the dead man says, "care about that, if nothing else. By trying to come out through the center of the black hole, you may rupture the seamless fabric of time and space itself. You may destroy everything. Past and present and future. The explosion may extend the funnel of gravitational force to infinite size, and all of the universe will be driven into the hole."

Lena shakes her head. She knows that the dead is merely another one of her tempters in a more cunning and cadaverous guise. "You are lying to me," she says.

"This is merely another effect of the Galaxy Called Rome. I am responsible to myself, only to myself. The universe is not at issue."

"That's a rationalization," the leukemic says, seeing her hesitation, sensing his victory, "and you know it as well as I do. You can't be an utter solipsist. You aren't God, there is no God, not here, but if there was it wouldn't be you. You must measure the universe about yourself."

Lena looks at the dead and the dead looks at her; and in that confrontation, in the shade of his eyes as they pass through the dull lusters of the neutron star effect, she sees that they are close to a communion so terrible that it will become a weld, become a connection ... that if she listens to the dead for more than another instant, she will collapse within those eyes as the *Skipstone* has collapsed into the black hole; and she cannot bear this, it cannot be ... she must hold to the belief, that there is some separation between the living and the dead and that there is dignity in that separation, that life is not death but something else because, if she cannot accept that, she denies herself ... and quickly then, quickly before she can consider further, she hits the controls that will convert the ship instantly past the power of light; and then in the explosion of many suns that might only be her heart she hides her head in her arms and screams.

And the dead screams with her, and it is not a scream of joy but not of terror either ... it is the true natal cry suspended between the moments of limbo, life and expiration, and their shrieks entwine in the womb of the *Skipstone* as it pours through into the redeemed light.

XIII

The story is open-ended, of course.

Perhaps Lena emerges into her own time and space once more, all of this having been a sheath over the greater reality.

Perhaps she emerges into an otherness. Then again, she may never get out of the black hole at all but remains and lives there, the *Skipstone* a planet in the tubular universe of the neutron star, the first or last of a series of planets collapsing toward their deadened sun. If the story is done correctly, if the ambiguities are prepared right, if the technological data is stated well, if the material is properly visualized ... well, it does not matter then what happens to Lena, her *Skipstone* and her dead. Any ending will do. Any would suffice and be emotionally satisfying to the reader.

Still, there is an inevitable ending.

It seems clear to the writer, who will not, cannot write this story, but if he did he would drive it through to this one conclusion, the conclusion clear, implied really from the first and bound, bound utterly, into the text.

So let the author have it.

In the infinity of time and space, all is possible, and as they are vomited from that great black hole, spilled from this anus of a neutron star (I will not miss a single Freudian implication if I can), Lena and her dead take on this infinity, partake of the vast canvas of possibility. Now they are in the Antares Cluster flickering like a bulb; here they are at the heart of Sirius the Dog Star five hundred screams from the hold; here again in ancient Rome watching Jesus trudge up carrying the Cross of Calvary ... and then again in another unimaginable galaxy dead across from the Milky Way a billion light-years in span with a hundred thousand habitable planets, each of them with their Calvary ... and they are not, they are not yet satisfied.

They cannot, being human, partake of infinity; they can partake of only what they know. They cannot, being created from the consciousness of the writer, partake of what he does not know but what is only close to him. Trapped within the consciousness of the writer, the penitentiary of his being, as the writer is himself trapped in the *Skipstone* of his mortality, Lena and her dead emerge in the year 1975 to the town of Ridgefield Park, New Jersey, and there they inhabit the bodies of its fifteen thousand souls, and there they are, there they are yet, dwelling amidst the refineries, strolling on Main Street, sitting in the Rialto theatre, shopping in the supermarkets, pairing off and clutching one another in the imploded stars of their beds on this very night at this very moment, as that accident, the author, himself one of them, has conceived them.

It is unimaginable that they would come, Lena and the dead, from the heart of the Galaxy Called Rome to tenant Ridgefield Park, New Jersey ... but more unimaginable still that from all the Ridgefield Parks of our time we will come and assemble and build the great engines which will take us to the stars and some of the stars will bring us death and some bring life and some will bring nothing at all but the engines will go on and on and so after a fashion, in our fashion — will we.

Agony Column

GENTLEMEN:

I enclose my short story, "Three for the Universe," and know you will find it right for your magazine, *Astounding Spirits*.

Yours very truly,
MARTIN MILLER

DEAR CONTRIBUTOR:

Thank you for your recent submission. Unfortunately, although we have read it with great interest, we are unable to use it in *Astounding Spirits*. Due to the great volume of submissions we receive, we cannot grant all contributors a personal letter, but you may be sure that the manuscript has been reviewed carefully and its rejection is no comment upon its literary merit but may be dependent upon one of many factors.

Faithfully,
THE EDITORS

DEAR EDITORS:

The Vietnam disgrace must be brought to an end! We have lost on that stained soil not only our national honor but our very future. The troops must be brought home and we must remember that there is more honor in dissent than in unquestioningly silent agreement.

Sincerely,
MARTIN MILLER

DEAR SIR:

Thank you for your recent letter to the Editors. Due to the great volume of worthy submissions we are unable to print every good letter we receive and therefore' regretfully inform you that while we will not be publishing it, this is no comment upon the value of your opinion.

Very truly yours,
THE EDITORS

DEAR CONGRESSMAN FORTHWAITE:

I wish to bring your attention to a serious situation which is developing on the West Side. A resident of this neighborhood for five years now, I have recently observed that a large number of streetwalkers, dope addicts and criminal types are loitering at the intersection of Columbus Avenue and 24th Street at almost all hours of the day, offending passers-by with their appearance and creating a severe blight on the area. In addition, passers-by are often threateningly asked for "handouts" and even "solicited." I know that you share with me a concern for a Better West Side and look forward to your comments on this situation as well as some kind of concrete action.

Sincerely,
MARTIN MILLER

DEAR MR. MILLOW:

Thank you for your letter. Your concern ~or our West Side is appreciated and it is only through the efforts and diligence of constituents such as yourself that a better New York can be conceived. I have forwarded your letter to the appropriate precinct office in Manhattan and you may expect to hear from them soon.

Gratefully yours,
ALWYN D. FORTHWAITE

DEAR GENTLEMEN:

In May of this year I wrote Congressman Alwyn D. Forthwaite a letter of complaint, concerning conditions on the Columbus Avenue — West 24th Street intersection in Manhattan and was informed by him that this letter was passed on to your precinct office. Since four months have now elapsed, and since I have neither heard from you nor observed any change in the conditions pointed out in my letter, I now write to ask whether or not that letter was forwarded to you and what you have to say about it.

Sincerely,
MARTIN MILLER'

DEAR MR. MILNER:

Our files hold no record of your letter.

N. B. Karsh
Captain, #33462

DEAR SIRS:

I have read Sheldon Novack's article in the current issue of Cry with great interest but feel that I must take issue with his basic point, which is that sex is the consuming biological drive from which all other activities stem and which said other activities become only metaphorical for. This strikes me as a bit more of a projection of Mr. Novack's own functioning than that reality which he so shrewdly contends he apperceives.

Sincerely,
MARTIN MILLER

DEAR MR. MILTON:

Due to the great number of responses to Sheldon A. Novack's "Sex and Sexuality: Are We Missing Anything?" in the August issue of *Cry*, we will be unable to publish your own contribution in our "Cry From the City" Column, but we do thank you for your interest.

Yours,
THE EDITORS

DEAR MR. PRESIDENT:

I was shocked by the remarks apparently attributed to you in today's. newspapers on the public assistance situation. Surely, you must be aware of the fact that social welfare legislation emerged from the compassionate attempt of 1930 politics to deal with human torment in a systematized fashion, and although many of the cruelties you note are inherent to the very system, they do not cast doubt upon its very legitimacy. Our whole national history has been one of coming to terms with collective consciousness as opposed to the law of the jungle, and I cannot understand how you could have such a position as yours.

Sincerely,
MARTIN MILLER

DEAR MR. MELLER:

Thank you very much for your letter of October 18th to the President. We appreciate your interest and assure you that without the concern of citizens like yourself the country would not be what it has become. Thank you very much and we do look forward to hearing from you in the future on matters of national interest.

MARY L. McGINNITY
Presidential Assistant

GENTLEMEN:

I enclose herewith my article, "Welfare: Are We Missing Anything?" which I hope you may find suitable for publication in *Insight Magazine*.

Very truly yours,
MARTIN MILLER

DEAR CONTRIBUTOR:

The enclosed has been carefully reviewed and our reluctant decision is that it does not quite meet our needs at the present time. Thank you for your interest in *Insight*.

THE EDITORS

DEAR SENATOR PARTCH:

Your vote on the Armament Legislation was shameful.

Sincerely,
MARTIN MILLER

DEAR DR. MALLOW:

Thank you for your recent letter to Senator O. Stuart Partch and for your approval of the Senator's vote.

L. T. WALTERS
Congressional Aide

DEAR SUSAN SALTIS:

J think your recent decision to pose nude in that "art-photography" series in *Men's Companion* was disgraceful, filled once again with those timeless, empty rationalizations of the licentious which have so little intrinsic capacity for damage except when they are subsumed, as they are in your case, with abstract and vague "connections" to platitudes so enormous as to risk the very demolition of the collective personality.

Yours very truly,
MARTIN MILLER

DEAR SIR:

With pleasure and in answer to your request, we are enclosing a photograph of Miss Susan Saltis as she appears in her new movie, *Chariots to the Holy Roman Empire*.

Very truly yours,
HENRY T. WYATT
Publicity Director

GENTLEMEN:

I wonder if *Cry* would be interested in the enclosed article which is not so much an article as a true documentary of the results which have been obtained from my efforts over recent months to correspond with various public figures, entertainment stars, etc., etc. It is frightening to contemplate the obliteration of self which the very devices of the 20th Century compel, and perhaps your readers might share my (not so retrospective) horror.

Sincerely,
MARTIN MILLER

DEAR SIR:

As a potential contributor to *Cry* I am happy to offer you our "Writer's Subscription Discount," meaning that for only $5.50 you will receive not only a full year's subscription (28% below newsstand rates, 14% below customary subscriptions) but in addition our year-end special issue, *Cry in the Void,* at no extra charge.

SUBSCRIPTION DEPT.

DEAR CONTRIBUTOR:

Thank you very much for your article, "Agony Column." It has been considered here with great interest and it is the consensus of the Editorial Board that while it has unusual merit it is not quite right for us. We thank you for your interest in *Cry* and look forward to seeing more of your work in the future.

Sincerely,
THE EDITORS

DEAR CONGRESSMAN FORTHWAITE:

Nothing has been done about the conditions I mentioned in my letter of about a year ago. Not one single thing!

Bitterly,
MARTIN MILLER

DEAR MR. MILLS:

Please accept our apologies for the delay in answering your good letter. Congressman Forthwaite has been involved, as you know, through the winter in the Food Panel and has of necessity allowed some of his important correspondence to await close attention. Now that he has the time he thanks you for your kind words of support.

Yours truly,
ANN ANANAURIS

DEAR SIR:

The Adams multiple murders are indeed interesting not only for their violence but because of the confession of the accused that he "did it so that someone would finally notice me." Any citizen can understand this — the desperate need to be recognized as an individual, to break past bureaucracy into some clear apprehension of one's self-worth, is one of the most basic of human drives, but it is becoming increasingly frustrated today by a technocracy which allows less and less latitude for the individual to articulate his own identity and vision and be heard. Murder is easy: it is easy in the sense that the murderer does not need to embark upon an arduous course of training in order to accomplish his feat; his excess can come from the simple extension of sheer human drives ... aided by basic weaponry. The murderer does not have to cultivate "contacts" or "fame" but can simply, by being *there,* vault past nihilism and into some clear, cold connection with the self. More and more the capacity for murder lurks within us; we are narrow and driven, we are almost obliterated from any sense of existence, we need to make that singing leap past accomplishment and into acknowledgment and *recognition.* Perhaps you would print this letter?

Hopefully,
MARTIN MILLER

DEAR SIR:

Thank you for your recent letter. We regret being unable to use it due to many letters of similar nature being received, but we look forward to your expression of interest.

Sincerely,
JOHN SMITH For the Editors

DEAR MR. PRESIDENT:

I intend to assassinate you. I swear that you will not live out the year. It will come by rifle or knife, horn or fire, dread or terror, but it will come, and there is no way that you can AVOID THAT JUDGMENT TO BE RENDERED UPON YOU.

Fuck You,
MARTIN MILLER

DEAR REVEREND MELLBOW:

As you know, the President is abroad at the time of this writing, but you may rest assured that upon his return your letter, along with thousands of other and similar expressions of hope, will be turned over to him and I am sure that he will appreciate your having written.

Very truly yours,
MARY L. McGINNITY
Presidential Assistant

Final War

" 'Twas a mad stratagem,
To shoe a troop of horse with felt ..."

—*Lear,* Act III

H ASTINGS HAD never liked the new Captain.
The new Captain went through the mine field like a dancer, looking around from time to time to see if anyone behind was looking at his trembling rear end. If he found that anyone was, he immediately dropped to the end of the formation, began to scream threats, told the company that the mine field would go up on them. This was perfectly ridiculous because the company had been through the mine field hundreds of times and knew that all of the mines had been defused by the rain and the bugs. The mine field was the safest thing going. It was what lay *around* the mine field that was dangerous. Hastings could have told the new Captain all of this if he had asked.

The new Captain, however, was stubborn. He told everyone that, before he heard a thing, he wanted to become acclimated.

Background: Hastings' company was quartered, with their enemy, on an enormous estate. Their grounds began in a disheveled forest and passed across the mine field to a series of rocks or dismally piled and multicolored stones which formed into the grim and blasted abutments two miles away. Or, it began in a set of rocks or abutments and, passing through a scarred mine field, ended in an exhausted forest two miles back. It all depended upon whether they were attacking or defending; it all depended upon the day of the week. On Thursdays, Saturdays and Tuesdays, the company moved east to capture the forest; on Fridays, Sundays and Wednesdays, they lost the battles to defend it. Mondays, everyone was too tired to fight. The Captain stayed in his tent and sent out messages to headquarters; asked what new course of action to take. Headquarters advised him to continue as previously.

The forest was the right place to be. In the first place, the trees gave privacy, and in the second, it was cool. It was possible to play a decent game of poker, get a night's sleep. Perhaps because of the poker, the enemy fought madly for the forest and defended it like lunatics. So did Hastings' company. Being there, even if only on Thursdays, Saturdays and Tuesdays, made the war worthwhile. The enemy must have felt the same way, but they, of course, had the odd day of the week. Still, even

Hastings was willing to stay organized on that basis. Monday was a lousy day to get up, anyway.

But, it was the new Captain who wanted to screw things up. Two weeks after he came to the company, he announced that he had partially familiarized himself with the terrain and on this basis, he now wanted to remind the company not to cease fighting once they had captured the forest. He advised them that the purpose of the war went beyond the forest; it involved a limited victory on ideological issues, and he gave the company a month to straighten out and learn the new procedure. Also, he refused to believe his First Sergeant when the First Sergeant told him about the mine field but sent out men at night in dark clothing to check the area; he claimed that mines had a reputation for exploding twenty years later. The First Sergeant pointed out that it was not twenty years later, but the Captain said this made no difference; it could happen anytime at all. Not even the First Sergeant knew what to do with him. And, in addition to all of these things, it was rumored that the Captain talked in private to his officers of a *total* victory policy, was saying things to the effect that the war could only be successful if taken outside of the estate. When Hastings had grasped the full implication of all of this, he tried to imagine for a while that the Captain was merely stupid but, eventually, the simple truth of the situation came quite clear: the new Captain was crazy. The madness was not hateful: Hastings knew himself to be quite mad. The issue was how the Captain's lunacy bore on Hastings' problem: now, Hastings decided, the Captain would *never* approve his request for convalescent leave.

This request was already several months old. Hastings had handed it to the new Captain the day that the new Captain had come into the company. Since the Captain had many things on his mind at this time—he told Hastings that he would have to become acclimated to the new situation—Hastings could understand matters being delayed for a short while. But still, nothing had been done, and it was after the election; furthermore, Hastings was getting worse instead of better. Every time that Hastings looked up the Captain to discuss this with him, the Captain fled. He had told the First Sergeant that he wanted Hastings to know that he felt he was acting irresponsibly and out of the network of the problem. This news, when it was delivered, gave Hastings little comfort. *I am not acting irresponsibly,* he told the First Sergeant who listened without apparent interest, *as a matter of fact, I'm acting in quite a mature fashion. I'm trying to get some leave for the good of the company.* The First Sergeant had said that he guessed he didn't understand it either and he had been through four wars, not counting eight limited actions. He said that it was something which Hastings would have to work out for his own satisfaction.

Very few things, however, gave Hastings that much satisfaction, anymore. He was good and fed up with the war for one thing and, for another, he had gotten bored with the estate even if the company hadn't: once you had seen the forest, you had seen all of it that was worthwhile. Unquestionably, the cliffs, the abutments and the mine field were terrible. It might have been a manageable thing if they could have reached some kind of understanding with the enemy, a peaceful allotment of benefits, but it was obvious that headquarters would have none of this and besides, the enemy probably had a headquarters, too. Some of the men in the company might have lived limited existences; this might be perfectly all right with *them*, but Hastings liked to think of himself as a man whose horizons were, perhaps, a little wider than those of the others. *He* knew the situation was ridiculous. Every week, to remind him, reinforcements would come from somewhere in the South and tell Hastings that they had never seen anything like it. Hastings told them that this was because there had never *been* anything like it: not ever. Since the reinforcements had heard that Hastings had been there longer than anyone, they shut up then and left him alone. Hastings did not find that this improved his mood, appreciably. If anything, it convinced him that his worst suspicions were, after all, completely justified.

On election day, the company had a particularly bad experience. The president of their country was being threatened by an opposition which had no use for his preparedness policy; as a defensive measure, therefore, he had no choice on the day before election, other than to order every military installation in the vicinity of the company's war to send out at least one bomber and more likely two to show determination. Hastings' company knew nothing whatever of this; they woke on the morning of the election cheerful because it was their turn to take the forest. Furthermore, the tents of the enemy seen in the distance were already being struck, a good sign that the enemy would not contest things too vigorously. The men of the company put on their combat gear singing, goosing one another, challenging for poker games that night: it looked as if it were going to be a magnificent day. All indications were that the enemy would yield like gentlemen. Some of the company began to play tag, leaping through the abutments, comparing them to the forest that would soon be theirs.

Then, from all conceivable directions, airplanes came; they wandered, moaning, a few hundred feet above the surface of the cliffs and apparently waited. When all of them were quite sure that no others were coming (there would have been no room for them anyway), they began to methodically drop bombs on the company. Naturally, the pilots and crews of the airplanes were terribly excited and, as a result, they misplaced their fire quite badly, missing direct hits on the company more often than not. After a while, there was so much smoke around the vicinity of the cliffs that the pilots were unable to see at all, and they drifted over and peevishly sent excess bombs on the mine field. Hastings, lying on his back, guessed that the First Sergeant had been proved right because, just as everyone had been telling the Captain, the mine field did not go up. It took the bombs quite nicely, as a matter of fact, not heaving a bit. When every plane had released its bomb (some had to actually go over to the forest and drop one on the enemy; there was no other space left), they flew off in a dazzle of satisfaction, leaving the largest part of the company choking with laughter. Those that were not choking were unable to because they were dead. The point seemed to be that here it was the company's day in the forest, and now their own or some other force had come in and had screwed everything up. In the distance, the enemy could be seen holding cautious formation and then, with no hesitation whatsoever, they put themselves into lines and marched briskly away from the forest, taking the long route back to the cliffs.

The new Captain got up on an abutment and made a speech; he said that this had been the first step in a whole series leading to mass realignment. The company applauded thinly, wondering if there was any chance that he might have a stroke. Then everybody packed up and went over to the forest; all of them, of course, except those who were dead. Hastings stayed with a work detail and labeled all of them so that headquarters, if they ever sent anyone up, would know who in the company had failed to take the proper precautions and was therefore to be permanently removed from the master roster list and placed in the inactive files, never to be bothered by formations again.

It was the election day disaster that caused certain men in the company to begin behaving in a very bizarre fashion. News received through the First Sergeant that headquarters believed that the president had won re-election had no effect upon the decision of these men to take up indefinite residence in the forest; they told anyone who asked them that the whole thing was a futile proposition and the company was always going to come back there, anyway. They refused to make formations and had friends answer for them; they covered their tents with mud and pitched them in the shadow of trees; they washed their garments in the rain and, furthermore, they told everyone in the company that they were fools not to join them. One morning, lining up in the cliffs, the First Sergeant noticed for the first time that five men were gone. He became furious and said he would not stand for it; he told the company that he had been through four wars, not including eight limited actions, and there was simply no basis, ever, to performances of this sort. The First Sergeant said that he was going personally to lead the company back to the forest to shoot those five men. They were all prepared to go, looking forward to the objective really, when a misguided enemy pilot flew uncertainly over the forest and, perhaps in retaliation, dropped thirty-seven bombs on it, blowing every tree to the ground, leaving the earth quite green and shuddering and completely decimating his own troops. They were unable to fight for a week because the enemy had to ship reinforcements, and when they finally got back to the forest, they could find, of course, no trace of their five men at all; only a few belt buckles.

It was right then that Hashngs decided that the matter of his convalescent leave had come to a head. He had had the idea and he knew that it was covered in regulations: *he was entitled to it.* Army manuals noted the existence of something called convalescent leave: if it wasn't for situations such as these, well then, for what was it? *They had to deal with it.* One morning, he carefully re-drafted his original request with a borrowed pencil on the back of an old letter from his fiancee and brought it again into the First Sergeant. Hastings reminded the First Sergeant that he had originally put this request in months ago. The First Sergeant, groaning, said that the Captain could not possibly look at it because he was still getting acclimated to the situation. But, the First Sergeant added, he had been talking to the Captain on and off and he had some promising news: the Captain had been saying that he would probably be completely familiarized by Christmas. It was only a matter of taking time to get hold of a situation. Hastings said was that a fact and, mumbling promises to himself, left the headquarters tent; he told the Corporal with whom he slept that he hoped to be out of this, sooner or later. Most of the company were still gathering for hours around the belt buckles, looking solemnly, telling each other that it was a damned shame what the Army did to people. Hastings, looking it over again, decided that he had written a strong appeal: how *could* it be ignored?

Gentlemen (Hastings had written), listen: I am applying for convalescent leave as I have already done because I have been in vigorous combat and, while adding little or nothing to the company effort, have driven myself to the ridges of neurasthenia. What fighting skills I do possess and what morale I have acquired through recommended reading materials have fallen to a very low point because of the discouragement involved in the present situation. We are capturing and capturing again one forest and some wasted hills. The forest is bearable; the hills are not, but in the exhaustion of this repeated effort, both have leveled to a kind of hideous sameness; *now there is no difference.* Indeed, everything has become the same, as is common now in cases of great tension occurring under stress situations to certain limited individuals. Recently, I have had cold sweats, nausea, some vomiting and various nervous reactions including migraine of relative severity that has cut my diminishing effectiveness even further. Most of the time, I can barely lift a rifle ... and for all of these reasons, I am repeating my ignored request of three months duration that I be given convalescent leave for a period of several weeks to months for the purposes of renewed vision. Ideally, I would like to go back home, see my civilian friends, share my experiences with them, but if it is found that I cannot be sent there due to problems with transportation allotments and the like, I would settle for being sent alone to the nearest town where there are women and where it is possible to sleep. I would even be willing, if the nights were quiet, to go to a place without women; as a matter of fact, this might be the best action at this time. I am certainly in no condition for relationships, not even those of the fragmentary kind necessitated by copulation. Hoping that this request meets with your attention and approval; hoping that you will not see it as the frenzied expression of a collapsed man but only as the cool and reasoned action of the professional soldier under stress, I remain yours truly, Hastings, 114786210. P.S. I wish to note that my condition is serious; how serious only a qualified professional judgement could determine. If this request is not met with your prompt attention, therefore, or not, at least sent to a competent psychiatrist for an opinion, it is impossible for me to predict what the scope of my reactions will be: *I can no longer control my behavior.* I have been brought up all my life to believe that institutions are the final repository of all the good sense left in this indecent world; at this point in my life it would assume the proportion of a major disaster if I were to learn that the Army, one of our most respected and ancient institutions, were not to be trusted. P.P.S. Please note that the mines here are *already defused*; inform the Captain that they need not worry him.

✳ ✳ ✳

On the other hand, the *first* request had been good, too. The day that the *old* Captain's reassignment to headquarters came through, all of the men in the company had come to his tent to stand around him, giving him notes and wishes of good will. Hastings had given him his request in a sealed envelope, and the Captain had taken it for another farewell message and placed it carefully in his knapsack; he told Hastings and the others that he was moved by their display of affection and he hoped that any of them who came into his territory later in the war would drop in and say hello; he would like to find out personally how everything was going. After all of this was over, the old Captain had crawled into his tent, saying, over his shoulder, that the company had given him an experience that he simply would never forget. The company smiled at the Captain's closed tent and wandered off to play poker. (They had been in the forest that day.)

Hastings thought that he would join them and then decided that this would not do; he would have to force the issue, and so he crawled, quite respectfully, into the Captain's tent and, finding him wrapped in an embryonic ball on his bunk, told him that he had a few things to explain. Hastings told the Captain that he had submitted a request for convalescent leave and not a good will message. At this, the Captain's legs kicked from the ball he had made of himself, and he told Hastings that he felt that he had very little consideration. Hastings said that this might all well be true, but he *was* a sick man and he then outlined the substance of his request. The Captain wrapped himself up intently and thought about it, said that he could court-martial Hastings. He added cheerfully that, since he was not legally in command of the company now, Hastings could be placed in the stockade for divulging confidential material to an outsider. Hastings kneeled then and asked the Captain what the proper thing would be to do, and the Captain said that he hadn't the faintest idea. He suggested that Hastings recall his request and, as a concession, court-martial proceedings would be dropped. He said that the appeal itself was unexceptionable; the new Captain, if one ever came, surely would approve it.

Hastings took his envelope and left the Captain, went back to his tent singing an Army song and fixed up his pegs neatly, but by the time he had all of them firmly in the ground, he found himself stricken with a terrible intimation. He went back to see the Captain, learned that he was in the officers' latrine, and waited outside there until the Captain came out. Hastings asked the Captain if headquarters or the new Captain might think that his request was a joke. The Captain said that he could not speak professionally but from what he had gathered from summation, he saw nothing funny in it at all; it seemed quite serious, quite to the point. Hastings said that the Captain might feel that way but, after all, he had been heading up the war, maybe at headquarters, they did not glimpse the urgencies. The Captain said that headquarters was filled with understanding people: they were people who had approved his own request for transfer, and they could be counted upon to comprehend the necessary. Hastings said a few unfortunate words about possible prejudice against enlisted men, and the Captain's face became bright green: he said that he suddenly realized that he had not finished his own business in the latrine. Hastings could not follow him in there, of course, but

36

he waited two hours until the Captain came out and tried to pursue the matter. But the Captain, walking away hurriedly, said that he did not know what Hastings was talking about: he did not even know what this request was, had never heard of it in fact; and then he said that, upon consideration, he realized that he did not know Hastings either; surely, he had never seen him before. The Captain ordered Hastings to return to his proper company, wherever that might be. Hastings explained that theirs was the only company within two hundred miles, and the Captain said that Hastings was obviously an AWOL with energy. Then, he ran briskly away.

Hastings gathered that there would be very little point in following and instead went back to his tent. His tent mate was sleeping inside, and Hastings methodically demolished the tent, wrapped it around the Corporal, picked all of this up, groaning, and threw it into a tree. The Corporal hit with a dull noise. When he came out rubbing himself, he said that he was shocked at this; he did not know that Hastings was the type. Hastings shrugged and said that some men changed personality under stress. He wandered away, not breathing very hard, and bought a pencil from someone, took some toilet paper from the latrine and began a very serious letter to his fiancee. He had just brought matters through the Captain's second flight when the sun set violently, and he had to put everything away. He slept quite badly in the mine field that night (he did not feel like returning to his tent; not quite yet) and in the morning, found that his letter had been somehow stolen. Hastings had a good reputation as a letter writer, and men in the company were always stealing his correspondence, trying to get useful phrases. Hastings did not care about this particularly, except that lately he had begun to feel that he had only a limited number of things to say and they were diminishing rapidly. This theft, then, intensified his gloom, and he almost decided to seek another interview with the Captain but then he said: *The hell with it. We'll give the new man a chance. That is the least we can do.* Looking sadly at the enemy tents, Hastings again decided that he was in a highly abnormal situation.

Headquarters (wrote Hastings some time later on the back of a letter from an old acquaintance), I am forced to take this most serious and irregular action because of the prejudicial conduct of the recently installed Commanding Officer concerning my re-request for convalescent status. As you may or may not know, I originally placed this request several months ago and rewrote it last week because of the failure of the Commanding Officer to pay any heed, whatsoever. This Commanding Officer has subjected mc to an exposure of terrifying inadequacy without precedent in a Captain of this Army and has imperiled my entire image of your institution. He has never confronted me concerning either request but has relayed statements through the First Sergeant (who is a war veteran with great sympathy for my position) that I am behaving irresponsibly. Headquarters, I ask you, is it irresponsible of me to request a convalescent leave? I have been fighting this war for a considerable period of time now, exposing myself over and over again to the same dreary set of experiences while around me the company ebbs and flows and the reinforcements creep in darkly. The reinforcements tell me again and again that they do not think that there is any sense to this engagement, and I am compelled to agree with them. This entire action has acquired the aspect of nightmare, I am sorry to say, and although I am not an unstable man, I have found myself becoming, not neurasthenic as previously noted, but truly psychotic. This is terrible ritual, gentlemen, terrible sacrifice, really deadly convolution of the soul. Also, they are stealing my correspondence. I have not been able actually to mail a letter for months, even to tell my fiancee that I have terminated our engagement. Gentlemen, I *like* my fiancee and what is more important, after two years of distance, I now wish to make an arrangement to spare her of me. What more significant proof can I provide of insanity? Hoping that you will give this request the most serious consideration and hoping that you will review the folder of the Commanding Officer here very thoroughly indeed, I am sending this letter out by and through devious and covert means. Yours truly, Hastings, serial number posted.

When he was finished, Hastings took the letter to the officers' section and gave it to the First Sergeant, who was cleaning some bits of litter from the top of his desk. He gazed dully at the First Sergeant and asked if it could be submitted through special channels, around the Captain. The First Sergeant gave him a look of wonderment and said that the letter could not possibly pass: it was not written in code as all direct communications to headquarters were compelled to be. Furthermore, the First Sergeant said, he had received exciting news from headquarters: there were plans to start a newspaper which would be distributed by airline to the company; this newspaper would tell them how they were progressing in their battle. The First Sergeant said that headquarters considered it a major breakthrough in morale policy. And, in addition to all of this the First Sergeant whispered, there was one other piece of news which had come through from headquarters which he was not authorized to disclose but which the Captain would make the subject of an address to the troops on this day. The First Sergeant said that this would probably be a revelation even to Hastings, a real surprise from headquarters. Hastings, still thinking about the newspaper, asked if it would contain anything except statistics, and the First Sergeant said there would probably be some editorials written by military experts. Hastings said that he wanted to awaken the Captain. The First Sergeant said that this was impossible because the Captain was already awake; he was drafting his speech, and he was too excited to deal with Hastings now. The First Sergeant added that he agreed that this was a shame. Hastings said that he was at the end of his rope. The Sergeant said that things were getting better: he recommended that Hastings learn headquarters code if he was serious about the message and then re-submit it, and he handed him a book. Hastings saw that the book was really a folder containing sheets of typewriter paper, and he asked the First Sergeant what this was. The First Sergeant explained that this was a copy of his short novel detailing his experiences as a veteran of four wars and eight limited actions. Hastings asked what the hell this had to do with learning code or with sending his message, and the First Sergeant said that he was astonished; he said that Hastings was the only man in the company so far to be offered his novel; and he added that everything in it contained the final answer, if it was only studied. The First Sergeant then said that the convalescent leave business was Hastings' problem, anyway; he had never cracked the code completely himself, and he doubted if it were possible to solve it.

When he came back to his tent, still carrying the First Sergeant's novel in one hand, Hastings decided that he had reached a moment of major crisis. There were obviously no points of reference to this in his life; he was definitely on his own. All of the company were getting up one by one, discussing the push to the cliffs which they were going to make later in the day. Some of the reinforcements insisted that to achieve the cliffs would be to attain a major objective, but older members of the company gently explained that the battle was probably endless. When they heard this, the reinforcements sat tearfully and had to be persuaded to strike their tents. The First Sergeant came out after a while and called a formation, saying that the Captain was going to address them. When they heard this, the company, even Hastings, became very excited because the Captain had never talked to any of them before; he had always been at the end of the marches, saying that he had to be acclimatized. Now, apparently, he had completed his assessment of the situation, and everybody was very anxious to find out what he had learned. Also they were curious, some of them, about his rear end and figured that at one time or another they would probably be able to get a glimpse of it now. Standing in the ranks, Hastings fondled the First Sergeant's novel and his letter and made a decision: he would present both of them to the Captain just as soon as he had finished talking. He would wait until the end of the Captain's speech that was, only if the speech was very interesting: if the Captain had nothing to say or only detailed how he intended to further familiarize himself, he would go up to him in the middle and simply hand him the letter. At least, he would have the man's attention. This would be a new element in the situation, right away.

Preceded by the First Sergeant, the Captain came from his tent and, walking carefully, came in front of the company. No one could see his buttocks because all of them were facing in the same direction. The Captain stood there, nodding, for several minutes, making some notes in pen on fresh paper, beaming at the motion. Hastings found this frightening. He had never before noticed how small the Captain's face was; at this distance it was seen to be covered with a hideous stubble superimposed over the features of a very young boy. In spite of all this evidence, he had not been convinced, apparently, because he wore a wedding ring. The Captain backed carefully against a tree and leaned against it, smiling at the company. "Some of you," he said, "have brought it to the attention of my First Sergeant that you are unhappy.

"More than unhappiness. I know that you are vitally concerned. You're concerned because you see no point in what you're doing. You're concerned because you can't see how what you are doing affects anything or anybody else. You're worried about this. This is serious. It is a real problem.

"It's a legitimate matter of concern, all right. When a group of men such as yourselves cannot feel dignity in the work they do, cannot feel that what they do is important to a much larger number of people, they break down. They become nervous. They begin to function in a cold sweat, and sometimes they do not function at all. I have noticed this about one or two of you. But even those I do not condemn. In fact, I have all kinds of sympathy for men in this predicament; it is not pleasant. I know what it can be like. But now and for all of you, this part of your life is over."

The company cheered thinly. Hastings folded his letter and put it away.

"The situation, in fact," said the Captain, "is now entirely changed; more than you would have ever thought possible. *General war has been declared.* The enemy, who have become increasingly provocative in recent weeks, bombed one of our ports of installation last week, reducing it to a pulp. How about that? As a result of this action, the president of the country has declared that a general and total state of war now exists between the countries of the enemy and ourselves. At this moment, troops all over the globe are actively pouring in and out of our military installations; their weapons at the ready!

"*Now, what does this mean?* I'll tell you what it means. Gentlemen, you are the first. But, you are only the beginning. What you have gone through will be absorbed, will be a spearhead. And when we go out today, we go into these fields with the entire Army, with the country behind us. You are some lucky bunch of fellows. I congratulate all of you, and I congratulate you individually."

After the Captain had finished, he stood against the tree, apparently waiting for the company to disperse, so that he could return to his tent without anyone having seen his rear end. Hastings, weeping, drifted behind him, stood in a clearing, destroyed his letter. The trunk covered the Captain's behind from that angle, too. *I do feel better, already,* Hastings told himself, *I feel better already.* But when the Captain finally gave a cautious look in all directions and started backing slowly from the tree, Hastings took his bayonet and threw it at him, cleaving the left buttock of the Captain, bringing forth a bright scream.

"I still feel lousy," Hastings said.

The Captain had never liked Hastings. Hastings walked in the middle of formations, telling everyone as they went over the mine fields that they were absolutely harmless, a fraud. No one would have taken *any* precautions going over the mine field, if it had not been for the Captain running behind them. Some of the men picked up stones and threw them at each other; some men said the war would never end. When things got utterly out of hand, the Captain would have to shout at the troops, at distances of hundreds of yards he found himself bellowing and, even then, the company would not listen. All of this traced back to Hastings. He was destroying the morale of the company. The Captain suspected that, beneath all of this, Hastings was trying to sink the progress of the limited war.

In addition to saying that the mine field was just as safe as a playground, this Hastings was a letter writer. He wrote letters to everyone; now he had written a request to headquarters (which was peculiar enough already; the messages coming from headquarters now were enough to confuse anyone, let alone a Captain just trying to get acclimated), giving his situation and asking for convalescent leave; he cited obscure regulations. The Captain knew, of course, that if he forwarded this material to headquarters, two or three field grade officers would come out in a jeep, capture Hastings and place him in a hospital for mental cases, and the Captain wanted to spare Hastings this. He was governed, then, by common, if causeless, feelings of mercy but nevertheless, there was Hastings, insisting that his form go through. The Captain did not know what to do with him. In the first place, he had only been with this company for six weeks and he was having all he could do to get acclimated to the situation; in the second place, he badly missed his wife and the cottage they had had in officers' quarters on a small post in the Southern tier. Furthermore, the Captain found himself wondering at odd moments in the night whether the war effort would truly be successful. There seemed to be some very peculiar elements about it. The bombing was so highly irregular, and some of the pilots did not seem to be very interested; they dropped bombs on their own side and also flew out of pattern. In addition, some of the men in the company had become attached to a certain part of the terrain; they were maintaining now that the entire purpose of the war was to secure and live permanently within it. The Captain did not know what to do about this. Also, Hastings waited outside of his tent often, trying to find out what he was doing with the leave request, and the Captain found that his free rights of access and exit were being severely limited, above and beyond the Army code.

The Captain had nothing against the war. It was all working out the way the preparation courses had taught. Certainly, it had its strange facets: the enemy also seemed to be attached to the forest part of the map and fought bitterly for the retention of certain cherished trees, but things like this were normal in stress situations anyway; after a while, all conflicts, all abstractions came down, in a group of limited men, to restricted areas. The Captain had been trained to see things in this fashion, and he had also been given a good deal of instruction in the intricacies of troop morale. So, he understood the war; he understood it very well. There was no doubt about that. *However*, the Academy had neglected to prepare him for Hastings. There was no one like Hastings at the Academy, even in a clean-up capacity. The Captain had taken to writing his young wife long letters on stationery he had borrowed from his First Sergeant (a war veteran of four major conflicts and eight limited actions), telling her all about the situation, adding that it was very odd and strained but that he hoped to have matters cleaned up by the end of the year, that is, if he was ever unleashed. Other than this, he did not write her about the war at all but instead wrote at length about certain recollections he had of their courtship, entirely new insights. In the relaxation of the war, he found that he was able to gather astonishing perceptions into the very quality of his life, and he told his wife the reasons for his action at given times, asked her if she understood. *We will get to the bottom of this,* he often reminded her, *if only you will cooperate.* His wife's letters in return were sometimes argumentative, sometimes disturbed; she told him that he was wasting his energy in the forgotten wastes, and that all of his strength was now needed to become acclimated to a new situation. When he read these letters, the Captain found that, unreasonably, he wanted to cry, but his bunk was too near to that of his First Sergeant, and he was ashamed. None of the officers wanted to be caught crying by the First Sergeant, a combat veteran.

Meanwhile, the Captain found that his communications with headquarters were being blocked for days at a time, and also that his messages, when they did come, were increasingly peculiar. Sometimes, the Captain succumbed briefly to the feeling that headquarters did not truly understand the situation, but he put such thoughts away quickly. Thinking them or putting them away; it made no difference, he was almost always depressed. *Continue on as you have done, worry not,* headquarters would tell him three days later in response to a routine inquiry. Or, *we are preparing new strategy here and ask you to hold line while formulating.* Such things were highly disturbing; there was simply no doubt about it.

One morning near Christmas, the Captain went through a near-disaster, a partial catastrophe. The First Sergeant came into his tent and told him that Hastings was thinking of submitting a letter to headquarters directly on the subject of his convalescent leave. The Captain said that he could not believe that even Hastings would be crazy enough to do something like that, and the First Sergeant said that this might well be true but, nevertheless, Hastings had brought in some kind of a letter that morning and asked to have it forwarded. The Captain asked the First Sergeant if he could see the letter, and the First Sergeant said that he had told Hashings to go away with it but that Hastings had promised to come back later. The Captain put on some old fatigues and went out into the forest in real grief; he looked at Hastings' tent, which was of a peculiar, greyish shade, and he sighed. Hastings was sitting outside the tent on his knees with his back to the Captain, scribbling something in the dirt with a stick. The Captain decided that he was ill; he did not want to have anything whatever to do with Hastings. Instead, he went back to his tent intending to sleep some more, but when he got there, the First Sergeant was waiting for him with astonishing news. He told the Captain that somehow a message *had* gotten through on Hastings because some Corporal was up from headquarters saying he had orders to put Hastings away in the asylum. When the Captain heard this, he felt himself possessed by absolute fury, and he told the First Sergeant that he was running this company and he refused to take treatment like this from anyone. The First Sergeant said that he absolutely agreed with the Captain and he would go out to deal with the Corporal, but the Captain said that, for once, *he* was going to handle the situation the way it should be. He told the First Sergeant to leave him alone, and then he went over to a clearing where the Corporal sat in a jeep and told him that Hastings had been killed a few hours ago in an abortive attack and was being buried. The Corporal said that that was a rotten shame because everyone in headquarters had heard the story and was really anxious to find out what kind of lunatic this Hastings was. The Captain said that he could tell him stories but he would not and ordered the Corporal to return to his unit. After the Corporal had explained that he was in an administrative capacity and therefore not at all vulnerable to the Captain's orders, he got in the jeep and said that he would go back to his unit and report what had happened. He asked the Captain if Hastings had had any special characteristics which should be noted in a condolence letter. The Captain said that Hastings had always been kind of an individualist and forceful in his own way; also he was highly motivated, if somewhat unrealistic. The Corporal said that this would be useful and he drove away. For almost an hour, the Captain found himself unable to move from the spot, but after a while, he was able to remember the motions of walking, and he stumbled back to his tent and began a long letter to his wife. *I gave an order today in a very difficult capacity,* he began it, but he decided that this was no good and instead started, *I have become fully acclimated to the situation here at last and feel that I am at the beginning of my best possibilities: do you remember how ambitious I used to be?* After he wrote this, he found that he had absolutely nothing else to write and, thinking of his wife's breasts, put the paper away and went for a long walk. Much later, he decided that what had happened had been for the good; it was only a question now of killing Hastings, and then he could begin to take control.

The First Sergeant had nothing to do with things, anymore. He slept a twisted sleep, crawling with strange shapes, and in the morning, the First Sergeant awakened him, saying that headquarters had just sent in a communique declaring that a total-win policy was now in effect; war had been declared. When the Captain heard this, he became quite excited and began to feel better about many things; he asked the First Sergeant if he thought that it meant that the company was now unleashed, and the First Sergeant said that he was positive that that was what had happened. The Captain said that this would definitely take care of Hastings; they could work him out of the way very easily now, and he added that he had studied the morale problem of troops; now he was going to be able to put it into effect. Troops, he said, were willing to get involved in anything, but if they felt they were being used to no good purpose, they tended to get childish and stubborn The Captain felt so good about this that he invited the First Sergeant to forget things and look at one of his wife's recent letters, but the First Sergeant said that he felt he knew the Captain's wife already and, besides, he had to make preparations for the war; he had real responsibilities. The First Sergeant explained that this would be his fifth war, but since each one was like a new beginning, he felt as if he had never been in combat before and he wanted to make some notes. The Captain said that this was fine, and then, right on the instant, he decided to make a speech to the company. He requisitioned two sheets of bond paper from the First Sergeant and sat down to draft it, but he found himself so filled with happy thoughts of Hastings' impending assassination that he was unable to keep still, and so he decided to speak extemporaneously. He knew that he could deal with the company in the right way. When he was quite sure that he was in the proper mood to make the speech, he ordered the First Sergeant to call a formation, and when the First Sergeant came back to tell him that all of the men were assembled, he walked out slowly behind the First Sergeant, knowing how good a picture he was making. He stood near a tree for shelter and smiled at all of the men, especially Hastings, but Hastings, looking at something in his hands, did not see the smile and that, the Captain decided, was Hastings' loss. It was one more indication, this way of thinking, of how well he had finally become acclimated. Everything, after all, was only a matter of time.

"You men," the Captain said, "are plenty upset because you see no purpose in this whole operation. In fact, it seems absolutely purposeless to you, a conclusion with which I am in utter sympathy. It is no fun when emptiness replaces meaning; when despair replaces motive. I know all about this; I have shared it with you over and over.

"Today, we mount another attack and many wonder: what is the point? it's all the same; it always was. We've been back and forth so many times, what the hell's the difference, now?

"In line with this, I want to tell you something now, something that will, I am convinced, change the entire picture in your minds and hearts. *Something is different*; things have changed. We are now in a state of war with the enemy. Our ports of installation were bombed last night; in return, our president has declared that we are now in a position of total war. How about that?

"Before we have finished our mission now, ten thousand, a million men will have shared our losses, our glories, our commitments, our hopes. And yet, because these began with us, essentially we are the creators of the war.

"Are we fortunate? I do not know. Such is our responsibility. Such is our honor."

After the Captain had finished, he stood near the tree for a long while, marveling at his speech. There was no question but that it had gotten right through to the middle of the situation; it left no room for any doubt of any kind. Surely he had, just as he had promised, become fully acclimated and now, *now* there was no stopping him at all. And it took care of that Hastings; it took care of him but good. The next step for Hastings was darkness. Therefore, the Captain was enormously surprised when he saw Hastings, grinning hysterically, come toward him, a bayonet shining in his hand. It just showed you, if you didn't know it well already, that there was just no predicting anything with enlisted men. Before the Captain could move, Hastings raised his arm and threw the instrument at the Captain.

"What are you doing?" the Captain screamed. "I'm your Commanding Officer in the midst of a war!"

"I still say I'm not crazy!" Hastings screamed.

"We're in the middle of a war!" the Captain said, dying.

But Hastings, apparently quite mad now, would not listen.

The First Sergeant had never liked Hastings or the Captain. Both of them were crazy; there was no doubt about it. Hastings, a Private, told everyone in the company that the mine fields were a sham, quite safe, really, and the Captain insisted that they were ready to fire. When the company walked over the mine fields, Hastings cursed to the troops that they were a bunch of cowards, and the Captain, his stupid ass waving, fell to the end of the formation and screamed at them to keep going. The two of them were wrecking the company, making the entire situation (which had had such potential, such really nice things in it) impossible. The war *was* peculiar, there was no question about this, but there were ways to get around it and get a job done. But the two of them, Hastings and the Captain, were lousing things up. The First Sergeant found himself so furious with their business that after a while he could not even keep his communiques straight: all the headquarters messages were getting screwed up in the decode because he was too upset to do it right and no one would leave him alone. There was no sense to most of the messages; they all seemed to say the same thing anyway, and the First Sergeant knew that headquarters were a pack of morons; he had decided this three days after he had taken over his job and began getting their idiotic messages. Meanwhile, the new Captain would not leave him alone; all that he wanted to talk about was Hastings. It was Hastings, the Captain said loudly to the First Sergeant, who was fouling everything up. He asked the First Sergeant if there might be any procedures to get Hastings to keep quiet, because everything that had gone wrong was all his fault. Over and over again, the Captain asked the First Sergeant to figure out a way to get rid of Hastings *without* giving him convalescent leave. All of this was bad enough for the First Sergeant but then, on top of all of this, there was Hastings himself hanging around all the time, trying to find out things about the Captain, asking if the man had yet initialed his request. All in all, it was just ridiculous, what they were doing to him. When the First Sergeant decided to do what he did, he had every excuse in the world for it. They were a pack of lunatics. They were out of control. They deserved no mercy.

One morning, for instance, around Thanksgiving, the Captain woke the First Sergeant to say that he had figured out the entire situation: Hastings was insane. He was investing, said the Captain, terrible dependency in an effort to become a child again and his functioning was entirely unsound. The Captain asked the First Sergeant if he felt that this was reasonable and whether or not he thought that Hastings belonged in some kind of institution. The First Sergeant, who had been up very late trying to organize some confusing communiques from headquarters in relation to the Thanksgiving supper, said that he was not sure but that he would think some about it, and if the Captain wanted him to, he would even check into Army regulations. He added that Hastings might have combat fatigue, something that he had seen in a lot of men through the course of four wars and eight limited actions; some men were simply weaker than others. The point here was that the First Sergeant was trying to be as decent to both the Captain and Hastings as any man could be, but there were limits. Later that day, Hastings found him sitting behind a tree and told him that he had figured out the whole thing: the Captain was obviously mad. He suggested that the First Sergeant help him prepare a report to headquarters listing all of the peculiar actions of the Captain and asked for some clean paper to do this. Hastings added that he thought that most of the Captain's problem could be traced back to his shame over his rear end. The rear end made the Captain look feminine, said Hastings, and the Captain was reacting to this in a very normal, if unfortunate, fashion. The First Sergeant said that he didn't know enough about modern psychiatry to give an opinion on that one way or the other. Hastings asked the First Sergeant to simply *consider* it, and the First Sergeant said that he would do that. After a while, Hastings left, saying that the First Sergeant had hurt him.

In all of this, then, it could be seen that the First Sergeant had acted entirely correctly, in entire justice. He was in a difficult position but he was doing the best he could. No claims could be made against him that he was not doing his job. But, in spite of all the times the First Sergeant repeated this to himself, he found that, finally, he was getting good and fed up with the whole thing. There were, he decided, natural limits to all circumstances and Hastings, headquarters, the Captain and the war were passing theirs; after a point simply no part of it was his responsibility, any more.

This, the First Sergeant told the officers who knew enough to listen, was his fourth war and eighth limited action, not counting various other difficulties he had encountered during his many years in the Army. Actually, this was not entirely true, but the First Sergeant had taken to feeling that it was, which was almost better. The truth of the situation, which the First Sergeant kept to himself except for occasional letters to his wife was that he had worked in a division motor pool for fifteen years before he had been reassigned to the company, and that reassignment had been something of a fluke, hinging on the fact that the company had, before the days of the limited war, been established as a conveyance unit, and the First Sergeant had absent-mindedly been assigned as a mechanic. That things had worked out this way was probably the fault of headquarters; at least, the First Sergeant did not question them on *that* score.

Early in the career of the First Sergeant, he had accidentally shot a General while in rifle training. The General, fortunately, had only lost an ear which, he had laughingly told the First Sergeant at the court-martial, he could spare because he never heard that much that was worth hearing, anyway. The General, however, claimed that the First Sergeant had had no right to shoot at him when he was in the process of troop-inspection, even if the shots had only been fired from excitement, as was the claim of the First Sergeant's defense. The General said that he felt the best rehabilitative action for the First Sergeant, under all the principles of modern social action, would be to be shot himself, although not in the ear. When the First Sergeant heard this, he stood up in court and said that for the first time in his life, he was ashamed that he had chosen to enlist in the Army.

When the head of the court, a Major, heard this, he asked the First Sergeant to stay calm and state, just off the record, what he wanted to do with his life. When the First Sergeant said that all he wanted to do was to make an honorable career and a First Sergeancy (at this time he had been considerably less, a Private in fact), the Major advised the General that the First Sergeant would probably have to be treated differently from the run of the mine soldier, and the General said that he found the First Sergeant's testimony very moving. It was agreed to fine the First Sergeant one month's salary every month for the next five years and send him to automobile training in the far North. The General said that he could think of some places right off the top of his head where the First Sergeant might do well, but he reminded him that he would have to remember to cut down very sharply now on all of his expenses as he would be living on somewhat of a limited budget.

The First Sergeant learned to live frugally (even now, he was still forgetting to pick up his pay when headquarters delivered it; he was always astonished) and repaired vehicles for fourteen years, but inwardly, he was furious. Because of his duties in the motor pool he lost out on several wars and limited actions, and, also, his wife (whom he had married before he enlisted) was ashamed that he had not been killed as had the husbands of many of her friends. As a result of this, he and his wife eventually had an informal separation, and the First Sergeant (who *was* by then a First Sergeant) took to telling people just being sent into the motor pool that he personally found this work a great relief after fighting one war and three limited actions. They seemed to believe him, which was fine, but the First Sergeant still had the feeling that he was being deprived of the largest segment of his possibilities. He moved into a barracks with a platoon of younger troops and taught them all the war songs he knew.

In September of his next to last year in the Army, the First Sergeant fell into enormous luck. He often felt that it had all worked out something like a combat movie. A jeep for whose repair he had been responsible exploded while parked in front of a whorehouse, severely injuring a Lieutenant Colonel and his aide-de-camp who were waiting, they later testified, for the area to be invaded by civilian police. They had received advance warning and had decided to be on the premises for the protection of enlisted men. As a result of the investigation which followed, the aide-de-camp was reduced to the rank of Corporal and sent to give hygienic lectures to troops in the far lines of combat. The Lieutenant Colonel was promoted to Colonel, and the First Sergeant was sent to the stockade for six weeks. When he was released, he was given back all of his stripes and told by a civilian board of review that he was going to be sent into troop transport. The head of the board said that this would extend his experience considerably, and told him that he would be on the site of, although not actually engaged in, a limited action war. Standing in front of the six men, his hastily re-sewn stripes trembling, the First Sergeant had been unable to comprehend his stunning fortune. It seemed entirely out of control. Later, getting instructions from an officer, he found that he would take over the duties of a conveyance First Sergeant in an important action being conducted secretly on a distant coast. As soon as he could talk, the First Sergeant asked if he could have three days convalescent leave, and the officer said that regulations would cover this; he was entitled to it because of the contributions he had made.

The First Sergeant borrowed a jeep and drove several hundred miles from post to a dark town in which his separated wife worked as a waitress. He found her sitting alone in the balcony of a movie house, watching a combat film and crying absently. At first, she wanted nothing at all to do with him, but after he told her what had happened to him, she touched him softly and said that she could not believe it had worked out. They went to a hotel together, because her landlady did not believe in her boarders being with other people, and talked for a long time; and for the first time, the First Sergeant said that he was frightened at what was happening as well as grateful. He had been away for so long that he did not know if he could trust himself. His wife said that finally, after fifteen years, she felt proud, and she told him that she knew he would do well. Later on he remembered that. But he never remembered answering her that only distress can make a man.

They went to bed together and it was almost good; they almost held together until the very end, but then everything began to come to pieces. The First Sergeant said that he would probably not be able to write her letters because he was going to an area of high security, and she said that this was perfectly all right with her as long as the allotment checks were not interrupted. When he heard this, the Sergeant began to shake with an old pain and he told her that the jeep had blown up because he had deliberately failed to replace a bad fuel connection. She told him that if this were so, he deserved anything that happened to him. He told her that nothing he had ever done had been his fault, and she said that he disgusted her.

After that, both of them got dressed, feeling terrible, and the First Sergeant drove the jeep at a grotesque speed toward the post. In the middle of the trip he found that he could not drive for a while, and he got out and vomited, the empty road raising dust in his eyes, the lights of occasional cars pinning him helplessly against dry foliage.

When the First Sergeant came to the company, they were just at the true beginning of the limited war, and he was able to get hold of matters almost immediately. The first thing that he learned was that his predecessor had been given a transfer for reasons of emotional incompetence and had been sent back to the country as the head of a motor pool. The second thing he found out was that his job was completely non-combatant, involving him only in the communications detail. When the First Sergeant discovered that his duties involved only decoding, assortment and relay of communiques from division headquarters to the company and back again, he felt, at first, a feeling of enormous betrayal, almost as if he had been in the Army all his life to discover that there was absolutely no reason for it at all. The Captain of this company communicated with headquarters from one hundred to one hundred and fifty times a day; he tried to keep himself posted on everything including the latest procedure for morale-retention. Other officers also had messages, and in the meanwhile, enlisted personnel were constantly handing him money, begging him to send back a hello to relatives through headquarters. The First Sergeant found this repulsive but the worst of it was to trudge at the rear of formations while in combat, loaded with ten to fifteen pieces of radio equipment and carrying enormous stacks of paper which he was expected to hand to the officers at any time that they felt in need of writing. In addition, his pockets were stuffed with headquarters communiques which the Captain extracted from time to time. It was a humiliating situation; it was the worst thing that had ever happened to him. When they were not in battle, the First Sergeant was choked with cross-communiques; it became impossible for him to conceive of a life lacking them: he sweated, breathed and slept surrounded by sheets of paper. He took to writing his wife short letters, telling her in substance that everything she had said was absolutely right. In what free time he had, he requisitioned a stopwatch and tried to figure out his discharge date in terms of minutes, seconds and fifths of seconds.

Then, at the beginning of the first summer, the First Sergeant had his second and final stroke of luck, and it looked for a long while as if everything had worked out for the best after all. He stopped writing letters to his wife almost immediately after the Captain was called back to headquarters and a new, a younger Captain was assigned to the command. This new Captain was not at all interested in communications; he told the First Sergeant the first day he was in that before he got involved in a flow of messages, he had first to become acclimated to the situation. That was perfectly all right with the First Sergeant; immediately he saw the change working through in other things; it was magical. Messages from headquarters seemed to diminish; there were days when they could be numbered in the tens, and the First Sergeant found that he had more time to himself; he started to write a short novel about his combat experiences in four wars and eight limited actions. Also, his role in combat had shifted drastically. Perhaps because of the new Captain's familiarization policy, he was permitted to carry a rifle with him, and now and then, he even took a cautious shot, being careful to point the instrument in the air, so that there would be no danger of hitting anyone on his own side. Once, quite accidentally, he hit one of the enemy's trees (they were attacking the forest that day) and destroyed a shrub; it was one of the most truly important moments of his life. Meanwhile, the new Captain said that he would contact headquarters eight times a day and that would be that.

The First Sergeant moved into one of the most wholly satisfactory periods of his life. His wife's letters stopped abruptly after she said she had been promoted to the position of hostess, and he quietly cut his allotment to her by three dollars a month; no one seemed to know the difference. He went to bed early and found that he slept the night through, but often he was up at four o'clock because starting each new day was such a pleasure. Then, just as the First Sergeant had come to the amazed conviction that he was not by any means an accursed man, Hastings came acutely to his consciousness.

Hastings, who was some kind of Private, had put in for convalescent leave months before, during the bad time of the First Sergeant's life, but the old Captain had handled the situation very well. Now, the new Captain said that he had to be acclimated to the situation, and so it was the First Sergeant's responsibility to deal with Hastings, to tell him that the Captain could not be distracted at this time. For a while, Hastings listened to this quietly and went, but suddenly, for no apparent reason, he submitted *another* request for leave. From that moment, the difficult peace of the First Sergeant was at an end. Hastings insisted that this message had to reach the Captain, and the First Sergeant told him that it would be forwarded, but the Captain refused to take it because he said that he was in an adjustment stage. So, the First Sergeant kept the request in his desk, but then Hastings began coming into the tent every day to ask what action the Captain had finally taken. The First Sergeant knew right away that Hastings was crazy because he had a wild look in his eye, and he also said that the Captain was a coward for not facing him. In addition to that, Hastings began to look up the First Sergeant at odd times of the day to say that the Captain was functioning in a very unusual way; something would have to be done. When the First Sergeant finally decided that he had had enough of this, he went to the Captain and told him what was going on and asked him if he would, at least, look at this crazy Hastings' request, but the Captain said that it would take him at least several months to be acculturated to the degree where he would be able to occupy a judgmental role; in the meantime, he could not be disturbed by strange requests. Then, the Captain leaned over his desk and said that, just between them, he felt that Hastings was crazy: he was not functioning like an adult in a situation made for men. When he heard this, the First Sergeant laughed wildly and relayed this message to Hastings, hoping that it would satisfy him and that now the man would finally leave him alone, but Hastings said that all of this just proved his point: the Captain was insane. Hastings asked the First Sergeant if he would help him to get the Captain put away. *All* of this was going on then; the Captain saying one thing and Hastings another, both of them insane; and in addition to this, the limited war was still going on; it was going on as if it would never stop which, of course, it would not. The First Sergeant would have written his wife again if he had not completely forgotten her address and previously thrown away all of her letters.

Hastings and the Captain were on top of him all the time now, and neither of them had the faintest idea of what they were doing. Only a man who had been through four wars and eight limited actions could comprehend how serious the war effort was. Three days a week the company had a *forest* to capture; three days a week they had the cliffs to worry about, and on Mondays they had all of the responsibility of reconnoitering and planning *strategy*, and all of this devolved on the First Sergeant; nevertheless, neither of them would leave him alone. The First Sergeant had more duties than any man could handle: he supervised the officers' tents and kept up the morale of the troops; he advised the officers of the lessons of his experience, and he had to help some of the men over difficult personal problems; no one, not even a combat veteran such as himself, could handle it. He slept poorly now, threw up most of his meals, found his eyesight wavering so that he could not handle his rifle in combat, and he decided that he was, at last, falling apart under the strain. If he had not had all of his obligations, he would have given up then. They were that ungrateful, the whole lot of them. Hastings, the Captain; the Captain, Hastings: they were both lunatics, and on top of that, there was the matter of the tents and the communications. One night, the First Sergeant had his penultimate inspiration. In an agony of wild cunning, he decided that there was only one way to handle things. And what was better, he knew that he was right. No one could have approached his level of functioning.

He got up at three o'clock in the morning and crept through the forest to the communications tent and carefully, methodically, lovingly, he tore down the equipment, so that it could not possibly transmit, and then he furiously reconstructed it so that it looked perfect again. Then, he sat up until reveille, scribbling out headquarters communiques, and he marked DELIVERED in ink on all of the company's messages to headquarters. After breakfast, he gave these messages to the Captain, and the Captain took them and said that they were typical headquarters crap; they were the same as ever. The Captain said then that sometimes, just occasionally, you understand, he thought that Hastings might have a point, after all. The First Sergeant permitted himself to realize that he had stumbled on to an extremely large concept; it was unique. Nothing that day bothered him at all.

The next morning, he got up early again and crept through the cliffs to the communications tent and wrote out three headquarters messages advising the Captain to put his First Sergeant on the point. When the Captain read these, he looked astonished and said that this had been his idea entirely; the First Sergeant led the column that day, firing his rifle gleefully at small birds overhead. He succumbed to a feeling of enormous power and, to test it, wrote out no messages at all for the next two days, meanwhile keeping the company's messages in a DELIVERED status. The Captain said that this was a pleasure, the bastards should only shut up all the time like this. On the third day, the First Sergeant wrote out a message ordering that company casualties made heavier to prove interest in the war effort; two men were surreptitiously shot that day in combat by the Junior-Grade Lieutenants. By then, the First Sergeant had already decided that, without question, he had surpassed any of the efforts of western civilization throughout five hundred generations of modern thought.

Headquarters seemed to take no notice. Their supply trucks came as always; enlisted men looked around and cursed with the troops and then went back. They did not even ask to see the First Sergeant because he had let it be known that he was too busy to be bothered. The First Sergeant got into schedule, taking naps in the afternoon so that he could refer daily stacks of headquarters messages in the early morning. One morning, he found that he felt so exceptionally well that he repaired the equipment, transmitted Hastings' request for convalescent leave without a tremor, affixed the Captain's code countersignature, and then destroyed the radio for good. It seemed the least that he could do in return for his good luck.

This proved to be the First Sergeant's last error. A day later, a Corporal came from headquarters to see the Captain, and later the Captain came looking for the First Sergeant, his white face stricken with confusion. He asked who the hell had allowed that Hastings to sneak into the tent and thus get hold of the equipment? The First Sergeant said that he did not know anything about it, but it was perfectly plausible that this could happen; he had other duties and he had to leave the radio, sometime or other. The Captain said that this was fine because headquarters had now ordered Hastings' recall and had arranged for him to be put in a hospital. The Corporal had come up to say something about a psychiatric-discharge. The First Sergeant said that he would handle this, and he started to go to the Corporal to say that Hastings had just died, but the Captain followed and said that this was not necessary because he himself had had Hastings' future decided; he would take care of things now. The Captain said that Hastings was not going to get out of any damned company of his any way at all; he would make things so hot for that lunatic now that it would not be funny for anyone at all. The Captain said that *he* was in control of the situation and there was no doubt about that whatsoever. The Sergeant left the Captain's presence and went outside to cry for half an hour, but when he came back, he found the space empty, and he knew exactly what he was going to do. He stayed away from the Captain until nightfall and, as soon as it was safe, dictated a total war communique. In the morning, breathing heavily, he delivered it to the Captain. The Captain read it over twice and drooled. He said that this was the best thing that had ever happened to anyone in the entire unfortunate history of the Army. He said that he would go out immediately and make a speech to his troops. The First Sergeant said that he guessed that this would be all right with him; if he inspired them, it could count for something in combat.

The First Sergeant did not even try to listen to the mad Captain's idiotic speech. He only stood behind and waited for it to finish. When Hastings came over after it was done and cut the Captain's rear end harmlessly with a bayonet, the First Sergeant laughed like hell. But later, when he went to the broken equipment, wondering if he could ever set it up again, he was not so sure that it was funny. He wondered if he might not have done, instead, the most terrible thing of his entire life. Much later and under different circumstances, he recollected that he had not.

The Wooden Grenade

I

STEIN, AN obsessive, carried a large dummy hand grenade in: the right pocket of his converted Army fatigue jacket. This instrument, which he had found in a surplus store two years ago while hunting for a rifle, he now carried with him everywhere he went, squeezing it through the fabric, stroking it with his fingertips and at private moments during the day removing it to better inspect its contours. He had no interest in rifles. All of the shapes of his grenade were varied and beautiful to him, and at night, when his door was secured, he would stare at it, sometimes for hours.

The counting, however, had started only recently. Now, he counted objects and actions, furiously added and subtracted numbers. Sixty, no, 'sixty-one steps, he measured, and four nails in the opposite wall as he climbed the last flight of stairs in a condemned tenement one gray October morning. One hundred and twenty-five divided by seven is seventeen point eighty-three, times ten equals one hundred seventy-eight point three and the wall was green: that much was obvious, although one could not tell specific qualities by the light of one bulb in the exhausted hallway. If four steps, he thought, made twenty-five yards, then one step would make six and one-half. All of this Stein considered as he ascended with groans, fondling his grenade while two stricken children far beneath leaned upwards in the well and cursed him twelve times each. They knew that he was from the Government and, solemnly, Stein knew that they were right to swear. At the top of the flight he paused, wavering in dimness, rubbing his eyes with one' hand while he looked for numerals on the doors. Counting vigorously, he saw opposed apartments and a third angle between; this last bore the number *forty-two* but the others were not as clear. One had a number *three* hanging by a staple with a blank scar where the other number would have been, and the other door was barren — Stein knew that they would not maintain their apartments in this building, not with the landlord in jail and *three* contractors assuring the

Municipal Board that each of the others was the most dangerous. The contractors were the whole problem, Stein thought furiously, and he took his notebook from under his arm and made an entry with a pencil, the strokes uneven because of his limited vision. *Three contractors,* he wrote, *and three apartments. Is this rule of three symptomatic?* He closed the book with a snap, hearing it echo for several yards and, half bending, removed his grenade from his pocket, shielding it with his cupped hands. In the glow of the shattered bulb it acquired an infinity of colors and Stein rubbed his thumbnail over it, bringing one surface to a high polish. He could, if he wished, pull an imaginary pin and hurl it down all the flights,' in which case it would explode and bring the fire: the consuming fire virgin in its purity that would lift the tenement into the air and hurl it, mumbling with dread, into some primal sea, as the tenants gasped with wonder and blew free of their history. Or, he could replace the grenade in his pocket and come to terms with the building for the next quarter-hour, knowing that at any 'instant he could extract his instrument, show it to the woman whom he was about to interview, and say: *It's all over now, Mrs. Silver; better hold your ears, honey.* The latter choice was more temporarily seductive but he replaced the grenade with a moan: it had never looked better than it did this morning.

"Hoo! He's a big mother," one of the children below whistled to his friend. Stein began to stumble through the hall, looking for the right apartment. *Yes I am,* he mumbled, *and I'll blow you and your friend and your tenement all off the face of this perished earth.*

"Can't do that," he heard the other child say softly, "this one official."

The apartment numbered *three* was the place to start, and he hit the door flatly with both palms, three times. *Yes, the three was symptomatic;* it had all kinds of significance: the three wishes and Trinity and the third, the prodigal son, cast to the lost countries, all of it was clear as a result of his perception. When he heard nothing inside the door, Stein hit it again, slapping his fists against it briskly. Instantly, the door was snatched open as if the occupant within had been standing behind it for a generation, testing his resolve for a moment precisely like this. Stein looked at the caverns of an old man's face and reeled: it did indeed look like a minefield.

"I'm sixty-five years old," the man said. "Just got my first Security check, day before last." "That's fine," Stein said. "Does Silver live here? I have an appointment."

"Got me a check that says Government right on it in printing," said the old man, running his tongue over his lower features. It was long and amazingly mobile. "Told me, m'wife did, before she died, that those bastards in the Federal Building would never come across; no loot from the Government! she said. Guess I proved a thing or two."

Over the shoulder of the old man, Stein could see the apartment's kitchen: it was streaked with pastels and scotch-taped to the walls were several hundred pictures of female breasts; detached from their owners, they had the curious look of a battery of artillery. The old man followed his glare and grinned at the pictures. "Betcha your pop's no fool," he said, "even though he's living' with his black brothers, old pops knows what's good in this world. Ain't that right, son?" He winked at the pictures. "Seen better'n that, you betcha life, son."

With difficulty, Stein looked away from the breasts and at his feet, rubbing his hands together as If the grenade were there. "I'm looking for a Mrs. Silver," he said. "I'm from the Government."

A look of terrible cunning came into the old man's eyes; he began to close the door. "Ain't gettin' my Social Security, son," he said. M'wife said you fellas be knockin' down doors, trying to take away m'money. M'wife's dead."

"I'm in a different branch," Stein said quickly, patting his grenade through his coat pocket, "I have other business. "

"No foolin' the old scout Johnny. Ain't no branches, *just one Government.* You can't touch my Security! Worked forty-seven years I did." .

Clamping the grenade hard, Stem could feel, even through the layers of the jacket, a distant warmth, a puppy's affection. He wondered what the old man would do if he took out the grenade and showed it to him. "I just want to see someone named Mrs. Silver."

"Government fellas," the old man said, closing the door. "Smart young Government whippersnappers come 'round lookin' to take back the old man's money. Ain't no young buck gonna have the brains to do. that." From the inside, Stein could hear the creaking of panels as the old man leaned. "Gonna hole up and drink on Government money till I die." Stein heard puffs of laughter, long gasps. "Government ain't gettin'. in my way *no more.*"

Alone in the hall, Stein shrugged and tilted his warm right hand at the ceiling. With the light from the apartment gone, it was quite dim again and, sighing, Stein lit a match and, peering through his dark glasses, went to the door of the opposed apartment.

"Screw," said one of the children below, "now he fixin' to put this place to fire."

"No. no," the other said; "he just tryin' to find a way for himself."

Stein flicked the match and threw it down the well, he spasmodically hit at the door of the other apartment with both hands, knowing that this was the *second* time that he had done this today and that, therefore there must follow at some time, a third. The door was flung open. A sweating cheek came out toward him then another; then Stem saw the entire face of a woman plastered over a fine, trapped delicacy which flickered at him from the corners of the half-closed eyes. "Me Silver," the woman said, "what you want?"

"Mrs. Silver? I'm from the Government. I — "

"I expected you," the woman said. She grabbed Stein by the shoulder, dragged him into a long, long corridor at the end of which he could sense kitchen smells and an accretion of dishes. "I've been waiting for you." Twirling in her grasp, rubbing his grenade, breathing absently through his mouth, Stem hopelessly followed.

II

Four years ago, Stein's grenade had hit. The entire situation had started then. There were just two of them in the enclosure when it happened, the Sergeant and Stein in his private's fatigues, steel pot absurdly jammed so deep on his head that his ears were blocked. All up and down the range that day, privates in fatigues were experimenting with their new grenades, fondling them, stroking their surfaces, half-burying them to gloat in the stand; looking with lust at their discovered possibilities, they waited for the Sergeants to come in for the fire. The Sergeants went with vast weariness down the rows of cubicles; they supervised the pulling of the pin and at the top of the throw they would shout for the private to release; then the grenade would go out fifty, sixty, seventy yards into the mud where it ticked and erupted. All up and down the range, then, the grenades were exploding in an intricate rhythm; two would hit at the same time and there would be a flash and roar, a pause, perhaps, of three seconds and another two would throw; then four more would hurtle into their smoke; it was all a delicate and precise business. In the last stall on the third line, Stein kneeled with the grenade in his right hand, staring. He knew that at any moment he could take the pin and diminish his life by ten-count; after, the entire line would be an inferno, but he tried not to think of this. Looking sadly at his grenade, knowing that he had the power in his hand to destroy, Stein found it all too much to contemplate: one twitch, one misplaced synapse, and it would all be in flames; Captain, Basic Training, Sergeants and the Company.

This mixture of conscience and terror which kept the grenade lying shyly at his knee was such a narrow thing: Stein could feel it disintegrate as he squeezed the grenade and thought what an excellent thing it would probably be if all of them were to be pulverized. He waited, sweating in his clenched uniform, for the Sergeant to come in. On the far left, in the tower, a Lieutenant with a megaphone bellowed for synchronization of the fire, and Stein heard him as if from a great distance, then suddenly with power and immediacy, this shifting all as if in the first instants of true sleep. He was in a state of near-collapse; that was evident. This Lieutenant was two hundred yards away, but the megaphone injected him into every aspect of the field, into the helmet of every private. Looking at the grenade, Stein felt waves of potential lashing at him.

This was the point that he had reached when the Sergeant came into the cubicle behind him, a small grim man wearing heavy combat belt and boots as if some undeclared and buried war had raged on these plains since the edge of the last engagement; there was an exhaustion about him which frightened Stein, gauging as he did the weariness of the small Sergeant from the way his feet lurched as he came into the cubicle and from the movement of his throat every time the grenades roared. It was not something he would have expected. The Sergeant detatched his canteen, had a careful drink of water, examined Stein. "Jesus Christ," he said, "look who they're giving grenades. Will you stop *staring* at it for God's sake?"

"I wasn't staring."

"You certainly *were* staring. You could knock out the fuse with your eyes. Hey," the Sergeant said, "you know why the Lieutenant's so nervous up there?"

"No."

"They're all misplacing the fire. Your whole company. The whole lot of you scared stiff."

Stein, astonished, rolled the grenade absently with his fingers, hoping that the Sergeant did not notice. "I'm scared too," he said.

The Sergeant squatted gracelessly in the sand, leaned toward Stein and picked up the grenade delicately. "I've thrown a thousand of these things," he said confidentially.

"Yes?"

"Got in the trenches on Midway once stuck with a load of them; needed to blast out Japs and threw them one after another. Exposed, opened the whole position," the Sergeant said almost cheerfully, "and the Japs came down. Then one blew up on me; put me in the back lines for months. Know how many operations I took?"

"I don't know," said Stein.

"Had *six* for the damage that thing done. What do you think of that?"

"I think they're very dangerous," Stein said, looking at the trees, at the line of smoke which drifted from the near horizon and hearing the bellowing of the megaphone Lieutenant, the cries of the men as the grenades hit, throwing fire against yards of sand. "I don't like them.'"

"You don't like them," said the Sergeant. "I'm scared *sick* of them." He paused. "So don't think that just because you all been lucky today those things ain't murder. Jesus," murmured the Sergeant, "I don't know how they give people like *you* stuff like this. They're *combat. I wouldn't touch them.*"

Stein said nothing, looked away from the Sergeant, clamped his hands. Over the man's left shoulder he could see the dry grass and trees of the rear range; somewhere in the distance beyond that was the road over which the trucks and cars occasionally passed, the trucks filled with men like-embryos hunched over the rear panels, stripped to the waist and sobbing with exhaustion: KP details on the way to post. The cars, when' they murmured by, were bright, insolently ornamented and fast; the post was on the outskirts of a college town and Stein could see the opaque faces of young men and girls, laughing as they looked upon the range. They were amused by the Army. In the far distance, Stein now imagined that he could hear this laughter, wavering under the horizon, against the organs of the field, from all the spaces where the cars were and where they had gone, and it covered. the range, assaulting him. Now, in a small pocket of time, as the Sergeant reached toward the grenade to tell him what to do, he saw an officer's vehicle pass gracefully. On the rear parapet of the jeep was a young Captain in dress khakis looking at the range with binoculars moving them up and down in rapid, polished strokes. Stein restrained an idiotic impulse to brandish his grenade and wave. The officer leaned perilously and said something to his driver; the jeep began to pick up speed and in an instant it was moving very quickly, but the Captain still remained on his parapet, looking at the range. Stein, in his fatigue, imagined that he could see the eyes of the Captain through the binoculars, the clenching of his hands as he moved the instrument up and down and told his driver: *Follow the road out of here; follow it fast.*

"Softball," the Sergeant was saying, "you know softball?"

"Yes."

"I don't mean *rules;* I mean how to throw a ball. Quick and sharp."

"I think I know that," Stein said. On the parade ground before Reveille he had thrown stones in the darkness, practicing a windup that morning. The stones had clattered on ridges of the field and Stein had been unable to judge how he was throwing: *can't toss a grenade like that,* he had muttered in the darkness, hearing the stones collide.

"Then take this," the Sergeant said with a sigh of disgust. He handed Stein his grenade; after the fingers of the Sergeant had touched it, it seemed to have an entirely different composition, be tilted at a different angle to his hand. From its surface seemed to come an odor of smoke. "Practice throws," the Sergeant Said. He put his knees in the sand and looked up at Stein, his eyes hollow and vaguely pleading.

Stein lifted the grenade and jerked his arm listlessly several times, looking away from the Sergeant. When he turned back, the eyes of the Sergeant had become absolutely blank and the man leaned forward and put Stein's index finger on another surface, sullenly moved his arm for him while Stein shuddered at the horrid rasp of skin. "All right," the Sergeant said, panting, looking down the line at the cubicles and the invisible troops crouched howling inside. "I got *my* insurance. You might as well kill us now as later." Glancing at the walls of the cubicle, the Sergeant said, "Go on. And when you throw it, throw it! I don't want my wife getting that damned insurance; not until I finish this enlistment, at least, and get into her a few more times." Unreasonably, the Sergeant giggled. "I got two years left on this hitch," he said, "then I re-up again. You want *me* to throw that thing? I don't care. It don't mean nothing to me. Don't tense up when you throw it. Stay calm. You know what it was like after Midway, lying all taped up in the hospital? No one came in to see me for a month, and then it was an re-enlistment officer. You going to throw that grenade? Listen, if you don't, *I* will and — "

"*No!*" Stein said, his voice sounding peculiarly unresonant and distant in his ears, the voice of a departed man, someone, perhaps, of whom he had once read seated in a comfortable chair: *poor son of a bitch.* "I want to throw that grenade. I *have* to!"

"Then throw it," said the Sergeant, his eyes blinking. He crouched again to his haunches, blew on his hand, looked dully at Stein. "Bum down the blasted range, college boy."

Stein, hearing this, brought the grenade into the air and lofted it, feeling as if his arm were essentially detached; feeling that only his arm had anything at all to do with this, he brought the grenade back slowly. It was too slow to gather momentum and the Sergeant shouted something but Stein, by then, at the top of his swing, with a graceless gesture of two fingers, had disengaged the pin. It fell noiselessly in a small arc into the sand and as Stein saw this in the comer of his vision, he felt an instant of pure freedom, an infinite stroke of time in which he existed alone with the grenade, the range somewhere far below where it rattled to the frantic voice of the Sergeant. He felt the instrument bounce against his palm, looked far down at the row of trees where it was going surely to be placed. Then, at last, he heard the Sergeant screaming at him to throw the grenade, and Stein thought, *he's really scared.* Then the grenade fell from his hand. It cleaved like a knife through the damp surface of his palm and fell. Stein looked at it with disinterest. It had been a silly thing to happen. The grenade lay half-toppled beneath; it seemed impossible that it was going

to go off. It looked like an artifact. Stein reached with a foot to turn it over for examination.

The Sergeant screamed suddenly and dived on top of him, slapped him sharply in the temple and Stein fell with a gasp away from the grenade, to the other side of the pit. The Sergeant was on top of him, holding him desperately by the shoulders and burying his face in the sand; Stein choked and realized that the Sergeant was putting him in deeper and deeper. Stein had the sudden impression that he was far below all sense of action; sand was in his nostrils and ears and all he heard was a thick, whirring absence of sound. He stretched an arm forward to pull some grains from his ear. Then, with a series of maddened and ferocious explosions, the grenade erupted. There were successions of high, white, furious flashes, and atop him, the Sergeant muttered and bucked as if he were about to enter the sand. Stein, pulling free of the trap then with a groan amidst the fragmentation, wondering, saw this. The men down the line were running at him. Some of them were crying.

III

In the induction station two months before that, it had been like this: the man sitting next to Stein was almost thirty and his features were already lit with certain intimations of a waiting and unique disaster. The two of them had sat rigidly against one another there in the empty room for some time, all alone on the bench, far back from the Recruiting Sergeant and his telephone, and finally the man had said, not looking at him but staring out the window at the feet of many people lurching on to their meals, "What they get *you* for?"

"I don't know," Stein said quietly, "I don't really know." Did anyone know? he thought, looking at the precise frieze in front of him. You vanished into a series of situations; out of them another individual came to a pass that looked final but was, of course, only another prologue. It was all too abstract. "It wasn't something I could get away from," he said. "I mean to say, I had no dodges."

The man looked as if he were about to spit at him but then he considered the Sergeant ahead carefully, as if he were measuring him for some gloomy meeting. The Sergeant was talking into his phone, looking in their direction every now and then with a vaguely reminiscent stare; it appeared that he had momentarily forgotten their business but would surely, in just an instant, remember, and to their regret.

"Let me tell you what I'm in for," the man said, "I'm in because of some very strong suicidal tendencies." He folded his hands and thought for a moment, apparently satisfied with what he had said. "Because that's always been the pattern," he added, "that and the stupidity. I never was too bright, being blocked by neurotic tendencies. And I didn't save myself when I could have; They got me for two years now."

Stein said nothing, grimacing, turning to look out the window. He thought he could see a crowd of girls, bright dresses shimmering in the heat, hurrying to lunch, shouting at one another and he felt a wave of exhausted lust; their circumstances, after all, were not nearly so different from his own.

"They're trapped, too," he said to the man. It was a new insight. "You're damn right. The General on the phone there is worse in it than we are. But he likes 'it.'"

"I mean the girls."

The man looked at the floor delicately, rubbed his shoetip. "What girls?"

"The girls outside. They're in offices; we're in the Army. It's the same thing."

"Oh, is it really?" the man said quietly, moving away from Stein a trifle. "It's exactly the same thing, of course. I'm too neurotic to have thought about it until you caught it for me, of course."

But Stein felt an explosive restlessness within; it was something new, he had definitely seen something he had not seen previously. If he sat in one enclosure outside his chosen possibilities, surely all of the girls swiveled their way through a series of others and, if that were the case, was not communion possible? *He had never before considered women in that way.* There had always been a high elevation, a great distance and purpose in their circumstances; nothing simple. Now, he was not so sure. *Why, that's the trouble,* he thought with excitement, *that's the whole trouble! It's simple!* "I never saw before," he said.

"Well, reach down and feel."

"It's all the same," Stein said with astonishment. "It's all the same."

"That's what I said the day I went for my physical. But it isn't. What are you talking about, anyway?"

"Forget it," Stein mumbled, embarrassed. But his vision was clearer. In his hand was a duffel bag with his induction papers; he was waiting for a Corporal to come and lead them to the ceremony, close the shutters and be done with it. He had put himself there and yet it was not too late. It might be a court-martial offense to leave, to tell the Sergeant at the desk that he had reconsidered the matter and wished to postpone induction. But then again, there might be crevices of mercy in the institution that he had not fathomed; surely the Sergeant might see what had happened. They could go out into the corridor and discuss it like gentlemen, the Sergeant and Stein, and then the Sergeant would come back and destroy Stein's folder, send him back to the girl-strewn streets with a favoring sigh. *You beat the game.* But then again, possibly and more likely, the as-to-the-moment friendly Sergeant might lean back in his chair, regard him with malicious glee and order his arrest. *We got you.* It could easily go that way. Stein got to his feet and put the duffel bag on the bench, brushing it against the man's hip. "I've got to talk to him about something," he said.

"You're not quite steady, are you?"

Stein went to the desk and waited for the Sergeant to put the telephone down while he looked through the window, looking for the legs of the girls. From this new angle in the center of the room, Stein could see only the sky, a blank wedge which covered the entire window. Momentarily, he shuddered. "What is it?" the Sergeant said absently, still on the phone.

"I want to talk to you about something."

"Looking forward to the South, huh?"

"Look," Stein said urgently, "I haven't been sworn in yet."

"You have to understand," the Sergeant said into the phone, "that there's only so much meat we can ship. If I tell you two, it's two. What do you want to do-replace the whole Fifth Army?"

"In the first place," Stein said, "I'm a voluntary induction."

"And if I tell you two, you'll like it," the Sergeant whispered into the telephone. "Some times are good; some aren't so good. *You'll make do with what I send you!*" He paused for a moment, looked over Stein's shoulder to the man sitting on the bench. "Anyway, one of them's experienced. He was in Korea."

"I want to hold back my draft," said Stein.

"Wait a minute," the Sergeant said to the telephone. He turned to Stein. "Son, when you're in, you're in," he said. "That's the way it is. Now sit down and wait."

Stein looked into the clear eyes of the Sergeant and said, "Do I have to?"

"Yes," said the Sergeant. "Yes?" he said into the phone. "Yeah, it was tough luck for that one all right, no doubt about it."

Stein returned to the bench and moved somewhat closer to the man. "You were in Korea?" he asked.

"Yes indeed," the man said. His voice now was at an absolute variance with the sense of his words; it was as if an insistent child had crept within his glazed skin and was engaging in an intense series of disturbed motions. "Couldn't get enough of it. Missed the Army the whole ten years I was out. Now I'm going to be happy again."

"I just tried to get out of here," Stein said pointlessly.

The man giggled. "Well, here you are," he said.

"What can I say? I had a bad basis for coming in myself. You know, those office girls outside — "

"Might lay you," the man said shockingly, "and you just found that out after you walked in here. Well, that's too bad, son; that's really too bad."

"No, it isn't that," Stein said, looking at the scarred benches, the chipped walls, the dents in the floor; signs, he imagined, of a generation of men who had passed through this room as now he was, deep in their own false visions and dreams. "I didn't mean that at all," and he saw the wall on his right where someone had scrawled in what looked like charcoal: *You're screwed when you were born, private.* It seemed to be recent work. "It was something else."

"Something else," the man said. He paused and seemed about to say something else but then he said nothing at all, following Stein's glance to the message on the wall. When he saw it, he began to shudder. The two of them looked at it together for a long time and then the man began to nod vigorously as he rubbed and rubbed his hand. "You ain't kidding," he mumbled, "you ain't kidding. And all of us are privates. All of us. All of us. All of us."

IV

In the enclosure, then, it must have been this way. He had paused at the top of his swing looking far up and down the line, sensing on some low plane of perception that all of them-the men, the Lieutenants, the quivering Sergeant himself-were enjoying this. Now the grenades were roaring continuously; there was no pause in the thunder and Stein could see that there was a kind of structured destruction in the air; it was controlled; it was under a strong hold, but it was there. Near one of the scarred trees, a small fire was bitterly resisting the flailing and curses of two Corporals who had backed to a safer distance. Every time a particularly loud grenade erupted, the Corporals would nudge one another. Yes, Stein thought, heaving the grenade above his head, they were enjoying this too: the death was there, but also the promise, and some of it was beautiful. At the top of his swing he froze. It was as if he had become aware, after a very long and difficult time, that he had always been listening for a particular sound which was now about to be heard. He knew that this was to be the instant of its coming' but that he had to maintain absolute control to hear that sound. Stein did not know what it was; it was something far beyond the roar of the grenades and the yammering of the megaphone; it seemed to be in the form of a cry or whisper relating profoundly to his history, and he knew that if he held his position and waited, he would hear it. But this grenade could not be thrown for, if it was, the sound, when it came, would blend at once into the roar and would be gone, and with its unheard echo the most essential because undiscovered part of himself. Stein disengaged the pin, squeezed his grenade and waited. In just an instant it would be finished. The Sergeant screamed. But Stein did not hear him, did not hear the Corporals or· the megaphone, heard nothing; waiting in a frozen posture for that first music which would redeem him and bring him again to the surface of his unknown possibilities, an entire man. Fragmentation began.

V

"Now," said the woman named Silver, "now, I am going to tell *you* something." Across from Stein, a giant print clung damply to one of the walls — a horse and rider caught in an iron frieze, the animal about to throw the bearded man brutally into the mud but being restrained by a sharp spike on the man's left boot. Paralyzed by rage and pain, the horse appeared to be dribbling saliva; the man held one arm above his head in defiance and triumph. *They shouldn't have such things,* Stein thought tiredly, listening to the cadences of the woman's voice, *they should not have this contradictory tableau poised over violence and torture; it can excite people. Where do they get such things?* It was obvious that either horse or rider would be dead by nightfall. A drab sun was ·painted near the horizon; it was close to dusk, and the stables were near. Harshly, he withdrew from the print and turned to the woman sitting next to him on the couch; her legs were posed as if for scuttling flight but studded with painful scars and veins, her hands folded babylike into a large yellow pillow, her face bright with clear sorrow, and listened to her voice, hearing only that sound in an immense, empty sadness. When it was time, he said, 'What can you tell me, Mrs. Silver. What can you tell me?"

"Make you see *clear.*"

Stein pressed in his pocket and squeezed. "We *are* clear," he said, "that's our job. Now, You've got a father, right?"

"Most people do, but not like *this* one."

Hand in pocket, Stein continued. "The point is, the man *is* your father; he's over seventy. And now he's applying for Government compensation because, he's broke."

"Ain't broke," the woman said stubbornly. "Got it socked away, he does."

"Not to our knowledge. Now, as his only daughter and making a good salary — "

"I'm a *maid,* Mister."

"Whatever you are, you declared five thousand dollars last year." Stein allowed his hand to drift, completely enclose his object; it huddled inside like a sparrow. "Now, you're in a position to help him; under the law you've *got* to help him, don't you, Mrs. Silver?" *Ah,* thought Stein. *The spike on the heel of the boot of the rider.* "You talk easy, Mister. I got things to say, too."

Rubbing, Stein said, "We don't want to make anything difficult, Mrs. Silver. We just want to make our role clear in such a circumstance." *Good Lord,* he thought.

"I want to talk now."

"Go ahead," said Stein, stroking furiously, hoping that the woman could not see what he was doing. But he knew that his action was of no concern to her at the moment, and perhaps this was the real, the true, the concealed trouble after all.

"Trouble with you people from the Government is that you come in to *talk.* Sometimes, you got to listen."

"I'm listening."

"I'm an orphan. Let me tell you about my father. Let me just tell you about that man. My father left me and my mother when I was two years old. I'm lucky I didn't have to go to no orphanage because my mother, she killed herself to keep a home going. *I knew you was coming up here to ask me questions!* My mother died when I was in high school."

"I'm sorry to hear that," Stein said. He hunched lower against the cushion on which he was sitting and half-turned his right side into the wall, slipping his hand all the way down into his pocket. The woman did not notice. "Still, a lot of people have unfortunate childhoods. It's nothing new."

"Now, when my mother died it was just like this: I just come home from school one day and she was *stiff on the floor* with her bag in her hand. She was trying to go out to work, but a stroke hit her. My aunt and I had to make all the arrangements and we sent a telegram to my father's brother because we knew he knew where my father was and after fifteen years, we wanted that man to *see what he had done.*"

"Now you have to understand, Mrs. Silver, that a lot of things we do really aren't our fault. Because your father was the kind of man he was, what happened had to happen."

"I don't know what you're talking about," the woman said. "You ain't even listening to my words. Now, the next day, my aunt and I went down to the parlor to see her laid out, and you know what the man at the door told us? He said my father had come in and had come right out again; he got sick, he told the people there he was her husband and he *couldn't take it!* Couldn't take it!" the woman shrieked, "for fifteen years he couldn't take *nothing,* not even himself, and then he couldn't even see her dead! Well, that was the end of *him.*"

"But that just shows you're stronger than your father," Stein said. "Maybe that's why he's in his present situation — because he isn't very strong at all. The strong have to take care of the others." He turned to the woman, facing her. "Some of us are weak."

"That was the end of him," the woman said. "I ain't seen him and I don't want to hear nothing of his troubles and they'll lay me out, too, before I'll give him a cent. Now, that's my piece, you understand? *Do you?*"

My God, Stein thought, leaning back again into the cushions, removing his sopping hand from his pocket, patting the pages of his notebook. She lives on the fourth floor of a stinking tenement with perhaps three thousand (a good number) dollars in the bank and a few more here and there, in front of a print of a dying horse with an old television set and five or six pieces of furniture and no history at all. None whatever. *You have no history.* Mrs. Silver, he considered saying, and perhaps her eyes would opaque: *don't need none of that.* There's no point in any of this, he thought, beginning to crouch his legs to leave. There is no inducement, no lie, no fiction, no myth or religion in the universe that can compel me to stay longer and hear an (orphaned) woman sack her past. *This is something we cannot do!* Stein thought absently, looking through the window at the roof of another tenement on which he saw children playing amidst the blank surfaces, heard their cries. Further down the street, he knew with fragments of his gathered sense that there were a thousand sweating, beaten men and women sitting on porches drinking, plotting murder, vanishing after some moments to perform mechanical coupling; waiting, all of them, for the clean, the pure fire that would, by common destruction of all of the cubicles of the city, liberate them from their unique disaster. It was only morning and they were coming out to the stoops; later there would be more and more, and by the time the sun had come down there would be an attentive army sweltering against backdrop, waiting to move and yet unable to march because of their lack of a single vision — there were no barriers that they could not wreck if only they truly wanted. He got up smelling that flame, thinking furiously: *three times seven are twenty-one; fourtimes six are twentyfour; fivetimesfive-aretwentyfive. As we increase, we also reduce.*

"All right," he said, "you've told me the situation and I've listened, but the position of 'the Agency in this regard is clear."

The woman rocked back in her chair. "I knew you weren't listening."

"I was so listening. The position of the Agency, however, is established by law and we'll communicate with you by mail indicating exactly what the fixed amount of your contribution will be."

"Contribution!".

"I think I'm just upsetting us," Stein said quickly. "There's no point in my staying, is there? I just hope you understand my situation as well as you understand yours," he added meaninglessly and closed his notebook carefully, looking at the door.

The woman got up with a scream and poised herself against him, her eyes thin and lined with rage. *Like the Sergeant.*

"I ain't got no one," she said, "and I don't want no one! That's the way it is; I've accepted things!

They're going to knock this building down and make me move and *I'll accept that!* Now, why don't you and your goddamned city leave me alone and accept things, too? Why don't you leave us alone, me and my father! He made out! Why don't you leave *him* alone?" She began to sob and wandered away from him, standing finally in front of the window where the glare made her features invisible, an impenetrable mask. "There isn't no right to interfere."

Stein stood alone in the center of the room, matching her breathing gasp for gasp, and reached again in his pocket. He took out his grenade and showed it to the woman. "You see that?" he said.

"See what?"

"This thing."

"It looks like a chunk of rock."

"It's a grenade," Stein said, waving it. "It's a *real grenade!* I could blow everything up, you know that? You want me to?"

"Are you crazy?"

"I could blow everything to *pieces,"* Stein said wildly, "is that what you want me to do? 1 can't just *listen to* this, forever." .

"You work for the Government!"

"I'll blow the Government up, too!" "You're *crazy.* What kind of people they sending up to this place?"

"Do you want me to blow it up?"

The woman moved away from the window, edging along the wall, past the print to the door, her tongue flailing. "Stop it!" she said. "Stop it!"

With a shudder, Stein put his grenade away. "You don't want me to do it," he said. *"You want to live. You don't really mind it at all."*

"Get out of here!"

"No," Stein said, straightening his pocket. "You didn't mean a thing you said. I was just testing it. It's not real."

The woman flung open the door. "Get out!" she screamed, "I'll get the police!"

"I knew it; I knew it," Stein said. He leaped toward the door, his arms flailing at the woman. "You really didn't want it at all." He fled into the hallway's night like an assassin, feeling his grenade. "You have to be honest," he said, turning to the woman.

The door cracked shut, leaving Stein in darkness. The bulb had been extinguished, and for a long time he only stood there, breathing heavily, feeling the power against his hip. Conditions surely were becoming clear; the testing was to begin. After a while, he went to the door of the old man and, pressing his right side into the soft plaster, he knocked.

He knocked and knocked.

He knocked three times.

Anderson

HE IS elected President of the United States by an overwhelming margin. A mandate. Fifty-eight percent of the popular vote, five hundred and twelve votes in the Electoral College. Inexplicably, his opponent wins Nebraska. On the day after the election, Bitters whooping in the huge suite says that the first action of the administration will be to settle with those hayseeds. Anderson looks at him quizzically. "I don't want to punish anyone."

"What the hell," Bitters says, "don't you have any sense of humor?"

✳ ✳ ✳

"I have a gloomy premonition that we will soon look back on this troubled moment as a golden time of freedom and license to act and speculate. One feels the steely sinews of the tiger, an ascetic 'moral' and authoritarian reign of piety and iron."

—Robert Lowell, 1967

✳ ✳ ✳

Winding down. Everyone knows that it is on the line now; this is the time when men and boys get separated. It is a time for greatness. Fourth and one on the ten-yard line, thirty-six seconds left on the stadium clock, no time-outs, game hanging in the balance. Anderson perches over the center, his eyes filled with alertness, his chest heaving with the excitement of it all, the lacerating cold turning warm inside, each exhalation truly a burst of fire. He has never felt so alive as at this moment when truly he is dead, the ball coming into his hand, he scurries and sees the middle linebacker shooting through unblocked, coming upon him, eyes huge. Anderson gives an eh! of woe and cocks the ball for a desperation pass, try and get it into the end zone anyway but his foot slips and even before the linebacker hits him he feels himself falling to the hard Astroturf and then the man is upon him, grunting.

Even as the horn sounds, Anderson hears not only the game but all circumstance spilling from him. He knew that it was going to be very difficult but could not surmise that it was going to be like this. Not quite. Sounds are all around him as he spirals out. Down and out. Game to go on the two. In coma, he hears the sound of engines.

✳ ✳ ✳

Anderson, awakening from an unrecollected dream of loss, plots his moves, considers his fortune, then opens his eyes to look at the lustrous plaster of the bedroom as his wife tumbles all over him. This is not characteristic of Sylvia.

Petulant, demanding, she seizes him. Wearily, he commits himself. Foreign policy, ceremonial pens, the medal of freedom, state banquets, it is just another of the obligations of office.

Sylvia is inflamed by the idea of touching a President: she has never shown so much interest in the act as in this last year. Anderson does as he can, serves as he will, utters oaths of office, does as he must, holds to the center. He is a moderate. Sylvia capsizes upon him mumbling. Anderson charts his own release, thinking of ICBMs as convulsively, absently, he climaxes.

✳ ✳ ✳

Anderson lights a cigarette calmly and blows out the match, tosses it, inhales, then in a single graceful motion pushes in the swinging doors of the Circle Bar and walks through. In the poisoned darkness the two Lump brothers stand glaring at him, hands on their holsters. Half-consumed whiskey bottles stand behind them over the deserted bar. The bartender has dived for cover, the customers, no fools they, have filched out a side door. "All right," Anderson says, "this is it. One at a time or both of you, I don't care."

"Taste lead," Tom, the older one, says. His gun is in his hand and poised to fire when Anderson shoots him in the wrist. Tom Lump shrieks and falls. His point thirty-eight clatters to the crude surface of the bar.

"Next," Anderson says, the gun cocked, drawing down on Charles. The tall Lump stares at him; his eyes shift, his expression weakens. Slowly he raises his hands.

"I'll take you on with fists," Anderson offers, "right outside. Let's go."

On the floor Tom whimpers. "Listen," Charles says carefully, "we don't want any trouble here. You got us wrong."

"Not wrong, just drawn down," Anderson says. He holsters his gun. "Okay," he says. "Any arguments?"

Charles Lump says, "I got nothing to do with this. Tom brought me along for the ride, I ain't got nothing against this town and I'm the first to say so. Anything this town wants to do is okay with me, so there."

"Oh shut up," Tom says weakly, "you're in this with me up to the hilt. I'm going to bleed to death here you don't stop talking and get me a doctor."

"You can get to a doctor out of town," Anderson says. He throws down his cigarette, carefully stomps it out with a circular motion. No fires when the marshal is around. "Get up."

Charles turns, shrugs elaborately. On the floor Tom begins to dry heave, then vomits brightly. "Pack him over a horse and get him out," Anderson says, "there's a doctor over in Bluff City twenty miles west, you ought to be able to get him there before he passes out if you get going now."

There is no spirit left in either of the Lumps. Charles nods, bends, yanks Tom to his feet and lurches him past Anderson, out the swinging doors. Anderson watches them carefully, joins them then as they saddle up their horses, Tom clumsily in an attitude of prayer. Charles unhitches.

"There will be another time, Anderson," Tom says weakly.

"This isn't the way it ends."

"Shut up," Charles says, helping him mount with a push.

"Just get those reins and let's get outta here."

"I had hoped for more from you than that," Anderson says carefully. "Maybe a little more fight next time, eh?"

"Maybe," Tom says. "Nothing ever ends. It replicates. It goes on and on."

"For Christ's sake shut up," Charles says. "Let's just get the hell going."

"Got nowhere to go," Tom says. He seems to be edging into delirium. "Anywhere we go, got to come back and face it.

Unless we die out of it, Charlie. I think maybe I'll do that."

"Ain't so easy," Charles says. He glares at Anderson. "Ain't going to be so easy for you either; this is a tough country."

Anderson stares back flatly, showing the outlaw his inner strength and Charles Lump drops his eyes, coughs, shakes his head, mounts his horse and taking the tether of the other, moves slowly away. He does not look back.

Hands on hips, gun dangling from his index finger, Anderson watches them all the way out of Tombstone. Their figures and the horses diminish to small, concentrated blobs of darkness that blend at last with the landscape to leave him there eternally and as always, alone. Soon enough it will be time to turn and face the silent crowd who have massed behind him; he knows to pay them homage but for the moment Anderson does not need them, needs none of this at all, needs only the proud and terrible isolation which has been imposed on him in the role which he so humbly but gracefully has assumed:

The Avenger's front man.

Some years ago Anderson had begun to feel it all slip away, not only his career which had been slowly drained from him for many years but his very sense of self. All of his life, through the great times and the years of sorrow, he had been sustained as had most of those he knew by the belief that destiny was benign, that life was a sentence with a structure and that nothing so terrible could happen that would not yield salvation in the nick of time.

But the decade shook that faith. It shook faith but good, shock, implosion, the feeling of circumstance turning upon itself and there had been a period, it must have gone on for years, when Anderson had found himself questioning the sense of it all, when paralysis had settled like a cloak upon him; for a long time he had been unable to perform all but the simplest actions. Sex, sleep, panels, conventions. Never an introspective man—but not nearly as stupid as a lot of them took him to be; that was his secret and his strength—he had found it hard to handle, like an undiagnosed, dreadful virus hanging on at the lip of reason.

It was the riots, the war, the circling anguish and the bewilderment, the terrible settling anger in this country that he loved and to which he had dedicated his life and purpose.

Anderson could not get a handle on it. Surely it would have to be the times and not himself, because this should have been the best period of his life. Sylvia and he had the understanding, he had the travel and the conventions, physically he might not be all that he had once been, a little shaky in crowds maybe, not as certain in bed as he had once taken for granted but the sense of decay which cut from the center had to do with politics.

They were making shit of everything decent, of everything for which he stood, and it was too easy to say that they were communist dupes. That wasn't it at all. Anderson knew the truth by now; RED CHANNELS had sucked him in but he had outgrown that: there might be fifty practicing communists left. Underground there were fifty thousand or a million of them hiding but they were not coming out and they were not practicing their deceit. No, it was the kids themselves and the war and the outside agitators from the Congo running around to the ghettos on expense accounts inciting to riot. God *damn* it; he was a man of reasonable sensitivity but there was such a thing as going too far.

He went to the back lot to discuss it with the Lump brothers one morning. The Lumps hadn't been heard from in years and years: they had gone into the can along with Republic Studios but they were still there for pain and conversation, bored and lonely like most of the old characters, still hanging around the commissary and waiting for the big turnaround. Everyone was waiting for the big turnaround about then, Anderson too, but no one had looked up the Lumps for a long time and they were almost pathetic in their eagerness to talk. "Jesus *Christ*, Anderson," Tom said, extending his damaged wrist, the one that had been shot and had never properly healed, "It's good to see you. We never thought we'd see you again." Charles grabbed Anderson's free arm and rubbed it passionately. "Maybe you got some work?" he said.

"Yeah," Tom said, "work, we're ready. Got out equipment and everything. Ready to go."

"No work," Anderson said. He shrugged. "Just some questions."

"Hell," Tom said. "We were hoping for work. Soon as we seen you, we said this is it. We're going into that town again.

You can even shoot up the other hand if you want."

"Afraid not," Anderson said. "No town, no shooting." He squatted on his haunches in the old easy posture, the Lumps leaned over him, their faces beckoning and doglike. "Where did it go wrong?" Anderson said. "We were at the height of our power, we controlled everything. Then we started to pull out piece by piece, and we lost our power, the President got shot, the kids went crazy on us, and the whole thing started to come apart."

"Forget the President," Charles Lump said, "that was a good one; it was a move in the right direction."

"Maybe," Anderson said. He thought about it. Images of the city in the sun, the fallen roses. "Maybe it was but it wasn't civilized."

"Country ain't civilized unless things like that *do* happen," Charles Lump said. He spat. "You think it's easy taking lead on the back lots for thirty years? Got to be some point or purpose."

"But it's no answer."

"Ain't no answer," Tom said. "Bunch of tethered horses and old film that ain't been shown for years. Don't even show it in *television*."

"We were kind of hoping *you* might have an answer," Tom said painfully, flexing his wrist. "Least we could ask, you being the marshal who shot us up and threw us out of town and all that. If you don't have an answer, Anderson, who in hell does?"

"It's out there," Anderson said. "I know it is." A palpable sense of mystery seems to invade him; maybe it was for this that he went to see the Lumps. "I guess I'll go look for it."

"Well, you carry the news back when you get it," Charles said. "We'll be waiting. Maybe there'll be a little action in it for us, too."

Anderson stood. He waited politely for the Lumps to straighten but they remain crouched. Arthritis has caught their joints, sucked their motion. "Well," he said awkwardly, "guess I'll be seeing you."

"Sure thing," Charles Lump said. He extended a hand.

Anderson touched it, then patted old Tom on his shoulder.

"Sure was good times back then," Tom said.

Anderson nodded. He strode from the back lot but when he was back in his rental car heading toward Pasadena he came to understand that he had no real destination. Open-mouthed he drove the freeway for hours. Fortunately circumstance took him one more time.

✳ ✳ ✳

At the cabinet the Soviets' latest ultimatum is discussed.

Some suggest withdrawal while others counsel invasion or at least a fierce reply. Anderson shrugs, waves his hands.

"Whatever you say, whatever you think." It is all too much for him, poised as he is on the edge of a new idea.

✳ ✳ ✳

Forbes, the White House doctor gives him an unscheduled and unexplained physical. Sylvia's instigation? Rumors he is losing his grip? News reports that he seems to be tottering and losing the thread of his speeches? Anderson submits wearily. Bowels, digestion fine, he tells Forbes, mind focused and clear. In the sack? Forbes says shrewdly, his eyes glittering with interest. "No difference," Anderson says. It is an answer to cover everything. Forbes squeezes the sphygmomanometer bulb furiously until the constriction forces metal and then releases: in the expiring hiss Anderson hears the sound of a crowd. State has fumbled. He will get a chalice with the ball again.

✳ ✳ ✳

At three in the morning he gets the call from Bitters, acting for the Joint Chiefs, he says. Tracers in Alaska have found activity, radar had subsequently picked up a convoy of jets of undetermined origin streaking over the Pacific toward the Golden Gate Bridge.

"It doesn't look good," Bitters says.

"What the hell does that mean?" Anderson says. He has slept badly, moving from one convolute dream to the next, sound stages of memory inhabited by goblins and archetypes and for a moment he thinks that this is yet another dream but the speaker phone glints, Bitters' whining, melodramatic voice is not the voice of recollection. "Are they aggressive forces or not?"

"Well we don't know. They're *moving* aggressively."

"Is it possible the radar is wrong?" These things have happened, Anderson knows.

"No. We've ordered a retaliatory strike force into the air as a matter of fact."

"You did all this without clearing?"

"It's in the statutes," Bitters says nervously. He has been with Anderson for a long time. Since the Senate campaign as a matter of fact. Anderson has never been able to figure out exactly how Bitters has insinuated himself so deeply into his political life and the administration but it was never worth the trouble of confrontation. Get along, go along. He had been a good appointments secretary anyway.

"Then why are you clearing it with me now? Why don't you just go ahead and deliver the payload? Isn't that what you want?"

Bitters says nothing. That is the key to his power; he responds only to those questions which he can answer, ignores the rest. Anderson has come to admire the quality; he has learned a bit of it himself. "Well," he says, "what am I supposed to do? Wake the Premier and tell him what's going on here? Is it an international crisis or not?"

"I'm just advising you of the situation," Bitters says.

Anderson reaches out and cuts the connection. For an instant he is insanely attracted by the idea of going back to sleep. The bombers will meet on their suicide collision or they will not; the retaliatory strikes will begin or they will not … but in a few hours it will all be over anyway and either way it goes there will be no penalty for him. None whatsoever.

The idea lunges at him like a lover, casts tentacles heavy with desire over him; it is with an effort that Anderson drags himself from the iron compulsion and stumbles from the bed.

He hits switch after switch, floods the room with light. The entire mechanism of this government is his to command, the awesome technology that can spirit his voice to the Premier or a hundred thousand missiles to deadly target is waiting to serve, but at this moment, in this room, it is to Anderson as if none of it exists, as if all of it, the situation, the Presidency itself, is hallucinatory and that if he were to fully concentrate he would be fourteen years old and back in his Omaha bedroom, peeping at the more benign shapes of the night.

Shakily he pours himself a drink from the bottle by his bedside, thinking of the sounds of the flatlands as they poured through his bedroom. There were no planes in the sky then, no missiles, no bombers, no retaliatory strike forces or warheads or Joint Chiefs. No Bitters. There were only he and hope in the darkness but that was a long time ago to be sure and of no moment. What is happening now is that he is in the grip of some kind of international crisis and he cannot find a position.

What would a President do? Anderson thinks about it.

There was that Henry Fonda film which dealt with something similar but he had never seen it, just heard about it. Actually he was pretty weak on movies in which he had not acted, he was too busy making films in that time to watch them, and there are serious gaps in his background, important matters hence which he will never come to understand. The phone lights and he thinks about ignoring it, then sighs and activates. "All right," Bitters says, "this has been discussed and the decision is that there's no alternative but a full retaliatory strike."

"What if it's a mistake?"

"Everyone knows the rules of this. There's no mistake anyway; we've checked it visually. Those jets are a thousand miles outside circumference in a target zone."

Circumference. Target zone. Anderson has always admired the cool language of the military; they seem to have a handle on things. "So you want the bombers ordered up."

"That's already done."

"What if I countermand?"

"That would he unwise."

"For God's sake," Anderson says, "you're talking about the end of the world, don't you know that?"

"You're talking about the end of San Francisco regardless."

"So does attacking them bring it back?"

"Does not attacking them save the rest of the country?

This is just the first step. They're testing our will."

"What if it's just a bluff?"

"They're over the perimeter. You don't understand that this is very serious business."

"The fate of the world is my concern."

"Unless you countermand, then," Bitters says and cuts the connection. Anderson looks at the speaker in amazement. The dull sound of transmission warns him that he must cut his own end. What the hell do I do now? He thinks. He cuts the connection. What have I gotten myself into here? I didn't want any of this. I was just doing a favor for some friends.

What the hell kind of ambitions did I have anyway? I wanted to save the world, not to end it. This is craziness. I'm an old man, I need my rest. I should be asleep now.

"Take them out," Tom Lump says wisely, clutching his withered hands. Tom and he have become more intimate in recent days; unlike his brother he feels free to come into the Presidential bedroom and engage in reminiscence, now offer advice. "What the hell else can you do? They've strayed."

"This could be the end of the world, Tom."

"Oh come on," Tom says calmly. "Shoot. The world isn't going to end. All that we've heard since 1946 is that if we did this, if we did that, the world would end and nothing much has happened except that every time we didn't take that stand they'd nibble another piece off. If we'd just gone ahead and acted like men from the start they wouldn't be putting bombers over us now but that doesn't mean we have to back off."

Tom spits, rubs his heel over the spot. "Awful sorry to do that in your bedroom," he says. "The White House and all. I mean this is the President I'm talking to, I mean to show a little respect."

"It isn't that simple you know," Anderson says, "I used to think it was but it's different once you get into this office; you see all kinds of problems—"

"Shoot again," Tom says wisely, "we've heard that kind of crap from anyone who ever came into the government; they campaign that they're going to clean things up, change them, stop putting up with what got us here and the next thing you know they're talking about the powers and problems of office and the humility of leadership and the complexity of the times and the *next* thing you hear it's the same crap all over again until someone else shoots them or blows them out." Tom clutches his emaciated wrist. "Long time ago when something had to be done you just went ahead and *did* it," he reminds Anderson. "Wasn't kind and hurt like hell but I'm still walking around and it sure cleaned up the problem, didn't it? You were right to do it and I'm the first one to say it. You had no choice. It was a lucky thing you spared my life but you could have cut me down and my brother too in that street and it would have served us right.

"That was the movies," Anderson said. "That wasn't really happening, that was film. Wasn't it? You can't take that kind of stuff all that seriously, Tom."

"Really?" Tom says. "Seemed real enough to me. Seems real enough right now. Can't pick up a coffee cup in this hand, hurts all night and real bad when I get up in the morning. I reckon it was real."

"It wasn't," Anderson says. But maybe it was, he thought.

It was certainly as real as this. He had lines which made more sense than anything going on here and the heat under the camera had been terrific. The pain was real, later, in the daily rushes it carried. "I've got to make a decision here," he says.

"I've got to face up to it."

"Seems to me the decision is made. All you got to do now is let events take their course."

"I'm the President. I'm supposed to control events."

"That's just stuff you heard on television," Tom says.

"That's just stuff you seen in the movies."

"What does that mean?"

"You start to talk about what's real, what's *not* real," Tom says, "you ought to think about that Bitters."

"What?"

"He don't seem so real to me," Tom says. "Seems to me that he's carrying on like something out of the movies. Where the hell did he come from, huh?"

Anderson stares at him.

"Just think about that," Tom Lump says, "just think about that."

He winks and vanishes.

Anderson can't think about it. Not now. If Bitters isn't real what is he then, a figment of his imagination that he has dragged from the Nebraska Senate campaign clear on, a dozen years later, to the White House and nuclear crisis?

What is he, a hallucination, someone be has invented to blame for the acts which he cannot accept himself? No, he will not even think about it; what he has to decide now is if this is all some kind of psychological test. Maybe that is the answer.

Forbes and Sylvia and Bitters are in on it; probably the Lump brothers too. They are testing his will and resolve.

Anderson knows all about the rumors from the press digests Bitters puts in front of him: that he has gone senile, retreated behind a wall in the White House, lost his grip, allowed matters to be taken out of his hand. The cut down in public appearances suggests that he might be a babbling fool. There are those who say that he has become a drooling oldster; that a stroke or irreversible kidney damage has done him in.

Now, it is possible that he *has* been showing symptoms and that they have banded together to test him. That is a possibility: under the 25th Amendment the determination of a President's capacity to govern can be made outside of him and they have grouped to see if he really has lost his marbles. That would explain everything: the way that Sylvia is making insatiable sexual demands and the Lump brothers checking into the Presidential quarters and now this damned nuclear strike which was made up to see if he could control himself in a crisis. He had no evidence after all that any of this was happening, just a couple of calls from Bitters (who according to Tom might be imaginary, in which case *none* of this was really going on except inside his own head but he could not tangle with the meaning of that; better to say that Bitters was real. Sure he was real; no one could invent someone like that hard, ungiving man).

They were trying to find how he would react. Forbes and a team of shrinks were probably monitoring everything to get a sense of the situation. And in that case, Anderson thinks sullenly, the hell with all of them. He kicks off his shoes, sits on the bed. It would serve them right if he *failed* their goddamned test. It would serve them exactly right if he were to collapse under all of these pressures deliberately heaped on him: the sex, the crisis, the suspicions and the complaint and they had to invoke the 25th and put the vice president whoever the hell that was in. Maybe they would get a good dose of the situation and see exactly what he'd been dealing with all of this time. They'd have to have someone else play President for them and let's see if *he* would do any better, Anderson thinks bitterly. He stares at the telephone for a long time, pondering his next move.

His next move is going to be a big one and he wants to make sure that it will be exactly right for the situation. No margin for error now.

Could he have invented Bitters and dragged him through a dozen years? Why, that would make him crazy.

It surely would.

After the holocaust, Anderson thinks, it will be wonderful.

No more problems, questions, conflicts. Simple resolution.

Plans have been made in a top-secret fashion for decades to spirit the leaders of government and industry underground at the first indication of nuclear strike and so he will be sped to an enormous shelter just south of Roanoke, Virginia, where luxurious quarters have been hollowed out miles under the surface for a luxurious existence while waiting for the fallout to clear. Several hundred of them will be in this most ornate and homelike of all the shelters; a small city underground with the appurtenances of modern living and he will still very much be the President. Anderson knows how it will be there.

They will leave him alone and he will have miles of glistening underground corridor to explore should he ever become bored. Millions of dollars have been spent over the years on this shelter; it is packed with devices to amuse. His old films are there, a screening room, light and speed and sound.

It may be possible, he thinks, to come to terms with the key questions of his life underground. In these dozens of years he has not had much time for contemplation, the kind of pondering in which a man must engage as he nears the end of his days. It had been his hope before politics intervened to use time to read and think but neither the Senate nor the White House were places where a man could come to terms with philosophy. Among the questions that he would consider in the deeps, Anderson supposed, were: the true weight of his marriage, the sense of his career, the influence of having been a fantasy figure upon his own inner life (could fantasy figures have fantasies themselves?) and the question as to whether being a wish fulfillment figure had made him capable of wishes. A lot had to do with the acting, of course: you took direction, first from your agent, then the scriptwriter and producer, then the director himself; you were always following someone's conception of what you should be and why and you tend to be measured as an actor in how well you came up to others' expectations. But that could be dangerous because all of his life he had been working for the others.

Could that be the reason for Bitters? So that even here, at the pinnacle, he would have someone to work for?

Well, goddamn it, maybe it was time that he did something for himself, looked for his own goals and desires. Struck out.

But that left another hard question: if you played it their way for almost three quarters of your life, doing what they wanted you to do to their satisfaction, could it be said at the end of this that you had anything inside independent of them?

Did he *have* any goals and desires? Or was it just a matter of being a people pleaser, a box office winner? He would give this some thought too while he prowled the corridors and networks of the gleaming underground city. He would not let possibilities of the slightest substance whisk by.

✳ ✳ ✳

Anderson sees himself on the rim of the underground city.

He has left quarters early, before the full fluorescence that in the controlled, timeless environment would be "day"; in the controlled seventy-six-degree temperature pouring from the canisters he walks in golfer's clothing past the tightly closed cubicles of his sleeping brethren, past the darkened cafeteria and recreation quarters, the closed library, past the exercise courts and into the deeper network. The tunnels fan here like flowers, open up like tumors, the lighting spurts uncontrolled reds and purple. Determinedly, Anderson walks through this, wallowing in the silence, fixated on his goal, which is the great, gray space into which the tunnels feed and where the network ends. The space is framed by a high wall which dwindles into the fading light; in the wall are carved the letters and numerals which cryptographically instruct the engineers on how to maintain. Anderson has access to the codes but will never study them. Senseless. Technology has always mystified although he has enjoyed its benefits no less than any other American. It made him a fortune, put him in power.

Now, on the stone floor into which the tunnels empty, Anderson stands, faces the wall and in the gray light deduces the sense of this greatest adventure of his life. Not two weeks ago he was the President in the country at the height of power; now he may be President but he lives with two hundred others underground and for all he knows the rest of his constituency is dead. Communications with the outside do not exist. Communication links with other shelters were planned but do not work. For all Anderson knows he may be with the last on earth but he does not want to deal with this complexity. The reality, the sheer weight of his present environment involves and amazes; for now they are all he needs to know of circumstance. He stands looking at the wall.

"Position," Bitters says. He has followed him all the way out here. "You know what to do."

Anderson knows what to do. He has always known; that is his strength and curse. "Only one more chance," Bitters says.

"And Tom?"

"Right," Bitters says. "For Tom."

For Tom, then. He always knew that it would be this way, didn't he? It would come to this. Anderson crouches. Position.

"Now," Bitters says. His face is obdurate, magnificent in the stricken light. "Now."

Now. Fourth and one on the ten-yard line, thirty-six seconds left on the stadium clock, no time-outs, game hanging in the balance. Anderson perches over the center, his eyes filled with alertness, his chest heaving with the excitement of it all, the lacerating cold turning warm inside, each exhalation truly a burst of fire.

As Between Generations

I RUN MY father. For months, years, I have wanted to do this; now I cannot stand it any longer and I push him through the streets of the town, waving the whip, screaming at him. His senile legs patter, his ancient mouth drools, he is pulling the cart to the best of his effort, he moans, could I please not hit him so often and so hard. But I am remorseless; I cannot bear any longer the culmination of all the things that he has done to me and now at last I am seeking retribution. It is not very nice of me but it is the custom.

People line the streets as I run him. It is not an unusual event. On a fine Sunday such as this, maybe ten or twenty sons or daughters will run their fathers, through the clear dry light of morning and into the dank afternoon but for the moment I am the only one; the others, perhaps, waiting until I have finished as a gesture of respect After all, I have been so patient for so long. I deserve full attention, without competing interests.

The route is one mile long, down the main street and although I am not performing the major exertions, I am puffing when we are barely halfway through, probably with emotion and short-breathed as well because of the things I have been screaming at him.

"Come on, you son of a bitch," I bellow as we pass Third Street, "take that and that and that," and slash him deeply, watching the blood run in aged streaks down the dull surfaces of his back. He is 78 years old. "That's for the time you wouldn't let me go with you to park the car!" I say, slashing him, "the time you said that I should stay with Mother in the restaurant because it was mans work. And that's for the time when you cut my allowance, you cocksucker, cut me down to 75 because you said you didn't like my associations. My associations, damn you!" I shriek and bring the whip down fully, "when you have not known for thirty years the quality of my inner life, the quality of my dreams, the very rubric of my existence. You dared to say that to me!" He pants and increases his pace.

The crowd cheers thinly as we stumble by and once again I bring down the whip, urging him to greater and greater speed. "Remember when I was necking with Doris in our living room and you came in in your pajamas, you old son of a bitch, and told me to grow up! Remember that! I never forgot that, you evil old man," I say, clouting him once again, "and for all the times when you did it to Mother when she was tired and sick and distracted, for all the times you laid your hands on her and carried her away I give you this," and slash him the hardest one yet, a streak of pain that makes the blood dance and I hear his high whining moan. Oh it is wonderful, wonderful, the music of his blood, the singing of his cries, the harmony of his pain, the fullness of my release and it all seems to blend together: sun, street, clouds, cart, whip, memory, loss and retribution as we go winding through the path of the city toward the climactic events that surely lie ahead.

II

I am driving my son. I have waited for this for thirty-six years, now at last my time has come, the loathsome spawn. He screams in agony in the cart behind me, moaning and sobbing as the whip joggles in his hand, his humiliation visible to all of those who have come to see us. Many fathers have driven their sons in this town: now it is my turn. It has been too long, too long. I can barely control shouting my release to the sun.

It was raining a little while ago but now it is clear. Everyone can see us; his torment, his guilt, his horror, his effort—and it is time, time that all of this happened because I could not have borne it any longer. He cries in rage behind me as the whip once again harmlessly grazes my flesh. "That's for you, you whelp," I murmur, "that's for the time when you called me an old fart right in front of your mother because I wouldn't let you go out in the rain. Because I wouldn't let you go to your disgusting movies."

Behind me, the cart sways and I know he is near unbalancing. "Good, good," I shriek back at him, "take it, choke on it. That's for the time you borrowed fifty dollars from me at college and said you only needed it for a week and then squandered the whole thing on pinballs and asked for more and never said thank you. That's for the time you broke in on your mother and me when you were seven years old, broke in on us at four in the morning and my lead full and heavy within me and you came in to say you couldn't sleep. Take it, take it you bastard!" and fling these words back to him, back to his teeth, knowing that behind me he has been impaled upon the sword of his humiliation, the very bleakness of his history, consuming him as he moans, crouches, tries to drive himself beyond guilt and mumbles in the clutches of his vulnerability. Oh I deserve it, I deserve it. It is high time.

Alongside, the crowd cheers. They wave at me, tip their hats, smile, teeth glinting in the sun. They share with me the power of the destruction I have brought upon him and I smile back at them, lift a hand, tilt an eyebrow, urge my legs to greater haste so that behind me the graceless sway of the cart, quickening, will toss him to the bloodless stones themselves and tear him, ungracious heart to spent limb and leave him empty, rolling, a darkening husk upon the pavement, waiting, waiting then in the night for the dogs of the prairies to come in from the South and scenting his imminent bones, tear out the very core of him.

Death to the Keeper

PIPER: THE disastrous consequences of George Stone's live (?) appearance on the INVESTIGATIONS show of October 31 are, of course, very much on my mind at the present time. I can find little excuse or explanation for the catastrophic events which have followed so rapidly upon its heels: the gatherings which the press so helpfully informs us are "riots," the general upheavals in the national "consciousness" and that climactic; if ill-planned, assault upon the person of our Head of State last week. No American more than I, William Piper, deplores these events; no American is more repelled by their implications. It was truly said that we are a land of barbaric impulses; our ancestors were savages and our means consequently dramatic, this is to say, theatrical.

But at the point at which *I*, William Piper, become implicated in these events, implicated to the degree that responsibility is placed upon *my* shoulders, at the point at which I am held responsible for these disasters simply because I permitted the renowned and retired actor George Stone, for private and sentimental reasons, to utilize the format of our INVESTIGATIONS show to act out a dramatic rite which was the product of his sheer lunacy; it is at that point, as I say, that I must disclaim. I disclaim totally.

How was I to know? In the first place, I had not seen or dealt with George Stone for the past 14 years and, following his reputation as it curved and ascended through the media, thought him merely to be a talented actor, superbly talented that is to say, whose appearance on our show would function to divert our audience and to educate them well, that joint outcome to which INVESTIGATIONS, from the beginning was dedicated. In the second place, although I was aware that Stone had gone into a "retirement" — somewhere around the time of the assassination, I did not connect the two, nor did I realize that Stone had, gone completely insane. If I had, I certainly would have never had him on *my* production, and you can be sure of that.

Piper is not an anarchist. Piper does not believe in sedition. While INVESTIGATIONS, product of my mind and spirit, came into being out of my deepest belief that the Republic had no answers because it was no longer asking questions, the program was always handled in a constructive spirit; and it was not our purpose to bring about that mindless disintegration which, more and more, I see in the web of our country during these troubled days. That is why I feel the network had no right to cancel our presentation summarily, and without even giving us a chance to defend ourselves in the arena of the public spirit.

And the recent remarks of our own President when he chose to say during a live press conference, which no doubt was witnessed by some seventy millions, that the present national calamity could be ascribed wholly to the irresponsibilities of "self-seeking entrepreneurs who permit the media to be used for any purposes which will sell them sufficient packages of cigarettes," were wholly unfortunate and, to a lesser man, would have been provocative. Not only is Piper no self-seeker, Piper has nothing whatever to do with the sale of cigarettes. We sold spot times to the network; what they did with their commercials was their business. I have not smoked for 17 years, and had no knowledge or concern with what products the network had discussed during our two-minute breaks, being far too busy setting my guests at ease, and preparing to voyage even deeper into the arena of the human heart.

"Self-seeking entrepreneurs" indeed! The very moment the announcement of the thwarted attempt to enter the White House and kill our beloved President was flashed upon the networks, I prepared a statement urging the nation to be calm, and repeating the facts of Stone's insanity. It was I, William Piper, who in the wake of the hurried and inaccurate reports as to the size and true intentions of the invading forces, called a press conference and there offered my services to the Administration in whatever capacity they would have me. Is this the performance of a seditionist?

But there, has been no peace. Ever since Stone's spectacular public, plunge some seven weeks ago, ever since his convulsions and death (now, blame *me;* say that I gave him poison) it has been Piper, Piper, Piper. Had Stone lived, the accusation would have gone where It belonged: on his curved, slightly sloping shoulders, and *he* would have had much to answer, crazy or not. But because of his unfortunate· demise, everything explodes upon the "entrepreneur" who happened to be merely helpless witness to convulsion. Is this fair?

But it is not the purpose of this introduction to be self-pitying or declamatory. Piper spits at such gestures; Piper transcends them. It is only, as it were, to set the stage for the revelations which follow; such revelations speaking for themselves and which publication will fully and finally rid Piper of this incipient curse. Thanks to the production skill and merchandising genius of Standard Books, Incorporated, I have been assured that this small publication will receive the widest distribution imaginable, being fully covered for foreign rights in all countries of the Western world (that is about all that one can expect) and with a fair chance of subsidiary, that is stage and motion picture rights, being taken up as well. The dissemination of this volume will serve, once and for all, to perish all doubts of Piper's patriotism and, as well, will free him, I am sure, of that threatened business for sedition which is now working itself laboriously (but successfully) through the network of the appellate division. They don't have any kind of case; my lawyer assures me they have no case at all.

Let me explain the background of this.

In the aftermath of that INVESTIGATIONS segment during which George Stone, once a renowned actor, attempted to reenact the assassination of our martyred President and ended by dying before the cameras; in the aftermath of that it was necessary, of course, for his environs to be searched, his personal effects placed under government security, and the whole history of his psychosis, needless to say, to be traced. Because the performance occurred on those very premises where Stone had spent the last years of his tragic life, and due to my own heroic efforts to have these premises secured, government and military authorities were able to make a total inventory at once. Billboards were seized, posters, newspapers, political works, magazines, personal paraphernalia of all kinds, stray bits of food secreted within hidden places of the wall, and so on. Also found was the journal which follows.

This journal, kept by the actor during the week immediately preceding his appearance on the INVESTIGATIONS program proves, beyond the shadow of any man's doubt, that the actor was completely insane, that his appearance was plotted with the cunning of the insane for the sole purpose of assaulting the precarious balance of the Republic, and that William Piper and INVESTIGATIONS were, from the start, little more than the instruments through which George Stone plotted insurrection. Why then, you ask, was this journal not immediately released to the public, thereby relieving all innocent parties of responsibility and halting, before they began, so many of these dread events?

There is no answer to that. Our Government refuses to speak. Indeed it has not, to this day, acknowledged the *existence* of such a journal, stating over and again through its mouthpieces that the actor "left no effects."

The Government is monolithic; the Government is imponderable. Nevertheless, and due to these most recent events, the Government, mother of us all, must be protected from itself. A carbon copy of this journal, hidden in the flushbox of Stone's ancient toilet, was found by employees of INVESTIGATIONS during a post-mortem examination of the premises three weeks ago, and immediately placed into Piper's hands. Piper, in turn, hastens to release it to the widest possible audience.

Let me make this clear again: *this journal will prove without shadow of doubt that Stone was insane and perpetrated a massive hoax through the persona of the late President, and that all of us were ignorant and gloomy pawns he moved through the patterns of his destiny.* There is no way to sufficiently emphasize that point. It will recur.

The hasty publication of this journal, with foregoing textual matter by William Piper, has led to disgraceful rumors within and without the publishing field that said journal is spurious, is not the work of George Stone, and was prepared by the staff of William Piper solely to relieve himself of present dangers. Having the courage of my format, I will come to grips with this mendacity forthrightly by acknowledging its existence and by saying that it is scurrilous. How could this journal possibly be spurious? It was found above Stone's own toilet seat. Besides, it exhibits, in every fashion, the well-known and peculiar style of this actor; its idiosyncrasies are his, its convolutions are the creation of no other man. Its authenticity has been certified to by no less than Wanda Miller who, as we all know, lived with the actor during those last terrible years, and was privy to his innermost thought. If *she* says it is the work of Stone, how can we possibly deny? I therefore present, with no further comment, the journal of George Stone. Present difficulties notwithstanding, and with all sympathy for the embattled Administration, I must point out that this should bring, once and for all, an end to this business. How could I possibly have had anything to do with Stone's performance? I was merely the focus, the camera, the static Eye. The vision, the hatred, the pointlessness of all of it was Stone's own, as in the creation of all madmen. "Re-enact and purge national guilt by becoming the form of the martyred President and being killed again!" Yes, indeed! Is such nonsense the product of a sane mind?

And now let it speak for itself.

STONE: Yes, here it is: I have it right here. I wrote it down somewhere and I knew it was in this room. Well, I found the little son of a gun. Right under the newspapers on the floor. I must remember to be more organized. Wanda won't like it if I don't get organized. She's warned me — rightly — many times about this. Live and learn, I say; live and learn. I WILL NOT SCATTER MY SHEETS.

Anyway, I've got it. The whole memory, just as I transcribed it yesterday. Or the day before. July 11, 1959. It is July 11, 1959, in Denver and Stone is acting Lear again.

He — that is, I — am acting him half on history and half on intention, trapped in all the spaces of time, the partitions of hell. Space is fluid around me, shifting as it does defined only by rows, by heads, by dim walls, by my own tears and tread. Sight darts crosswise. I act Lear as only I, George Stone, the flower of his. generation, can, while the cast stands respectfully in the wings like relatives at a baptism, while lights twitch and hands wink.

For I, George Stone, *am* Lear. It is the Gloucester scene and old Earl, my familiar and my destiny, stands behind, playing mutely while I rant. He is fat, he is bald, he is in fact old Alan Jacobs himself, familiar as God, as empty as death … but no matter; I am alone. I extract the words carefully, reaching inside to make sure that what they mean is still there; the *burning, the burning.*

" … I know thee well; thy name is Gloucester; I shall preach to thee, so listen …"

And the burning leaps, the burning leaps.
"… When we are born, we cry that we are come
To this great stage of fools … this a good block;
It were a madness to shoe a troop of horse
With felt; so when I steal upon these sons-in-law,
Then, kill, kill, kill, kill, kill, kill!"
Do you hear me, Jacobs?
"Kill, kill, kill, kill, kill, kill!"

I wheel upon the bastard; I take old Earl by the shoulders, and I move to vault him on the sea. He trembles in my grasp, and I feel his false surfaces shake; he gasps and groans but no matter for I am beyond his objection: I drag him to the sheer, clear cliff and topple him over, send him shrieking ten stories searching for the ground until he hits with a thud and in an explosion of sawdust, his brains spill free and then, cotton as they are, turn green in the fading light. *So much for Lear.*

Sa, sa, sa, sa. For I can kill, I *can* kill and now, against that wooden sky I scream murder so that they can hear; so that all of them can hear. No more of this magic, I say; no more of these imprecations against the nailed skull: in Lear, no one kills; no one *ever* kills, but *let us have no more magicians.*

Attendants come.

They have detected something in the wings, something they were not supposed to see. Ah, here they are: eight of them in a row, carrying a jacket of mail for my:. arms, my legs. They are coming for the old King; greet the world. I flee.

From stage center to left I go, nimble as light, stuffed like a porpoise. The spot cannot pin me; oh, boy, I transcend vision itself. *Sa, sa, sa, sa.*

Stone is acting Lear again. In Denver, in the vault of the unborn, in all the Denvers of the skull, in the sun of the city itself while the Keeper walks straight through those who love him. Perpetual Lear; perpetual Stone.

He had such plans, he did, that no one knew what they were. But they would be the terror of the earth.

On the other hand, does this make much sense? All of this is fine for me, fine for Wanda: we know what's going on here, and that Jacobs business in Denver was just terrible (did I kill him?) prefiguring, as it did, so much which followed. But I am no impressionist; not me, not George Stone. Got to get the material in shape *circumspectly;* from one thing to the next, all in its place and at last to end with something meaningful. So let me structure the materials as I structured a role; let me resist that impulse which is simply to implode my own skull; sprinkle this stinking cellar with thoughts and curses. Where is Piper? He promised to be here three days ago. The profligate louse; you can trust him for nothing but this time I have the goods and he'll be here. My reputation. That alone makes it worth it. STONE RETURNS TO PUBLIC LIFE ENACTING HIS OWN CREATION BEFORE YOUR EYES. Yes, that should do it. He loves that. But why isn't he here yet? Oh, Wanda, Wanda; I'll grasp a proper grasp to show you what I think of *you!*

We need an organized journal. Part one, part two, but first, by all means a prospectus. Begin with the beginning:

THE BEGINNING

So. It began like this: it was, for me, as if the worst of us had risen to confront and destroy the best; that the blood ran free in heaven because the worst said *they wouldn't take it any more; don't need none of this crap.* It was a shattering, because nobody politic can exist forever in two parts. Oh, I had it figured out so elegantly. I had it made.

For me it was like this: it was benefit Friday for the Queens chapter of one league or another; the curtain was scheduled to rise at two, and at one I was comfortably settled in full costume, fully prepared with nothing to do for an hour but sit and get in some serious time on the gin which I had thoughtfully stocked at the beginning of the run. I sat there for a while, drinking like that, and listening to the radio, and after a while the Announcement came through. I shut off the radio and went down the hall, looking for the stage manager.

Oh yes, he had heard it too; he had a television set in his office, and now they had broken into all kinds of programs with the Word. Yes, he believed that it was true; someone like the Keeper was bound to get it one of these days, and besides, every man elected in the even number years ending with 0 since 1860 had died in office. He had known the Keeper wouldn't make it from the start. And it looked how he was right, not that it gave him any pleasure and not, thank God, that he had any idea what was really going on. I left the stage manager.

Back in my own room, whisk close the door,

listen some more and came the Second Announcement. The Keeper was dead.

I corked the gin and put it away, put my feet up and began to think the thoughts I have mentioned above, the best and worst and coming together and all of that. They certainly made me feel better, because my legs got numb right away, and I was convinced that if anyone was part of the best, I was. Didn't the notices say so? *Everybody knows Stone.*

After a while, the stage manager came into my room, and said that he had decided to call off the performance. Would I make the announcement? "After all it's your play," he said. "Nobody else should do it. They'll feel better if they hear it from you."

"Why not just pipe it in and let them go home? Much easier."

"Can't do that. Equity rules, you know. Anytime there's a major change in a performance, a member of the cast has to announce it, from the stage."

"This isn't a change, it's a cancellation."

"Fight it out with Equity. There's no precedent. You do it."

"Can't say I want to."

"Who does?"

So I did it.

Can one explain the barbarity of that occasion?' The theatre was virtually filled, then, and the news. did not seem to have come to die audience; they, were all sitting there in a spray of contentment, waiting for the curtain to rise on the eminent George Stone in MISERY LOVES COMPANY (doesn't it?), and there I came as the house lights darkened, to stand before the curtain with the servile tilt' of the jester. They quieted, and a spot came on me.

"Ladies and gentlemen," the jester said, "I have an announcement. I am most entirely sorry to say, that this performance will be canceled."

That seemed to sit fairly well: a few stirrings but nothing drastic. The jester, pleased with his success, decided, however, that they deserved in the bargain to understand the cancellation (not being caused by the jester's health), and so he hastened to serve them:

"As you might know," he said, "our Keeper has been shot in the Southlands, and it appears that he was killed instantly. While we await official notification, it seems certain in the interim that he is no longer with us. Our new Keeper is already at the helm, of course, and will serve us well."

There was a faint murmur, and the lights began to tremble upward again; the jester looked out into the full eye of the house and noted that they were confronting him.

They were confronting him.

"A most terrible tragedy," he said helpfully, "and I am sure that all of you could be induced to join in a moment of prayer for the departed Keeper."

Not a good ploy. There were no bent heads, no shared mutterings during which the jester could make graceful exit. Instead, they continued to look at him. *And look.*

And the jester had an insight then, in that moment when all of the barriers were down and that ancient and most terrible relation between actor and audience had been established, killers and prey ... the jester realized that they were staring at him as if *he* were the assassin. If he wasn't, why had he interrupted their revels with such news? What had he done? How long had it taken him and how, then, had he been able to return to this stage so quickly?

Well, he had given the news, hadn't he? He, the perpetrator, had made it known. So, then —

It was a difficult period for the jester, and it lasted several seconds until, by sheer heroic will, he compelled himself to take his handsome, if slightly gnarled, frame off the stage and into the wings. He hardly wanted to do so, of course; what he wanted to do — that is, what *I* wanted to do, what *I* wanted to say — was to confront them in return and have it out, lay it on the line. *Excuse me,* I wanted to say: *excuse me, ladies and gents, but I cannot be held responsible for drastic acts committed by lunatics in a distant place. I am, after all, only an actor, an occupation never noted for its ability to perpetrate with originality.*

That is what I might have said ... but, to be sure, I said nothing at all. The moment passed, the confrontation went under the surface to muddle with other things. They rose, and as I watched them — having decided that it would, after all, be a mistake to leave the stage — they left.

And, oh god, I hated them, then. I hated their greedy need for a perpetrator as I hated my own tormented and quivering mind; I despised them and shuddered at how close these had come to evicting some final ghosts. But they were right.

They were right, you see; it was as simple as that, and as deadly. Oh, it took me a long, long time to apprehend that knowledge which they had so easily and effortlessly assimilated. *I* was the killer. The killer of their Keeper.

You can imagine the effect that it had upon me; it was simply catastrophic. I was appalled. It was appalling. It shocked· me to the core of my innocent actor's being.

What happens? I asked myself in the empty theatre, uncapping my bottle of gin; *what is going on, here? We must define some limits and stay within.* Easier methods by far to dispose of a Keeper; quiet strangulation or death by pater; poison in the tonic and leeches in the bed. *This was going too far,* I said. I sat before the media and wept for the whole three days, and shortly thereafter I left MISERY LOVES COMPANY.

I left the play, found myself a proper slut to bed and plan with; and a fortnight after that I came to my present quarters, this reeking, stinking abandoned theatre, once a whorehouse, before that a slaughtering mart. A rich, a muddled history: this building is descending into the very earth of the lower East Side of Manhattan; in two hundred years it will peep shyly through a crown of mud.

But that has nothing to do with me. I lie here content with my notes, with my intentions, and with Wanda; always Wanda. Together, then, we work out my condition, my final plan and the plan becomes fruitions through the corpus and instrumentation of William Piper. Ah, Wanda, Wanda; I'll make my skull a packing case for your scents, for my waters. I'll toss you a touch to make the alter jump.

My condition. All of it, *my condition*. For the Keeper's death, too, was an abstraction, and it did what nothing else could have done; sped me gaily to the edge of purpose; found me a proper slut and a proper tune. And now, to be sure, a proper destiny.

For the secret shorn bare is this: *it made everything come together*. Without it I was nothing, a child trapped in dim child's games; but with it, *ah — with it,* I moved to new plateaus, new insights on the instant. *No one ever killed a King but helped the Fool.* Focused so, with edge and purpose at last, I feel within me wandering, the droning forebears of a massive fate.

So endeth THE BEGINNING. We move forward jauntily now, a fixed smile on our anxious face; the old, worn features turned blissful and unknowing, toward the sun.

So, before the act be done; before Piper and his technicians come to unroll the final implements of purpose, chronologize a little; we explain, ourselves. Writing, this late at night as I must, I can make little order; the entries flickering in time and space would be the ravings of a madman were I not so sane. Barriers must be smashed in any event; fact and fantasy must be melded together; As the Keeper knew. Wow, did he know!

But one last terror remains in these rooms, then, and that must be this: that when it is all over and when police come for my belongings, find this and turn it upon a fulfilled, grateful world, these notes may be taken as clinical offering; may, indeed, be found by Piper and his troops themselves and disseminated as "culture." Oh, I know your tricks, Piper; I, know the corridors of your cravening soul and you will try, you will, to reduce these to pure casenotes, more symptomology. But if this be so, be forewarned, Piper: I will not be a document, I will not be a footnote. Not me, George Stone; *I Will purge the national guilt by being the Keeper and plunging, at last, the knife into myself; take that, you bastard, and I'll free you all.*

So, chronologize a little.

My name is George Stone. I am an actor. I am ,the greatest actor of my time. Read the notices. Look at my Equity card. It checks out.

I know more than that. Thirteen seasons ago, when I was young and full of promise, I acted in repertory theatre on the black and arid coast of Maine ... a cluster of barely reconverted buildings on some poisoned farmland, a parking lot filled with smashed birds and the scent of oil; those dismal seawinds coming uninvited into an the spaces of the theatre. From this; I learned everything I know about the human condition.

How could I not? Life, you see, is a repertory theatre; each of us playing different roles on different nights, but behind the costume, always the same bland, puzzled face. Oh, we wear our masks of so many hues night after night that the face is never seen: tonight a clown and last night a tragic hero and tomorrow perhaps the amiable businessman of a heavy comedy of manners, and next week … off to another barn. But underneath the same sadness, the unalterability: the same, the same, the same.

And so I know: I know what you wore Thursday and what the stage manager plans for you Monday night; I know while you pace the stage this Saturday, all activity, pipe clenched firmly in your masculine jaws, that crumpled in your dressing room lies the faggot's horror. *I know you.* The power of metaphor is the power to kill. You deceive me not for I know 'all of your possibilities.

Enough, enough. *As* always, I move from perception to abstraction, from the hard moment to the soft hour. Oh, I must stick to the subject, *I must stay in the temple, the temple of the Keeper.*

Last night, I became 38.

It was a poor enough birthday for the old monarch. Wanda brought me a cake, Wanda cut a slice and I ate it, Wanda blew out the candles, Wanda gave me congratulations. She too ate some, let me give her a pat and then, reaching, we tumbled to the slats and made our complex version of love; the bloat-king's fingers tangling through her hair. It was not a bad birthday, but it was hardly a good one.

Here it is: I got it down just the way it happened. Word by word. Wanda and I had a talk, after my party, and several matters were discussed freely and frankly:

STONE: Wanda? Seriously, now. What do you think of me?

WANDA: How's that?

STONE: Do you think this idea of mine is crazed, Wanda? A little mad? This matters to me, you being my world and all, you know. Is this a sane conceptualization; my re-enactment?

WANDA: I don't get it.

STONE: You go out of doors, Wanda; these days I never do. You have perspective. You know things. The national guilt is really bad, isn't it? They really need a purge, right? You haven't mislead me into —

WANDA: What do I have to do after all this time to prove to you that I'll never betray you?

STONE: I know; I know. But seclusion under such pressure must lead to difficulties. I am so frightened —

WANDA: You'll simply have to trust me.

STONE: I do; I do. But I'm not a machine. I tell you, I am not merely an actor, I *suffer.*

WANDA: Of course you do.

STONE: You could hardly imagine the reach of my passion were you not living with me. Consider what I have taken upon myself. The burden of a nation. The lost Keeper. All of that.

WANDA: Sure.

STONE:, I'm no martyr; my uses are concentrated into the fact of my *humanity.* You do believe in the reality of my quest, don't you? (Anxiously) You share, don't you?

WANDA: Always, George. Anything at all. You really should rest now. You're being overanxious again. Everything will be just fine when Piper comes, you can be sure of that.

STONE: (Cunningly) What's in it for you? WANDA: Huh?

STONE: Surely there's something in it for you, isn't there? A fat contract. Notoriety. A contract for your memoirs. Even if national guilt weren't so terrible, you'd *say* it wonldnt you?

WANDA: I don't know how you can say that of me, George.

STONE: Oh, it's easy; I've lived in the world a long —

WANDA: I'm really insulted that you think so of me. In fact, I think I'm going to bed., Good night.

STONE: Wanda —

WANDA: You'll feel better in the morning, George. (Exits)

STONE: She's as guilty as the rest of them.

My little closet drama. Wanda is suspect as well, of course, but happily enough, I do not care; a fine and grotesque mutuality, this: conceived for purposes as limited as they are relevant. And, as always for the jester, things voyage to a conclusion now. Nothing is eternal — not even Wanda's delights — and this will end after all. We have outlived our possibilities, she and I. Perhaps my intentions were misguided. But I needed someone … an assistant, we shall say. I shall *always* need someone so terribly. *Piper.*

Wanda is coming in now.

Later: time for metaphysical notation. For I am sick, sick of metaphor; Wanda fed me and combed my poor, tumbling hair and pressed my hands to tell me that Piper was coming tomorrow, tomorrow with equipment and technicians. The broadcast will be tomorrow night. There is no time, then, for constructions; we must go to the heart of the issue. For I will tomorrow kill the Keeper, and the last that can be asked is that you know who I am. *Curse you, Piper, but I have my notes.* "He, finds the whole concept fascinating, George," she said to me. "Particularly this feeling that the national guilt must be purged He agrees With you there." I bet he does. Fortunately, Wanda has been intermediary from the first — I will have nothing to do with minor relationships, and everything is worked through her, my bland familiar — and the rich implications of Piper's agreement, viz., national guilt need never be explored. Only exploited.

There is so little left to me. Twenty-four hours from now, then, where will I be, after Piper's machines have wrung me through? I must do it now, now, I must make it clear; *I must somehow trace the origin to the roots, past the trickling, brown earth and the green stems into the gnarled, poisoned bases of life themselves, the liquid running thick in them, bubbling and choked like blood.*

I first learned that genocide existed in Europe when I was 10. My mother, a husky tart named Miriam — but we won't get into *that,* not here, not Ever — told me that l might as well face facts beyond the neighborhood: Jews were being killed in Europe by the millions while she hustled and I froze, and someday, if it and the Jews lasted long enough, I might find myself, some day, interceding for them. This news shook and grieved me for days; I wrote a long one-act play about an abstract, persecuted Jew; obscurely, I felt my mother responsible since, after all, she had broken the news.

But not long after that, I met for the first time two of the participants in my mother's vigorous scenario ... a mixed pair of Schwartzes, who tenanted and barely ran a gloomy candy shop on a nearby corner, put up a sign in the window announcing that they were members of a refugee organization, displayed scars which, they stated, were caused by beatings administered by the milder bigots, and generally made concrete Miriam's whispered injunction.

I was not moved at all.

I wasn't moved; I didn't give a damn. They were two raddled Jews; they raised prices in the store by a fifth, which was hardly justified by their curiously bland and self-indulgent tales of horror; even the exemplification was drab. The worst things had happened not to them but to people they had *heard of*. So one day, in a capitalistic outpouring of patriotism, I overturned the candy counter directly on Schwartz-pater's thigh, and ran. And I took my business elsewhere.

Was that the first inkling of my condition?'

Call the Keeper.

Well, this then: once I took an acting course in a great university: I was 17 and wanted to understand why I was gripped by what has always possessed me. (As my obituaries will remind you, I left the course and the university at the end of the fourth week, but that is not the point. Nor is Miriam's reaction relevant.) The instructor warned us in an early lecture that the act of drama was but this: that it began in the particular and moved toward the general; originating as it did in the passion and moving later to the implications. We listened well; we took notes. *Remember*, he said, *when a role is acted, don't worry about what you mean; think about how you feel. Find an image and work from that. Leave the meaning to the professionals. Just feel, feel.*

Ah, yes. Is there some way I can inform the gentleman that my most stunning roles — moving through the decades of my greatness and culminating in the Lear of Denver, the greatest and least human of all Kings, they called me — emerged from the most intricate, the least applicable convolution? Is there?

Does that inkle to my condition?

I call the Keeper.

And this too: I took a wife. The year was 1953. Her name was Simone Tarquin. She was a designer in that repertory on the coast of Maine. She was 22, she was accomplished, she was lovely, my darling, in the rocks and curling waters. *How she rose to greet me —*

We met in July; I thought I loved her. She knew (she said) that she loved me in June, in all the springs of her life, and that was good enough for me; quickly, quickly, we chose to marry; I had had no time for women in those twenty-five Struggling Years; there was too much to do and too much to flee, and the conceit of having one of my own, at last, to play with for as long and lavishly as I chose was a pretty, pretty, pretty one. In the fall I had a contract at a university theatre; Simone would undertake graduate design on the other side of the country. So, our maddened lover's plans went like this: she would telegram . her resignation and join me in the Midwest to type or file in a reconverted barracks; in the night we would build and fondle until a summons came from the East, saying that our time was up; we had transcended suffering. We might even have a child during the struggling period, just to fill out ,the picture. That was the way it was; we had it figured out. Ah, God.

I have not said that I was a virgin in those days; so I was, but she was not. Solemn confessions were traded during the premarital experience, and agreed to be of no consequence at all. But we decided to defer consummation; after all, there was no reason to further dishonor her (my thoughts). One Saturday, license in hand, we were married before the cast and crew; we said farewell to them and with noisy enthusiasm went straight to the nearest motel, a gloomy, shabby structure four miles from the barns themselves. We parked the car. We removed our luggage. We checked in. We entered our room. We placed down our luggage. We undressed. We had at one another.

And, yes, I can block the scene; yes I can dredge through the channels of memory for the perfect, frozen artifact; yes, it is there like a horrid relative, ready for resuscitation on all necessary occasions and sometimes unbidden between. Yes, yes, yes, *it happened this way:*

SIMONE: Well, here we are.
STONE: Yes.
SIMONE: Naked, too.
STONE: Indeed.
SIMONE: So come here.
STONE: Yes. One second.
SIMONE: What's wrong with you, anyway?
You look kind of funny.
STONE: (Opening windows, inhaling deeply, fanning himself and knocking a fist against the wall) Kind of warm in here, wouldn't you say?
SIMONE: Silly. They have air conditioning. (She hugs herself.)
STONE: Probably isn't working.
SIMONE: Anyway, there's plenty of air now. Why don't you come here?
STONE: One minute.
SIMONE: What's wrong? You seem kind of cold all of a sudden.
STONE: Nothing is wrong. *Nothing.*
SIMONE: (Showing herself) Don't you like me?
STONE: What a question …
SIMONE: (Some unprintable, if not untheatrical gestures) Well?
STONE: Of course I like you. I low you. You look lovely.
SIMONE: So then …
STONE: So, I love you.
SIMONE: Why are you lighting that cigarette? Stop it!
STONE: Well, it's already lit, so that's that. Might as well finish it now. Be right with you. (He puffs grotesquely.)
SIMONE: (After a pause) I don t like this, George. What do you think I am, the blushing virgin? I *told* you, I've been around. I'm no teenager and I know what's going on. Now either get that miserable cigarette out or …

STONE: (Trying to be cheerful) It's almost done now.

SIMONE: *What's wrong?*

STONE: Don't be dramatic, Simone; I'm the actor here. Nothing's wrong. I love you. I'm just a little warm — I meant to say cold — in here.

SIMONE: Then come here. (More theatrical gestures)

STONE: I'm, coming. Coming now. (Disposes of cigarette) See?

SIMONE: Closer.

STONE: Like that?

SIMONE: Not quite. More like *this*. And *this*.

And *this*.

At this point our curtain falls chastely for some moments or hours; the scene behind is as predictable as it is monolithic and dull but there are limits to this playwright's gift for metaphor, and one has been reached now. Of course, one could do this scene in mask and symbol, showing Simone gripping a large, earless rabbit, but such is too tasteless even for that commedia dell' arte the sensibility likes to play in the vault in that noon of dreams. No, no: better to let the curtain fall. After some period of time — perhaps allowing audiences to think about matters and even to do some experimentation of their own — it rises.

SIMONE: (In a state of some agitation, twisting to her side of the bed, holding the sheets closely around her and looking wildly toward the corners of the room) What's wrong with you? What's wrong with you? *What's wrong?*

STONE: Ah —

SIMONE: Oh boy, do I see it now!

STONE: Ah —

SIMONE: It figured. Goddamn, did it figure! STONE: (Really speechless; this ingratiating and benevolent presence unable to make connection with his audience for one of the few times on record.) Ah — now, look Simone. Ah, Simone —

SIMONE: *Actors!* You keep away from me! ,

STONE: (He can respond to that.) You bet I will.

SIMONE: Are you crazy? What's inside there?

STONE: I don't know. Nothing's inside, all right? Nothing. Is that what you want to hear?

SIMONE: I want to hear nothing from you.

STONE: You won't! You won't then! But the others will. Everybody will hear of me. I'll fix them. (He is distraught.)

SIMONE: Wow. *Wow!*

STONE: Let's get out of here.

SIMONE: I'll buy that. I'll just *buy* it, friend. That's the ticket.

STONE: Go — ah — go into the bathroom and dress. SIMONE: Turn your back. (He does so and she exits hurriedly stage left, gathering garments as she does, exuding a faint mist, tossing various parts of her body.) And I want you ready to leave, by the time I come out.

STONE: I'll be ready.

SIMONE: Good; *good* for you.

STONE: I'll be ready; I'll be ready. I'll be so damned ready you never saw anything like it in your whole life, you bitch!

The curtain falls. Or, it does not fall — for somewhere, right now, it is yet open, the actors staggering through the banalities; in all of the rooms of the world, the mind, it goes on right now. You as well as the jester have lived through it all too many times; all have dreamed its horrid possibilities on wedding eves;, speak to me not, then of divisions in lives. For as it ends, it yet goes on, leaving nothing more to play: I have no interpretations, nor shade, nor form to all of this, nor perspective against which to place it: it is done but it *is* undone, for at this moment it is going on, it goes on right now; it goes on ...

Does that abate my condition?

Call; call the Keeper.

Only this, only this must be said, which is: that I wanted *all* women that night but not this woman, that I wanted all flesh, but not that flesh, that I wanted the mystery but not the outcome, and in touching that flesh — in touching Simone's breasts, those wonderful abstractions which had dazzled and goaded and seized me with groans as their clothed representation glided past me so many times — that when I touched them, I found those breasts tough, resilient, drooping bags empty of mystery and redundant of hope; they were flesh, mere flesh freed of that which entrapped it: say too that I found her arms of stone, her thighs of wood and her lips, like clay, mere clay; and pressed against her, holding her like a tumbled doll, I knew that by wanting everything, I had taken nothing; by being possessed of the totality, I had lost the elements; by seeking God, I had lost my soul and that in the dream of all flesh, I had lost my flesh.

And so, I too had had a dream: I dreamed that in the wanting of the fullness; I had lost the oneness, and that entering the cave of time, I had lost, the lamp of self and that the light, all of the light, was one. *Light, light, give him some light give the old King some bulb of hell.*

But there was more, too: it took me a long time to see that there was something else as well, and in the years to come, I learned; I learned by dint of cunning to enter and haunt their channels; I learned with Wanda how to do it and I did it; I did it with luck and skill (by closing my eyes and making pretty pictures); and now, as I lie with Wanda again and again, I lie, afterward, shaken and empty beside her and wonder how, it would have been with Simone. Because the secret was all in the pictures; once you knew how to make the pictures, everything else would fall into place.

Suppose I had done it with her, then; suppose I had found the way and had. taken Simone shuddering in our night: *would I then have found a fullness in the oneness, instead of the oneness outside this fullness? Would I? Would I?*

Where are you now, Simone?

Where are you, my darling, absolved, annulled these many years and never *to.* be seen again? I dream you then to be in a cave by the sea or in a paneled kitchen staring absently for the Time; perhaps you have become a dressmaker's doll, but it does not matter; it does not matter for you are gone and gone. *Gone, gone; lost, lost.*

It is done. Could you have saved me, Simone? Could you have rescued me through your flesh, through your wholeness from the noisome spaces of this tenement; the shape of my days, the flow of my disaster? Could I have held you, could I have found salvation in you? Could I?

Could I? What could I have done? *What there was to do I did not; what I did I should not have done.* Is there anything ever done that would make any difference at all? Oh God, sometimes, dear, I think that I cannot bear it any longer; this filthy slut, this horrible life, these raving notes, this pointless re-enactment: oh, the twisted plans and the despair and the rage, I am so sick of it, I am so. sick, listening to my tinny, tiny voice reverberating in the chambers of self; my own voice imploring, wheedling, ranting, going to periods of cunning, apologizing, searching, … *I cannot bear it anymore.*

Oh God, to live through it again with Piper; to implode with him in the reach of the Eye, and to be done with it, to be no more, no more.

Call the Keeper, I want the Keeper, give me the Keeper. Where is our Keeper? We have lost our Keeper.

Death to the Keeper, death to the Keeper.

Call the Keeper and give him death. Call the Keeper and give him dread. Let him know; let him know.

Let him know love.

Know love.

Love, love, love.

Death, death, death.

Love, love, love.

Death, death, death.

PIPER: That evening, on the INVESTIGATIONS format, George Stone, representing himself as the image of the fallen Keeper, re-enacted the assassination, thereby seeking to purge his country of "national guilt." The dismal outcome, of course, made necessary the publication of his journal.

I am so sure that his journal establishes beyond controversy the sole responsibility of the actor for the grievous events of today, and the complete victimization of Piper that I will say no more about it; no more; no more. Only one last irony remains: Stone felt that his act would *purge* us of "national guilt."

Purge us? One can only say, from this lamentable aftermath, that the precise opposite was accomplished. The attempt upon the person of the present President was disgraceful, and the ragged shouts of the fanatics scurrilous as their leadership was damning, should convince us of the opposite. Certainly, there are things which should not be meddled with.

Say I; says Piper: if there is poison on the shelf leave it there; leave it sit, fester, mold for the spaces of eternity; do not touch it for once touched, if the poison runs free, it becomes the communal blood and riots and danger and sedition trials and trouble with the press and loss of great sums of money and then they all go out to get you just like they've been wanting to get you for thirty years but this time they have the chance and so the rotten stinking bastard sons of bitches never give you a moment's peace but Piper doesn't care because Piper has the *truth* and as long as man tells the truth he will be free — that's what I say to them, the hell with them, the hell with all of you, just get off my back before I get you in real trouble, Piper knows, Piper thinks, Piper functions.

Piper, Piper, Piper, Piper, Piper, Piper.

State of the Art

H ERE WE all are, at this elegant sidewalk cafe perched on the edges of what appears to be a ruined Paris. Hard to tell; outside of this circle of brightness, much is opaque. Originally we were supposed to gather in the Algonquin, but that hotel was demolished seventeen years ago to make way for Intervalley Seven. "Disgusting," Dostoevski says, thudding his heavy tumbler against the table, "the ruination of the environment, the nature of man to impress his internal corruption upon the landscape. I tell you, we are fast approaching the end of time."

Dostoevski is gloomy. The twenty years in Siberia have warped his soul and given him a somewhat grimmer outlook on humanity than, perhaps, events will justify. Nevertheless he must be attended to. All of us attend to one another with extreme courtesy, but Dostoevski deserves our good wishes. He contributed many important works to the literature and besides the change has discombobulated him. Siberia was not good for his personality; I must concede that. "Of course," I say gently, draining the last sparkling dregs, "but still, technology is not an absolute. A neutral quality like sex can be turned in any direction; so can machinery. Watch; the environment may change but it will also become more pleasant." I signal for a waiter. The service is abominable in this cafe, but then they have not been on the main line for years. Something about deliveries being undependable; the impossibility of getting good staff. A waiter shuffles over, his clothing glistening with dirt, and shrugs as I give him the order. Another mug for Dostoevski, an aperitif for Gertrude Stein, a little more wine for myself. Hemingway will pass this round. Shakespeare is now in the men's room having more difficulty with his bowels; perhaps a little cheese and crackers. The others, another round as previously. We make quite a group hunched around this small table, blocking the aisles, giving the cafe a reputation for seediness and disruption even beyond its wont, but we are customers, and the waiter, grumbling, goes off to the kitchen. "But you've certainly got a point, Fyodor," I add pleasantly, "and you're entitled to your opinion. I *defend* your opinion."

"The hell with all of it," Hemingway says. He stands, tucks his writing pad under his arm, heads toward an exit. "I have listened to the merde. All this afternoon I have been possessed by nothing but merde. Now it is time to go off and do good things. To feel richly, to know greatly. To conquer feeling with hope." He is in one of his sulks again. Really, despite all our efforts, we have been able to do very little with him. The man is simply not companionable. "I am off for sunlight," he says and staggers through the aisles, leaving us with his share of the check as usual, and stepping off into the Rue de la Paix is hit by a passing streetcar which dismembers him thoroughly and leaves him in small pieces on the sidewalk.

Gertrude Stein giggles a little and raises a napkin to her lips, fondling Alice Toklas' hands. "Ernest never did have any taste," she says, "and all his gestures fail as gestures." She shakes her head, puts the napkin down, leans over toward Alice's ear and disappears into some intense conversation as pedestrians and gendarmes outside gather around the ruins of Ernest. The streetcar has stopped and from its windows, faces look out incuriously, mumbling. "Like petals on a wet, black bough," Ezra says, speaking for the first time this afternoon, and goes back to his jottings. Now the crowd covers Ernest and it is difficult to see what is going on. I assume that in due time they will put him into one of the conveyors for reprocessing. It hardly matters. None of this matters. My relationship with Ernest has not been a happy one, and although I am embarrassed to admit this, I am not entirely sorry to think that he is dead.

Shakespeare returns from the men's room simultaneously with the appearance of the waiter carrying our glasses, and they almost collide. "Bloody fool!" Bill says, collapsing into a chair. "You stink up everything!" And the waiter, with the air of a man who has suffered greatly and has now passed tested limits, balances the tray on one hand, takes off a glass of wine and throws it into Bill's face. "Bastard!" Shakespeare says, but his expression does not change, his eyes revolving flat and dead above his cheekbones. Incontestably, the man is drunk. In any other condition he would knock the waiter unconscious.

But nothing will happen this afternoon. The moment of tension passes, the waiter looks toward the sky and, recovering his control after a moment, puts the glasses before us. As he bends near me, I ask him quietly for the check. The waiter's face suffuses with rage, but somehow I am able to convince him that I mean no insult and he says that he will go off to the kitchen and see what he can do. Truly, I am the only one of us who is able to deal with the common, ordinary realities of the afternoon, the others being abstracted into their private roles or sorrows, but in all honesty I am getting somewhat tired of this and for the first time it occurs to me that I am becoming bored with my companions and our afternoon routine and that I may bring it to a halt. I would hardly be missed if I did not appear at the table at one o'clock. But if I did not, I wonder, who would order the drinks?

I think about all this, looking out idly toward the street where, even though only a few moments have passed, there is no sign of Ernest's recent tragedy. Pedestrians whisk by quickly, automobiles honk their scattered way past, a fat patrolman with a cheerful expression paces in front of the cafe, hands on hips, looking at the sun. The one conveyor clanking its way on the street-edge is clean and empty; Ernest is already gone. It is depressing to think that for all of his bombast his death has had so little effect upon the world, but then, as most of my companions would advise me, it is very difficult to make any kind of permanent change in the landscape. Technology has done this to us, and also the alienation effect which progressively separates men from the consequences of their acts, the products of their labor.

As if catching my thoughts, which have taken a rather stricken and metaphysical turn, Dostoevski looks up at me and winks. "It is difficult, is it not, my friend," he says, "to see so much and do so little, eh? The Czars would have had a word for this kind of condition, but I call it refractory."

"He's just pouting," Gertrude Stein says. "He thinks he's sufficient when he is really insufficient, is that not so, Alice?" Beaming Alice nods; the two old lesbians clasp hands again and recommence their incessant laughter. Really, I cannot stand them — their presence at the table is a constant embarrassment and most of the waiter's hostility, I know, is directed toward them — but what can I do? Paris was their idea, after all, and a good suggestion it was. If we had not gone to Paris we might have ended up meeting in New York or Berlin and with the Algonquin demolished, how many places are there left which are really good for our discussions? I nod judiciously and turn my gaze from them. It is better at most times not to see too deeply, as my friends have advised me, and with some difficulty, I have made progress with this advice.

"I believe," Shakespeare says heavily, "I believe that I am suddenly very ill, oh you fools," and to our astonished gaze — Bill never complains; he has always been the heartiest of the lot — stands swaying in the dense little spaces of the cafe, his skin turned a sudden vigorous orange color. "It must be the wine, the heat, the afternoon, the pain oh my friends," he says, "oh let me unbutton here," and tugs at his waistcoat; in the midst of his struggles, however, a spasm of some violent kind hits him and he collapses heavily over the table, bringing it to the floor in an incandescence of cups, saucers, glasses, beer, wines, liqueurs. Into the middle of this he plunges, and rolling once on the floor lies still.

Standing, Fyodor eyes him with disgust and then takes a large watch out of his pocket. "I believe the old bastard has died," he says, checking the time, "but if you will excuse me, I really have had enough of this. There is a great deal of work to be done and I hope to conclude an important subsidiary deal on *Crime and Punishment* before sunset." He turns to leave.

I am offended by his coldness, by the total lack of regard which it is now clear was his only true feeling about our afternoons, but before I can ponder this further or remonstrate with him, the waiter has appeared flanked by two police and a large angry man who must be the owner of the cafe and who looks at Shakespeare's corpse with revulsion. The waiter whispers desperately into the owner's ear; he seems to be trying to explain that he had nothing whatsoever to do with this occurrence. The owner shrugs him off. "I'm quite sorry," he says to us as the police stare solemnly, "but we cannot allow this anymore. You have been stinking and drinking up my cafe, the last cafe of Paris, for many weeks now and the disgrace is intolerable. My staff is at their wits' end and my wife threatens to leave me." He kicks the corpse. "You are all impounded for further investigation," he says.

"This is disgraceful," says Gertrude. "Alice, help me!" And Fyodor, with the ancient cunning of the prison camps, tries to slink toward the exit, but the police are efficient and determined in the way that even post-technological gendarmes can be and before I can quite grasp what has happened we are all in handcuffs. Fyodor too, and being led away.

"We will give you a full report," one of the police says to the owner, "we can give you our assurances of that."

"This is an outrage," Fyodor says. "You can slap chains upon us and your machinery "but you will never, never, imprison the free, lunging, human soul, and flings himself at the nearest police but is knocked unconscious by one mild blow — Fyodor is quite frail for all of his bombast — and topples to the floor, dragging all of us with him. We seem to be hooked on the same chain.

I feel Shakespeare's corpse, already cooling underneath me, to the left and right I absorb the struggles and kicks of Alice and Gertrude, I raise my head to see that old Count Leo too, just returning from a brisk walk, has somehow been hooked and chained, but my gaze passes through and then beyond all of them; looking upon the street I see with precision I have never had before the movement of the conveyor and then, as the mass around me begins to roll in that direction, I understand that in the absence of proper police procedures, we are all going to be taken there instantly, and it is with relief — how I always knew in the deepest of my Fyodor's aspects that it would be with relief! — that I feel Gertrude's dark kiss upon me and in that way we are all carried out.

The Only Thing You Learn

In Memory of Cyril M. Kornbluth

HELLO, VOYAGER. you come into the bar cautiously, not looking for trouble but ready for anything that you might find, you tell yourself, the token in your left pocket emitting its precious waves of secret and solace as you squeeze it, then let it go. Your posture is poised toward ruin but ready for flight. You are neat and fleet, ready for anything, but willing to stay and fight it out too if you must. There at the end of your bar is the target, just as they had promised in the dusky half-light of the Seven Moons, your target in sailor cap and shapeless jacket, drinking red top and beer chaser wedged in that corner, his eyes curiously alight. You are drawn to him instinctively, not only by the sense of mission you must undergo, but by that necessity in his eyes, you tell yourself that you have never seen anyone quite as open, as charmed, as needful as this man whose glance now passes from you disinterestedly, swinging left to right, then down to the shot-glass as he shrugs and drinks. Three hookers in working garb are scattered on the right side of the bar as you approach, none of them displaying any interest in the target — or in anything else — as you glide past, on the other side there are two drunken bums, their heads in their hands, listening to the private and integral sounds of their consciousness, whiskey glasses drained before them. The bartender looks at you incuriously as you come down the line of stools on the left, past the drunken bums, and take your seat beside the target. His sailor cap is oddly peaked, his brown eyes alight with something other than inebriation, but he does not seem willing to make eye contact and in that furious, broken instant during which you assess the situation, you think that despite the assurances of the ancient ones, their pledge that nothing can possibly go wrong, you might have once again, voyager, taken yourself over your head, entered a situation you cannot resolve. It is difficult to say.

What he's having, you tell the bartender who is looking at you. And buy him a round too.

Money, the bartender says. Joint like this, you put your money on the bar first. Rules of the house. In his voice is the stentorian sound of the Reptiles; he seems to be vocalizing in their ancient and frightening tongue. Of course they would have put an agent in here, they would allow no corner of the sector to be unoccupied, undefended against precisely this kind of immersion. You do not let this knowledge frighten you.

Of course, you say. In your right pocket, the strange coins and bills seem to emit a strange warmth, something like that of the token but occupying their own heat and substance. You thrust your palm in there, remove a handful, shake them out on the bar in an indiscriminate outpouring. The bartender retreats a little at the sound of the coins, then fixes you with an unwavering gaze. Beside you, the target sits unmoving.

Is that enough? you say.

The bartender shuts, tilts a hand in an either-or gesture, limps back along the railing, and obtains glasses. You hear for the first time the thin racket from the television set above the bar, a comedy of some kind turned down very low, the old black-and-white television hazed toward a kind of omnipresent blur, the figures of the actors only dimly visible. From the television set comes the quiet sound of shrieking which may be part of the live audience in attendance but then again might be the interior of your own astonished and trapped heart, fluttering against the walls of your being. The hookers glance at the television set now and then, the drunken bums pay no attention whatsoever, being too deeply drawn into their own substance, you think, to be concerned with decor. Beside you, the target raises his glass, drains the last of the beer, shakes his head, then stares at you as the bartender comes banging down the rail, places shot-glasses before you, contemptuously up-ends a bottle and fills them with orange liquid. What do you want? the target says.

Your instructions have been very specific. You adhere to them at all perilous costs. That is up to you, my friend, you say. The bartender goes away, returns with two trembling glasses of beer, places them in front of you, takes coins and bills, moves away. The token sends out odd glares of heat from its hidden place. What do you think I want? you say.

I know who you are, the target says. There is no preamble to this statement, no edging into it, the aspect is one of shocking bluntness. You had been warned that this would probably be the case, the target has been pushed far, far beyond the rim of his patience. You're one of them. You're part of them. Another one come to torment me, to haunt.

You say nothing. It is time to drink, to put the liquid and its chaser into you, to obtain as much as possible the riot of their own chemistry. You do this, quickly and solemnly, fixing the target with your hopeful and sparkling gaze as the chill and warmth begin to spread through you and then the target does the same, drinking quickly and convulsively, slamming shot-glass and then beer on the counter.

Lies, he says, it's all lies. It's all part of the same swindle. Give me the feeling that I'm at the center of things but I'm not. I'm not. You're just using me for something I can't even understand and I don't know — He stops. It is as if the speech, extracted from him in wrenching syllables, has astonished not its auditor but the target himself. Your instructions on this possible reaction are also quite clear. You have, within the limits of the situation, been given the most explicit procedures and it is within your responsibility to follow it or to face your own terrible penalty.

I'm not one of them, you say now. I'm from the other side. I've come to offer you surcease. Freedom, possibly. The means of freedom rest within your hands. It is within your means.

You look at the target calmly, seriously, while the target finishes the contents of the shot-glass and the beer, then waves his arms at the bartender. Enough of this, he says. I'm getting out. I'm checking out. I'm in over my head here but I have the sense to know it.

You know nothing, you say. Nothing at all. You don't even have the language to express your lack of knowledge. You feel the rage and disgust coming upon you, just as had been predicted, but still, within you, there is the terrible, serene knowledge with which you carried yourself back across the centuries.

Here, you say. Here.

You reach into your left pocket, remove the token, place it on the gleaming surfaces of the bar. It lies there in its phosphorescent glare, leaking power, hints of the millennia and its wastes glinting from it. Even the hookers seem to be entranced, gaining sudden respect for this colloquy, they stare at you and the target with new interest. The drunken bums, oblivious of this as the Reptiles themselves, continue to brood and nod in their vomitous stupor. The bartender, respectful, flicks a towel at the television set and observes all of this with great patience. It is fortunate that this is a neighborhood bar in a bad area and that incoming traffic is light to nonexistent because it is not clear how the token would deal with new entrants or how, for that matter, they would deal with this unleashed power.

Here, you say. Here it is. The sign of the centuries. Reach out. Take it in your hand.

The target looks at the token with an intensity as to minimize your own attention through all of this. You have never, in all of your experience, seen an attentiveness like this. Are you crazy? the target says. You want me to touch that. He gestures at the token. Touch that He recoils, his arms flailing again. Get out of here, he says. Get out of here now. That thing can explode. It can destroy the world. It can — Why don't you try it? you say. See what it can do. You put an exploratory finger on the token, push it toward the target. Small rays of power seem to pour from it and strike the target in the eyes although this may be illusory. You have been carefully warned about the phenomena in this place, how the surreal, the imagined, the extant can mingle in dangerous and unpredictable fashion.

Anyway, you say, it's up to you. It's your decision. It rests in your hands. The decision is yours.

You stand, your instructions completed, and adjust your clothing, then move slowly down the arc of the bar, moving without urgency but determination toward the door, the bartender now saying, Hey, mister, come back here. You can't leave that thing here. You can't—

Yes I can, you say. I can and I must. Behind you, you hear the target beginning to murmur, then scream as the terrific heat of the token, now unleashed by instruction, absorbs him, but you will have nothing of this. Abandoning caution in the rising clamor behind, you sprint toward the door, then out, the strange, swaddling air of this planet gripping you as you stumble toward the checkpoint. Behind, you hear voices, louder and louder sounds, sudden screams, then the whump! of great flame and ignition but you do not turn.

Oh, you do not turn. You have absorbed your lessons well, terror of the reptiles no less than dedication to your duties impels you as you sprint toward the rendezvous point. Enormous, transmogrified, the target and his cohorts behind you scream for you to stop but it is too late for them, perhaps too late for you as well as you feel the bowl of circumstance closing tightly around you. Oh, voyager, we had it planned this way from the start. The rendezvous will never occur; here you were detailed, here you stay. Be lost, voyager. You shriek with a rage to match that of your target as now, at last and as predicted, the hundred years of fire begin.

Leviticus: In the Ark

I

CONDITIONS ARE difficult and services are delayed. Conditions have been difficult for some time, services have been delayed more often than being prompt, but never has it weighed upon Leviticus as it does now. Part of this has to do with his own situation: cramped in the ark, Torahs jammed into his left ear and right kneecap, heavy talmudic bindings wedged uncomfortably under his buttocks, he is past the moments of quiet meditation that for so long have sustained him. Now he is in great pain, his body is shrieking for release; he has a vivid image of himself bursting from the ark, the doors sliding open, his arms outstretched, his beard flapping in the strange breezes of the synagogue as he cries denunciation. *I can no longer bear this position.* There must be some Yiddish equivalent for this. Very well, he will cry it in Yiddish.

No, he will do nothing of the sort. He will remain within the ark, six by four, jammed amidst the holy writings. At times he is sure that he has spent several weeks within, at others, all sense of time eludes him; perhaps it has been only a matter of hours ... well, make it a few days since he has been in here. It does not matter. A minute is as a century in the Eye of God, he remembers — or did it go the other way? — and vague murmurs that he can hear through the not fully soundproofed walls of his chamber inform him that the service is about to begin. In due course, just before the adoration begins, they will fling open the doors of the ark and he will be able to gaze upon them for a few moments, breathe the somewhat less dense air of the synagogue, endure past many moments of this sort because of his sudden, shuddering renewal of contact with the congregation, but, ah God! ... it is difficult. Too much has been demanded of him; he is suffering deeply.

Leviticus turns within the limited confines of his position, tries to find a more comfortable point of accommodation. Soon the service will begin. After the ritual chants and prayers, after the sermon and the hymn, will come the adoration. At the adoration the opening of the ark. He will stretch. He will stand. He will stretch out a hand and greet them. He will cast light upon their eyes and upon the mountains: that they shall remember and do all his commandments and be holy unto him.

He wonders if his situation has made him megalomaniac.

II

Two weeks before, just at the point when Leviticus' point of commitment to the ark loomed before him, he had appeared in the rabbi's cubicle and made a plea for dispensation. "I am a sick man," he had said, "I do not think that I will be able to stand the confinement. Also, and I must be quite honest with you, rabbi, I doubt my religious faith and commitment. I am not sure that I can function as that embodiment of ritual which placement in the ark symbolizes." This was not quite true; at least, the issue of religious faith had not occurred to Leviticus in either way; he was not committed to the religion, not quite against it either, it did not matter enough … but he had gathered from particularly reliable reports going through the congregation that one of the best ways of getting out of the ark was to plead a lack of faith. Perhaps he had gotten it wrong. The rabbi looked at him for a long time, and finally, drawing his robes tightly around him, retreating to the wall, looked at Leviticus as if he were a repulsed object. "Then perhaps your stay in the ark will do you some good," he had said; "it will enable you to find time for meditation and prayer. Also, religious belief has nothing to do with the role of the tenant. Does the wine in the goblet conceive of the nature of the sacrament it represents? In the same way, the tenant is merely the symbol."

"I haven't been feeling well," Leviticus mumbled. "I've been having chest pains. I've been having seizures of doubt. Cramps in the lower back; I don't think that I can — "

"Yes you can," the rabbi said with a dreadful expression, *"and yes you will,"* and had sent Leviticus out into the cold and casting light of the settlement, beginning to come to terms with the realization that he could not, could not under any circumstances, escape the obligation thrust upon him. Perhaps he had been foolish to have thought that he could. Perhaps he should not have paid credence to the rumors. He returned to his cubicle in a foul temper, set the traps to *privacy* and sullenly put through the tape of the *Union Prayer Book, Revised Edition: For the High Holy Days.* If you really were going to have to do something like this, he guessed that a little bit of hard background wouldn't hurt. But it made no sense. The writings simply made no sense. He shut off the tapes and for a long time gave no further thought to any of this, until the morning, when, in absolute disbelief, he found the elders in his unit, implacable in their costume, come to take him to the ark. *Tallis* and *tefillim*.

III

In the ark, Leviticus ponders his condition while the services go on outside. He has taken to self-pity during his confinement; he has a tendency to snivel a little. It is really not fair for him, a disbelieving man but one who has never made his disbelief a point of contention, to be thrown into such a position, kept there for such an extended period of time. Ritual is important, and he for one is not to say that the enactment of certain rote practices does not lend reassurance, may indeed be a metaphor for some kind of reality which he cannot apprehend ... but is it right that all of this should be at his expense? He has never entered into disputation with the elders on their standards of belief; why should they force theirs upon him?

A huge volume of the Talmud jabs his buttocks, its cover a painful little concentrated point of pain, and cursing, Leviticus bolts from it, rams his head against the beam forming half of the ceiling of the ark, bends, reaches, seizes the volume, and with all his force hurls it three feet into the flat wall opposite. He has hoped for a really satisfying concussion, some mark of his contempt that will be heard outside of the ark, will impress and disconcert the congregation, but there simply has not been room enough to generate impact; the volume falls softly, turgidly across a knee, and he slaps at it in fury, little puffs of dust coming from the cover, inflaming his sinuses. He curses again, wondering if this apostasy, committed within the very place in which, according to what he understands, the spirit of God dwells, will be sufficient to end his period of torture, release him from this one kind of bondage into at least another, but nothing whatsoever happens.

He could have expected that, he thinks. If the tenant of the ark is indeed symbol rather than substance, then it would not matter what he did here or what he thought; only his presence would matter. And fling volumes of the Talmud, scrape at the Torahs, snivel away as he will, he is nevertheless in residence. Nothing that he can do will make any difference at all; his presence here is the only testament that they will need.

Step by tormenting step Leviticus has been down this path of reasoning-after-apostasy a hundred times during his confinement. Fortunately for him, these are emotional outbursts which he forgets almost upon completion, so that he has no memory of them when he starts upon the next; and this sense of discovery — the renewal of his rage, so to speak, every time afresh — has thus sustained him in the absence of more real benefits and will sustain him yet. Also, during the long night hours when only he is in the temple, he is able to have long, imagined dialogues with God, which to no little degree also sustain him, even if his visualization of God is a narrow and parochial one.

IV

The first time that the doors had been flung open during the adoration and all of the congregation had looked in upon him, Leviticus had become filled with shame, but that quickly passed when he realized that no one really thought anything of it and that the attention of the elders and the congregation was not upon him but upon the sacred scripts that one by one the elders withdrew, brought to the podium, and read with wavering voice and fingers while Leviticus, hunched over naked in an uncomfortable fetal position, could not have been there at all, for all the difference it made. He could have bolted from the ark, flung open his arms, shrieked to the congregation, "Look at me, look at me, don't you see what you're doing!" but he had not; he had been held back in part by fear, another part by constraint, still a third part from the realization that no one in the ark had ever done it. He had never seen it happen; back through all the generations that he was able to seek through accrued knowledge, the gesture was without precedent. The tenant of the ark had huddled quietly· throughout the term of his confinement, had kept himself in perfect restraint when exposed; why should this not continue? Tradition and the awesome power of the elders had held him in check. He could not interrupt the flow of the services. He could deal with the predictable, which was a term of confinement and then release, just like everyone who had preceded him, but what he could not control was any conception of the unknown. If he made a spectacle of himself during the adoration, there was no saying what might happen then. The elders might take vengeance upon him. They might turn away from the thought of vengeance and simply declare that his confinement be extended for an indefinite period for apostasy. It was very hard to tell exactly *what* they would do. This fear of the unknown, Leviticus had decided through his nights of pondering and imaginary dialogue, was probably what had enabled the situation to go on as long as it had.

It was hard to say exactly when he had reached the decision that he could no longer accept his position, his condition, his fate, wait out the time of his confinement, entertain the mercy of the elders, and return to the congregation. It was hard to tell at exactly what point he had realized that he could not do this; there was no clear point of epiphany, no moment at which — unlike a religious conversion — he could see himself as having gone outside the diagram of possibility, unutterably changed. All that he knew was that the decision had slowly crept into him, perhaps when he was sleeping, and without a clear point of definition, had reached absolute firmness: he would confront them at the adoration now. He would force them to look at him. He would show them what he, and by implication they, had become: so trapped within a misunderstood tradition, so wedged within the suffocating confines of the ark that they had lost any overriding sense of purpose, the ability to perceive wholly the madness that they and the elders had perpetuated. He would force them to understand this as the sum point of their lives, and when it was over, he would bolt from the synagogue naked, screaming, back to his cubicle, where he would reassemble his clothing and make final escape from the complex ... and leave *them,* not him, to decide what they would now make of the shattered ruins of their lives.

The long period of confinement, self-examination, withdrawal, and physical privation had, perhaps, made Leviticus somewhat unstable.

V

Just before the time when the elders had appeared and had taken him away, Leviticus had made his last appeal, not to them, certainly not to ,the rabbi, but to Stala, who had shared to a certain point his anguish and fear of entrapment. "I don't see why I have to go there," he said to her, lying tight in the instant after fornication. "It's stupid'. It's sheer mysticism. And besides that, it hasn't any relevance."

"But you must go," she said, putting a hand on his cheek. "You have been asked, and you *must.* " She was not stupid, he thought, merely someone who had never had to question assumptions, as he was now being forced to. "It is ordained. It won't be that bad; you're supposed to learn a lot."

"*You* go."

She gave a little gasping intake of breath and rolled from him. "You know that's impossible," she said. "Women can't go."

"In the reform tradition they can."

"But we're not in the reform tradition," she said; "this is the high Orthodox. "

"I tend to think of it more in the line of being progressive."

"You know, Leviticus," she said, sitting, breathing unevenly — he could see her breasts hanging from her in the darkness like little scrolls, *like little scrolls,* oh, his confinement was very much on his mind, he could see — "it's just ridiculous that you should say something like that to me, that you should even *suggest* it. We're talking about our tradition now, and our tradition is very clear on this point, and it's impossible for a woman to go. Even if she wanted, she just couldn't — "

"All right," he said, "all right."

"No," Stala said, "no I won't stop discussing this, *you* were the one to raise it, Leviticus, not me, and I just won't have any of it. I didn't think you were that kind of person. I thought that you accepted the traditions, that you believed in them; in fact, it was an encouragement to me to think, to really think, that I had found someone who believed in a pure, solid, unshaken way, and I was really *proud* of you, even prouder when I found that you had been selected, but now you've changed everything. I'm beginning to be afraid that the only reason you believed in the traditions was because they weren't causing you any trouble and you didn't have to sacrifice yourself personally, but as soon as you became involved, you moved away from them." She was standing now, moving toward her robe, which had been tossed in the fluorescence at the far end of his cubicle; looking toward it during intercourse, he had thought that the sight of it was the most tender and affecting thing he had ever known, that she had cast her garments aside for him, that she had committed herself trustfully in nakedness against him for the night, and all of this despite the fact that he was undergoing what he took to be the positive humiliation of the confinement; now, as she flung it angrily on herself, he wondered if he had been wrong, if that casting aside had been a gesture less tender than fierce, whether or not she might have been — and he could hardly bear this thought, but one must, after all, press on — perversely excited by images of how he would look naked and drawn in upon himself in the ark, his genitals clamped between his thighs, talmudic statements by the rabbis Hill and Ben Bag Bag his only companions in the many long nights to come. He did not want to think of it, did not want to see her in this new perspective, and so leaped to his feet, fleet as a hart, and said, "But it's not fair. I tell you, it isn't fair."

"Of course it isn't fair. That's why it's so beautiful." "Well, how would *you* like it? How would *you* like to be confined in — "

"Leviticus," she said, "I don't want to talk to you about this any more. Leviticus," she added, "I think I was wrong about you, you've hurt me very much. Leviticus," she concluded, "if you don't leave me right now, this moment, I'll go to the elders and tell them exactly what you're saying and thinking, and you know what will happen to you *then,*" and he had let her go, nothing else to do, the shutter of his cubicle coming open, the passage of her body halving the light from the hall, then the light exposed again, and she was gone; he closed the shutter, he was alone in his cubicle again.

"It *isn't* fair," he said aloud, "she wouldn't like it so much if this was Reform and *she* were faced with the possibility of going in there someday," but this gave him little comfort; in fact, it gave him no comfort at all. It seemed to lead him right back to where he had started — futile, amazed protest at the injustice and folly of what was being done for him — and he had gone into an unhappy sleep thinking that something, something would have to be done about this; perhaps he could take the case out of the congregation. If the ordinators were led to understand what kind of rites were being committed in the name of high Orthodoxy, they would take a strong position against this, seal up the complex, probably scatter the congregation throughout a hundred other complexes ... and it was this which had given him ease, tossed him into a long, murmuring sleep replete with satisfaction that he had finally found a way to deal with this (because he knew instinctively that the ordinators would *not* like this), but the next morning, cunningly, almost as if they had been informed by Stala (perhaps they had), the elders had come to take him to the ark, and that had been the end of that line of thought. He supposed that he could still do it, complain to the ordinators — that was, after his confinement was over — but at that point it hardly seemed worth it. It hardly seemed worth it at all. For one thing, he would be out of the ark by then and would not have to face it for a very, very long time, if ever. So why bother with the ordinators? He would have to take a more direct position, take it up with the congregation itself. Surely once they understood his agony, they could not permit it to continue. Could they?

VI

In the third of his imaginary dialogues with God (whom he pictured as an imposing man, somewhat the dimensions of one of the elders but much more neatly trimmed and not loaded down with the paraphernalia with which they conducted themselves) Leviticus said, "I don't believe any of it. Not any part of it at all. It's ridiculous."

"Doubt is another part of faith," God said. "Doubt and belief intertwine; both can be conditions of reverence. There is more divinity in the doubt of a wise man than in the acceptance of fools."

"That's just rhetoric," Leviticus said; "it explains nothing."

"The devices of belief must move within the confines of rhetoric," God said. "Rhetoric is the poor machinery of the profound and incontrovertible. Actually, it's not a matter of doubt. You're just very uncomfortable."

"That's right. I'm uncomfortable. I don't see why Judaism imposes this kind of suffering."

"Religion *is* suffering," God said with a modest little laugh, "and if you think Judaism is difficult upon its participants, you should get a look at some of the *others* sometime. Animal sacrifice, immolation, the ceremony of tongues. Oh, most terrible! Not that everyone doesn't have a right to their point of view," God added hastily. "Each must reach me, each in his way and through his tradition. Believe me, Leviticus, you haven't got the worst of it."

"I protest. I protest this humiliation."

"It isn't easy for me, either," God pointed out. "I've gone through cycles of repudiation for billions of years. Still, one must go on."

"I've got to get out of here. It's destroying my health; my physical condition is ruined. When am I going to leave?"

"I'm sorry," God said, "that decision is not in my hands."

"But you're omnipotent."

"My omnipotence is only my will working through the diversity of twenty billion other wills. Each is determined, and yet each is free."

"That sounds to me like a lousy excuse," Leviticus said sullenly. "I don't think that makes any sense at all."

"I do the best I can," God said, and after a long, thin pause added sorrowfully, "you don't think that any of this is easy for me either, do you?"

VII

Leviticus has the dim recollection from the historical tapes, none of them well attended to, that before the time of the complexes, before the time of great changes, there had been another kind of existence, one during which none of the great churches, Judaism included, had been doing particularly well in terms of absolute number of participants, relative proportion of the population. Cults had done all right, but cults had had only the most marginal connection to the great churches, and in most cases had repudiated them, leading, in the analyses of certain of the historical tapes, to the holocaust that had followed, and the absolute determination on the part of the Risen, that they would not permit this to happen again, that they would not allow the cults to appropriate all of the energy, the empirical demonstrations, for themselves, but instead would make sure that the religions were reconverted to hard ritual, that the ritual demonstrations following would be strong and convincing enough to keep the cults out of business and through true worship and true belief (although with enough ritual now to satisfy the mass of people that religion could be made visible) stave off yet another holocaust. At least, this was what Leviticus had *gathered* from the tapes, but then, you could never be sure about this, and the tapes were all distributed under the jurisdiction of the elders anyway, and what the elders would do with material to manipulate it to their own purposes was well known.

Look, for one thing, at what they had done to Leviticus.

VIII

"I'll starve in here," he had said to the elders desperately, as they were conveying him down the aisle toward the ark. "I'll deteriorate. I'll go insane from the confinement. If I get ill, no one will be there to help me."

"Food will be given you each day. You will have the Torah and the Talmud, the Feast of Life itself to comfort you and to grant you peace. You will allow the spirit of God to move within you."

"That's ridiculous," Leviticus said. "I told you, I have very little belief in any of this. How can the spirit — ?"

"Belief means nothing," the elders said. They seemed to speak in unison, which was impossible, of course (how could they have such a level of shared anticipation of the others' remarks; rather, it was that they spoke one by one, with similar voice quality — *that* would be a more likely explanation of the phenomenon, mysticism, having; so far as Leviticus knew, very little relation to rational Judaism). "You are its object, not its subject."

"Aha!" Leviticus said then, frantically raising one finger to forestall them as they began to lead him painfully into the ark, pushing him, tugging, buckling his limbs. "If belief does not matter, if I am merely object rather than subject, *then how can I be tenanted by the spirit?*"

"That," the elders said, finishing the job, patting him into place, one of them extracting a rag to wipe the wood of the ark speedily to high gloss, cautiously licking a finger, applying it to the surface to take out an imagined particle of dust, "that is very much your problem and not ours, you see," and closed the doors upon him, leaving him alone with scrolls and Talmud, cloth, and the sound of scrambling birds. In a moment he heard a grinding noise as key was inserted into lock, then a snap as tumblers inverted. They were locking him in.

Well, he had known that. That, at least, was not surprising. Tradition had its roots; the commitment to the ark was supposed to be voluntary — a joyous expression of commitment, that was; the time spent in the ark was supposed to be a time of repentance and great interior satisfaction ... But all of that to one side, the elders, balancing off the one against the other, as was their wont, arriving at a careful and highly modulated view of the situation, had ruled in their wisdom that it was best to keep the ark locked at all times, excepting, of course, the adoration. That was the elders for you. They took everything into account, and having done *that,* made the confinement, as they said, his problem.

IX

Now the ritual of the Sabbath evening service is over, and the rabbi is delivering his sermon. Something about the many rivers of Judaism, each of them individual, flowing into that great sea of tradition and belief. The usual material. Leviticus knows that this is the Sabbath service; he can identify it by certain of the prayers and chants, although he has lost all extrinsic sense of time, of course, in the ark. For that matter, he suspects, the elders have lost all extrinsic sense of time as well; it is no more Friday now than Thursday or Saturday, but at a certain arbitrary time after the holocaust, he is given to understand, the days, the months, the years themselves were recreated and assigned, and therefore, if the elders say it is Friday, it is Friday, just as if they say it is the year thirty-seven, it is the year thirty-seven, and not fifty seven hundred something or other, or whatever it was when the holocaust occurred. (In his mind, as a kind of shorthand, he has taken to referring to the holocaust as the H; the H did this; certain things happened to cause the H, but he is not sure that this would make sense to other people, and as a matter of fact wonders whether or not this might not be the sign of a deranged consciousness.)

Whatever the elders say it is, it is, although God in the imaginary dialogues has assured him that the elders, in their own fashion, are merely struggling with the poor tools at their command and are no less fallible than he, Leviticus.

He shall take upon himself, in any event, these commandments, and shall bind them for frontlets between his eyes. After the sermon, when the ark is opened for the adoration, he will lunge from it and confront them with what they have become, with what they have made of him, with what together they have made of God. He will do that, and for signposts upon his house as well, that they shall remember and do those commandments and be holy. Holy, holy. Oh, their savior and their hope, they have been worshiping him as their fathers did in ancient days, but enough of this, quite enough; the earth being his dominion and all the beasts and fish thereof, it is high time that some sort of reckoning of the changes be made.

Highly unfair, Leviticus thinks, crouching, awaiting the opening of the' ark, but then again, he must (as always) force himself to see all sides of the question: very possibly, if Stala had approved of his position, had granted him sympathy, had agreed with him that what the elders were doing was unjust and unfair ... well, then, he might have been far more cheerfully disposed to put up with his fate. If only she, if only someone, had seen him as a martyr rather than as a usual part of a very usual process. Everything might have changed, but then again, it might have been the same.

X

The book of Daniel, he recollects, had been very careful and very precise in giving, with numerology and symbol, the exact time when the H would begin. Daniel had been specific; 'he had alluded to precisely that course of events at which period of time that would signal the coming (or the second coming, depending upon your pursuit); the only trouble with it was that there had been so many conflicting interpretations over thousands of years that for all intents and purposes the predictive value of Daniel for the H had been lost; various interpreters saw too many signs of rising in the East, too many beasts of heaven, stormings of the tabernacle, too many uprisings among the cattle or the chieftains to enable them to get the H down right, once and for all. A lot of them, hence, had been embarrassed; many cults, hinged solely upon their interpretation of Daniel and looking for an apocalyptic date, had gotten themselves overcommitted, and going up on the mountaintops to await the end, had lost most of their membership.

Of course, the H had come, and with it the floods, the falling, the rising and the tumult in the lands, and it was possible that Daniel had gotten it precisely right, after all, if only you could look back on it in retrospect and get it right, but as far as Leviticus was concerned, there was only one overriding message that you might want to take from the tapes if you were interested in this kind of thing: you did not want to pin it down too closely. Better, as the elders did, to kind of leave the issue indeterminate and in flux. Better, as God himself had (imaginarily) pointed out, to say that doubt is merely the reverse coin of belief, both of them motes in the bowels of the Hound of Heaven.

XI

The rabbi, adoring the ever-living God and rendering praise unto him, inserts the key into the ark, the tumblers fall open, the doors creak and gape, and Leviticus finds himself once again staring into the old man's face, his eyes congested with pain as he reaches in trembling toward one of the scrolls, his cheeks dancing in the light, the elders grouped behind him attending carefully; and instantly Leviticus strikes: he reaches out a hand, yanks the rabbi out of the way, and then tumbles from the ark. He had meant to leap but did not realize how shriveled his muscles would be from disuse; what he had intended to be a vault is instead a collapse to the stones under the ark, but yet he is able to move. He is able to move. He pulls himself falteringly to hands and knees, gasping, the rabbi mumbling in the background, the elders looking at him with shocked expressions, too astonished for the instant to move. The instant now is all that he needs. He has not precipitated what he has done in the hope of having a great deal of time.

"Look at me!" Leviticus shrieks, struggling erect, hands hanging, head shaking. "Look at me, look at what I've become, look at what dwells in the heart of the ark!" And indeed, they are looking, all of them, the entire congregation, Stala in the women's section, hand to face, palm open, extended, all of them stunned in the light of his gaze. "Look at me!" he shouts again. "You can't do this to people, do you — understand that? You cannot do it!" And the elders come upon him, recovered from their astonishment, to seize him with hands like metal, the rabbi rolling and rolling on the floor, deep into some chant that Leviticus cannot interpret, the congregation gathered now to rush upon him; but too late, it has (as he must at some level have known) been too late, from the beginning, and as the rabbi chants, the elders strain, the congregation rushes … time inverts, and the real, the long-expected, the true H with its true Host begins.

Police Actions

❝YOU COUNTRYMEN,❞ the general said, "so good-hearted, so sincere, so convinced of your righteousness, so clumsy and devoted in all of your duties and for these reasons the most wicked and dangerous nation who ever worked out a policy. He took a sip of wine, motioned to the waiter for a check, smoothed lint from his fatigues (retired, he still came to our cafe in combat gear, prepared for the destabilization which might occur at any time), sighed. "It is not so much that self-righteousness that makes you such a complicated and mesmerizing factor," he said, "for that, we must address your love of pornography and the censor alike, of damnation and religious revivals, of urban retrieval and urban destruction, those marvelous contradictions embedded in your history and responses that you work out so catastrophically on helpless subjects like ourselves." He sighted an imaginary pistol, pulled the trigger with insouciant grace. Boom. "Someday I would like to come to your country, see your enclaves, harass your women," the general said. "Of course someday I would like to ski Switzerland, learn Esperanto, foment a true revolution of the spirit overseas. We do not get what we want, *n'est'ce pas?*" The waiter leaned to whisper confidentially while, politely, we looked away although we could sense the urgent sibilance of information dutifully given. "Of course, of course" the general said, "these warnings are unnecessary. My good friends here know I am merely speculating, talking idly, the ravings of a peculiar old man in the sun-spattered cafe of an occupied and defeated country. Is that not so?" He grinned. We made conciliatory, noncomplicitous gestures. In the square, the birds lofted as if in response to rifle fire.

It is difficult to sort out matters in the midst of self-protection.

But the general was only one of the many counselors and advisors we met in our wanderings that year. It was a restless time, a time to seek some balance, some vaulting perspective that might protect us against the strange new times at home. It was not that we were in flight, we assured ourselves, not flight so much as a search for accommodation with those urgent, millennial versions of ourselves that were coming. The general was one of the curiosa, one of the exhibits of the tour, and he struck us, as perhaps he knew, as being a kind of bad example, a representation of an embittered general in a defeated country overrun and humiliated by our superior firepower. But unlike most of the defeated, he retained his insouciance, not to say a certain style which we found illuminating.

Afterward, later this was, when we had obtained some kind of control over the situation and our emotions, our waiter recognized us on the street and sprinted over. All those months since he had served us and yet his recall was perfect. Out of uniform, he seemed both taller and undefined, a set of features in search of attitude. "Do let me apologize for the general," he said, seizing one of us by the elbows in a gesture combining obsequiousness and insistence in a peculiar way. He is not himself. He is a poor representation of the man he was; he has not been well for many years. He dreams of the invasion, takes responsibility for its outcome, feels that had he performed differently, commanded firmly, showed determination in the eyes of the enemy there would have been a different outcome. The poor man takes no note of ordnance, of superior firepower. He is quite mad, do you understand? There is no other way to explain this."

Standing there, shouting these explanations so fervently, the waiter-in-mufti seemed to be an emblem of what we must have sought on these tours, some proof then that the world was so disordered, so filled with private grief and misapprehension that we simply were not responsible. We bore no blame for what had happened, let alone for the future. But none of this enabled us to deal better with the waiter, who at last had to be dragged off by security monitors, his voice having become enormous, threatening, appalling. Dragged away at high speed by loyal troops, he gesticulated wildly, gestures oddly those of a man displaying handfuls of silverware, plates of appetizer, he seemed motivated in ways both unique and characteristic. But this of course was not for us to meditate on; darkness came to the city, and instructions were issued that we should be in the hotel long before that hammer of dusk struck. The country is under control and yet there is no way of accounting for the private treacheries of the irresponsible in the unpatrolled corridors of their city.

The "we" is not a narrative device, not a provincialism. It is a literal expression. At this post-millennial time, we had come together in the first true shock of purpose and had come to understand that not only was there preservation in our number but that individual identity was dangerous. Identity, that curious and reflexive advancement of the self, had proved again and again to be the source of so much of our trouble; with the assertion of individual demands came exposure, flight, desire, entrapment and sometimes dreadful retaliation. It was the collective we that would bear salvation, and so our little group had massed that spring to bury our histories and idiosyncrasies in a shared, compassionate circumstance. We would go through the continents as a conglomerate and show our enemies that there was a different kind of countryman, a humble and quasi-autonomous collective rather than the prideful and dangerous adventurers cursed by the general. We is not to be construed as I; there is for the intent of these memoirs no I at all, and it is surely this reserve, this calm and dedicated ascendancy of the group that matters. We are not like the others. We are the post-millennial example of the New Country, and it is in that spirit that we went forth, put up with abominable hotels, insolent agents, rifle fire at dusk, obscene and terrifying notes left in our quarters and other paraphernalia and exemplification of the brutal state of our world.

Earlier, before his denunciation, the general had led us on a tour of his beloved city, his own quarters, the markets which until recently had been so colorful and filled with pulsing energy, now closed by the obdurate curfew. "This is what you have done," the general said, "you must take responsibility for this. No one else can be blamed." His gestures were forceful, enormous, determined; this was at a time when we had not yet quite taken him for mad and gave credence to his bearing, his thunderous denunciations. "Some admission, some partial confession might have saved a lot of trouble." he pointed out.

There was nothing to say to this. We had been under strict orders from embarkation. No prolonged contact, no real conversations with the populace. We could not be prevented from traveling nor assuming a collective identity, but we were under close orders. Do not jeopardize our reputation. Even among ourselves, conversation was brief, and what relationships we had were furtive, cursed with hostility, impotence and real fear. Meant to cling, we found ourselves atomized at this time, the need for a composite self driving us further into inner cells of necessity.

"You sicken me," the general said. "I dismiss, I denounce, I renounce you utterly." He made a threatening gesture, yet from his eye darted a complicitous wink. "I am only playing," that wink said, "I am acting the role of a disaffected military leader of a defeated country in order to enhance your tour of what you regard as some back lot of reality. At any moment, I am prepared to tell dirty stories of my people."

Or were we reading too much into that tic? It is difficult to tell at such distance. We find our way these days into recollection even more laboriously than we forge for a future; pinned amongst absolutes we become ever more cautious with the accumulation of time. This is my theory.

"And such is my renunciation," the general added. He saluted. Impelled by some larger perspective of my own, I winked in return. The general appeared startled.

"Come, come," the tour guide said. Our guide, native in all cases and indigenous to the culture, is that anomaly: a credible outsider permitted by agencies to take responsibility for our lives. "Enough of this. Let us go on." We wandered toward the boarded marketplace. There seemed to have been much implied by this exchange, but at such a distance it is hard to sort any of it out.

We must avoid at all costs the delusion that we are the occupying force," I cautioned my companions during one of our few unsupervised moments on tour. "We are not our government, we are not responsible for its acts. In fact, we are in flight from our government, we are a neutral, observing force seeking independence from our leaders. We reject guilt. We are not the conquerors. None of this was our decision, none of it was of our making; we have no connection to it at all." I could see their disbelief. The speech was not going over well. In every eye too I could see the image of complicity, in every curious and attending feature, a slash of recrimination. In the hammering of the engines drawing us toward the gate, I could hear grenades. "None of this is our fault." I said, but my voice sounded flat and unconvincing, sounded that shrill and defensive tone which I had heard in official addresses and which made it impossible, no matter how fast and determined our flight, to escape identification.

In the lobby, we gathered around our guide. "I must tell you to watch for ordnance, for sudden attack," he said. "You must keep to yourselves and remain alert at all times. There are threats; I cannot be more specific than that, but you would be advised, well advised, to stay indoors. We are arranging for a flight to the capital and from there direct to the southernmost part of the continent; this will be best for you, best for all of us. "There are problems," he said, "which cannot be disregarded, and we are trying to save the situation if possible. For the moment, we advise you to stay indoors, although civil authority cannot force you."

There were murmurs not so much of fear but outrage, then the babbling questions. Why, why? Why were they focused upon us? We were, if anything, delegates in contravention of the ugly policies they hated. "I am not authorized to answer," the guide said, "but I can tell you that there are some who have found aspects of your statements to be altogether defensive, and in their defensiveness they confirm a sense of outrage. No one can account for the responses of a large population, a difficult, subordinate and defeated country such as this, but there is, I must tell you, a good deal of anger and it is felt that it might go out of control."

There might have been a good deal more—our guide was well launched and his pleasant, pedagogical features seemed to be adjusting toward an ever more detailed explanation despite his claimed reluctance to analyze—but it was at that moment that the appalling flashes of heat and light began. The artificial plants in the lobby liquefied. This disconcerted the clerks, and the ceiling collapse which followed seemed somehow implied by their disorder; the collapse was of such stunning and flabbergasting force as to make further exchanges, even of the most knowledgeable kind, impossible.

Of the aftermath, of the shocks and disasters that sped some of us more deeply into the times ahead while hastening others so quickly out of the millennium, there is little to report; our own awareness is necessarily dim, comes back only in small fragments and hints of recovery. But it has been handled so well, laid out with such documentary insistence by the journalists that none of this should be at all necessary.

No, none of that. We merely felt that you would appreciate a report from the interior, a report from a survivor who can claim to have tried so fervently—if with so little appreciation—to give a different impression of a country that has been so severely misunderstood and whose latter days I now suspect are going to be filled with such difficulty.

I did the best I could to tell the tale.

This was the year of Polar Star. Polar Star was the emblem under which the divided city would be made whole again, the under- and over-classes stitched into a pleasing tapestry of bright and concordant hue in which the infrastructure would bring its own renewed spaces to bind. Polar Star was the accord toward which all of us had struggled for these decades, and now, at last, the restoration would begin.

Oh yes, this was the year of glowing and ambient parties filled with the sound of theremin, heavy percussion, the whisk of invisible dancers. How we stared from the secluded and heavily guarded roofs of the structures which had been safe, how we stared upon the city! How we watched the stars wink and dazzle, the beams of apparatus casting sullen light into the hidden spaces. How long could this polarization continue? We wondered. Sleek in their hidden places, the breasts of privileged women would bounce and bounce while we turned our tortured, more concernedly academic perspective to the teeming, unknown places beneath and said, "Unless there is some attempt to bind these enclaves, we are doomed. We will no longer be able to afford our lives." That was the year Polar Star was to make its first administrative conceptualizations under the Federal banner.

And was then delayed. The new President announced a "moratorium" to consider all Federal agenda. (Although we knew what he really had in mind, the real focus of the delay.) That was the year that Polar Star was to swing open the gates that partitioned us, but instead the hearings disclosed a massive, almost uncontrollable diversion of funds away from Polar Star and into the tributaries of the contractors. Protection, the integrity of the process demanded that the project be put on hold until all corruption had been isolated and controlled, or so the President announced. This was wise thinking, good politics, and all of us—liberal, conservative, reconstructionist and rebellious alike—could do nothing other than accept the agenda. Some were fervid, others were reluctant. Some were highly qualified. A few abstained, fearing the effects of delay. But our sympathies throughout remained with the aims, the ideal of Polar Star. It was only the practice that had sparked those fires of division.

That was the time in which we at last abandoned the idea of underclass... The sociology of our generation, the fury and anguish surrounding the millennium had purged us of such stereotypes. "There is no underclass," we said to one another. "The 'underclass' is a myth; the term 'underclass' was invented to rationalize oppression." There were, we agreed, only various versions of ourselves, trapped in contesting versions of our own lives, some of them seemingly with no end of travail, others with means of flight or assimilation. Assimilation was our goal under Polar Star. "There will be no 'underclass,'" the manifestos and curricula had stated. "There will be no 'overclass' either. There will be no 'ruling class.' There will be the leveling of difference, the accession of opportunity."

The plans were elaborate, blueprinted; model cities soared into history at the Exposition under the Polar Star banner. We were committed to that goal. It was only the means that defied us, the means by which the old squalor of corruption and kickback, leverage and connection were influential. Under the circumstances, that moratorium was inevitable. We congratulated ourselves upon our willingness to accept the hard and heavy truths of the situation. After our abandonment of stereotypes, after our willingness to accept shared humanity, renewed responsibility, nothing seemed beyond us. The delay of Polar Star was worrisome. There was no question about this. But that delay was only in the interests of a smooth and proficient, an incorruptible and smoothly functioning operation. We were sure of this. We had confidence in our leaders. Newly elected, newly installed, departing the dock of the millennium into the strange and dangerous waters ahead, the President was our coxswain, his gallant associates, the crew and we, we were the landscape toward which they so energetically moved.

That was the year of the easy lay, the quick seduction, the restoking and reassembly of desire, the quick surfacing of new possibilities. Polar Star had made us fluid, had made us come to understand that soon enough all would be entitled to the pursuit of happiness, that barriers outside would fall and, responsively, the barriers of limitation would fall within. Sexual transmission of disease was no longer a factor: all who were going to die had done so, studies assured us. Would soon enough assure us. Reassured then by the most respectable journals of medicine, we were out for a good time. In that year, bouncing and neatly jouncing at our parties, moving our pieces of paper, assigning LED codes at our functional spaces, we had the feeling of being on the lip of massive resolution, of participating in the last period of human strife before true accord. We held breasts tentatively to our lips and made intelligent, concerned sounds as nipples slowly pursed. Cocks and cunts intertwined gracefully in the arbors patrolled by respectful silent security and automatic dogs. A hundred virgins a night fell to the swords of desire.

That was the year Dora became pregnant as an expression of affirmation, as a statement of hope for the metropolis itself. "I will raise my child in Clifton," she said, "I will put her on hobbyhorses in the playground, nurse her openly in Central Park, teach her to read from the graffiti in public facilities. She will be a child of the city and she will flourish." Dora's husband, a sculptor and solemn bureaucrat in the Western division of Polar Star, grinned. In his little eyes glistened querulousness, then panic, then—as we stared— a kind of numbed assent, this being after all the reaction so many had at that time. Numbed assent was what we felt in that year as we huffed and puffed, humped and jumped, played and wooed at our protected parties, waiting for the walls to come down, waiting for the winds of the metropolis to blow across while knowing at the same time that these enclosures were perhaps the best of all spaces we could inherit and Polar Star, which held such promise, also held a kind of portent with which even the most imaginative of us could barely contend.

That was the year before the full extent of the scandals was known. At that time it seemed they were localized, contained, that Polar Star essentially lay intact and that it was only the modus operandi that corrupt elements had compromised. Little did we know the dimensions of the difficulty, or that in the months following how the extent of debasement and venery would be displayed from every basement, every fax, every sideways ticker. In our essential innocence, and it is important to note that we were innocent, that it was not malevolent, that even our seductions, our sexual pledges, our lies and misgroupings were only a function at worst of immaturity and unwillingness to grasp the consequences, we thought that the structure was reparable, that there were ways in which it could be made to last and that it was possible for the process to work.

We were good people. We were not, we felt, malevolent. If Dora was stupid, she certainly wished the throngs beyond the security gates no harm. If she romanticized what she could not see, she did not have the heart of an assassin. We all felt this way, that we were good people, that Polar Star was the expression of our goodness and health and decency. In those months before the full extent of misdeed had been exposed, we still believed in the possibility of concord because it came from that belief in ourselves. We had been born that way, educated toward that end all our lives.

How could we have known otherwise?

And that was the year too of odd premonitions. Gliding against one another in the huge and glowing heart of those parties, listening to the distant sounds, watching the tongues of flame to the north and south of us, we would feel the thickening waters of remorse and morning apprehension, feel that slow, clamping stir in the gut which signaled our mortality. Smile as we might, commit ourselves as we could to the coxswain, there were moments for all of us on those rooftops and later in the thick enclosures of our bedrooms when we saw another vision of the metropolis, when we struggled from dreams in which Polar Star had been obliterated, done in by its own sentimentality and manipulation, and we had nothing, nothing to stand between us and the disaster but the certainty and purity of our hearts. We had good hearts. We had been raised to be good people. We knew we were good. We knew that the others for whom Polar Star had been conceived were good also, and that was why we would no longer use that pejorative term, "underclass." We knew that our motives and theirs were confluent and benign, but we could not nonetheless keep that clamp from the gut, the fold from the unspeaking heart.

For we knew. We must have known. We could not forever shield our plans from our plans. But how we tried! We tried and tried. We were good people. We had the larger interests of the country at heart.

That was the year before the year in which the gunfire and the huge lights winked and blazed, roared and stumbled, the year before that time when parties became hopeless and we were forced to consider the unavailing manner of all options.

It was the time before that clangorous summer when Dora said to any of us who would listen, "We lied and lied, we talked our way around everything. We all knew, but we never said even to ourselves what Polar Star was," How could that be, though? How could we have known what Polar Star was? It was urban retrieval gone wrong, that was all, the best of motives, leading only to the worst of outcome. None of this had been planned. Desperate measures led to desperate responses, but this was not the coxswain's original intention.

"Murderers," Dora said, "we're all killers, we set this up, we pulled this lousy job." But that was after the miscarriage and its pathetic aftermath, and by this time Dora was clearly not sane. It was possible to discount everything she said. It was, in fact, necessary to make that discount.

And so we did. We ignored her. We were polite, tolerant, we did not wish to ostracize, but at the same time we were firm. "Listen," we said, "we are decent, we are good, we are sensible people." Our voices were firm, our faces judicious and tolerant. "We had no choice, no control," we added. "Besides, the word 'underclass' remains out of our lexicon." And so it did. We were not pejorative. We were kind people. We had full awareness.

So we were good to Dora, as good as could be under the circumstances, and we protected her as best we could from her own self-destructiveness. We looked forward to the time when Polar Star would permit us to take down the gates and reclaim all of our city. Our city.

"Killers," Dora screamed. But the sculptor had left her, all of us, in exhaustion, had left her, really. She was almost impossible to tolerate, and no matter how great our ingestion of palliatives, she still appeared ugly.

Report to Headquarters

G ENTLEMEN: WITH considerable difficulty I have managed to compile the following primitive glossary of the X'Thi. Working under great pressure and in difficult circumstances as I have been, this was not an easy job and may be riddled with inaccuracy. Nevertheless, considering that I was able to assemble it within two cycles and *under exceedingly embarrassing personal situations* I think that it is a job of some quality.

Conditions here remain as stated in previous reports, and I hope that the rescue party is continuing with all due haste. I do not know how much longer I can hold out in these circumstances irretrievably alien, although they are, of course, trying to do everything to make me comfortable. Mooning season is approaching, however, I am warned by the X'Thi, and with it their apparent "decampment" (I think that this is the equivalent I am seeking) and they cannot take me with them. What am I supposed to do then, gentlemen? Stay here with diminishing supplies and die? You can understand my problem. You must render me help.

AZAPLI: The act of triring or having just trired, the retraction of tentacles; the tendency of tentacles to constrict the blood vessels when extended, leading to vascular suffering and, in extreme cases, sudden death. For this reason the X'Thi trire as little as possible, although triring is inevitable during Hok, a metaphysical situation. They are trying to reduce Hok, however.

BLOLOMITE: The principal substance of reduction, that substance which appears to be a metaphor for the Cosmic Jolt which, the X'Thi believe, resulted in the creation of the universe and their own central, crucial role in it. Blolomite can neither be seen, touched, tasted, heard nor felt but it is the major source of all energy. During Hok, Blolomite may be seen for brief flashes in the light of the paralleled moons.

COSMIC JOLT: That central, lurching force with which the X'Thi believe that the universe began; alternatively, that C.L.F. (I am using abbreviations in order to save transmission time and costs and hope that you appreciate this gesture) with which the universe will end; their conception of the known universe, and all of time for that matter, as being a loop or thread suspended between the poles of Cosmic Jolts. The interval between the first Cosmic Jolt and the second appears to be calculated, as neatly as I can manage this, as being in reductions of sixty to seventy trires.

A panic appears to have been created by the landing of the vehicle upon Coul's Planet; the impact sprang up little filaments of Blolomite and many of the X'Thi took this to be the second and the more jarring of the Cosmic Jolts. It may have been for this reason, the impact and the panic, the assault of the X'Thi upon the vehicle, which caused me to use the reactor. I regret this very much. I have communicated this regret to the X'Thi. They have accepted my apology. I do not believe that they will seek retaliatory action since they are a gentle and spiritual people, but cannot guarantee this.

COUL'S PLANET: I do not believe that there is any megalomania in my referring to this rather bucolic if gaseous world as the above. As *Coul's Planet*. The naming of territory after its discoverer has an old and honorable tradition dating back to the maritime industry and also from the early days of interplanetary survey. Coul's Planet, along with the remainder of the universe, was, as stated by the X'Thi, formed from the Cosmic Jolt an unimaginable interval ago and will similarly terminate in another. In another Cosmic Jolt. In the meantime it is composed of a series of noxious gases suspended by light gravity above a liquefied core: methane, hydrogen and nitrous oxide in equal parts circulate rather energetically around the unseen core. Here at the heart of Coul's Planet I reside, surrounded by the friendly steel and metal alloy bulkheads of this ship which protect me from the environment and which also through an intricate series of viewscope devices permit me to remain in contact with the X'Thi, the lords of this planet. I am located, to the best of my knowledge, some twenty-five hundred miles north of the equator, rather near to one of the snow-capped poles. The X'Thi have no name for their own planet. The stupid creatures. They say that its name is ineffable, known only to the Creator of the universe. Therefore I have given it its proper name.

DECAMPMENT: Shift of Coul's Planet in the cosmos which, according to the X'Thi, results in a necessary redistribution of gaseous materials which would otherwise become stagnant. Forming waste. Reconstitution of Blolomite during the decampment renders the planet safe until the next period, but grave shocks to the environment force the X'Thi into their annual rite of displacement which takes them to the northern pole through this period of readjustment. They cannot take me with them and that is why recovery efforts must be accelerated and why you must do everything within your power to save me from the horrors of unreconstituted Blolomite, slowly encircling this little craft in their dread dread tentacles which I *cannot retract*.

DISPLACEMENT, RITE OF: See DECAMPMENT.

E: That cosmic sound (emanating of course from the Cosmic Jolt) with which all creation began. According to myth of the X'The, "E:" was the shout of the Creator as, in his anguish, he caused Coul's Planet to be.

HOX: Apparently a religious festival preceding decampment. (See DECAMPMENT, DISPLACEMENT.) Alterations in the eco-geological balance signaling the advent of decampment cause physical changes in the environment. Blolomite appears in dull flashes of energy, suddenly revealed to the naked eye. One can, during Hok, reach out and physically touch the Blolomite or endure the illusion that it can be touched as seen in the vibrating, varying light swinging from the equator to the poles, revealing the substance in all its dull luster, recapitulating as it were the appearance of the planet as it might have been during the Cosmic Jolt. During Hok the normally tight sociopolitical patterns of the X'Thi are deliberately altered; there is a relaxation of stricture, prurience occurs, random contacts between individuals, a shattering of the socioeconomic sector so that all elements of the culture interweave and intermix during this celebration. During Hok even the lowest and humblest of the filthy creatures may cohabit with the rulers; even the rulers are allowed to throw off the necessary dignity of their office to fornicate with the populace: all of them fornicate and cohabit together; it is this which brings Hok to its climax and in the general exhaustion, guilt, debilitation which follow, the decampment and its consequent displacement then occur; but through all of this and after I will be confined to this vessel, the simulated bulkheads, the thick metal shielding, unable to participate because exposure to the deadly gases of Coul's Planet would instantly kill me; all I would be able to do would be to rotate slowly in the contrived weightlessness of the ship, penitent, suffering, awaiting rescue and then, *after* Hok, in the darkness after decampment when all of them have gone to the poles and it is as if I will be the only individual left on the surface of the world … well, you should surely see why I await the rescue party with such unusual eagerness and anticipation and why it is all I can do to keep myself from tearing at the very bulkheads with frustration and rage; I can hardly bear the emotional exhaustion of Hok which, the X'Thi assure me, is almost upon us. *How much more of this can I stand to take?*

COUL, LEONARD (see also COUL'S PLANET): The discoverer of Coul's Planet. The intrepid and solitary voyager out of the Service who has dedicated his life to adventure, to the search for and achievement of new terrain, who has cheerfully, steadfastly, unblinkingly accepted the loneliness and danger of his trade, who has asked (until the moment of this disastrous event) absolutely no assistance from the Service but has merely accepted his duty as a given condition, now thirty-seven years old and fallen upon difficult times but still, still, gentlemen, of good courage and spirit, continuing his negotiations with the X'Thi, working upon this glossary which is a keyhole into their consciousness, performing his tasks within the difficult confinement of the ship uncomplainingly … all the time putting to one side any consideration of his wizened genitals, his tormented psyche, his diminished and abused consciousness which has put up with more, more, I must tell you, than any of you would conceive. Who, nevertheless, is Coul to complain? Hok comes upon him; Cosmic Jolts lay both before and ahead of him, somewhere in the middle of that great Loop of possibility he hangs doing his tasks, keeping up his optimism, knowing that in his hour or hours of need ye will not abandon him but will save him from all of this.

PARALLELED MOONS: Two moons track Coul's Planet, revolving around it in tandem much as Coul's possibilities may be said to darkly devolve around his core. The moons are linked yet separate, they are in similar orbits following duplicate trajectory separated only by a small wisp of space; for this reason they are referred to as "paralleled," although certain of the X'Thi disagree with this, saying that "simultaneous" would be a better mode of reference. The Cosmic Jolt has both an origin and a conclusion, the X'Thi (they are in their way a rather mystical people although they have no organized religion) state, all of the universe may be perceived as a duality, within each of us are not only (in many cases) paired organs but opposed motives, and these paralleled moons are projections of that duality, circling, circling Coul's Planet in the perpetual night of its sky. During Hok, Blolomite is revealed in Hashes in the light of the paralleled moons (see BLOLOMITE). The paralleled moons, however, are composed of the same gaseous substance as is Coul's Planet; that is to say that it would be very difficult to get hold of them, even if they were not so impossibly distant, so impossibly huge.

TRIRE: See AZAPLI.

X'THI: The cheerful residents of Coul's Planet. The natives of Coul's Planet I should say rather; indigenous to its ecology and terrain, that essentially ebullient population whose rather arcane linguistics are at least mapped in this glossary, that essentially ebullient population With whom I have been in almost constant contact since my crash-landing and subsequent unsuccessful escape attempts from Coul's Planet some time ago.

The X'Thi are mystical without being religious, efficient without being organized, proprietary without being domineering; it can be said that they combine both the best and worst traits of their ecology in so being, although again this may merely be a projection of my own admittedly limited view of them and they may be both more or less than can be readily ascertained. What is there to be said of the X'Thi? Their physical appearance is amorphous; dimly glimpsed through the viewports of this sinking vessel they take on different colors and aspects with the changes of the day; part of this having to do with their own rather chameleon-like ability to partake of features of the terrain, part of it having to do with my own rather dazzled perceptions which due to hunger and increasing flight cannot be trusted as to consistency. The X'Thi themselves testify that their changing aspect may be due not to difficulties in sight or terrain but to the presence of Blolomite itself throughout the atmosphere: Blolomite has the sinister ability to distort reality into changing shapes and aspects; coming from the Cosmic Jolt and being put in place by the squawking "E:" of the Creator (whose identity, gentlemen, is unknown at the present time, the Creator being ineffable), it partakes of many qualities which may be beyond our ken and it can be said that to live on Coul's Planet as I have been forced to for this period of time may simply mean to be *immersed in Blolomite* as strange as this thought may be, immersed in Blolomite and circling forever dimly under the light of the parallel moons, the parallel moons streaking the heavens in their very duality. The X'Thi say that they cannot sustain me much longer in this environment, that as the time of decampment approaches they must more and more attend to their own difficult and necessary tasks preceding said decampment, that they will have to abandon me to my own devices in order that they may protect themselves. There is, they assure me, nothing at all personal about this abandonment, they are rather fond of me, they are fond of Leonard Coul, abandoned voyager in their midst, but their own survival is paramount and they must go about it in their own way. After all, Coul's Planet, the Cosmic Jolt, Hok and the decampment were around long before I was (to say nothing of Blolomite) and will Similarly survive me by a good long period; they must pay proper obeisance to their traditions because without their traditions, where are they? An unanswerable question, gentlemen. Hok will begin, in glimmers of Blolomite as seen in the light of the parallel moons the Cosmic Jolt may be apperceived but the X'Thi will be gone, they will all be gone and I will be here alone, always alone, *unless efforts are made to speed up the rescue party at all costs,* to accelerate, that is to say, its efforts. In the meantime there is nothing to be done but to continue on my routine and essentially timekilling tasks, maintenance of the environment, eating, sleeping, the preparation of this glossary and so on. What will I do when Hok comes? The answer to that is unspeakable and I will cheerfully leave that question to you, gentlemen, being unable, quite, to deal with it myself.

Y: That cosmic sound (emanating, it is said, from the second Cosmic Jolt) with which creation will end. (See E.) According to the myths of the X'Thi, the Creator will cry "Y:". as Coul's Planet comes to an end, imploding toward ash in the Sickly light of the wasted moons, small scraps of Blolomite dancing in the gases as in that explosive "Y:Y:Y:" all that the X'Thi will ever know shall end.

The Shores of Suitability

COMMON EXEGESIS of Killers of the Rulers *portends the interrelationship of post-Joycean rhetoric with post-Shavian political pluralism. Relate this confluence. Elaborate and discuss. Exemplify.*

The Old Hack is having a nightmare. In it, he has returned to academia and is seeking a master's degree at Extension U., which, he hopes, will enable him to find work as an assistant instructor of English. All right, it is a long shot, but he is almost out of ideas. The markets are really hell, and foreign sales have dried up. And he is having big trouble delivering on the one outline he has sold. So the Old Hack has enrolled in English 353A: *Science Fiction and the Archetype*, because in the catalog it seemed to be an easy three points (no paper required). If he knows anything, he knows science fiction. Right? Well, doesn't he? Now he is taking the final examination in this graduate-level course, which appears to focus on an old Ace Double, *Killers of the Rulers*. He is especially qualified to deal with this book. He wrote it back in 1957 between wives at the old place on West 89th Street. Even so, the exam is giving him trouble. Big trouble.

❋ ❋ ❋

The subtheme of colonic usurpation in its Jungian relevance creates a multileveled tension in Killers of the Rulers, *which points toward the induction of three distinct archetypes. Name these archetypes. Elaborate and discuss. Discuss further how a Freudian approach would defeat consummation of the Blue Alien Incursion.*

The Old Hack is not sure exactly how he got into this. It all seemed so simple when he enrolled. The reading list, which included many of his old favorites, indicated this would be a snap, to say nothing of the pleasant surprise of finding *Killers of the Rulers* right in there between *More than Human* and *The Forever Machine*. But he suspected that things had begun to go wrong from the start. In the first session the young instructor had begun by speaking of a Manichean influence in the birth of American science fiction, and how the great Fifties novels were an extension of the Fabian theory of Socialism as propounded by the works of G. B. Shaw. The Old Hack had briefly thought of identifying himself when his book came up in November. "I wrote that one," he could have said (it had been written, as had all of the Ace Doubles, and too much of his other stuff, under a pseudonym), but by then he was totally confused. It did not seem wise to admit writing *Killers of the Rulers*, particularly if he could not understand a word the young instructor was saying about it.

Produce a 1,000-word monograph interrelating the empire building of Killers of the Rulers *with the more pacific vision of* More Than Human. *Be specific. In what way does Melville's "Bartleby the Scrivener" inform and influence both works as controlling response? Why does* Heartbreak House *not apply here?*

Heartbreak House. That's what West 89th Street had been. It was there, drunk and up against a deadline, that he wrote *Killers of the Rulers* on the kitchen table. The Old Hack hadn't even started it until the weekend before it was due. There had been all that excitement about him and Mabel Sue, and, besides, for a $750 advance (payable in halves) why should he get all upset about churning out this stuff to their convenience rather than his? Even then the book kind of lurched along, what with Betty (wife number one) crying and coming out of the bedroom now and then only to throw another of his paperbacks at him while he sat there typing. Finally he gave up, turned to the Cutty Sark, and took down that 1952 issue of *Worlds of If*, which he used to bloat up his novelette.

In the end the book was not what he had promised in the outline, but what the hell? Everyone lied and cheated in the small things (he had tried desperately to explain this to Betty); the important commitment was to getting the work done, and to holding on to enough of the advance money to have a good blowout. Despite all the screaming, he had been only three days late, thanks to the Cutty Sark, but then the bastards took a month to deliver the check, by which time he was well embarked on that disastrous series of events that ended with Mabel Sue's calling him a drunken liar and throwing his typewriter *and* the carbon of *Killers of the Rulers* out the third-story window.

Neologic devices in Killers of the Rulers *account for, as in* Finnegans Wake, *much of its subnarrative power. Present and discuss five such devices. Analyze two of them. Describe how they function as a metaphoric combine of the Blue Aliens.*

In his dream, the Old Hack brings his blank essay booklet up to the proctor midway through the three hours. "I can't stand it," he says shakily. "I can't stand it anymore. Just take me away. I'll be good." The proctor stares at him mercilessly through goggles of glittering glass. "Help. Help," the Old Hack whimpers as he tumbles like a stone through various levels of his dream world.

He finds himself awake and fifty-seven in his own bleak room at dawn, his hopes for an assistant instructorship at the college destroyed, the empty pages of *Grandsons of the Killers of the Rulers* littering the floor beside him, and this novel— his masterpiece, he had told the editor to clinch the contract, the crown of his career—three months overdue today. And counting.

Hop Skip Jump

IN THE distance Constanza thought she could see the Battery, the extreme southern tip of Manhattan with boats prowling the waters, the thin lights and suggestion of ships curving toward the night; nearer were the heavier, blooming lights of midtown Manhattan, the suggestion of motion within. But in the tight confinement of the car itself, looking at the George Washington Bridge, it was possible to believe that the city did not exist, that it was just the two of them, the suspension bridge itself only a suggestion against the night that held them.

"It's going to make a pretty blaze," Frank said.

He pitched the directional signal upward indolently, cut to the right lane of the upper roadway to take the parkway exit. "Chicago was nothing to the way this will be. This still is the big town." His smile, she knew, would split the night if she looked, but she was lacing away, staring through the passenger window, looking at the poles as the car skirted them. "We shall utterly consume all things off the face of the earth," Frank said happily, "and that's the prophet Zephaniah. Always liked Zephaniah. They thought he was a crank, you know. Now he's a minor Book."

Constanza shuddered, drew the shawl around her. The heater was on, the car a furnace gathering fumes from the engine core and expelling them through the flaps near her legs, but she was cold in a way heat could not reach, cold in a way that was not to be touched. As cold as any city in the ashes of their long fire. Frank was giggling now, singing a little against the bland noises that came from the radio, mumbling about fires and lyres and sires tuning the dire night, breaths and deaths and quests from the city, and it occurred to Constanza, possibly for the first time, that this was the principal difference between Frank and herself: He loved his work. She was the more competent, possibly even the one who had better reasons, but Frank wallowed in the implication, in the fire, in every lush and splendid exercise of conflagration. He would sing all through it; even if the devastation were to claim him he would go smiling as long as he were the focus, if he could take the credit. But for Constanza it would be different; pieces of her would be extinguished, and she could not keep from feeling a trace of pity. "Do you ever think about it?" she said.

He looked up from the wheel, the car wavering on the descent.

"Think about what?"

"Watch your driving. Concentrate on the road."

He shut off the radio. "What are you talking about?"

"Don't have an accident. Not with what we're carrying."

His eyes were wide and bewildered. "I don't understand," he said. "You talked to me, I didn't say a word. I'm watching the road, you're the one who's talking —"

"Oh, all right," she said, "you're right, you're right, just watch the road, don't get us into trouble, don't put us into a girder, we'll blow up everything north of Harlem, and we'll never be able to get out of it alive. They'll never understand —"

Frank sighed, a deep, confused sigh, and Constanza faded, drew further into herself on the seat. He was right, of course; she was the one who was acting in a silly and misdirected fashion. The one who was falling apart. Frank was doing fine, in control, the car gliding neatly into the merge lane and then at a steady and controlled burst was taking the center on the sparse midnight roadway, moving up to sixty. Local streets would be easier, less exposure there. At the end, assuming they got to the water, ignition and upheaval would be routine. Frank was right; she should shut up. The cold clawed at her suddenly. "I'm cold'" she said. "Give us some heat!"

Frank reached out, moved a switch. "Don't be afraid," he said. "There's nothing to be afraid of."

"I'm not afraid."

"San Francisco went okay, didn't it? We thought we were goners on the Golden Gate when the cops picked us up, but it was just a routine check and we were free. Chicago was beautiful; nobody thought it would go that easy. We're doing fine, Countess, it'll work just as well here."

"It's too big. It's New York, it's —"

"It's just another place," Frank said. "They're all the same, it's just a matter of numbers. Abilene, Corpus Christi, Schroon Lake, the training camps, those were just a body count. Chicago and San Francisco were the same, only bigger. All of them are the same: sinners in heat, snakes in darkness, the Devil's legions. There are just more of them here."

"It all happens so fast." She was talking wildly. She knew it. They had warned her of this, too, the possibility of panicky upheaval, her tendency toward hysteria. That was why they had teamed her with Frank: Frank was a steady guy, his eye was on the sparrow, he was a solid citizen, steady with his hands and with the fuses. "Chicago went in ten seconds. It was there. Boom! It wasn't there. It took so little—"

"And the same here. Set the fuses, wire the incendiaries, go, go, go! It's all the fire, Countess."

"That's not what I meant," she said. They were coming up on the Ninety-sixth Street exit, only a couple of miles to go now. No traffic at all in the density and the damp; it was as if on this midnight the roadway had been laid out for them. Maybe it had. Frank's hands were steady, his eyes were fixed on some tunnel of perception, his white sleeves billowed in the heavy gusts from the heater. The Dodge hit a bump, and she heard the thin clang from the trunk, the equipment rolling loose, reminding them. "So many people," she said. "Seven million."

"Ten million," Frank said with satisfaction. "Ten million sinners. Ten million heathens, celebrants of the darkness; ten million who have known corruption and are unacquainted with grief. But we'll change that. We'll change that — "

"It's too much. What are we doing?"

"Don't forget the little towns, too," Frank said, "or that trial run at Schroon Lake, Oh, boy, we've come a long way."

"No," Constanza said. The word seemed to have been dragged from some reservoir of unconsciousness, spoken out of herself. "No, I can't go through with this. We have to stop. This isn't San Francisco or Chicago."

"It's the biggest town of all, Countess. That's why."

"Frank," she said, "let's give it up. Get off at Ninety-sixth Street and turn it around. We'll go back. Tell them it's all my fault. I'll tell them. Get someone else. I'll take all the blame. I must—"

"Calm down. You're going to be all right. You've been fine until now. It's no big deal —" She put her hand on his wrist. Warm but unyielding, steel under the sleeve, the white on white. "There's a parking area at Ninety-sixth Street," she said, "remember?"

"I remember everything."

"Pull it in there. Pull it in there, and stop the engine. I'll give you everything. I'll give you what you want, Frank, if you'll just bring it to a stop."

His hand twitched. "You're a sinner, too. You're asking me to sin. You're offering me your flesh for their flesh." His voice cracked on the second flesh, "I can't. I won't."

"Don't you want to? Don't you want to touch me, really touch me? You know you do, the lies they tell, the things they gave us to do, that's just to keep you from knowing what you really want, what you really need—"

He was jumping and quivering under her touch, the car swaying, but the car was slowing, too, as they came up on the Ninety-sixth Street sign, and she could tell; yes, she could tell. She had him now. She had him. "Forget the fuses," she said, "forget the bombs, forget the bodies just this once, just think of me, of what you're going to do soon —"

"What will we tell them?"

"We don't have to tell them anything," she said with a shocking sense of discovery. "We can stay. We can just live here, like the rest of the sinners. Find our way. Trade weapons for food. We'll be free, no one will find us, they won't want to find us, the committee, they'll just get replacements. But that will take time, the training takes a long time, and in the meanwhile —"

Trembling, trembling everywhere, Frank guided the Dodge into the rest area, the brakes quivering, the frame shaking, the incendiaries bouncing. "Meanwhile, we'll be sinners. We'll join them in the nakedness of their captivity —"

She reached out with her free left hand, stroked his inner thigh. "Yes, the nakedness of their captivity." The car pitched, Frank braked, foliage grabbed them, they were against the trees. The car bumped, sagged. The engine rumbled. Constanza reached out, cut the ignition, reached to clasp his cheeks and draw him upon her.

His tongue was moist, desperate. "But why?" he whispered, as the engine ticced to silence, as she came over him fully as the sounds and the force of her own desperation overtook.

"Why are you doing this for the sinners? What do you care?"

"Because," she said, placing his left hand on her breast, "because they cannot discern their right hand from their left, the sinners," showing him what she could do with her right hand and her left. "Nor can their cattle."

"Book of Jonah," Frank said, heaving on her. "Final verse."

"Also much cattle," she corrected herself.

They were well beyond words, well beyond thought when, furious but paralyzed by shock, the archangels so came upon them.

To Mark the Times We Had

THE SCENE is the stage of a theater of indeterminate age and location; it is dimly lit. An ACTOR is speaking; somewhere to his left, the PRODUCER sits listening.

ACTOR. I shall do such things — I know not what they are — but they shall be the terror of the earth.

DIRECTOR. No good.

ACTOR (After a pause). Oh, that this too, too sullied flesh should thaw, melt, resolve itself —

DIRECTOR Doesn't work. Cut it.

ACTOR (*Angrily*). Our revels now are ended, and these, our players—

DIRECTOR. Say, thanks a lot. We'll be in touch now.

ACTOR (Frantic). Ask not what your country can do for you but what you can do for your country. We shall never fear to negotiate, but we shall never negotiate from fear. Ask not what your country can do for you but what you can do for your country.

DIRECTOR (Thoughtfully). Do you do more of that?

ACTOR. Oh, yes. Lots more. We will land a man on the moon. Think of me as the man who accompanied Mrs. Kennedy to Paris. I thought I'd give my brother a little legal experience before he applies for a job. I—

DIRECTOR. Well, it's something we can work with. (Pause) Oh, all right.

What the hell, we'll give it a try. (Goes offstage. returns with top hat, cane, hands them to ACTOR. Presidential seal lowered as backdrop.) Good luck.

ACTOR, Uh, before we start this, shouldn't there be a contract?

DIRECTOR. Later, later.

ACTOR. But Equity—

DIRECTOR (Fiercely). Screw the union; do you want the job or don't you?

ACTOR (After a pause, reluctantly). I want the job. (Puts on top hat, twirls cane.) We all want the job. I was trained in classics, though.

DIRECTOR. Then shut up and do the job (Exits)

ACTOR. But just a moment. (Silence. ACTOR starts offstage to pursue DIRECTOR, then shakes head stops, returns to center stage. Fixed spot hammers him into place.) Damn it anyway.

OFFSTAGE FEMALE VOICE. Ready?

OFFSTAGE MALE VOICE. Ready as I ever will be.

OFFSTAGE FEMALE VOICE. All right, then (Pause). You can't say the city of Dallas doesn't love you now, Mr. President (Sound of shot).

ACTOR. God damn it. I should have known (*Clutches throat*). Damn open calls! (*Second shot; blackout*)

What I Did to Blunt the Alien Invasion

1. I talked to them. "Be reasonable." I said, "Consider the conditions here. Consider the nature of our circumstances. We are struggling toward a kind of equivocal democracy, equivocal poise, equivocal justice: Marx's alienation effect is only an intermediary stage on the road to Nirvana." And so on and so forth. A modicum of learning, a flutter of pedantry, even some scatology now and then to show the great comic vision which, ultimately, underlies the human condition. They nodded solemnly but did not make their position clear.

2. Carried the word to the President, to Congress, to the press as best I could. Not only through letters to the editor, not only through the vox populi sections of the newspaper and by phone calls to the district office of our congressman, but through the great common network of our evolving democracy, the talk shows, "Alien invasion," I said. "Creatures from the far Centauris, from the proximate Centauris coming in disguise to infiltrate our customs, our cities, the interstices of cur lives, disguised as fellow citizens, dogs, horses, houseplants. Against their cunning we must be unavailing, nonetheless I think you are entitled to know. The full story." Also small notices in the classified sections of the local daily, not much but all I can afford, all THOSE WHO ARE OF THE ALIEN INVASION PLEASE CALL (my number) or write post OFFICE BOX (my post office box). I did what I could, certainly, to bring alertness to the populace. My modest funds, my lack of true credibility, all of these were very much against me; but nonetheless, within limits, I tried.

3. Discussed the issue with Susan. I made no attempt to hide my distress or my growing awareness that perhaps between the loathsome, threatening presence of the alienness and all of those circumstances which are our democratic way of life, I stood alone. "I don't know what you're trying to tell me, George," she said.

"If the aliens are coming, why are you the only one who knows this? The rest of us haven't heard a word." "I don't know," I said. "How can I possibly know?" There is, after all, only so much of an accounting one may give, and yet the woman is endlessly demanding. "Perhaps the rest of the population is narcoticized or drugged," said. "Perhaps it is only for me to carry the tale." And so on and so forth. Even within the context of a difficult living situation, a situation built, I think, up' on my need to reach out to Susan, to humor her, to treat her as if she were a sensible, rational woman and not the raving, neurotic pain that I know her to be... even within that context, I tried to be ultimately reasonable. "You can see why I'm somewhat preoccupied," I said. "You can understand now why you may find me somehow abstracted on various occasions. I'm trying to work out a plan to blunt the alien invasion. This takes all of my mental powers." She laughed and laughed and it was at this point in our dialogues, usually although not exclusively, that she would begin to hurl objects at me. I do not wish to discuss this any further. Of the true and mordant nature of our relationship, of the dark and tumbling necessity of our connection, I will inform in another context. At this time we are dealing with the public rather than the private (and hence irrelevant) consequences of our activity

4. Remonstrated with myself. Had genuine agonies of conscience, cris de coeur in the deep insertion of the night. "Perhaps it is a delusion," I was driven so far by the insensible Susan as to admit. "Perhaps there are no aliens, let alone an imminent invasion; I have concocted all of this out of heavy drugs, phantasms, and the need to establish some aura of personal significance. But no, no, this cannot possibly be; the corporeal reality of the aliens has been proven over and again, and I have no reason whatsoever to fantasize." I am of course compressing this internal monologue significantly while at the same time preserving its essence. It is of the essence which I am speaking now. "No, I have examined the issue wholly and profoundly and I know that it is only I who can sound the warning," I concluded. Would conclude these remonstrances and heaving internal monologues composed of equal parts self-revulsion and determination. "It is not internal disintegration but objective necessity. That necessity can be proven by the very conditions in which we find ourselves. The times bespeak invasion," Well, don't they? How much doubt can there be about the nature of dislocation?

5. Rendered pictures of the aliens for talk show hosts or congresspersons who might want physical evidence. Using Crayola™ and perspective drawing, rendered them as they had appeared in my hallway on that fateful afternoon in June of 199 — when all of this began. Eight-feet aliens with thin lips and square shoulders, the aspect of soccer goalies or perhaps a new breed of astronauts, all of them with intense, winking blue eyes and highly concupiscent genitalia of the requisite kinds. Whiskers and cilia, representative balloons to display their dialogue, which came in only slightly fractured English with what seemed to be a cockney accent. "Are you serious?" Susan said, seeing a cache of these drawings one night, looking as she so often looked in places which were none of her

business. "What are these things, what has happened to you?" Pointed at the representations of genitalia and with crooked forefinger made an inexplicable but wholly repellent gesture. "This is too much for me," she said. "It's one thing to have a living arrangement, strictly business and all that and another, quite another to realize that you are living with a homeboy lunatic." And further statements of a kind which cannot be paraphrased and need not be included in this otherwise true bill. The pictures, faithful reproductions of the aliens as they appeared to me on that doomed late Saturday, the cones and slants of dim summer light infiltrating the walls of this tenement, have been carefully preserved and are available at any time for inspection and further consideration,

6. Tried in the absence of *any fair response* from congresspersons, call-in hosts, co-vivant, or the corrupt, self-serving press to take the issue directly to the streets. "They are already among us," I said, "eight-feet caterpillars with purple genitalia masquerading as people and they have so clouded our minds with dangerous drugs and global corruption that we do not notice, we think it is merely part of urban decay. When several hundred thousand of them, a critical number, have infiltrated the populace, they will have reached a kind of Heisenbergian mass and through use of the uncertainty effect will topple entropy itself. Oh, we must be alert, we must be alert, we must be aware!" I pointed out, gesturing somewhat floridly (but in a controlled and geometric fashion) in the park on that and other difficult evenings and I would like to say that I drew a crowd and some enlightened response but due to the *very dreadful and imminent conditions* created in part by the aliens themselves, I am afraid that I was unable | o elicit the kind of response which was deserved under the circumstances. Tried then in the presence of few and the absence of many to make the situation *entirely clear* but, met only by welling indifference and at last the tanks and brutalities of the guardians, was able to shout no more.

7. Tried to consider all parts of the issue, all phases, and alternatives. "Perhaps I *am* fantasizing," I told them when they had called me in for further investigation, "but that doesn't mean that it isn't true, that they aren't here, it just means that I have no hard evidence, that I cannot produce them. Not that I am fantasizing, you understand, although I wilt make that stipulation for the purposes of argumentation. I have a serious mission, this is serious business, we are talking about the *alienation effect*," but their faces were bleak and implacable; oh, I know something of bleakness and implacability, it must truly be conceded, although it is not these qualities alone which will suffice when they come tunneling through our streets, using their massive weaponry, dismembering our civilization.

8. Seized Susan in a sexual embrace and tried to convert her to understanding through *sheer will*, some Reichian orgone box of the spirit, performing upon her otherwise unprintable and desperate acts which need no explication within this difficult compass. "You've got to listen," I said as she struggled. "You've got to hear me out, you have to understand that there are aliens among us, they may even as I speak have seized me just as I seize you," and the desperate cries of her

resistance sped me only further on my way as I joined with her in an absolute cold infusion of knowledge, a spiraling knowledge of spiraling aliens as pointlessly she resisted the knowledge which would tree her.

9. Begged the aliens, as they clutched me, as they took me away, to heed my pleas for the sake of our destiny. "Behold truly, I will not betray my race before cockcrow," I said, "not one time, not twice, not *three* times," and invoked what frail Scripture I knew to try to change their course, our destiny, "Comfort me with apples," I said, "and leave us time and season," but beggars, like betrayers before cockcrow, cannot oppose with reason that which is implacable and doom ridden, although I tried and tried. 10. Offered my services as administrator, "All right," I said to them, in the consultation room, being allowed as was their policy (they said) one interview in which to make my position known. "You need an intermediary, someone you can trust, someone who can speak to both sides and surely I have done that throughout. Consider Retain," I said, "consider Quisling, consider the occupied territories. Consider how truly dapper and assimilated I will look in my eight-foot disguise," and so on and so forth; there are, after all, as many species of failure, as many varieties of submission as there are of success and it fell upon me — it has always fallen upon me, consider the condominium split with Susan — to make the best deal I can. "After all," I pointed out to them, "who better than me, who better than the prophet of Tompkins Square and the Marxian diocese would know how to manage the true destruction, the latter exculpation of Earth? Who, O friends and brothers? Who, then?"

Shiva

❝WE'LL TRY Paris," someone says. "Remember Paris." Sperber, trusted only for an apprentice assignment but still determined to be hopeful, huddles in the deep spaces of the extradimensional calculator, figuring out his further moves. Sperber has always been a thoughtful type, not impulsive, only reactive. That is one of the primary reasons for his participation in the program. Know your course, pull down vanity, move deliberately toward a kind of fruition. Still he thinks: How long can I remain hopeful doing stuff like this?

Still, he has. Remained hopeful, that is. Choice gleams like knives from the enclosure; shrugging, his life a cosmic shrug he thinks, Sperber is catapulted to Paris, 1923, finds himself with no real transition in a small café on the fringes of the Champs Élysées where he seems to be already engaged in profound conversation with the young Pol Pot and Charles de Gaulle, nationalists both, their expressions set intently toward a future that glows for them, even though Sperber knows better than they how problematic the situation.

"*Excusez-moi*," Sperber says in his miserable, poorly accented French, tugging on the sleeve of de Gaulle's brown jacket.

Even at this early stage of his life, de Gaulle seems to have taken on a military righteousness. "*Je* can stay only a moment. I am here to give you a glimpse of your future *s'il vous plait. Comment allez vous?* Would you like that portrait of your future?"

He hopes that the translator has done its wondrous work.

There is no way that he can express to De Gaulle in this perilous situation without the help of that device. Still, it seems—like so much else in post-technological 2218—something of a cheat. Form has taken function all the way to the grave; the extradimensional calculator has, for instance, subsumed the causes of research or serious speculation.

De Gaulle is unresponsive to Sperber's question. Perhaps premonitory apprehensions of the Fourth Republic have overtaken him; he seems distant, affixed to some calculation of a future that Sperber himself knows all too well. Saleth Sar (Pol Pot's birth name or at least the name he employed in his student days) brandishes a teacup, looks at Sperber with a kind of loathing.

"And me?" he says. "What about me? What *s'il vous plait* are you undertaking to give me? My French is not perfect but I am worthy of your attention, no? This certainly is true. Saleth Sar is worthy of his attention.

In his excitement at finally meeting de Gaulle, Sperber has almost ignored the general's old companion and rival in student debates.

"Pardon me," he says. "I meant to give no offense. I am a student, I am in this place to study and to learn. It is not possible for me to know everything."

"You do not have to know everything," Pol Pot says reprovingly, "but it is not correct to know nothing at all." He stares at de Gaulle sourly, takes the teacup from the general's hand, and places it with a thump on the table. "I think I will ask you to leave this table," he says. "You were after all not invited."

"I have to tell you that the Algerian intervention will come to a very bad end," Sperber says hastily. "Both of you must know this, also that the decision to leave Indo-China will lead in no way toward peace. Your intervention will be supplanted by ignorant Americans, the Americans will get in deeper and deeper, eventually the Americans will ignore the borders of Kampuchea and will commit severe destruction. No good will come of this, none at all. One country will be shamed, another sacrificed. You must begin to make plans now."

"Plans?" Pol Pot says. "What kind of plans are we supposed to make? You babble of destiny, of destruction. But it is this kind of destruction which must precede the revolution itself. It is vital that the revolution prevail, that is why I have been sent to Paris. To study texts of successful revolutions, to know the Constitution of the United States among other things."

Pol Pot, the admirer of democratic principles. Sperber had forgotten that.

Paris at this time was filled with future Communists who loved democracy, the United States, American music and sexual habits. It was betrayal, Americans not taking to Asian desires, which had tamed them into revolutionaries, anti-Bolsheviks. But Sperber had, of course, forgotten much else in his various missions; the lapse here was not uncharacteristic; lapses had carried him through all of these expeditions, making matters even more difficult.

De Gaulle shrugs much as Sperber had shrugged just subjective instants ago in the extradimensional calculator.

The Frenchman's face shines with confusion, the same confusion, doubtless, that exists in Sperber's own. "There is nothing I can do about this," he says. "Or about anything else for that matter."

Sperber knows then with sudden and sinking acuity that he has done all that is possible under these circumstances. There is nothing else that he can do. He has used the extradimensional calculator to detour to this crucial place, has warned the future leaders of consequence, has delivered the message as best as he can; now consequence—an extradimensional consequence, of course, one which has been imposed upon the situation rather than developed—will have to engage its own direction. It is a pity that he cannot bring documents, wave them in front of Pol Pot and de Gaulle, but the laws of paradox are implacable and no one may test them by bringing confirmation to the past. The speaker must make his point through fervor, through credibility. There is no supporting data.

"What are we supposed to do?" Saleth Sar says. "You surely cannot think to give us such an evaluation and simply disappear. We are not fools here, we are serious people. Even he is a serious person," he says pointing to de Gaulle, "even though like all of his countrymen he is full of grand designs and stupid dreams. Serious stupid dreams, however. You must take responsibility for that as well as much else."

Well, that seems fair enough. Perhaps that is so.

"*Regrette*," Sperber says. What else is there to say? In just a moment he will take the extradimensional calculator out of his briefcase, calculate the dials, and make his departure. He hopes that the café personnel will not take the calculator for a grenade or plastique; that they will not interpret his intentions as violent. His intentions are not violent, they are simply pedagogical in all of the better senses of that word.

✳ ✳ ✳

Next assignment: This one the standard interview (in all of its hopelessness) which no one in training can avoid. "Don't do this," Sperber therefore says to JFK, appearing in the President's private quarters at Hyannisport with the help of his speedy and selective instrument. "Don't go to Dallas to resolve a factional dispute, the factions are hopelessly riven, there is nothing that you can do but interfere and otherwise, if you go there, horrendous personal consequences may follow. I am not even talking about the future of the country."

Kennedy looks at him kindly, helps himself to another breadstick from the stack next to the table, seems to regard Sperber in a unique and favorable light. Jacqueline is ensconced upstairs, Dave Powers is pacing the corridors outside: This is a quiet night in the fall of 1963, quieter than most of them and therefore good for sitting by the calculator.

Sperber has come to Kennedy noiselessly, with no disturbance whatsoever.

"You're not the first from whom I've heard this, you know," Kennedy says. "There has been a whole group of you who have come in mysteriously with a similar plea over the past few weeks. It's a good thing I know I'm only hallucinating. Or are you really all emissaries from the future on some kind of training plan? That's what I'm beginning to believe but I can't get a straight answer out of any of you. It strikes me as the most reasonable guess; either that or you're all really extraordinary actors and Lyndon is even more demonic than I think, trying to make me crazy here. But I don't think I'm crazy; I have a rigorous, robust intelligence and know a hawk from a handsaw."

Sperber knew of course about all the others. Kennedy in the fall of 1963 was one of the most popular destinations: unlike de Gaulle and Saleth Sar in the café, who were really unusual and almost secret. Certainly, Sperber would never make his knowledge of that site public. Still, you could not use only the most popular destinies; you had to do some original warning and rebutting or risk falling into imitation, the inattentiveness of the assessors. Alternate history was not merely an odyssey; it was a work of art, it had to be particularly shaped.

"What can I do to convince you that I'm different from the others?" he said. "I'm a specialist, I work on historical causation, on first cause, on original motivation, it's been my field of study for years and if I didn't have this opportunity, I would be abandoning the future to mindless consequence. It's got to mean more than that."

"I can't get into arguments of this sort," Kennedy says. He rocks back in his chair, sighing a little as his weak back is momentarily shifted from axis, then recovers his purchase.

"All of you are so insistent, all of you seem so convinced that you carry the real answers." He smiles at Sperber, his fetching smile, the smile that has been preserved in all of the living and dead histories through the hundreds of years between them, then pats Sperber on the hand. "It's a fated business anyway," Kennedy says. "And if I'm not mistaken, if I understand this correctly, it's all happened anyway from your perspective."

"It's happened," Sperber says, wishing that he had managed a university education so that he could put this in more sophisticated terms. The trades were not a good place to be; this work was really too delicate for someone training fundamentally as a technician and yet that was the only way it could be financed. "It's happening and happening but there's a chance, just a chance, that if you avoid in the future the events which I know so well, that it can happen in a different way. I'm not doing this for recompense," Sperber says unnecessarily. "I have a genuine interest in improving the quality of our lives in the present."

"Well," Kennedy says. "Well, well, there's no answer to that then, is there? There's no canceling travel and political commitments at such a late time unless there's a proven disaster lying there and we know that that's not the case.

Sorry, pal," Kennedy says, patting Sperber's arm almost lovingly, "there's just no way around this. Besides, I'm getting a little tired of all these visits anyway. They're distracting and there's nothing that I can do to change the situation anyway."

"Je regrette," Sperber says in poorly stressed French, carrying over his response from an earlier interview, "je regrette all of this, Mr. President, but it's important for you to understand the consequence—"

"There is no consequence," Kennedy says; "there is only outcome," and Sperber in a sudden and audacious wedge of light, an extrusion that seems to come from Kennedy's very intellect, which fires and concentrates his features, bathing them in a wondrous and terrible life, understands that Kennedy is right, that Sperber has been wrong, that he has been pursuing consequence at a distance in the way that a platoon of guards with rakes might trail the line of a parade, clearing the landscape. Sperber was no more consequential to Kennedy than such a crew would be to the parade.

"Don't do it!" he says nevertheless, seizing the opportunity as best he can. "You still shouldn't do it, no matter how right you feel; you will be surrounded by enemies, taunted by a resisting crowd, then you will perish among roses. You have got to heed me," Sperber says, and jiggles the extradimensional calculator into some kind of response, already too late, but he is willing to try to get Kennedy to listen to reason even as the storm begins in his viscera and he feels himself departed through yet another wedge of history, spilled toward a ceaseless and futile present.

✳ ✳ ✳

Sperber takes himself to be addressing Albert Einstein in a hideous cafeteria in Einstein's student days, the unformed Alfred nibbling an odorous salami, calculations and obliterated equations on the table between them. "Don't do this," Sperber says in what he takes to be a final, desperate appeal, "don't do it, don't complete the equations, don't draw the conclusions: This will lead to the uniform field theory, it will lead to one devastating anomaly after the next, it will unleash the forces of atomic destruction upon a hapless and penitential humanity surrounded by consequence. Don't you understand this? Put it away, put it away!"

Einstein, another infrequent site, stares at Sperber with a kind of terror, not for him the cool insouciance of Kennedy, the political fanaticism of Saleth Sar and de Gaulle. Einstein is as fully, as hopelessly, astonished as Sperber was when informed, five or six subjective hours ago, of his mission.

"Change history?" Sperber had said. "I can't even spell history," and similarly Einstein shudders over his equation, stares at Sperber in a fusion of shyness and loathing. "I can't shape history, I don't even know myself," Sperber, the student, had shouted when informed of his mission, and the implacable sheen of their faces when they had responsively shoved the extradimensional calculator into his hands was like the sheen of the salami that Einstein held in one hopeless, hungry hand.

"I don't know of what you are speaking," Einstein said.

"Physics is too difficult a subject for me to understand; I can do nothing, don't you know this? I can do nothing at all." In Einstein's despair, Sperber can glimpse the older Einstein, the saintly and raddled figure whose portrait adorns the site, a musty extrusion from the journals, who played the violin badly at Princeton and blamed everyone else for the bomb.

"Yes you can," Sperber says, and resists the impulse to spout French again: the language of diplomacy, he had been told, but that was just another cracked idea of the assessors.

"You can do something, all of you could have done something, you have to take responsibility, don't you see?

You must take responsibility for what you have given us."

Sperber would have a great deal more to say but the sound of the assessors is suddenly enormous in the land and Sperber finds himself, however unwillingly, ground to recombinant dust in the coils of the calculator.

He is taken back.

He ponders the landscape, the faces of the assessors, neither unsurprisingly changed at all. The program is sustained, after all, by failure. What point in resisting?

"Oppenheimer is next," someone says to him. "Are you prepared for Oppenheimer?"

Well, no, in fact he is not, but Sperber tries as ever to be hopeful. He is Shiva after all, destroyer of worlds.

Rocket City

MARGE AND me, we took Dink and went down to Rocket City. Dink, he got into one of those retrograde simulators, and we didn't see him for o-three-hundred hours. He be flying to Phobos oldstyle, I guess, with the field monitor pouring in his head and all the music of the spheres; but Marge and me, we did walking. We walked through the turbofire and the second-stage exhibits. We walked by old three-level jobs and the actual pieces of craft that blew up on Ceres. It was a slow time in Rocket City, and I was able to get into conversation with one of the guides. "Listen to this, Marge," I said. "He be telling you things about this you never knew. How we flew the planets and dropped on Pluto; how we perched on the edge of the stars and now no more. He primed and full of tapes and stuff: he give the true story of the human destiny and condition and why we no turn outward but inward instead."

"I got no interest in that," Marge said. "What he be telling I be not wanting." But when the tour guide began to speak, she stood in place anyway, partnership being a matter of bearing up. Or under.

"The program was abandoned in the early twenty-fours," the tour guide said. He be a young fellow who know nothing about history, but those mnemonic devices mean they can tell you everything, just like the simulators can take Dink to Phobos. "The utter inhospitability of the environment to stellar exploration was confirmed by the findings of Vieter and Loeb, whose bio-mechanical researches did confirm that the organism could not stand the period of time necessary to reach even the Centauris. Faced with the prospect of becoming a race of planet-hoppers and dilettantes eternally confined to our solar system, authorities made the decision instead to dismantle the program except for the transfer voyages among the settlements. Hence the establishment of Rocket City so that replications and originals of the real devices of travel could be preserved for all time."

"It all sounds very sad to me," Marge said. "Why give up planet-hopping?"

"The stars they be a suicide mission," I said. "This very discouraging in terms of high expectations; continued flight within the solar system then be perceived as decadent, am I right?"

"Right," the guide said. "Psychotronic control's perception was that the non-abandonment of rocketry in the context of limitation to the solar system would have led to deadly warfare by the middle of the twenty-fours. Hence the devices were dismantled except for Rocket City, which was established in San Diego in 2453 so that our heritage should not be forgotten." The guide stared past us. "I got that right," he said.

"You," Marge said to me, "let us be looking for Dink. O-two-hundred hours in that simulator be addling his brain; he come out and not know he be Dink himself."

"In just a moment," I say. "This is very interesting." We only go down to Rocket City once a year, and Marge, she be hurrying to leave from the moment we hit the gate; but I think these visits an important part of preserving our human history and try to get as much from them as possible. With Dink scrambling off to the simulators since he be ten years old already, it be difficult for him to learn anything, and Marge has no interest in rocketry. "Talk about the stars as a suicide mission," I said.

"That's what they were. Certain aspects of the radiation that could not be kept out of the craft, no system being utterly self-enclosed, would have driven the crews insane and have caused them to destroy the mission. Vieter and Loeb proved this, and it was decided that it would be the most humane decision not to subject their theories to proof."

"I think that's a pretty good thing," Marge said. "It would have been cruel. They were pioneers and heroes."

"That is true," the guide said and went into a long speech on the background, but I be thinking of Dink again. Pioneer and hero, that what he wanted to be; that is why he crawls off to the simulators and dreams of stars every time in Rocket City. He would have been very good if it had not been for Vieter and Loeb. But then I can be telling from the look on Marge's face that she not want to listen anymore, and I cannot say that I blame her. Maybe she be thinking of Dink too. I nod at the guide, and we walk away. There is not to worry about hurting feelings, because the guides be close to simulators themselves, filled with penalyazyne and other concoctions from an early age to make good passageway for the mnemonics: obliteration and suppression of the personality from an early age, in other words. When they off duty, they swim in the tanks or lie in the barrows.

Marge and me, we walk through the gate and into the section where the thrust chambers and multi-leveled rockets be poised in rows against the dome. The arena be almost empty on this slow afternoon, and I look at the steel and circuitry and think how sad it is that most of us, we are now so uninterested in our heritage that this place be almost empty. Year by year there are fewer at Rocket City, and I am pretty sure that by the end of the twenty-fives it will be closed, leveled for more occupation. But while it be still around, it is important to pay our heritage respect.

I stare at the multi-levels and think of the men who centuries ago locked themselves into steel, surrounded themselves with filters, and hurled themselves toward Ganymede. They must have been strange and courageous, informed by the knowledge that they were going to the stars; even though that did not quite work, one can respect their dedication. Dink be the same way.

Marge had had enough. "We be getting that boy and out of here," she said. "O-three-hundred hours now in the simulators, and you know what it was like the last time."

I know what it was like. We begin to walk that way. "This an impressive place, though, Marge," I said. "This a memorial to the time when we be spacebound."

"We not spacebound," Marge said. "That be put away."

I do not argue. What is there to argue? She is right, and I have had enough of Rocket City myself; every time the crowds be less and the space between the ships greater. We stroll in our usual way to the simulator barn and pipe in the message for Dink. We wait and we wait. Finally he be coming out in that stunned way they emerge from the simulators, his eyes looking like the guide's. "Who be you?" he said.

Disorientation on release be common. "The engines be shutting down; we ready for Ganymede contact."

"Come along," Marge said, taking his hand. "Ganymede takedown come next time." He stumbled along with her, still weak and confused. The simulators, they do one good job.

"Ganymede touchdown," Dink say. "Big Jovian landscape. Moons as big as worlds. Oh, the darkness." They talk like that for some hundred hours after release, even longer before they throttle down. "Oh, the darkness," Dink, he say again, and Marge look at me over his little round head. I shrug, I be taking his other hand. We walk quick and fast out of Rocket City then, the night hard over San Diego outside the dome and the lights winking on the tastehouses and the slaughtering bins as clutching his strong spaceman's hands.

Marge and me, we take our twenty-eight-year-old son all the way, all the way, all the way home. His round head a spacer's. His cold eyes the stars.

Tap-Dancing Down the Highways and Byways of Life, etc.

HE CAME out of the hedges with an angrily uncertain expression, a hesitancy in his gestures. The gun, however, looked quite positive as he shoved it in my ribs. "Give me all your money," he said, "right now."

"This isn't very nurturing of you, Cecil," I said. "It also isn't legal."

"Don't give me 'nurturing,'" he said in a tortured whine.

"Just give me the money."

Carefully I put my hand in my pocket, fumbled for my wallet. "You'll regret this, Cecil," I said. "I know your parents.

They'll be ashamed of you —"

He reversed the gun and slammed me across the face with the butt. I do not mind saying that it hurt, but I took it with frozen expression, resolved not to show emotion. As he shifted the gun back to firing position, I could feel the blood crawling down a cheekbone. How humiliating, I thought. But of course, humiliation is part of the package here.

"Just shut up and hand it over now," he said. The gun shook in his hand. Overhead a helicopter prowled, rattling the sky. I could smell the gasoline fumes, leaching onto the pastoral, deserted suburban street. This civilization guards at all times against the illusion of beauty.

I opened the wallet and stroked the bills, took out the clumped hundreds. "Now," I said, "you should understand remorse —"

"Fool!" he said, snatching the wallet from my hand. "The whole thing!" He backed away two paces, clawed through it.

"Three thousand dollars," he said at length. "You're holding out on me. Where's the rest of it?"

"I gave you all I had, Cecil —"

"You're a liar!" he said. His face clutched in petulance, he looked as if he were going to cry, a most embarrassing posture for a man of his age and history. "I want it all!" He seized me by the throat, squeezed. The impact made me groan, and I could feel a fresh wave of blood cascading. "Give it to me!" he said.

I struggled in my pocket, removed the ten hundreds I had folded away separately. "Here," I said, suffocating in his grasp, barely able to articulate. "As if it will do you any good."

He released me, pushed me away, counted the money frantically. "There's *still* another hundred," he said. "You're holding out on me."

"That's all of it," I said. I stood shaking by the fence, the helicopter clattering overhead, feeling the pain now. "You ought to be ashamed of yourself, Cecil. A man of your background, your opportunities. Your parents will be horrified when I tell them—"

He looked at me with fury, and then, suddenly, centered the gun. "I told you to shut up!" he said. "You mention my name or my parents again, and I'll blow you away!"

"It's the truth, Cecil!" I said angrily, touched, felt the pain in my injured throat. "You're a disgrace to your heritage, and everyone should know about it. I'll tell—"

He fired the gun.

The bullet caught me squarely in the forehead, and I fell.

His receding footsteps mingled with the sound overhead.

I lay near the tangled bushes for a good fifteen or twenty minutes this time. I must have been dead when they finally pulled me up with the ropes, took me inside, returned me to the all-purpose institute, and performed the standard procedures. At length, cleaned up and given fresh clothing—the cuts on the face were superficial, but they had to do painstaking work on a bruised larynx—I was hauled in front of them and roundly chastised. "I know," I said, hoping to forestall more of it after the initial onslaught. "I shouldn't have done it."

"You're a fool," the examiner said. "You did *everything* wrong. You were even worse than the first time."

"Sometimes I have to be given a little more time," I said—rather sullenly, I suppose. "I may not be the quickest learner, but once I know, I really know—"

"You mentioned his name, you invoked a personal relationship, you mentioned his *parents*. You held out on him, not once but twice. That's really stupid—"

"I got angry," I said.

"You *can't* get angry if you want to survive, you fool. How many times must you be told that?"

"I'll be better," I said. The cut still stung. I ran a finger over it lightly. "I don't want to go through much more of this."

"Then get it *right*," the examiner said. "We have only so much time for each of you, you understand."

"All right," I said. I knew that I should be submissive, cooperative, but a tiny core of revulsion still persisted. "These are our streets, you know. It was my neighborhood."

"You *cannot* get ideological. That is the last thing—"

"All right," I said. "I know." I sat there quietly, nodded with agreement to everything that was subsequently said to me, and at length they let me go. It was agreed to run the circumstance immediately: the best lessons are not assimilated to be reenacted in the morning.

As soon as he came from the hedges, I knew I was in trouble. His eyes looked desperate, and the gun was shaking in his hand—probably because this was his first robbery. "Oh my God," I said, "please don't shoot! I'll give you everything."

"Give me the money," he said. With the cap pulled over much of his head and with the huge gun, he was a menacing figure, if one could look past the facts that I knew all so well.

I allowed the terror to fill me. "Here," I said, handing him my wallet. "Oh, here it is, just don't shoot me."

He clawed rapidly through the contents. "They told me you were carrying five thousand," he said. "Where is it?"

"It's all there," I said, "just count it again."

The clatter of the helicopter rattled the street; a shadow passed across us. I was careful not to look up, not to acknowledge the observation in any way.

He jammed the wallet into his pocket. "All right," he said, "turn around and start walking. Don't look back."

"Can't I just stay here?" I said. "You'll shoot me in the back—"

"Stop complaining! Just turn around and start walking."

"Oh Cecil," I said, "these cheap theatrics, these little scenarios of intimidation—"

He stared at me. "Don't use my name!" he said. "I hate my name!"

"Maybe if you stopped hating yourself, Cecil, you wouldn't do things like this—"

The gun began to waver in his hand. "Goddamn you!" he said. "Start walking. Get away."

"You ought to be ashamed of yourself," I said. "What your parents will say when I tell them—"

I never saw him aim and fire this time. But I do remember the impact of the stones as, most heavily, I went down.

They must have been furious this time. It was hours later before I found myself restored, and then they had left both bruises I had taken on the knees when I went down so rapidly. The examiner stared at me with loathing. "You'll never learn," he said. "You just never learn!"

"I'm trying," I said. "He got me angry. The business of turning my back to him and walking, it was humiliating—"

"Don't tell me about humiliation!" the examiner yelled. He stood, only five and a half feet but intimidating on the podium, his mustaches flaring, his face diffused. "You people infuriate me. You don't understand, you'll never learn. But I'm going to make you learn because that's our responsibility here."

"All right," I said, "I'll say nothing. Whatever he says, I'll accept. Whatever he orders, I'll do." I felt a sudden twist of pain coming from my legs. "I'm sick of being killed and killed, pistol-whipped and beaten up, you know."

"Not sick enough," the examiner said firmly. "We're running out of chances, you know. One more failure and you're going to fail altogether, we'll have to send you back."

"No," I said. "No, I don't want that."

"Think of what your parents will say."

"All right," I said. I meant it, I could feel my own features flushing. "I'll shut up. I won't say anything."

"It's in your hands," the examiner said. He was breathing hard, almost as hard as Cecil when he fired the gun.

"Ultimately you have to accept the responsibility, don't you see that?"

✳ ✳ ✳

Stumbling down the street, I thought I did. I thought that I saw his point. His point was well taken, urban existence is impossible, one must learn at all costs how to survive. The sound of the observing helicopter, tracking me, made me ill; the fumes started me gagging. I was sick of it. The examiner was right: there was a time for student folly, but there was also a time to grow up. I had to grow up. He came from the hedges, extending the gun. "Give me all the money," he said.

He was nervous and uncertain, but the gun was convincing. Enormously convincing. I knew what it could do now. I handed him the wallet, the money protruding from it. He snatched it from me, backed away, clawed through it in both hands. "All right," he said, "it's all there. Now lie down and close your eyes and count to 250. Slow. Don't move."

I pointed to the sidewalk. "Right here?"

"No dummy. In the goddamned *mud*. Over there."

I looked to the right, at the slimy substance, still drenched from the recent rain. "There?" I said. "It's dirty—"

He waved the gun at me, his control breaking. "Down!" he said. "Down, down, down in the mud!"

The helicopter's sound seemed to overwhelm us as it approached. We were completely in its shadow. Of course he never acknowledged its presence; he is programmed not to.

"Down!" he screamed.

I looked at the filth, at the gun, toward the invisible, implacable observing eyes in the copter. "Oh, the hell with it,"

I said. "Screw you, Cecil," I said. "I won't do it! I won't cooperate." I spat in his face. Even at distance, it landed solidly. He stared at me with fury, wiped at it, then raised the gun. You fool, I thought to myself. "Your parents will cry at your execution, Cecil!" I hurled at him.

He fired the gun. Flame from the muzzle, et cetera. Quite accustomed to the consequences by this time, I died quite neatly.

I wondered if they'd even bother to revive me this time. It seemed unlikely; I was hardly worth it to them. I'd never be able to live in their cities.

I just couldn't be a victim.

Coursing

THERE WAS this woman and her name was Maria. She lived in a console of the great ship *Broadway* and whispered to Hawkins in the night, promises of love and fealty, warmth and connection. Hawkins could not touch her, could not consummate the promise because she was a simulacrum, a collection of electrons and impulses in the bottle but she made dark periods lively indeed and they had promised that at the end of the voyage, if Hawkins were to do what he meant to, she would be waiting for him, the real Maria; and she would make all these things true. Hawkins did not really believe this, did not believe any of it but the light years were vast, the ship was vacant and full of the stink of antiseptic, and if he were not able to converse with Maria there would have been nothing at all. So he thanked them in his heart for their time and trouble, their cruelty and their manipulativeness, and let it go by. He let everything go by.

The twenty-fourth century was all accommodation.

Hawkins, a felon interred on Titan, had been given a conditional release to go to the Pleiades System and negotiate with the King of the Universe. The King of the Universe, through pulsar, had advised the inner clusters that he would destroy them greatly unless every knee bent and every tongue did give homage. The King of the Universe might have been insane, but very little was known of the Pleiades Cluster and it was assumed that any culture with technology advanced enough to make possible this kind of communication could not be dismissed out of hand. *Half* a hand yes—send them a felon to do the negotiating—but the last time an alien threat had been entirely ignored brought about the Slaughtering Hutch of a hundred years. The King might have been a child given access to powerful communications *matériel* or a lunatic acting out for therapy; on the other hand he might be exactly what he said, in which case the inner clusters had a problem. Hawkins, a failure, was half a hedge against riot. Keep a civil tongue, the Advisors had said, evaluate the situation, and try to buy him off; if he refuses to negotiate or turns out to be what he seems then you know where the self-destructs are. Try to get near enough to take the King down. There's enough armament on the *Broadway* to take down the Pleiades themselves. And have a good time; after all, the Advisors concluded, that's what it's all about, isn't it? Thirty-three Earth days is nothing for a man who has done half a lifetime; think of it as front-loading.

Hawkins lay in the ship's abscess, just inside the probes, and said to Maria, "This isn't going to work. They'll wipe me out as errata; we're an unidentified flying object."

"I love you," Maria said softly; "I want to hold you against me. You are the gentlest and most wonderful man that I have ever known and I want you to be mine, all mine."

"I have to get serious," Hawkins said; "there's no time for passion here."

"Don't put me off, you dark fool," Maria said. "Closer and closer. Touching in the night. You will pacify the King and return; we will meet on Ganymede and in the silence and the density we will hold one another. Oh, if we had only met earlier; none of this would ever have happened to you."

Hawkins said, "I don't want to think about what it would have been like if we had met earlier. I don't want to talk about that now." He reached for the volume switch and lowered Maria's voice to a soothing burble. For reasons which were quite sufficient the technicians had made it impossible for him to cut off Maria completely, but he was able at least to modulate; this made it possible for him to find some periods of sleep. In the intricate alleys of metal and wire he could still hear her voice, extract the shape of words. *Lover.*

Apposite. Breasts. Hawkins felt a regret which verged on pity, but he urged himself to be strong. He could not listen to her now. He was scheduled for a confrontation with the King of the Universe shortly. The King had scheduled it all. Hawkins would be brought before him in the dock of an artificial satellite and explain his condition, offer his terms. The King had stated that he had not been surprised; he knew that it would only be a matter of time until the Inner Cluster sued for mercy. The *Broadway* had been tracked all the way with farsighted devices, had been under the King's mighty surveillance since it had torn free of the sun outside the orbit of Jupiter.

Hawkins huddled in the ship and awaited judgment. He thought of all the alleys and corridors of his life which, like the alleys and corridors of the ship, seemed to work endlessly and musically against one another, bringing him to this tight and difficult center. If he had done this then he might not, instead, have done that; if he had served his time penitentially rather than with defiance they might have sought someone else to deal with the King. But then again defiance was good because they needed a man who would take a position and most felons got broken within the early months of their confinement. Then too there was Maria who had been given to inflame and console but with whom, instead, he had fallen into a difficult kind of love. It was not her corporeality but the electron impulses themselves, the cleverness and sophistication of the device, which had hooked him in. Someday, if he lived through this, he would try to explain it all to the technicians. He doubted if they would listen; creating their wonderful devices they had come only to hate themselves because they could not be part of them. If the twenty-fourth century was for accommodation, then it was also for paradox. It was a paradoxical age. The *Broadway* veered and the gray abscesses colored to flame; the King of the Universe materialized before him in holographic outline. "I thought this would be easier," the King said. "Of course I am at a good distance from this image so don't think of anything foolish."

Hawkins was thinking of nothing foolish, concentrating instead upon the holograph. The King was a wondrous creature; the form was avian but like no bird that Hawkins had ever seen, and the beak was set of fierce design. The King half-turned, seemed to preen, displayed feathers. "Do you like this?" he said. "I wanted an imposing design in which to appear."

"Then this isn't how you look?"

"This is *exactly* how I look," the King said, "and this is no time for conundrums. Can you give me any reason why I should not sack and destroy the Inner Cluster?"

"I have brought priceless gems," Hawkins said; "if you sack and destroy there will be none of them left. Also, as a creature of some sensitivity you would not want to destroy ten trillion sentient and vulnerable souls, would you?"

The King winked. "You don't believe me," he said. "You think that only a lunatic would address you over the light years, threaten destruction, call himself the King of the Universe."

"On the contrary," Hawkins said, "we take you very seriously or why would I be here?"

"I can't answer that," the King said. "I merely run things, not try to account for them; and I must tell you that I am sore displeased. I think I'll appropriate your gems and dematerialize you."

"Don't do it so quickly," Hawkins said. It was impossible for him to tell whether the King was serious or capable of such action, but the entire mission had been predicated on the fact that he might be, and his own condition was humbling. "Don't do it," he said again, pleadingly. "We're not without a history. There are elements of our tradition which are honorable. If not science, art; if not art a certain damaged religiosity." Why am I defending us? he thought; this was the civilization, those were the technicians who first imprisoned me and then sent me out with the simulacrum of a woman to tantalize and to die. Truly, the situation is indefensible. Perceiving this, knowing that his thoughts were moving toward hopelessness and failure, Hawkins reached out and moved the volume switch. "Tell him," he said. "Tell him the things that you tell me, Maria."

"He is a good man," Maria said. "I love him desperately. We talk in the night; he tells me many things. When he returns to Titan I will dwell with him in holiness and fealty forever."

The King fluttered. "Who are you?" he said.

"My name is Maria and I am the lover of this man, Hawkins. He is a good man."

"Where are you?"

"I walk on this ship and to and fro upon it. Where are you?"

The King said, "That is not the issue." His speech had slurred; he seemed to have lost that edge of high confidence with which he had threatened destruction.

"Show me yourself."

"That is not necessary," Maria said. "I am faithful to this one man."

"Abandon him," the King said, "and come to me instead. Perhaps we can work out something."

"I won't do that."

"Maybe something can be worked out," Hawkins said carefully. "It isn't absolutely necessary—"

"Offer him the diamonds, but don't offer him me."

"I don't want the diamonds," the King said. He sounded petulant. "I can have the diamonds *anyway.*"

She is a simulacrum, Hawkins thought, a memory, an instance, unpurchasable. But instead he said, "If you return with me to the Inner Cluster you can have her."

"Why return? I want her *here.*"

"Love is impossible in space," Hawkins said quietly. "The eternal vacuum, the interposition of organism upon the void makes love impossible. Accept my assurances on that."

"I cannot return with you," the King said after some silence. "I would burn in the vastnesses of space. I am unprepared for a journey of any sort, confined to my castle.

Leave her here."

"I'm afraid not," Hawkins said. "She would perish."

"Yes, I would perish," Maria said coldly. "I would most surely perish, Hawkins, if I could not have you. I am not property; I am your lover, I cannot be treated in this fashion."

"You can be treated in any way I want," Hawkins said.

"Remember the conditions. You were delivered to give me solace, not argument.

"Nonetheless," he said to the King, "as you see, it is quite impossible."

"Nothing is impossible," the bird said, "not to the King of the Universe," and the bird turned, opened both impenetrable eyes and clawed at the floor. "That is my demand," he said,

"leave her here and the diamonds and you may go. The Inner Cluster will be spared. Take the diamonds, in fact. I don't need them."

Hawkins said, "For the greater good, Maria, for all circumstances, I ask you—"

"I love you," the simulacrum said. "I know that I was made part of the equipment merely to convenience, to give you solace, but I am quite out of control and it's you I love. I don't want to deal with any bird."

"I'm not really a bird," the King said, "this is merely a form which I project. Actually, I can be anything at all. You would be most pleasantly surprised."

"Appearances mean nothing to me," Maria said. "I'm sorry but it's quite impossible. This wasn't how the situation was supposed to be but it's how matters have turned out, I'm afraid. No, Hawkins, I will not yield."

"Then neither will I," the King said. "I am not a paranoid Pleiadan but the true and invincible King of the Universe, and I will make good on my threats. I tracked you from Jovian orbit, Hawkins; I had hoped that it would be for better outcome."

Hawkins looked at the figure of the bird, the eyes and figures glinting in the tight spaces of the cabin; he listened to the continued murmuring of Maria, now plaintive as she explained why she could not leave him. Hawkins looked at one simulacra and listened to the other as the *Broadway* ebbed and dipped in station, thinking I am man, I am twenty-fourth-century man, era of accommodation and paradox, felon of the twelfth order; you are in a Hell of a spot now. A Hell of a spot, for she cares.

But he wasn't. He really wasn't, after all. As he heard Maria begin to shriek in passion, as he heard her say Oh, Kingo King o King he came to understand that for some dilemmas there is, after all, resolution; if not flesh, then steel is all. Oh Kingokingoking Maria cried, and as the Broadway grandly broke stasis he began to see the light of eternity open up to him. He's wonderful! Maria cried, O King!

There was this woman and her name was Maria; she loved Hawkins, she said, and first refused the impossible embraces of a mad Pleiadan but there was a grander design and she saw it saw it saw it *okingoking.*

Hawkins felt the tumble of paradox.

Just before the blankness, he mumbled, *faithless bitch.*

O flawless faithless one.

Blair House

TRUMAN DOES not quite know what to do. Does not know how to handle this. It is a new sensation for him; he has always been a decisive man; his enemies may take him for superficial, but in a difficult world of hard choices encircled by an increasingly powerful Communist threat the only sin is inaction. He ordered the bomb. He decided to run even when his own party was ready to dump him and beat that simpering clown Dewey, fair and square. Took the gauntlet in Korea. Stayed beneath the 38th parallel. Fired that lunatic MacArthur and made it stick. In retrospect all of this was easier than it seemed at the time; he had settle on a point and stuck to it. But this is a new situation.

This is an entirely new situation. The aliens have landed on the White House lawn and have demanded that he turn over the government to them or they will incinerate the planet. They claim they have the weapons to do it, and who would dispute them? Any group of eight-foot hanging marsupials that could travel from the Ceres system in enormous craft certainly possesses the technology to blow up a small planet near a forgotten star. At least this is what the scientists have told him. Where the hell is Ceres anyway? He cannot seem to keep this straight in his mind. Not that it matters anyway. Ceres system, spaceships, eight-foot marsupial aliens, it was all just a bunch of science fiction bosh until three days ago. Now he is up against it, though. There is no question about it.

Harry Truman sits in his working quarters at Blair House and says to Dean Acheson, his Secretary of State, "I'd like to call their bluff. I don't think they'll do it."

Acheson says, "I'll support you in a hard line if you want to take it." He stubs out his cigar. "on the other hand, they seem to have the capability to do what they threaten." The secretary's hand trembles slightly. The situation is upsetting him, there is no question about it. Acheson was the rock of his cabinet; he would have planted a bomb on Moscow at any time since 1945, Truman knows, and it has taken all of his force of personality to keep the man in place. Nonetheless he appears to be crumbling. It is a testimony to the power of the aliens, eight of them in three enormous spaceships. In the statements they have given to the world, wearing llife-support gear, standing outside their ships, they have succeeded in throwing quite a shock into everyone. Even Stalin has had no official comment on the episode. Sources deep within the network report that old Uncle Joe is gibbering.

"Did you contact Einstein?" Truman asks. "What did he say?"

Acheson shrugs. I certain postures, Truman thinks, he bears a discomfiting resemblance to Dewey. "He says that he's a physicist, not an astronomer, a sociologist or an exobiologist. He doesn't have anything to say at all."

"Coward," Truman says.

"Can you blame him?" Acheson takes out another cigar, look at his watch. "We've only got another three hours until their deadline," he says.

"I know that as well as you do," Truman says. He feels his famous temper about to explode. The situation is infuriating. He is the President of the United States, and yet he is being humiliated by a group of grotesque creatures with translator gear who look like inflated raccoons and who nest in the trees surrounding the White House lawn while they make threatening statements about the future of the planet. "Don't you think I know that I've got three hours? The Joint Chiefs want me to call their bluff. They're of the opinion that they don't have the armament, and anyway we can always incinerate them; they'd never achieve escape velocity."

"We know about the Joint Chiefs," Acheson says cautiously.

"MacArthur has offered to come out of retirement to lead the attack." Truman says. He slams the desk top. "Godamn it," he says, "at least I said I wouldn't run again before this happened. Otherwise the press would have said that it's some kind of stunt."

"I should go back to the war room," Acheson says.

"Don't want to be on the spot, eh?"

"There's no telling what the generals will do," Acheson says. "There's a great deal of panic."

"Go on," Truman says, "go on, get the hell back. I'm not asking you for advice anyway. I know I'm in this one alone.'

"I don't think they'd blow us up." Acheson whispers. "Besides, it may be a stunt. Maybe the Russians sent them over. Maybe they came from Hollywood. How do we know? We're just looking at a bunch of ships and raccoons."

"Go away," Truman says. Acheson stands, flicks cigar ash, leaves the office. Truman picks up the phone and tells the appointments secretary that he does not want to be disturbed for half an hour; then he goes to the couch and lies on his back, draws up his knees and stares at the ceiling. Sometimes he gets some of this best idea after awakening from one of his well-known cat-naps. He finds them as bracing as his morning constitutionals.

But there is no rest for him this time. The events of the last days waver across his consciousness: the landing, the panic, the ringing of the capital by Washington police and then army troops, the arrogant pronouncements in English which the aliens broadcast through loudspeakers. Then the insane press conferences with the aliens emerging from the ship to hang from branches and harangue the press on the corruption and instability of all Terran life, their decision that they must land and civilize the planet by running it. The cabinet meetings, the all night conferences. Fortunately he has been insulated from the impact this has had upon the country. The impact has been terrible, he gathers; most of the cities are being abandoned by millions heading for the mountaintops, and there is shooting, fasting and prayer on the farmlands. It is a damned good thing that he declared out a few months ago because whatever the outcome of this he is going to get the worst of it for sure. Even if he stands up to the aliens at the end, he has lost a great deal of ground by capitulating up to this point. Perhaps he should have let the Joint Chiefs us the atom bomb. But everything would have to have been evacuated through a radius of 500 miles, and that would make a terrible situation even worst.

Truman thinks of his political career. Up until three days ago it has been a remarkable adventure, unsullied by any feeling of doom. He had never expected to be put in a position like this; everything has worked out so nicely for him up until this point. The top of his ambition had been to sit in the Senate; even though he knew Roosevelt was failing, he had never viscerally expected to be President until the moment that he had gotten the terrible news. After that everything had fallen into place. He would have been beaten for sure this time out; everyone knew that the Republicans were going to get Eisenhower, but seven years of this was enough for any sane man. He had been looking forward to an honorable retirement, maybe even going back and serving in Congress after a couple of years back in Independence. Now this. It left him simply without a position, and this had never happened to him before. As long as you could make a decision, kick a critic, drop a bomb, hold fast on the Yalu, you could get through, but what were you supposed to do when you were confronted by a situation like this? No American President, not even Lincoln, had ever had to contend with a mess like this. The aliens might be clowns, all of this might be a Soviet plot rigged to make him appear foolish, but how could you take the risk? How could you put the lives of everyone on the planet at stake even if there was only a small chance that these marsupials from Ceres could do what they threatened?

Harry Truman uses the spittoon, curse. This thing must come to an end. He picks up the telephone and asks for Barkley; the old gent is in the Senate chambers where if course things have been in recess for three days. "Hold the fort," he says, "I'm going to go over and talk to them."

"Talk to who? Barkley says. He is a clean old fellow but not as sharp as he used to be. "The generals? That's the spirits. Roll right in. Take their bluff. I'm with you all the way, Harry if that's your decision."

"Not the generals, "Truman says. "The marsupials."

"The who?"

"The fellas on the godamned front lawn of the godamned White House!"

There is a thick pause. "Harry," Barkley says, "I don't know if that's such a good idea, Harry. They got spaceships, they probably got weapons. Maybe the telephone?"

"Got to do it in person. That's why I'm calling you. I just want you to kind of mind the store while I'm over there. If anything happens to me they'll know who to reach."

"Anything happens to you?" Barkley's voice quavers. "Harry, I don't think that's such a good thinking. If you want anyone to go over there and talk to them, why not get MacArthur? He's itching to get back into this."

"If the press talked to them, I can," Truman says angrily. "Goddamned MacArthur just wants to be back in the newspapers, get his career together. He's not getting anything past me. No, Alben, you don't have to do anything, I'm not asking you to come with me. Just stay where you are and let them know where they can reach you"

"Well," Barkley says hesitantly, "well, all right, Harry. This is pretty tricky stuff, you know. Those boys are supposed to come from another galaxy; they pack a hell of wallop, maybe."

"Same galaxy," Truman says. "Same godamned galaxy." He hurls down the phone, picks up his suit jacket and walks through the door of his office. Two secret service personnel dozing in straight chairs bolt up. "I'm going to take a little walk over to the White House lawn," he says. "I'm going to go alone. I don't want protection."

"Mr. President — "

"Think this is the only way," Truman says. He makes a dismissive gesture. "you sit tight." They subside on their chairs, apparently debating whether Truman has the authority to release them. "Don't worry about it," Truman says "there aren't any Puerto Rican nationalists in those spaceships, that's for sure."

He walks down the corridor, nods at the appointments secretary, out the door. Fortunately, he has been casual about his movements over the years that this attracts little attention; even in national crisis they are accustomed to a President who often strolls out for his own newspaper. Across the street he sees the three tall silver ships glinting in the late afternoon sun; shadows of the monument playing over them. There are no signs of activity; sometimes the aliens have come out to sun themselves on the rocket tips, but at the moment, apparently, they are all inside. Truman walks briskly though the gate and across the street. Traffic is sparse; there has been little movement in the capital — in the country itself — in these recent days. The guard at the White House gate comes to attention as Truman approaches, steps towards his. Truman waves him away. "Just going if for a little talk," he says.

The guard steps to one side. Truman walks to the lawn. He supposes that the aliens landed on the White House lawn because they did not know that the President had moved into Blair House weeks ago while repairs were made on the mansion. This is one of the strongest reasons, Truman supposes, to think that it is not a Russkie move because certainly the Soviets would have known about this. He walks across the grass to the nearest spaceship and gestures vigorously. He knows that the lawn is under constant surveillance; the Joint Chiefs have reported the presence of scanners. "Want to talk to you a little," Truman shouts. His voice carries easily in the late April afternoon. "Send out your representative."

A hatch opens and a raccoon's head peers out. "That's fine," Truman says. "Come on down. I just want to talk some."

A claw emerges from the access, makes gestures at the dead. "All right,"

Truman says, "I understand. Get some gear on and then let's discuss things a little." The hatch closes. Truman waits patiently, thinking of his political career. It has been an astonishing journey, and along the line he has certainly angered a good many influential people. Perhaps this is not the Soviets but Republicans; it is the kind of thing that the party of Taft, Stassen, Wilkie and Dewey would try. But then again and very possibly it is not a prank. If only he could have been sure of one thing or the other, he would not be in this position, he reminds himself. It is a very humiliating position, but it is not going to be entertaining much longer.

The hatch opens and a figure clambers out, bulky in gear, weaving on the platform. Truman waves. "Come on down," he says genially, "stand on the lawn. There no need for me to look up at you like this. You're always going to be taller than me, but lets' deal with this face to face."

The figure seems to shrug, continues on down the platform, walks across the lawn. Inside the helmet he can see the square raccoon's face, the intelligent eyes. Perhaps it is not a prank after all. "Come on," Truman says, "come over here." The figure closes the distance, stands a few feet away. "That's fine," Truman says, "isn't that better now? Now we can talk."

"You are the President?" The figure says. The voice through the translating equipment is without inflection but not unpleasant "Your are Mr. True Heart?"

"Truman," he says. "Listen, haven't these people to whom you've been talking gotten my *name* straight?"

"My apologies, Mr. Truman," the alien says. "There have been many names and faces. We have wanted to talk to you from the first. Why have you not come before now?"

"Well," Truman says, "that was not exactly my decision. I should have come from the outset. Look here, says reasonable, "what are you doing, dealing ultimatums to us, threatening our government and way of life if we don't capitulate to you and so on? It's ridiculous. That's not the way we do things in America."

"We are not threatening," the alien says, "We are merely distressed at circumstances. Your inhabitants seem unable to control their own lives. So we wish to assume control for your own good. It need only be a temporary measure."

"Yeah," Truman says, "yeah, well buddy, that isn't the way it happens. In a free land you don't turn over control to anyone else, and you don't take promises that it will only be a short while. Maybe you'd get a better response from the other side, but that's not how we operate."

"We do not wish to deal with the other side. The Russkies you call them? We have heard about them. We do not wish to deal with them but with you."

"Well, that's probably to your advantage. If you had been dealing with them instead of us, you probably would have been attacked days ago."

"To their disadvantage. We are invulnerable."

"Well, you might well be," Truman says, "but you haven't seen our armaments yet." He makes a deprecatory gesture. "Let's not talk about armaments, attacks," he says. "Let's be reasonable here. What do you want to take over this planet for? We've got a pretty decent situation, all things considered. So it can't be for our own good, and if you want to conquer us, you'd probably find we have more fight than you expect. Why don't you simply go back to where you came from and check with us in fifty years? You might be surprised how much further along we'll be."

"That is not possible. Those are not our orders. We are supposed to achieve a resolution now."

"Fine," Truman says, "here your resolution. We appreciate your offer of conquest, but we're simply not interested. Say that you were turned back with thanks."

"That will not work."

"Then say that you were turned back with threats. That should do it. Say that we have weapons for which you never had an accounting, that we're much more dangerous than you thought we were."

"Mr. Truman," the marsupial says, "that is an interesting offer but we have heard it already. Why should we take it from you?"

"Because I'm the President, go, godamnit," Truman says, "and an offer from the President carries more weight than from anyone else because of the office, the authority. We're negotiating here. You go back and take your friends home, and I'll do my best to keep things under control here and prove that we don't need outside supervision. Next time around, you'll see that I was right. That's my bargain. If you really have your best interests at heart, you'll take it."

"It is an interesting offer," the alien says. "It is the first time that we have been made it by someone in your authority. But precisely what guarantees do we have that you are telling the truth and that you are capable of self-governance?"

"You have the word of the President."

"Mr. Truman, to yourself you are the President but to us you are merely a symbol. In the cosmos you would be surprised of how little importance symbols are."

"You have my word," Truman says. "Come back in fifty years and it will be proven. Any difficulties you see will be solved. You will have been saved all the trouble and expense of what would be an ugly fight, let me tell you. We Americans don't take conquest either."

The alien pauses; the silence is very much reminiscent of the pauses in his conversation with old Barkley. "You are a courageous man, Mr. Truman," the marsupial says. "If your word is that strong, if it has the same power as your courage, then it must be taken very seriously. I will confer with my colleagues. Fifty year?"

"Right on the nose," Truman says. "Fifty years right on the button. You come back and you'll see."

"We will give it much consideration,' the alien says, "and you will know soon of out decision." I turn and moves back towards the ramp, wafting the faint odor of cinnamon. For the first time Truman thinks that these creatures may indeed be what they represent themselves to be. It is not only the smell but the aspect of their presence; a foreignness which goes far beyond anything he has glimpsed at the United Nations.

"Soon you will know our decision Mr. Truman," the alien says and mounts the ramp, turns, waves and disappears in the hatchway. There is the sound of clanging steel.

Truman shrugs and walks slowly away from the three ships, first moving backwards so that he can stare at them, then turning and moving briskly over the lawn back towards the gate. To turn your back on an enemy is to show strength; it might also be contempt, but this is a risk that he will have to take. At the gate he nods at the guard and trudges back across the street towards the Blair House. At least I made a decision, he thought. At least I made a clear choice, Now it's up to them. If they don't decide to take it … by God, Truman thinks, if they don't decide to take it, I'll tell the Joint Chiefs to do what they want to as my last act, and I'll resign and give this thing to Barkley. Let *him* run it. At least I'll be back in Independence before tomorrow is out.

He waves cheerfully to the guard outside Blair House, waves to his appointment secretary and goes back into his office. As he enters he hears for the second time in three days the pounding, the surreal hum, the sound of fires. He looks out the window in time to see the ships, one by one, gracefully ascend.

By God I *did* it. Harry Truman thinks. All they needed from the first was a stern talking-to.

The image of the fire bloom on the panes of his office. They'll be back in fifty years, Truman thinks suddenly. That was the agreement, fifty years.

Well, what the hell. In fifty years we'll have this whole damned place cleaned up, he thinks. Nothing to worry about.

Nothing to worry about.

"Come on, Alben," he says in a moment over the phone, "bring over a pint of bourbon and I'll tell you all about it." In the background he hears the thin sound of Senate cheering.

Fifty years *is no problem at all*, thinks Harry Truman.

Quartermain

ALL FLESH is as grass: "you know how it will be," the modal says. "You will wander upon the desert. You will contest with Satan. You will return to Galilee. You will find yourself riding upon an ass. A few small dazzlements, a few larger enchantments, mobs, publicity, betrayal and vengeance. You will be taken to a high place, lots cast over vestments and etc." Its voice drops to a confidential tone. "It will be extremely painful, Quartermain," it advises. "These things have a certain cheap, dramatic force but there is no way that you can be properly committed to the extreme and, I might add, embarrassing agonies. Are you sure you want to go through with this?"

"Of course I want to go through with it," I say. I should point out that I am at a final briefing, that I have passed the various levels of qualification and that the modal, an intimidating but harmless device, is trying to harass me. "Don't be concerned," I say, "I can handle any of this."

Lights blink across the modal; one gathers that it might shrug if a room-sized cube were capable of gesture. "Very well," it says, "you will do as you will. I must warn you, Quartermain, this is no easy business. A cheap religious fanaticism will carry you only so far. Wait until they drive in the nails."

"Wait until you hear my seven last words," I counter.

"I'm waiting," the modal says. "I'm waiting and waiting. I suspire in conclave after conclave, interview after interview and, Quartermain. I will be waiting yet. I have seen you come and I have seen you go."

"Believe this," I say, "I am different."

"I have heard that before," the modal says. "Truly I have heard that before."

✳ ✳ ✳

BLESSED ARE THE DEAD: "Your name is Nicholas Quartermain," Satan says with deadly earnestness. For the purposes of our encounter he has assumed the frame of a youngish woman, rather fetchingly attired in scant clothing and equipped with the postures of seduction. I must admit that I do not find him unattractive although, of course, I am not enticed. "You have come to replicate the apocryphal chronicles of Jesus of Nazareth in the hope that a satisfactory crucifixion and a necessary ascension will grant you credibility as a cult head, but I tell you, Nicholas, you are a fool. Better men than you have fallen on the road to Bethlehem, the very best have cursed their Father on the Cross. No one has emerged from these simulations since they began and you will be no different." Satan reaches into her low-cut dress, takes out a large, well-formed breast, shows it to me. "Why not stop now, save yourself a lot of trouble and have a good time? Better to fail here than in the court of Pilate and besides, I'm getting so *tired* of these encounters, these dialogues. Come on be reasonable."

I stare at the old Tempter with disdain. "Never," I say, "I cannot be distracted by such cheap devices."

Satan winks, drops the breast. "Why not be diverted by the fantastic?" She arches a finger; from the dim mist which surrounds us the hundred priests emerge whispering in robes of splendor; great mythic birds enchanting in their plumage and color whirl against the sudden bowl of sky. "You want miracles?" Satan says, "I give you miracles. It surpasses your bread-and-wine tricks any time. You have to understand that you're dealing with a professional here, Quartermain. Dazzlements are my oldest charm."

I watch the chanting priests, the wheeling birds. "This is an impressive demonstration, I agree," I say, "but this is not a matter of display. I am familiar with all of your divertissements."

Satan shakes her splendid head, makes a moue of discontent. "You dislike enchantment?" she asks. "Very well then, settle for rhetoric." She makes a gesture of dismissal, the priests and birds reluctantly dissolve and the sky closes in like a grey collar once again. "I can defeat you with rhetoric of the most rigorous sort since I was, as you know and as any study of the proper texts will reveal, His best loved just before the moments of the Fall. I am that part of Him split off to walk up and down upon the earth and to and fro upon it, to test those for whom conviction is the highest necessity. In fact," Satan says, again with that fetching moue, "you might consider me to be His assistant, Quartermain, and what do you say now to a little wrestling? Forty days and forty nights of wrestling? You'll have a few tales for the boys in the Nazarene, you obsessed little darling!"

I look upon her and I look upon her and after a long time the knowledge of my resistance seems to settle inside and the slow fire of shame burns through her cheekbones, melting the mask of seduction, but as the birds and the beasts of the empty spaces begin to flutter and congregate once more, I understand that this will not be easy. Thirty-nine nights and thirty-eight days to go. I have instructed myself to keep precise records.

✳ ✳ ✳

THOU SHALT BRUISE HIS HEAD: One must do something in the twenty-second, tra-la, to keep from being poisoned or going mad; my choice was to qualify for a Cult. Access, however, is controlled tightly, as would be expected in this highly alienated and stratified culture, and the simulations are so difficult that only one out of twenty or so, it is rumored, even *qualify*. Beyond qualification the chances are uncertain; Satan's testimony that no one has ever succeeded is — well — Satanic but it cannot be more than one out of a hundred according to the rumors. The only information would be from the cult heads themselves and needless to say they will not talk. The failures will talk and through the Inventories I talked to many of them but the counsel of failure is not to be trusted. "You haven't a chance, Quartermain," my Counselor told me. "For one thing the trials are manipulated, and for another you *believe* in the apocrypha. It is this belief that is going to *undo* you." Then she laughed and laughed, mad laughter from the bitch until I fell upon her and drained her dry but as I rose and fell, rose and fell, her hands tearing at my back like prosthetic claws I could see the defeat in her eyes: I was leaving her after the Simulations, regardless of their outcome, and I would be taken from the Complex forever. This could only depress her since we had, as may be obvious, an active relationship. "Oh you fool," my Counselor screamed in the throes of orgasm (then again it may only have been disappointment), "you fool, this is the twenty-second. Nobody believes in that shit any more!" But she was wrong, quite wrong: *lots* believed in that shit any more. The cult heads had a splendid and lucrative occupation. I was tired of living in the engines.

✳ ✳ ✳

I SHALL UTTERLY CONSUME ALL THINGS OFF THE FACE OF THE EARTH: So I wrestle and wrestle with Satan; she assumes many forms and arguments over the endless weeks to follow, a falcon and a sage, a technician and a wild beast, a stone, a bone, a crone. And I come through all of these struggles and impositions with my belief, if not my virtue, intact until finally on the fortieth day (I believe that it is the fortieth but by this time my record' keeping, needless to say, has become somewhat dishevelled) He appears Himself, a special appearance as guaranteed by all the apocrypha and looks at me lying on the desert floor in a rather exhausted condition and says, "Quartermain, what are you *doing?* Why have you done all of this to yourself?"

"For the splendor," I say. His form is ineffable and I will, hence, not attempt to describe it. "For the sacrifice and for the necessity, to commit myself to You as Your only begotten Son—"

He makes a dismissive gesture. "Do that in the temples," He says. "It's not necessary here, this is a confidential discussion." He squats in clouds of glory, clasps his hands, spits into the sand. "No, really," He says, "the outcome is impossibly humiliating and the question of Resurrection is still being debated. You have no assurance. All that awaits you are heat, dust, lepers, the misbegotten, the legions, the crucifix and a most miserably bleeding and sweaty ordeal. Why not get out now? You can call for an end to this ridiculous simulation and be resting comfortably in the recovery shack in just a few moments."

"It isn't really You," I say grimly. "It's him in another form. You've assumed another shape in order to tempt me. Get thee behind me, Satan."

"Oh come on," He says with a splendidly graceful gesture. "Really Quartermain, if you've gotten to the 39th day of this you ought to have more sophistication than that. We're working *together;* we're a team."

I lick my burning lips. "Is that supposed to unsettle me?" I say. "I knew that all along and it's merely another aspect of doubt. A Cult Leader must be able to subsume himself in mystery. It doesn't change anything. I'm not unsettled at all."

"Ah well," He says, "ah well," and rises from his crouch. "You are of strong stuff, Quartermain, or at least of stronger stuff than most of them, but if this doesn't unsettle you, the ass certainly will. No creature of the twenty-second century is really equipped to ride upon an ass. For any considerable distance to be sure."

'Til deal with that when the time comes," I say. "Right now I have another day on this bloody desert."

"And a very good day to you *indeed*" He says, and disappears, leaving me to my various cogitations and moanings which, considering the thirst, heat, starvation, pain, and humility which have been invoked upon me, are considerable. It is very hard to take a sense of dignity from all of this, but astonishments, as I have perhaps brought Him to understand, are few.

✳ ✳ ✳

COMFORT ME WITH APPLES: Long consultations with my Counselor resonate within memory as I founder in delirium on the desert floor. "You are an ambitious man, Quartermain," she said to me. "There is a core of obsession within you which profoundly fails to intersect with the sense of the times. This is no century for ambition. The machinery, the engines of the night have overtaken us all; it is best perhaps to give one's will to them. There are small escape hatches, possibilities offered: the lotteries, the Slaughtering Docks, the Technician's License and the Cult Leaderships, but they are, as we know, largely illusory, rigged against achievement and functioning largely as safety valves. It would be far easier for you if you were to accept your condition, give up; easier for me too because predictably I have fallen in love with you and your ambition works against the small layers of peace we might create as insulation. Come on, Quartermain," she said, offering me her hand, "come to me and rest. It really isn't that bad once you accept the circumstances. The machines don't want our souls, merely our respect."

I looked upon her, my gentle and wise Counselor, assigned to me many years ago to give comfort to me as I was to give comfort to her, each of us Counselor to the other in a relationship alternately stratified and affectional. It would be easy, I thought, easy to take that acceptance which she offered, to give into the will of the machinery and the dark administrators who controlled the complex. For a passing moment I felt more profound than any I had ever known, but in the next instant I had passed through as I had done so many times, and knew that it was impossible. "It is impossible," I said. "I want to be a Cult Leader. I want to have my servitors and the congregation; I have something to say, I want to disseminate that message. I do not want to give in, not when the will exists to be otherwise."

"Vanity of vanities," she said quietly, "all is vanity."

"So true," I said. "To give up is vanity, to struggle is vanity. To struggle is what I have elected."

"You are a fool," she said, "a self-dramatizing fool." Her eyes were moist.

"Come here," she said, "look upon the city; all of the greys and greens. The walls of the city were erected to guard us against the monstrous, the truly insane, outside of those walls anything may happen —"

"Vanity of vanities," I said. And thought of the desert outside those walls, the desert upon which, if I were strong enough, I would take the forty and assert the oath and return to toss one by one with casual strength all of the money changers from the temple. "The time, the season."

Her hands upon me insistent, her voice against me insistent. "You are a fool, Quartermain," she said, "and the price of your foolishness will be mightily extracted from you.

"Cult Leaders have their choice of women," I point out.

✳ ✳ ✳

FOR UNTO US A CHILD IS BORN: The fortieth day expires and, grumbling, Satan releases me; he has, after all, no choice according to the contract. I return to the city where food and water await me along with devotion of my followers, a small and hardy band who seem to have increased in my absence. They look at me with awe. "It wasn't that difficult," I say self-deprecatingly, "I was armored with the strength of my own innocence. Too, you have to consider the benefits." Nonetheless they remain unshaken in their devotion. I have returned gaunt and bearded and it is possible that an aura of the divine clings to me although the secret is that it is not faith but cynicism which has gotten me through the ordeal. "Rabbi," one of them says, "what do we do now?"

"We gather, we formalize, we recruit, we go upon the countryside, perform miracles, raise a dead man or two, redeem a harlot, comfort the sick, give grace to the graceless, find an ass, come into Jerusalem, attract the attention of the legions and so on and so forth," I say. "Eventually, sooner than we would like, we get to the grimmer parts but that does not have to concern us now. In fact," I say rising, "this does not have to concern us at all. Consider it merely as a journey, as a set of tasks to be completed for a pre-ordained goal." For me, if not for you, I think.

"Did you *wrestle* out there, Rabbi? a boy asks, his eyes round and devoted.

"Like a son of a bitch," I assure him.

UPON THIS ROCK: Peter, Paul, Mark, Simon Peter. Judas is the only problem; eventually I find a thin, sullen youth with a limp whose generalized rage seems easy enough, when the time comes, to direct toward betrayal. Assuming custody of the lot and giving them simple instruction I go upon the countryside. Loaves and fishes are easy, the Magdalene interlude only slightly embarrassing. (She misunderstands my motives initially. It has been so long since Counseling that I almost respond but fortunately hold myself in check and eventually the Magdalene understands.) Lazarus is noisome and disgusting, far fleshier and more odorous than might possible be inferred through the materials but discipline and a visualization of the many rewards of being a Cult Leader squeeze me through the vile episode. Peter follows me into the fields on the evening of this adventure and says, "Are you sure you want to go through with this, Quartermain?"

"Of course I'm sure," I say. I should point out—if it is necessary to point it out—that the disciples, congregation, observers and hangers — on are all professionals from the twenty-second who function in Simulation; they have their own reasons for being on the scene. "That was all settled in the desert."

"You seemed overcome with revulsion back there. And the really difficult stuff is still ahead."

"Nothing to it," I say. I give the trembling youth a clap on the shoulder. "After what I've been through already this is nothing."

"Very well," Peter says, "I'm just trying to help. We *are* disciples you know; we have that responsibility."

"Oh I know that," I say with a booming laugh. I am really quite giddy; who would not be, considering the situation? "I know you're there to help. And the best way that you can help is by *staying in place.*"

"Certainly," Peter says, "certainly, Rabbi," but I detect a bit of sullenness in his posture and am given to understand, as I should have understood from the beginning, that my goals and those of the disciples are not necessarily confluent. They are, after all, creatures of the Simulator and hence of the State. One must embrace this understanding and after a time one does.

✳ ✳ ✳

IN THE BEGINNING WAS THE WORD: The ass, a miserable creature, is taken from pasture and I am lashed on. Somewhat awkwardly I ride into Jerusalem surrounded by my ragged troops. (The texts give no hint of the essential indignity and anonymity of the enterprise; there are *many* riding on asses toward Jerusalem in this time. Only in retrospect did I assume stature.) I find crude quarters; Judas disappears upon predictable, mysterious business. The Magdalene comes to visit me during this interval in my tent, and when she drops her cowl I see to my surprise that she is my Counselor.

"Well, what did you expect?" she says. "There's a long commitment here. I had to come and be with you to see it through. Now come home before it's too late."

"What do you mean?"

"I mean it's time to stop. This is ridiculous, Quartermain. You've done very well up to this point but now the nails and the torment begin. You haven't really begun to suffer."

"Are you working for the Simulators?"

"Don't be ridiculous," she says, tossing her head in a gesture not unlike that of Satan a long time ago although I do not, for an instant, confuse the two. "I'm working for no one. I care for you. I have your interests at heart. Listen, you've shown a lot of courage and you've carried this on far longer than almost anyone. We can have a nice life together. It isn't so hard once you give up and accept the situation. And you've proven a good deal to yourself."

"Leave now," I say. "Leave before I become angry."

"Come on," she says, putting her hands on my shoulders. "Enter me. Let me show you what you'll be missing. Cult leaders must remain chaste you know."

"I must remain chaste," I say. Her breasts suddenly appear. "What are you doing?"

"Trying to help you come to your senses before it's too late, Quartermain.

This is insane." She rubs a breast against my nose. "Come on," she says, "it gets much easier once you accept the truth."

I hold her arms tightly, desperately wrench her away from me. She stumbles back. "Get out of here," I shout, "get out of here right now!"

Her eyes are luminescent. "You're really serious about this," she says. "You really *are*. You *believe* in this —"

"Don't you?" I say. "Don't we all?"

"You fool," she says, backing toward the tent flap, "don't you know that no one has *ever* become a Cult Leader this way? They told me the truth and I'm risking everything by carrying it to you but there's no other way. All of the Cult Leaders are State Employees, the stories of the Simulators are all lies, just to keep the masses in check, to make them believe there's a way out. Now get out of this before it's too late."

"And you too," I say, "you too. And after the life from which I saved you and the immortality you have been given. It is too unkind."

"You're mad, Quartermain," the Magdalene says. "You're filled with madness."

"Get thee behind me," I say and plunge toward her furiously, but the canvas drops and I am alone.

*** *** ***

BEFORE THE COCK CROWS: The crowd—much larger than before and more respectably garbed — shouts for Barabbas and Pilate says to me in his heavy accent, "You see, it is quite impossible. I gave you a fair chance, however. You must admit that."

I say nothing to him. There is nothing, after all, to say. I can hear Judas frantically counting his silver somewhere in the background. The crowd murmurs for the next step in the process and I move forward, lift my arms. "To the high place," I say, "to the high place now."

A blush spreads over Pilate's features. He leans toward me and whispers, "I've been authorized to make you a final offer. We can get you out of here quickly. There's no need for this, Quartermain. We're all on your side and really you've done admirably until now, there's no reason to suffer —"

"To the high place!" I scream and the soldiers seize me under the arms and take me away. There is an instant of hesitation as I brush through the crowd and for a harsh, shocking instant I fear that the soldiers too are authorized to make me a compromise but then common sense reasserts itself along with speed and I am carried away. Huge wooden blocks are fastened in place along my back. The soldiers cannot possible be part of an authorization. Not *everyone* can be in on this. They could not employ and manipulate thousands simply to divert one Quest. Or could they? The resources of the technicians are awesome. I may have misunderstood the situation.

*** *** ***

WHY HAS THOU FORSAKEN ME? The thieves, chatty in their dilemma, toss insults back and forth over me as I hang in difficult posture. Flashes of color below give me hope that the casting of lots has begun. "Ain't it a bitch?" one of the thieves says, "ain't it just a merry bitch? The things a man gets put through," and then he dies or at least he seems to die, his face slackens, drool appears, his body gives out and lies slack. "I had big plans," the other thief confides to me, "I didn't see no way to make it in the armies. But I guess there's just no way for the common folk, eh chief?"

"Before this night is out you shall dwell with me in heaven," I say.

"Ah," the thief says, "the same old bullshit, that's all you get."

FORGIVE THEM! In the blood haze one of the hundred priests in the guise of a bird appears before me. "Quartermain," he says, "I am prepared to make you a final offer. This is the last time. There is no Resurrection. There is no Church. There is nothing; you have been misled by the texts just like so many of them, so it would serve you to attend closely. We can get you out of here and make you a Lecturer in Metaphysics. With a high-level rating and much better domicile. Think of the comforts. Also the Counselor. She's very emotionally tied to you."

"Go away," I say.

"Quartermain, you're not being reasonable."

"Go away." The huge dark bird flutters, inclines. "I mean it," I say. "I'm not going to sell out now. I've gone too far."

"You're crazy. There's nothing beyond. Nothing."

"There's a Leadership."

"You'll be dead."

"In the Simulators?"

"Truth," the bird says. "This is no dream, you fool."

"Go away," I say for the third time. The bird shakes its huge head.

"You're a fool. Quartermain, you could have had it all."

"I have nothing if I yield. Upon this rock I will build my church."

"You were warned," the hundredth priest says and flies. Coma storms and lashed to the wood, I lose count of the breaths of my betrayal.

LIFT UP YOUR HEADS O YE GATES: The stone is rolled away on the third day but I am not there, of course. Nor on the fourth, fifth, or, tenth. On the fortieth they think to search the desert and there they find my bones, thus obviating any necessity for worship.

In the twenty-second you can't take anything seriously.

Playback

Did you ever read what they call Science Fiction? It's a scream. It is written like this: "I checked out with K 19 on Alabaran III, and stepped out through the crummalite hatch on my 22 Model Sirius Hardtop. I cocked the timejector in secondary and waded through the bright blue manda grass. My breath froze into pink pretzels. I flicked on the heat bars and the Brylls ran swiftly on five legs using their other two to send out crylon vibrations. The pressure was almost unbearable, but I caught the range on my wrist computer through the transparent cysicites. I pressed the trigger. The thin violet glow was ice-cold against the rust-colored mountains. The Brylls shrank to half an inch long and I worked fast stepping on them with the poltext. But it wasn't enough. The sudden brightness swung me around and the Fourth Moon had already risen. I had exactly four seconds to hot up the disintegrator and Google had told me it wasn't enough. He was right."
They pay brisk money for this crap?

— Raymond Chandler,
letter to H. N. Swanson,

Selected Letters of Raymond Chandler, edited by Frank McShane

I **CHECKED OUT** with K 19 on Alabaran III. On the portico, moving slowly against the cracked and ruined spaces of the enclosure, watching the slow, dangerously signatory implosions from the outer ring, I could feel not only the collapse of the project, but my own, more imminent ruin.

Ruin will not be enough, Google had warned me. If it were only a matter of ruin, it would have been accomplished a long time ago. They want to smear us, they want us utterly defaced.

"What is that supposed to mean?" I said. "What do I do now?"

She said nothing looking back at me, the high panels of her face drawn tightly as if to prohibit speech, block it at the source. They will respond to direct questions but are no good on abstractions, on open-ended cries of despair. As I well know. That should have been all right; all my life the abstract has been well dismissed. "How much longer?" I said, trying again. "Enough time to get clear?" K 19 shrugged. In this guise she was a tall and intense young woman, her brain packed with deadly secrets which one by one her mouth would promise to impart ... but no such knowledge would issue, that was not the program and I would hammer again on those panels to no outcome. "I do not understand the concept," she said. "What is time? What is your conception of that?" A horrid precision now in her step, she moved toward an unshrouded viewplate. "Out there, in here," she said, pointing. "No difference."

She froze in that position. I could see the slow enclave of psychic ice glazing her and then she was silent. In my side pocket the heat bar ticked faintly, sent slivers of warmth through the thin fabric, but I was still fixated on K 19, still touched by the possibility that somewhere in her closed and deadly face there would lurk the answer, an answer to take me from the portion, silence the Brylls. Not the heat bar or the poltext, then. A true answer.

"Do you remember?" I said. "You made a promise —"

"I remember nothing. There is no memory, there is only this."

Looking at her so, locked to that lesser desire which still intimated possibility, I could see that this was truth, came to understand in that concentrated moment that all along there had been nothing else, no imminence, grandeur, possibility, or disclosure, only this denial. And knowing that at last, I felt the beginnings of release, the snap of that fine and tensile emotional rope that bound us. Testing the force of that insight, I moved away from her, ducked under the refractory bands cast by the high binding rings , and stepped out throughthe crummalite hatch, seized instantly by the vacuum that snapped and skulked at the perilous enclosure.

Now, against the blurred firmament itself, undefended by the thin expanse of the dome. I could feel the half-forgotten swaddled in those caverns we make, I could feel the awful power of the heavens, understand that what stood between us and retrieval was little more than a set of assumptions, assumptions which at any time could be blotted as thoroughly as K 19 had destroyed whatever compact we had. Knowing this did not strengthen nor change a thing but the acceptance was in itself a kind of control. The Brylls have come a long way, worked hard, dedicated themselves, applied all of their awful technology, but that cunning of effort has not yet succeeded in taking from us all recollection. So we are sport for the trajectory of the Brylls' conquest.

Now and then there are these pure moments of recovery, and outside the enclosure, K 19 still behind, I had another, turned the power *on my 22 Model Sirius Hardtop*, watching the sheaves of light curl from the element, now drawing pure solar heat at reversed amperage, seeking the internal source that we had dragged from the vacuum.

What joys we had from the cosmos before the Brylls! Our Sirian hardtops, galactic entertainments, bustling travel, our dolefully comic cries: oh, cascades of stars, nebulae of grandeur thus informing our spirit and possibilities until those Brylls came to show us the real force of universal law and to illustrate the limitations of our own condition. Crammed in the vehicle, feeling the tremors of the engine, I thought too of the easy, gliding weight of the hardtop when it had made fast passage from Peking Festival to the port of Macon, the wharfs of Brooklyn to the Empyrean Tower. Times when I had chanted mantras of speed to the hardtop, before the change, the emergence, the debarkation of the Brylls ... and these shards of memory were knives, slaughterhouse of memory. *I cocked the timejector in secondary and* felt the rush, the sense of distances opening and then as the hardtop lifted —

❋ ❋ ❋

I *waded through the bright blue manda grass* toward the beckoning Bryll, feeling the pull of the mud as I tried to clamber away, retain balance. This more than anything else they enjoy, taking our dignity, making us cartoons, yanking from us the solemnity of our distress and placing us on a flat and colorful map where we deal with pale, exploded forms who may or may not be representative of the Brylls themselves. We do not know if it is submission or some parody of conquest. *My breath froze into pink pretzels* as I squeaked.

Beyond the rise, the ape snickered and pointed; the Sirius fell with a whoop and I could hear the ape's chuckling. "So little," it said in that mechanical voice, as refractory in its burning as the fire beyond the portico. "So little and so strong, so ugly and so nice, so nice and so distressed. What do you want?" They toy with us; if this is our vision of purgatory I think that it must be theirs of transcendence.

Here is where they want to go when they die, one might have said, and now all of them through the eons are dead. "Nice!" the ape said and I bounced, then fell to ooze. Stumbling for balance, I flicked on the heat bars. They had not plundered before the transfer; in their eagerness to bring me to the pink pretzels they had left weaponry behind and suddenly it was in my hand, the feel of it steady and reassuring.

Yes, I thought. I can at least take the ape. If this is my purgatory, then perhaps I can block their transcendence. We live in small snatches, now and then we are granted a glimpse of recovery. The ape waved with a scanty claw, winking, *and then there were others, jolting presences. No longer alone. The Brylls ran swiftly on five legs* from all directions.

It was as if in my focusing of the weapon I had panicked them, made them show their true aspect. Ringing me on all sides, almost offhandedly, they attacked. I could feel the imminence of their horror and then, once again, the darkness.

"They are treacherous," one said.

"No," I offered. "Listen to this. We are not treacherous. We are driven. You gave us no choice, you gave us at the end no dignity." But having spoken, knew it was unheard, knew that there was no way in which connection could be made, was locked once again in that place so well known to K 19 from which there was no emergence.

❋ ❋ ❋

"Using their other two to send out crylon vibrations," the ape said, and this time I could see, in the flooding light I could see the bowl of roof, beyond that transparency the stricken and venomous sun, and I tried to move but found myself locked into place. At the edge of vision the ape was talking to something else, oblivious. "They die," one said, "they die and they die and it is not enough." "Of course it's enough," I said, as if they could hear me.

"It's always enough, it was a sufficiency when we began," and tried to wave, tried to show them through the intensity of movement the thorough nature of my distress, but they wouldn't acknowledge me, I might have indeed been dead and they large solemn demons, blank devil and primate, assessing larger goals. "It wasn't enough for Google," it said again, "and it's not enough for you." The strangulation, as if an arm were laid across my throat.

The pressure was almost unbearable but the heat bar was there, they still had not taken it through all their insistence.

Somehow, yanked to a seated position, I felt the pain seize me like a fist *but I caught the range on my wrist computer* and said, "Listen here! Listen to me! You must not turn away from this, we suspire, we are creatures, we live and suffer."

Through the transparent cysicites of the atmosphere I felt as if I had caught their attention, told myself that I had their attention at last, could somehow break through.

"You've broken us," I said. "You've done it now."

"It's never enough—" The gorilla moved deliberately, its companion turning now.

The Brylls were coming.

I pressed the trigger.

❊ ❊ ❊

"Now what?" K 19 said.

She lay against me in terrain like knives, ice and slice sending tender, necessary slivers of pain, the two of us stretched one by one on heavy mesh like metal. We were in an enclosure, the air stale and heavy, and *the thin violet glow was ice-cold against the rust-colored mountains* in the distance.

"I don't know," I said. Her skin lay damp and open under my fingers, rising in small response as I clutched. "We're somewhere else now. We've been taken away."

"What did we do?"

"We were taken. They turned our breath into pink pretzels."

"Yes, but what did we *do?*" Once we had lain together in transaction, hovering, mild connection, but now, even as I felt her stillness, it was as if this had not happened. Far from me, distilling loss with every breath, K 19 said, "You have destroyed us."

"We were already destroyed."

"My name is Linda. Call me that, give me my name."

"It was over, Linda. Wherever we are, whatever has been done, it was over."

I could feel the stirring and then there were many sounds, perspective cleared, breath again began to pretzel. Looking toward the sounds, I could see the little forms, could see them scuttle, could see *the Brylls shrank to half an inch long*, hopping, scuttling. They ringed us with the eagerness of their necessity, showed us their incessancy.

"What is it?" Linda said. "Where are they?"

I pointed, drew the line of her attention, and then with her breath, her first frozen and intense knowledge, I reacted instinctively, did what some of us had tried at the beginning, *and I worked fast stepping on them*, lunging somehow to a standing position. Linda screamed as she saw what I was doing, pointed at the rust-colored sky, and I ignored the heat bars, consigned them to darkness along with the rest of my life, no transaction left now, and began to fight *with thepoltex*; the small rubber flange opening like a petal as I beat at them. If this was to be the final battle (and it was, my time was over, I knew that now), it would be as deprived of dignity as the rest but at least I could right the balance, struggle on.

Even as Linda tried pathetically to crawl away, I found myself pitched against them, grunting, heaving with that sole weapon left, seeing them pulp, listening to their brisk and intermittent cries as some — but not too many — of them died.

But it wasn't enough.

The sudden brightness swung me around and Linda, the mask clamped tightly, was holding the heat bar, aiming at me, maniacal and concentrated laughter pouring through.

Pouring through as fuel of my destruction.

And it was at that moment, then, and not an instant earlier nor a flash later, that I came to understand what had happened, the true nature of the Brylls, the deadly and insistent nature of their circumstance and plans.

"*And the Fourth Moon had already risen*," the thing in the mask said, "and it was time then, time for us if not for you and it would always in that extreme be enough."

If I had understood what was happening, *I* might have *hadexactly four seconds to hot up the disintegrator* of the heat bar.

But even then —

"*And Google had told me it wasn't enough*," I said. I believe I had lost control. I believe I had really lost control.

That flush of abandonment, the surge of separation, the conviction of utter disaster —

"Not for you," the thing that had been Linda K 19 said.

"Not for you, perhaps. But it is for us."

He was right.

Corridors

R UTHVEN USED TO have plans. Big plans: turn the category around, arrest the decline of science fiction into stereotype and cant, open up the category to new vistas and so on. So forth. Now, however, he is, at fifty-four, merely trying to hold on; he takes this retraction of ambition, understanding of his condition as the only significant change in his inner life over two decades. The rest of it—inner and outer too—has been replication, disaster, pain, recrimination, self-pity and the like: Ruthven thinks of these old partners of the law firm of his life as brothers. At least, thanks to Replication & Disaster, he has a brief for the game. He knows what he is and what has to be done, and most of the time he can sleep through the night, unlike that period during his forties when 4 A.M. more often than not would see him awake and drinking whiskey, staring at his out-of-print editions in many languages.

The series has helped. Ruthven has at last achieved a modicum of fame in science fiction and for the first time—he would not have believed this ever possible—some financial security. Based originally upon a short novel written for *Astounding* in late 1963, which he padded for quick paperback the next year, *The Sorcerer* has proven the capstone of his career. Five or six novels written subsequently at low advances for the same firm went nowhere, but: the editor was fired, the firm collapsed, releasing all rights, the editor got divorced, married a subsidiary rights director, got a consultant job with her firm, divorced her, went to a major paperback house as science fiction chief and through a continuing series of coincidences known to those who (unlike Ruthven) always seemed to come out a little ahead commissioned three new Sorcerers from Ruthven on fast deadline to build up cachet with the salesmen. They all had hung out at the Hydra

Club together, anyway. Contracts were signed, the first of the three new Sorcerers (written, all of them in ten weeks) sold 150,000 copies, the second was picked up as an alternate by a demented Literary Guild and the third was leased to hardcover. Ruthven's new, high-priced agent negotiated a contract for five more Sorcerers for $100,000.

Within the recent half decade, Ruthven has at last made money from science fiction. One of the novels was, a Hugo finalist, another was filmed. He has been twice final balloted for a *Gandalf*. Some of his older novels have been reprinted. Ruthven is now one of the ten most successful science fiction writers: he paid taxes on $79,000 last year. In his first two decades in this field, writing frantically and passing through a succession of dead-end jobs, Ruthven did not make $79,000.

It would be easier for him, he thinks, if he could take his success seriously or at least obtain some peace, but of this he has none. Part of it has to do with his recent insight that he is merely hanging on, that the ultimate outcome of ultimate struggle for any writer in America not hopelessly self-deluded is to hang on; another part has to do with what Ruthven likes to think of as the accumulated damages and injuries sustained by the writing of seventy-three novels. Like a fighter long gone from the ring, the forgotten left hooks taken under the lights in all of the quick-money bouts have caught up with him and stunned his brain. Ruthven hears the music of combat as he never did when it was going on. He has lost the contents of most of these books and even some of their titles but the pain fingers. This is self-dramatization, of course, and Ruthven has enough ironic distance to know it. No writer was ever killed by a book.

Nonetheless, he hears the music, feels the dull knives in his kidneys and occipital regions at night; Ruthven also knows that he has done nothing of worth in a long time. The Sorcerer is a fraud; he is far below the aspirations and intent of his earlier work, no matter how flawed that was. Most of these new books have been written reflexively under the purposeful influence of Scotch and none of them possesses real quality. Even literacy. He has never been interested in these books. Ruthven is too far beyond self-delusion to think that the decline of his artistic gifts, the collapse of his promise, means anything *either*. Nothing means anything except holding on as he now knows. Nonetheless, he *used* to feel that the quality of work made some difference. Didn't he? Like the old damages of the forgotten books he feels the pain at odd hours.

He is not disgraced, of this he is fairly sure, but he is disappointed. If he had known that it would end this way, perhaps he would not have expended quite so much on those earlier books. *The Sorcerer* might have had a little more energy; at least he could have put some color in the backgrounds.

Ruthven is married to Sandra, his first and only wife. The marriage has lasted through thirty-one years and two daughters, one divorced, one divorced and remarried, both far from his home in the Southeast. At times Ruthven considers his marriage with astonishment: he does not quite know how he has been able to stay married so long granted the damages of his career, the distractions, the deadening, the slow and terrible resentment which has built within him over almost three decades of commercial writing. At other times, however, he feels that his marriage is the only aspect of his life (aside from science fiction itself) which has a unifying consistency. And only death will end it.

He accepts that now. Ruthven is aware of the lives of all his colleagues: the divorces, multiple marriages, disastrous affairs, two- and three-timing, bed-hopping at conventions; the few continuing marriages seem to be cover or mausoleum—but after considering his few alternatives Ruthven has nonetheless stayed married and the more active outrage of the earlier decades has receded. It all comes back to his insight: nothing matters. Hang on. If nothing makes any difference then it is easier to stay with Sandra by far. Also, she has a position of her own; it cannot have been marriage to a science fiction writer which enticed her when they met so long ago. She has taken that and its outcome with moderate good cheer and has given him less trouble, he supposes, than she might. He has not shoved the adulteries and recrimination in her face but surely she knows of them; she is not stupid. And she is now married to $79,000 a year, which is not inconsiderable. At least this is all Ruthven's way of rationalizing the fact that he has had (he knows now) so much less from this marriage than he might have, the fact that being a writer has done irreparable damage to both of them. And the children. He dwells on this less than previously. His marriage, Ruthven thinks, is like science fiction writing itself: if there was a time to get out that time is past and now he would be worse off anywhere else. Who would read him? Where would he sell? What else could he do?

Unlike many of his colleagues, Ruthven had never had ambitions outside the field. Most of them had had literary pretensions, at least had wanted to reach wider audiences, but Ruthven had never wanted anything else. To reproduce, first for his own pleasure and then for money, the stories of the forties *Astounding* which moved him seemed to be a sensible ambition. Later of course he; did get serious about the category, wanting to make it anew and etc.... but that was later. Much later. It seemed a noble thing in the fifties to want to be a science fiction writer and his career has given him all that he could have hoped for at fourteen. Or twenty-four.

He has seen what their larger hopes have done to so many of his peers who started out with him in the fifties, men of large gifts who in many cases had been blocked in every way in their attempts to leave science fiction, some becoming quite embittered, even dying for grief or spite, others accepting their condition at last only at the cost of self-hatred. Ruthven knows their despair, their self-loathing. The effects of his own seventy-three novels have set in, and of course there was a time when he took science fiction almost as seriously as the most serious ... but that was later, he keeps on reminding himself, after breaking in, after publication in the better magazines, after dealing with the audience directly and learning (as he should have always known) that they were mostly a bunch of kids. His problems had come later but his colleagues, so many of them, had been ambitious from the start, which made matters more difficult for them.

But then, of course, others had come in without any designs at all and had stayed that way. And they too—those who were still checking into *Analog* or the Westercon—were just as miserable and filled with self-hatred as the ambitious, or as Ruthven himself had been a few years back. So perhaps it was the medium of science fiction itself that did this to you. He is not sure.

He thinks about things like this still ... the manner in which the field seems to break down almost all of its writers. At one time he had started a book about this, called it *The Lies of Science Fiction*, and in that bad period around his fiftieth birthday had done three or four chapters, but he was more than enough of a professional to know that he could not sell it, was more than ready to put it away when *The Sorcerer* was revived. That had been a bad time to be sure; ten thousand words on *The Lies of Science Fiction* had been his out put for almost two full years.

If it had not been for a little residual income on his novels, a few anthology sales, the freelance work he had picked up at the correspondence school and Sandra's occasional substitute teaching, things might have bottomed. At that it was a near thing, and his daughters' lives, although they were already out of the house, gave Sandra anguish.

Ruthven still shudders, thinking of the images of flight which overcame him, images so palpable that often they would put him in his old Ford Galaxie, which he would drive sometimes almost a hundred miles to the state border before taking the U-turn and heading back. He had, after all, absolutely nowhere to go. He did not think that anyone who had ever known him except Sandra would put him up for more than two nights (Felicia and Carole lived with men in odd arrangements), and he had never lived alone in his life. His parents were dead.

Now, however, things are better. He is able to produce a steady two thousand words a day almost without alcohol, his drinking is now a ritualized half a pint of scotch before dinner and there are rumors of a larger movie deal pending if the purchaser of the first movie can be bought off a clause stupidly left in his contract giving him series rights. Ruthven will be guest of honor at the Cincinnati convention three years hence if the committee putting together the bid is successful. That would be a nice crown to his career at fifty-seven, he thinks, and if there is some bitterness in this—Ruthven is hardly self-deluded—there is satisfaction as well. He has survived three decades as a writer in this country, and a science fiction writer at that, and when he thinks of his colleagues and the condition of so many with whom he started he can find at least a little self-respect. He is writing badly, *The Sorcerer* is hackwork, but he is still producing and making pretty big money and (the litany with which he gets up in the morning and goes to bed at night) nothing matters. Nothing matters at all. Survival is the coin of the realm. Time is a river with banks.

Now and then, usually during the late afternoon naps which are his custom (to pass the time quicker before the drinking, which is the center of his day), Ruthven is assaulted by old possibilities, old ambitions, old dread, visions of what he wanted to be and what science fiction did to him, but these are, as he reminds himself when he takes his first heavy one at five, only characteristic of middle age. Everyone feels this way. Architects shake with regret, doctors flee the reservation, men's hearts could break with desire and the mockery of circumstance. What has happened is not symptomatic of science fiction but of his age, his country. His condition. Ruthven tells that to himself, and on six ounces of scotch he is convinced, convinced that it is so, but as Sandra comes into the room to tell him that dinner is seven minutes away he thinks that someday he will have to get *The Lies of Science Fiction* out of his desk and look at it again. Maybe there was something in these pages beyond climacteric. Maybe he had better reconsider.

But for now the smells of roast fill the house, he must drink quickly to get down the half-pint in seven minutes, the fumes of scotch fill his breath, the scents and sounds of home fill all of the corridors and no introspection is worth it. None of it is worth the trouble. Because, Ruthven tells himself for the thirty-second time that day (although it is not he who is doing the counting) that nothing nothing nothing nothing nothing matters.

▢   ▢   ▢   ▢

Back in the period of his depression when he was attempting to write *The Lies of Science Fiction* but mostly trying to space out his days around alcohol, enraged (and unanswerable) letters to his publishers about his out-of-print books and drives in his bald-tired Galaxie — back in that gray period as he drove furiously from supermarket to the state border to the liquor store, Ruthven surmised that he had hit upon some of the central deceptions which, had wrecked him and reduced him and so many of his, colleagues to this condition. To surmise was not to conquer, of course; he was as helpless as ever but there was a dim liberation in seeing how he had been lied to, and he felt that at least he could take one thing from the terrible years through which he had come — he was free of self-delusion.

Ruthven thought often of the decay of his colleagues, of the psychic and emotional fraying which seemed to set in between their fifth and fifteenth years of professional writing and reduced their personal lives and minds to rubble. Most were drunks, many lived in chaos, all of them in their work and persona seemed to show distress close to panic. One did not have to meet them at the conventions or hang out with them at the SFWA parties in New York to see that these were people whose lives were askew; the work showed it. Those who were not simply reconstructing or revising their old stories were working in new areas in which the old control had gone, the characters were merely filters for events or possessed of a central obsession, the plots lacked motivation or causality and seemed to deal with an ever more elaborate and less comprehended technology. Whether the ideas were old or new, they were half-baked, the novels were padded with irrelevant events and syntax, characters internalized purposelessly, false leads were pursued for thousands of words. The decay seemed to cut across all of the writers and their work; those that had been good seemed to suffer no less than the mediocre or worse, and there was hardly a science fiction writer of experience who was not — at least to Ruthven's antennae — displaying signs of mental illness.

That decay, Ruthven came to think, had to do with the very nature of the genre: the megalomaniacal, expansive visions being generated by writers who increasingly saw the disparity between Spaceways and their own hopeless condition. While the characters flourished and the science gleamed, the writers themselves were exposed to all of the abuses known to the litterateurs in America and intelligent, even the dumbest of them, to a fault—they were no longer able to reconcile their personal lives with their vision: the vision became pale or demented. At a particularly bleak time, Ruthven even came to speculate that science fiction writing was a form of illness which, like syphilis, might swim undetected in the blood for years but would eventually, untreated, strike to kill. The only treatment would be retirement, but most science fiction writers were incapable of writing anything else after a while and the form itself was addictive: it was as if every potential sexual partner carried venereal disease. You could stop fucking but only at enormous psychic or emotional course, and *then* what? Regardless, that virus killed.

Later, as he began to emerge from this, Ruthven felt a little more sanguine about the genre. It might not necessarily destroy you to write it if you could find a little personal dignity and, more importantly, satisfactions outside of the field. But the counsel of depression seemed to be the real truth: science fiction was aberrant and dangerous, seductive but particularly ill-suited to the maladjusted who were drawn to it, and if you stayed with it long enough, the warpage was permanent. After all, wasn't science fiction for most of its audience an aspect of childhood they would outgrow?

This disparity between megalomania and anonymity had been one of the causes of the decay in his colleagues, he decided. Another was the factor of truncation. Science fiction dealt with the sweep of time and space, the enormity of technological consequence in all eras, but as a practical necessity and for the sake of their editors all science fiction writers had to limit the genre and themselves as they wrote it. *True* science fiction as the intelligent editors knew (and the rest followed the smart ones) would not only be dangerous and threatening, it would be incomprehensible. How could twenty-fourth century life in the Antares system be depicted? How could the readership for an escape genre be led to understand what a black hole would be?

The *writers* could not understand any of this, let alone a young and gullible readership interested in marvels that were to be made accessible. (Malzberg had been into aspects of this in his work but Ruthven felt that the man had missed the point: lurking behind Malzberg's schematics was the conviction that science fiction should be able to find a language for its design, but any penny-a-word stable hack for *Amazing* in the fifties knew better and Malzberg would have known better too if he had written science fiction before he went out to smash it.) So twenty-fourth century aliens in the Antares system would speak a colloquial Brooklynese, commanders of the Black Hole Explorer would long for their Ganymede Lady. The terrific would be made manageable, the awesome shaped by the exigencies of pulp fiction into the nearby. The universe would become Brooklyn with remote dangerous sections out in Bushwick or Greenpoint but plenty of familiar stops and safer neighborhoods.

The writers, awash in the market and struggling to live by their skills, would follow the editors and map out a universe to scale ... but Ruthven speculated that the knowledge that they had drained their vision, grayed it for the sake of publication, had filled them first with disappointment and finally self-hatred: like Ruthven they had been caught early by the idea of science fiction — transcendence and complexity—and however far they had gone from there, they still felt at the base that this was a wondrous and expensive genre. Deliberately setting themselves against all for which the field had once stood could not have been easy for them. Rationalization would take the form of self-abuse: drink, divorce, obesity, sadism, in extreme cases penury, drugs or the outright cultivation of death. (Only H. Beam Piper had actually pulled the trigger on himself but that made him an honest man and a gun collector.) That was your science fiction writer, then, an ecclesiastic who had been first summoned from the high places and then dumped in the mud of Calvary to cast lots with the soldiers. All for a small advance. That had been some of Ruthven's thinking, but then he had been very depressed. He had done a lot of reading and thinking about the male mid-life crisis.

Sandra and he were barely dealing with one another; they lived within the form of marriage but not its substance (didn't everyone long married end that way?). His sexual panic, drinking, terror of death and sense of futility were more characteristic, perhaps, of the climacteric than of science fiction. The poor old field had taken a lot of blame over its lifetime (a lifetime, incidentally, exactly as long as Ruthven's: he had been born on April 12, 1926) for matters not of its own making, and once again was being blamed for pain it had not created. Maybe.

It wasn't science fiction alone which had put him in the ditch at late midlife, Ruthven thought, any more than science fiction had been responsible for Hiroshima, Sputnik, the collapse of Apollo or the rotten movies of the nineteen-fifties which had first enticed and then driven the public away. The field had been innocent witness to much of these and the target of some but it was unfair to blame the genre for what seemed (at least according to the books he read) an inevitability in middle class, middle aged, male America.

It was this ambivalence—the inability to fuse his more recondite perspective with the visceral, hateful feeling that science fiction had destroyed all of their lives — which stopped *The Lies of Science Fiction*. Ruthven does not kid himself even if the contracts for *The Sorcerer* had not come in and his career turned around, he probably would have walked away from the book. Its unsaleability was a problem, but he knew that he might have sold it somewhere, an amateur press, and he had enough cachet in the field to place sections here and there in the fan magazines. It wouldn't have been much but it would have been more per diem than what Sandra was making or he from the correspondence school.

But he had not wanted to go on. His commitment, if anything, had been to stop. Ruthven, from the modest perspective of almost four years, can now admit that he was afraid to continue. He could not bear to follow it through to the places it might have taken him. At the worst, it might have demonstrated that his life, that all of their lives in science fiction, had been as the title said: a lie … a lie which would lead to nothing but its replications by younger writers, who in turn would learn the truth. The book might have done more than that: it could have made his personal life impossible. Under no circumstance would he have been able to write that book and live with Sandra — but the drives on the Interstate had made it coldly evident that he had nowhere else to go. If he were not a middle-aged, married science fiction writer, then what was he?

Oh, it was a good thing that *The Sorcerer* had come through and that he had gotten back to fiction. The novels were rotten but that was no problem: he didn't want to be good anymore, he just wanted to survive. Now and then Ruthven still drives the Interstate in his new Impala; now and then he is still driven from sleep to stare at the foreign editions … but he no longer stares in anguish or drives in fury; everything seems to have bottomed out. Science fiction can still do many things to him but it no longer has the capacity to deliver exquisite pain, and for this he is grateful.

Eventually someone else, perhaps one of the younger writers, *will do The Lies of Science Fiction* or something similar, but of this in his heart is Henry Martin Ruthven convinced: he will never read it. He may be dead. If not he will stay clear. Science fiction now is only that means by which he is trying to hang on in the pointless universe and that which asks that he make anything more of it (what is there to make of it?) will have to check the next bar because Henry Martin Ruthven is finished. He knows the lies of science fiction, all right. But above all and just in time, he knows the truths of it too.

□ □ □ □

Ruthven attends the Cincinnati World Convention as guest of honor. At a party the first night in the aseptic and terrifying hotel he is surrounded by fans and committee, editors and colleagues, and it occurs to him that most of the people in these crowded rooms were not born when he sold his first story, "The Hawker," to *Worlds of If* on August 18, 1952. This realization fills him with terror: it is one thing to apprehend in isolation how long he has been around in this field and how far the field in its mad branching and expansion has gone from all of them who started in the fifties, but it is quite another to be confronted in terms that he cannot evade. Because his career has turned around in the decade, most of these people have a good knowledge of his work, he is guest of honor, he is hardly ignored, but still —

Here and there in the packed three-room suite he sees people he knows, editors and writers and fans with whom he has been at conventions for years, but he cannot break out of his curious sense of isolation, and his conversations are distracted. Gossip about the business, congratulations on having survived to be a guest of honor, that sort of thing. Ruthven would almost prefer to be alone in his room or drinking quietly at the bar but that is obviously impossible. How can a guest of honor be alone on the first night of his convention? It would be, among others things, a commentary on science fiction itself and no one, least of all he, wants to face it.

None of his family are here. Felicia is no surprise: she is starting her second year of law school in Virginia and could not possibly miss the important early classes; besides, they have had no relationship for years. Maybe never. Carole had said that she might be in from Oakland, would do what she could, but he has heard that kind of thing from Carole before and does not expect her. The second marriage is falling apart, he knows, Sandra will tell him that much, and Carole is hanging on desperately (he surmises) much as Ruthven himself hung on years ago when, however bad it might be, there was nothing else. He wishes that he could share this with Carole but of course it would be the finish of him. There are hundreds of sentences which said to the wrong people would end his marriage on the spot and that is another of them.

Sandra did want to be here but she is not. She has been feeling weak all year and now at last they have a diagnosis: she will have a hysterectomy soon. Knowing what being guest of honor meant to him Sandra had offered to go regardless, stay in the room if she could not socialize, but Ruthven had told her not to. He knew that she did not want to come, was afraid of the crowds and the hysteric pulse and was for the first time in her life truly afraid of dying. She is an innocent. She considers her own death only when she feels very ill.

Not so many years ago, being alone at a large convention, let alone as guest of honor, would have inflamed Ruthven. He would have manipulated his life desperately to get even a night away alone, a Labor Day weekend would have been redemption … but now he feels depressed. He can take no pleasure from the situation and how it occurred. He is afraid for Sandra and misses her a little too, wishes that his daughters, who have never understood him or his work, could have seen him just this once celebrated. But he is alone and he is beginning to feel that it is simply too late for adultery. He has had his opportunities now and then, made his luck, but well past fifty and into what he thinks of as leveling out, Ruthven has become resigned to feeling that what he should have done can be done no more — take the losses, the time is gone. There are women of all ages, appearance and potential here, many are alone, others in casual attachments, many—even more than he might imagine, he suspects—available. But he will probably sleep alone all the nights of this convention, either sleep alone or end up standing in the hotel bar past four with old friends drinking and remembering the fifties. The desperation and necessity are gone: Sandra is not much, he accepts this, but she has given him all of which she is capable, which makes her flaws in this marriage less serious than Ruthven's because he could have given more. His failure comes from the decision, consciously, to deny. Perhaps it was the science fiction that shut him down. He just does not know.

Ruthven stands in the center of the large welcoming party, sipping scotch and conversing. He feels detached from the situation and from his own condition; he feels that if he were to close his eyes other voices would overwhelm him … the voices of all the other conventions. Increasingly he finds that he has more to hear from — and more to say to—the dead than to the living. Now with his eyes closed, rocking, it is as if Mark Clifton, Edmond Hamilton, Kuttner and Kornbluth are standing by him glasses in hand, looking at one another in commiseration and silence. There is really no need for any of them to speak. For a while none of them do.

Finally, Ruthven says as he has before, "It hurts, doesn't it? It hurts." Kuttner nods, Kombluth raises a sardonic eyebrow. Mark Clifton shrugs. "It hurts," Clifton says, "oh it hurts all right, Henry. Look at the record." There seems nothing more to say. A woman in red who looks vaguely like Felicia touches his arm. Her eyes are solemn and intense. She has always wanted to meet him, she says; she loves his work. She tells Ruthven her name and that she is a high school English teacher in Boston.

"Thank you," he says, "I'm glad you like the books." Everybody nods. Hamilton smiles. "You might as well," Kombluth says with a shrug, "I can't anymore and there's really nothing else." Ruthven shrugs. He tells the woman that the next scotch is on him or more properly the committee. He walks her over to the bar. Her hand is in his. Quickly, oh so quickly, her hand is in his.

□ □ □ □

At eight-fifteen the next evening Ruthven delivers his guest-of-honor speech. There are about three thousand in the large auditorium; convention attendance is just over ten thousand but 30 percent is not bad. Most attendees of modern world conventions are not serious readers now; they are movie fans or television fans or looking for a good time. Ruthven has thought for months about this speech and has worked on it painfully.

Once he thought — this was, of course, years ago that if he were ever guest of honor at a major convention he would deliver a speech denunciatory of science fiction and what it did to its writers. Later, when he began to feel as implicated as anyone, the speech became less an attack than an elegy for the power and mystery that had been drained by bad writing and editing, debased by a juvenile audience. But after *The Lies of Science Fiction* had been put away and the edge of terror blunted, the very idea of the speech seemed childish. He was never going to be guest of honor and if he were, what right did he have to tell anyone anything? Science fiction was a private circumstance, individually perceived.

Nonetheless he had, when the time came to plan, considered the speech at length. What he decided to do, finally, was review his career in nostalgic terms, dropping in just enough humor to distract the audience from the thrust of his intention because after bringing his career up to date he wanted to share with them his conviction that it did not matter. Nothing mattered except that it had kept him around until the coincidence of The Sorcerer, and *The Sorcerer* meant nothing except that Ruthven would not worry about money until he was dead. "Can't you see the overwhelming futility of it?" he would ask. "The Lies of Science Fiction" seemed a good title except that it would be printed in the convention book and be taken as a slap at the committee and indeed the very field which was doing him honor. Better to memorialize his book through the speech itself. Anyway, the title would have alerted the audience to the bitterness of his conclusion. He wanted to spring it on them.

So he had called it "Me and the Cosmos and Science Fiction," harmless enough, and Ruthven delivers the first thirty-two minutes of his thirty-five minute address from the text and pretty much as he had imagined. Laughter is frequent; his anecdotes of Campbell, Gold and Roger Elwood are much appreciated. There is applause when he speaks of the small triumph of the science fiction writer the day Apollo landed. "We did that" he remembers telling a friend, "at three cents a word." The audience applauds. They probably understand. This much, anyway.

Then, to his astonishment and disgust, Ruthven comes off the text and loses control. He has never hated himself so. Just as he is about to lift his head and explain coldly that none of it matters his voice falters and breaks. It has happened in the terrible arguments with Sandra in the old days and in the dreams with Kornbluth, Hamilton, Kuttner and Clifton, but never before in public, and Ruthven delivers the last paragraphs of his speech in a voice and from a mood he has never before known:

"We tried," he says. "I want you to know that, that even the worst of us, the most debased hack, the one-shot writer, the fifty-book series, C the hundreds and thousands of us who ever wrote a line of this stuff for publication: we tried. We tried desperately to say something because we were the only ones who could, and however halting our language, tuneless the song, it was ours.

"We wanted to celebrate, don't you see? We wanted to celebrate the insistent, circumstantial fact of the spirit itself, that wherever and in whatever form the spirit could yet sing amidst the engines of the night, that the engines could extinguish our lives but never our light, and that in the spaces between we could still thread our colors of substantiation. In childhood nights we felt it, later we lost it, but retrieval was always the goal, to get back there, to make it work, to justify ourselves to ourselves, to give the light against the light. We tried and failed; in a billion words we failed and faded again, but throughout was our prayer and somewhere in its center lived something else, the mystery and power of what might have been flickering.

"In these spaces, in all the partitions, hear our song. Let it be known that while given breath we sang until it drew the very breath from us and extinguished our light forever."

And then, in hopeless and helpless fury, Ruthven pushes aside the microphone and cries.

Icons

———

MY **HEMINGWAY** keeps mumbling about the ultimate *nada*, Smith said "and the darkness and the light." It keeps trying to go upstairs to lock itself in the bathroom with my carbine. I have to shut off the power but one of these days I'm not going to be home when it happens.

Jones nodded glumly. "My Hemingway wants to go running with the bulls," he said, "calls it the ultimate quest and so on but what it really wants is to be gored. It keeps on looking out the window staring at the pavement and I have to pull it back inside.

I shrugged. There was no point in admitting that my Hemingway slipped off while I was at the slaughtering docks yesterday and put a hole in its Plexiglas head. I had the same warnings as Smith and Jones. No one to blame. "Not good." I said.

"It's always the same damned things." Jones said bitterly. "They send these things out glistening with their white beards and leery eyes and they're marvelously entertaining for a few weeks typing and drinking away and speaking of the clean and just and next thing you know they're off in corners whispering about telescopic sights. I say it's disgusting."

"Design defect." Smith said knowingly, "built in the machines. Planned obsolescence. Self-destruction. Good turnover. A need for replacements all the time. It's all planned."

"Well I won't take it anymore." Jones said, "You have take a position make a stand."

"That's the ticket." Smith said. "Draw the line. Fight for truth. Stand up to the bastards once and for all."

They looked at me expectantly. I have their trust. In a way I am a the ringleader by unspoken consensus.

"Agreed gentlemen," I said. "One must take a stand."

We left the Juicer and took the tramway to the central offices of Icons Inc. located in the packing district. As soon as we arrived we could see the dimensions of the problem. The offices were ringed by thousands of demonstrators chanting in an ugly way for justice. Barricades had been established and the police were restraining the crowd. Many had brought their defective or imploded Hemingways to wave above their heads. The problem as we had suspected was quite widespread.

"Who would have known?" Smith said reverently. "There is still some spirit left in us— and outrage.

"There are limits." Jones agreed. "They cannot sell us defective Icons indefinitely. We can only take this stuff for so long."

We established positions at the rear and joined in the chant. Smith's face flushed with accomplishment. Jones seemed timorous, he lacks physical courage — a quality that he had hoped his Hemingway might have given him, more the pity.

"New Hemingways," we shouted. "Hemingways that live, not Hemingways that die." Gunshots were heard as here and there in the crowd defective Hemingways found their masters' weapons and did away with themselves on the spot.

An employee of Icons In., came out on a balcony. Even from this distance we could see him shaking. They usually assign a minor functionary to address rioters. "Be reasonable" the junior shouted. "Disperse. You are breaking the law."

"Justice!" we shouted. The police with their weapons holstered stood looking in the opposite direction. After all many of them had Hemingways too. "Go home!" the junior said but he was pelted by debris. He recoiled under a hail of garbage.

"All right," he bellowed suddenly, "we'll make an adjustment."

"No adjustments!" we shouted, quite caught up in the moment. "Justice." We knew that we would prevail. We always do in these confrontations. After all Icons is dependent upon our goodwill. Remember the Monroe riots and their outcome.

"Very well." The junior said. "We accept return of all Hemingways. For full credit."

We cheered.

"And we will apply the full cost of each toward the purchase of a Kennedy. Only taxation differential will be due."

We cheered again. Everyone thinks of the Kennedy with anticipation. Rumors are that models had been in production for years but were being help back purposely to manipulate greater demand.

"A Kennedy for everyone!" The junior screamed. "Everyone, *all* of you will know that they will fight any battle share any cause in the struggle for freedom. Friend and foe alike will know that a new generation forged from a hard and bitter peace —"

But he could no longer be heard so great now were the cheers.

I can't wait for my Kennedy. He will put strength in my spine sparkle in my eyes purpose in each dreary day. It will be like the early days with Hemingway before the terrible design defect manifested itself.

Smith tears, however that the Kennedy will also prove detective. "You can't trust these corporaton." He points out. "They probably have an obsolescence factor in the Kennedy as well. But Icons is clever."

"What do you mean? I ask.

"I mean, this time when it breaks down they'll have it arranged so it looks like *our* fault." Smith says bitterly. "Wait and see."

Jones and I however, disgusted with Smith's pessimism have threatened to do him damage if he doesn't shut up. If you can't trust a Kennedy what then?

Something from the Seventies

BUT WHY me? Winogrand said, this was in the interrogation room, a gad-
get-strewn place which reminded him of the way his industrial-arts class-
room had looked in high school. Maybe a little more threatening because the
industrial-arts guy was not a spotted alien with what appeared to be a heavy-duty
space weapon of an advanced type. I don't remember anything about the seventies, Winogrand said. I slept through the whole decade. The sixties blew me out.
It wasn't the drugs, he added, trying a fetching, self-deprecating *moue*, just the
intensity of the time. The assassinations and the sex and all of that stuff. But really
most of it's a blur to me.

Strange, the interrogator said, that's what we hear from the rest of you that
we've checked out on this. But, really, we can't accept excuses here. We're trying
to do some kind of comprehensive history and we can't have a ten-year gap in the
Amurrican century. That's what you call it, right? The Amurrican century. That
guy, Booth, that was his name for it.

Luce, Winogrand said. Henry Luce, the guy from *Time*. It's not Amurrican,
it's American. Actually, United States. America refers to a bigger place. Where do
you want me to start? Winogrand said. He peered over to the shadowed corners
of the room in which there seemed to be torture devices, strange implements
of an alien sort which he was convinced could do terrible things to Amurrican
extremities. That was the trouble with alien invasion and interrogation, it seemed
like a joke in the abstract but when you got right to circumstances, they weren't so
funny at all. One morning a simple account executive for Universal Steel, the next
somewhere in the bowels of what he guessed was an alien spaceship, talking to
some multitentacled creature who wanted to obtain information on a dry, senseless

time, a decade during which, as he tried to look back upon it, Winogrand had not had four minutes of continuous pleasure. Strung end to end as moments of pleasure never were, he might have had two hours of fun through the internment of the hostages. How could this make him an expert on the period and why had the alien snatched him of all people and put him to this horrid condition? He looked at the implements in the shadows again and shuddered. It was remarkable how plans seemed to unravel, tiny plans hardly voiced even to the self, and then your life was atomized into the chemical stink of an alien interrogation room. Well, that was the decade for you. There was the malaise speech, Winogrand said, that was in the summer of 1979. Right after the second gas shortage, the first having been in 1973, and just before the hostages got snatched in Iran. Carter said that it was all our fault, that the country had a stalking malaise because of the sixties assassinations and all the cynicism. He said we needed a spiritual revival. It didn't go over too well. You understand, most of us had spent June and July trying to get a tankful of gas, they reran that November and December of 1973 energy scam right past us again. What we didn't need was some guy shouting at us that our lousy lives were all our fault. It cost him the election.

Not the hostages? the alien said. Somewhere, the greenly tentacled creature seemed to have picked up a little history on its own; perhaps this was not a true interrogation but one of those traps which sneaky aliens were likely to pull, Winogrand thought. The papers had been full of sidebar stories after the invasion, dealing with the sneakiness and duplicity of the aliens. They told lies about their planet of origin and loved to load up the fade line at craps in the casinos. Perhaps deception like entropy was interstellar. We thought it was the hostages swept up at the American embassy in Iran who couldn't be rescued which were responsible for the troubles of your president.

Don't think so, Winogrand said. Look, when you've spent all summer trying to get a tank of gas and fighting 20 percent inflation, you don't need to hear some guy in a sweater telling you that it's all your own fault. Of course, that's just my theory, Winogrand said. Nothing is sure with this stuff, you know. Stupid politics, though.

So how did this Carter get to be president in the first place? the alien said. If he was so stupid, how did he become president?

Boy, Winogrand thought hopelessly, these creatures are really out of it, either that or they were faking a consummate stupidity which was hard to believe. Of course it could merely be a display of alien cunning. Watergate, Winogrand said, the presidential resignation in August of 1974. Then Ford pardoned Nixon. You know who these people are? You know what I'm talking about? The alien made quivering motions of agreement. Well, then, the pardon sunk Ford, Winogrand said. That was in September of 1974, exactly one month after Nixon had resigned on August 9 which led people to think that there had been some kind of a strict deal in the first place. Ford never got over the pardon and then in the first debate in October of 1975 he said that a bunch of Communist satellite countries in Eastern Europe were really free. That pretty much did him in since he did not have a major reputation for intellect in the first place. His idea for beating inflation was to make a speech in the summer of 1975 saying that they were going to print up a whole bunch of buttons saying WIN for WHIP INFLATION NOW, you get it? and everyone should wear one. That was his idea of high policy. I don't even want to think of low policy. Do you understand any of this?

More or less, the alien said. Watergate we've learned a lot about already. The question is why when those tapes were found out in July of 1973 which showed your president had taped every word spoken in his offices for four and a half years didn't Nixon at once dispose of them? We have no such parallel in our own history. It seems inexplicable, really.

Oh, it's not so inexplicable, Winogrand said. He was thinking of the pieta at Kent State, that famous photo taken in May 1970 after the Ohio guardsman had shot five students during the campus protests, the girl screaming over the body of the dead boy. The girl it turned out had been a runaway and seeing the picture in the paper was the first the parents had heard of her in a year. She had come home but then there were more troubles with drugs and somehow nothing had worked out for the girl. Nothing had really worked out for any of them, even though Winogrand had put the drugs and the peace signs away, had transferred to a university nearer home and had resolved to get a degree in something not very controversial. It's not inexplicable, Winogrand said, because Nixon had himself on tape probably promising Ford that he would make him vice president in October of 1973 if Ford would agree to a pardon if Nixon got jammed too tight. Ford would have known about that and it would have gotten *him* nailed for obstruction of justice if it had come out. So it was useful, I guess, to have a lot of things on a lot of people. That was the decade, Winogrand said. Everybody had something on everybody else. The FBI broke into the office of the psychiatrist of the guy, Ellsberg, who had stolen the Pentagon Papers to try to get something on him. On Ellsberg. If they could have found some interesting crazy stuff back then in 1971, they figured that they could get even with him for releasing that stuff proving that everyone in the Pentagon had known that Vietnam was a lost cause from the beginning. You get it? Getting something on someone was just an instrument of national policy, then. If everybody was wired, then everybody was protected. The Houston Plan, Winogrand said. The Plumbers. Deep Throat in the bowels of the White House, meeting Woodward and Bernstein at the Lincoln Memorial with fancy, private stuff on Nixon. The whole ten years was tattletale, that's all. If the sixties were the caldron with the lid off, the seventies were in the oven. The Philharmonic had had enough of Leonard Bernstein and his fund-raising for the Black Panthers so it got this real tight French guy, Boulez, in 1968 and until he got fired in 1977 Boulez wired the whole program with pots and pans and electrolysis.

This is very interesting, the alien said. It seemed in the half-light of the interrogation room to be drained now of malice, to be in the same broken, vulnerable, querulous posture that Winogrand had imagined himself occupying for most of that miserable decade. Really a strange, a miserable time, perched on his knees, not always metaphorically, waiting for first one humiliation, then the next to softly descend upon him. Wallace lying in the shopping plaza in Maryland in May 1972, shot by Bremer, paralyzed for life two days before Wallace won the Michigan primary anyway and then had to quit the race due to incontinance, paralysis, pain and an understanding of the mortuary arts. A sinkhole, that was what the seventies had been, Wallace lying on his back on the stones in the same posture as RFK in that kitchen in Los Angeles and the wife, Cornelia, over him screaming. A missed assassination, though, just like the two attempts on Ford, Fromme and Sarah Jane Moore two months apart in 1975. A cold decade, the seventies, but not as efficient for all of its sleekness, as the sixties. In the sixties people got put down, the seventies though were just for hanging around and around, sometimes until the eighties or even nineties. Bush had been chairman of the Republican National Committee during Watergate at Nixon's behest. McGovern had backed Eagleton a thousand percent in August 1972 when word got out about the shock treatments Eagleton had incurred and then three days later had dumped him from the ticket in favor of Shriver. No, it was not an efficient decade.

It had more bark than bite, though, Winogrand said pointlessly. I mean, you could tough it out, you could get through it. Not like the sixties. The sixties could kind of sneak around and sneak around on you and then burn out your brainpan but even though the seventies started out tougher with that failed *Apollo 13* and the secret bombing of Cambodia, they wimped out in the malaise speech. A clear arc toward extinguishment, Winogrand said. Is there anything else you need to know? Can I go now? Are we finished?

It's hard to understand you people, the interrogator said. You take all of your history so *seriously* and yet nothing happens.

I told you that to start, Winogrand said earnestly. I told you that it was a cold gray time. You said you knew, that everyone else had told you that too. Well, that's what it was. It was a cold gray time. The Oakland A's won three world championships in a row from 1972 through 1974 and then Steinbrenner and Martin and Jackson had the New York Yankee follies in the late seventies so it wasn't *all* a matter of recycling at a lower level. A few things changed. Even I changed, Winogrand said. He could feel the slow throb of change moving within him although maybe it was inertia or a kind of moral paralysis. There was no difference amongst all of these—change, fear, moral paralysis, sexual desire, the whole grabbag of virtues and vices—and that was another thing the seventies had taught him.

Believe me, Winogrand said, you don't want this place. The more you learn about it the less you can see, am I right? I'd like to be excused now.

His interrogator bobbed its tentacles in a way which seemed very much like a shrug of assent although of course, anthropomorphizing was pretty much a constant in the alien-human spatial relations which Winogrand had noted. What we can't understand, the interrogator said, taking testimony on this century of yours in decade-long testimony, cutting up the century and trying to get the picture here … we simply can't understand how and why you cling to any concept of linearity. Don't you see how disjunctive this is? Yet you seek for connections even when there are no connections.

Well, Winogrand said, and felt the full weight of the century coursing thickly through like sludge, like knowledge, like some river of testimony, well, that's how we were framed. We're a linear race. We believe in chronology. We hold to chronology as if it had consequence. Everyone, Winogrand said, but Nixon that is. I don't think that he's linear which is why he is still around. The shadows poked from the corners of the room, seeming to dazzle in the sudden heat and Winogrand felt himself beginning to slide away, toward a lucid and grateful consciousness. Well thank you, he heard the alien say, thank you for your time and trouble. We'll have to consider all of this but I think there's a very good possibility that we want no part of this. None at all. Too much malaise, the alien said. You should talk, Winogrand said and then, sinking into the reconstructed unconsciousness from which time and again they had hauled him, he felt himself on the lip of a profound but casual insight which seemed to wait for him like a net just below that abyss of sleep. *Linear*, he thought, that was the fallacy, and then he was out and the aliens going about their continuing work which consisted of trying to find some way of reordering the century. The trouble was that like a Chinese puzzle, it didn't seem to fit no matter *how* you placed those tubes of the decade. Of their eventual decision, then, the account executive remained blameless.

Le Croix

DEPERSONALIZATION TAKES over. As usual, he does not quite feel himself, which is for the best; the man that he knows could hardly manage these embarrassing circumstances. Adaptability, that is the key; swim in the fast waters. There is no other way that he, let alone I could get through. "*Pardonnez tout ils*," he says, feeling himself twirling upon the crucifix in the absent Roman breezes, a sensation not unlike flight, "*mais ils ne comprendre pas que ils fait.*"

Oh my, is that awful. He wishes that he could do better than that. Still, there is no one around, strictly speaking, to criticize and besides, he is merely following impulse which is the purpose of the program. Do what you will. "*Ah pere*, this is a bitch," he mutters.

The thief on his left, an utterly untrustworthy type, murmurs foreign curses, not in French, to the other thief; and the man, losing patience with his companions who certainly look as culpable as all hell, stares below. Casting his glance far down he can see the onlookers, not so many as one would think, far less than the texts would indicate but certainly enough (fair is fair and simple Mark had made an effort to get it right) to cast lots over his vestments. They should be starting that stuff just about now.

Ah, well. This too shall pass. He considers the sky, noting with interest that the formation of clouds against the dazzling sunlight must yield the aspect of stigmata. For everything a natural, logical explanation. It is a rational world back here after all. If a little on the monolithic side.

"I wonder how long this is going to go on," he says to make conversation. "it does seem to be taking a bloody long time."

"Long time" the thief on the left says. "Until we die, that's how long, and not an instant sooner. It's easier," the thief says confidentially, "if you breathe in tight little gasps. Less pain. You're kind of grabbing for the air."

"Am I" Really?"

"Leave him alone," the other thief says. "Don't talk to him. Why give him advice?"

"Just trying to help a mate on the stations, that's all."

"Help Yourself," the second thief grumbles. "That's the only possibility. If I had looked out for myself I wouldn't be in this mess."

"I quite agree," I say. "That's exactly my condition, exactly."

"Ah, stuff it, mate," the thief says.

It is really impossible to deal with these people. The texts imbue them with sentimental focus but truly they are swine. I can grasp Pilate's dilemma. Thinking of Pilate leads into another channel, but before I can truly consider the man's problems a pain of particular dimension slashes through me and there I am, there I am, suspended from the great cross groaning, all the syllables of thought trapped within.

"Ah," I murmur, "ah," he murmurs, "*ah monsieurs, c'est le plus*," but it is not, to be sure, it is not *le plus* at all. Do not be too quick to judge.

It goes on, in fact, for an unsatisfactorily extended and quite spiritually laden period of time. The lot-casting goes quickly and there is little to divert on the hillside; one can only take so much of that silly woman weeping before it loses all emotional impact. It becomes a long and screaming difficulty, a passage broken only by the careless deaths of the thieves who surrender in babble and finally, not an instant too soon, the man's brain bursts … but there is time, crucifixion being what it is, for slow diminution beyond that. Lessening color; black and grey, if there is one thing to be said about this process, it is exceedingly generous. One will be spared nothing.

Of course I had pointed out that I did not want to be spared anything. "Give me Jesus," I had asked and cooperating in their patient way they had given me Jesus. There is neither irony nor restraint to the process, which is exactly the way that it should be.

Even to the insult of the thieves abusing me.

□   □   □   □

Alive to the tenor of the strange and difficult times, I found myself moved to consider the question of religious knowledge versus fanaticism. Hard choices have to be made even in pursuit of self-indulgence. Both were dangerous to the technocratic state of 2219, of course, but of the two religion was considered the more risky because fanaticism could well be turned to the advantage of the institutions. (Then there were the countervailing arguments of course that they were partners, but these I chose to dismiss.) Sexuality was another pursuit possibly inimical to the state but it held no interest for me; the general Privacy and Social Taboo acts of the previous century had been taken very seriously by my subdivision and I inherited neither genetic nor socially-derived interest in sex for its own non-procreative sake.

Religion interested me more than fanaticism for a permanent program, but fanaticism was not without its temptations. "Religion after all imposes a certain rigor," I was instructed. "There is some kind of a rationalizing force and also the need to assimilate text. Then too there is the reliance upon another, higher power. One cannot fulfill ultimately narcissistic tendencies. On the other hand, fanaticism dwells wholly within the poles of self. You can destroy the systems, find immortality, lead a crushing revolt, discover immortality within the crevices. It is not to be neglected; it is also purgative and satisfying and removes much of that indecision and social alienation of which you have complained. No fanatic is truly lonely or at least he has learned to cherish his loneliness."

"I think I'd rather have the religious program," I said after due consideration. "The lives of the prophets, the question of the validity of the text, the matters of the passion attract me."

"You will find," they pointed out, "that much of the religious experience is misrepresented. It leads only to an increasing doubt for many, and most of the major religious figures were severely maladjusted. You would be surprised at how many were psychotics whose madness was retrospectively falsified by others for their own purpose."

"Still," I said, "there are levels of feeling worth investigating."

"That, of course, is your decision," they said, relenting. They were nothing if not cooperative; under the promulgated and revised acts of 2202, severely liberalizing board procedures, there have been many improvements of this illusory sort. "If you wish to pursue religion we will do nothing to stop you. It is your inheritance and our decree. We can only warn you that there is apt to be disappointment."

"Disappointment!" I said, allowing some affect for the first time to bloom perilously forth. "I am not interested in disappointment. This is of no concern to me whatsoever; what I am interested in is the truth. After all, and was it not said that it is the truth which will make ye?"

"Never in this lifetime," they cut me off, sadly, sadly, and sent me on my way with a proper program, a schedule of appointments with the technicians, the necessary literature to explain the effects that all of this would have upon my personal landscape, inevitable changes, the rules of dysfunction, little instances of psychotic break but all of it to be contained within the larger pattern. By the time I exit from the transverse I have used up the literature, and so I dispose of it, tearing it into wide strips, throwing the strips into the empty, sparkling air above the passage lanes, watching them catch the little filters of light for the moment before they flutter soundlessly to the metallic, glittering earth of this most unspeakable time.

□　　□　　□　　□

I find myself at one point of the way the Grand Lubavitcher Rabbi of Bruck Linn administering counsel to all who would seek it.

The Lubavitcher Sect of the Judaic religion was, I understand, a twenty or twenty-first reconstitution of the older, stricter European forms which was composed of refugees who fled to Bruck Linn in the wake of one of the numerous purges of that time. Now defunct, the judaicists are, as I understand it, a sect characterized by a long history of ritual persecution from which they flourished, or at least the surviving remnants flourished, but then again the persecution might have been the most important part of the ritual. At this remove in time it is hard to tell. The hypnotics, as the literature and procedures have made utterly clear, work upon personal projections and do not claim historical accuracy, as historical accuracy exists for the historicists, if anyone, and often enough not for them. Times being what they are.

It is, in any case, interesting to be the Lubavitcher Rabbi in Bruck Linn, regardless of the origins of the sect or even of its historical reality; in frock coat and heavy beard I sit behind a desk in cramped quarters surrounded by murmuring advisors and render judgments one by one upon members of the congregation as they appear before me. Penalty for compelled intercourse during a period of uncleanliness is three months of abstention swiftly dealt out and despite explanations that the young bride had pleaded for comfort. The Book of Daniel, reinterpreed, does not signal the resumption of Holocaust within the coming month; the congregant is sent away relieved. Two rabbis appear with Talmudic dispute; one says that Zephaniah meant that all pagans and not all things were to be consumed utterly off the face of the Earth, but the other says that the edict of Zephaniah was literal and that one cannot subdivide "pagans" from "all things". I return to the text for clarification, remind them that Zephaniah no less than Second Isaiah or the sullen Ecclesiastes spoke in doubled perversities and advise that the literal interpretation would have made this conference unnecessary, therefore metaphor must apply. My advisors nod in approval at this and there are small claps of admiration. Bemused, the two rabbis leave. A woman asks for a ruling on mikvah for a pre-menstrual daughter who is nonetheless now fifteen years old, and I reserve decision. A conservative rabbi from Yawk comes to give humble request that I give a statement to the congregation for one of the minor festivals, and I decline pointing out that for the Lubavitcher fallen members of the judaicists are more reprehensible than those who have never arrived. Once again my advisors applaud. There is a momentary break in the consultations and I am left to pace the study alone while advisors and questioners withdraw to give me time for contemplation.

It is interesting to be the Lubavitcher, although somewhat puzzling. One of the elements of which I was not aware was that in addition to the grander passions, the greater personages, I would also find myself enacting a number of smaller roles, the interstices of the religious life, as it were, and exactly as it was pointed out to me there is a great deal of rigor. Emotion does not seem to be part of this rabbi's persona; the question of Talmudic interpretation seems to be quite far from the thrashings of Calvary. Still, the indoctrinative techniques have done their job; I am able to make my way through these roles even as the others, on the basis of encoded knowledge; and although the superficialities I babble seem meaningless to me, they seem to please those who surround. I adjust my cuffs with a feeling of grandeur; Bruck Linn may not be all of the glistening spaces of Rome but it is a not inconsiderable part of the history, and within it I seem to wield a great deal of power. "Rabbi," an advisor says opening the door, "I am temerarious to interrupt your musings, but we have reached a crisis and your intervention is requested at this time."

"What crisis?" I say. "You know I must be allowed to meditate."

"Yes," he says. "Yes, we respect your meditations. It is wrong to impose. I should not," and some edge of agony within his voice, some bleating aspect of his face touches me even as he is about to withdraw. I come from behind the desk saying, "What then, what?" and he says, "Rabbi, it was wrong to bother you, we should protect, we will respect," and now I am really concerned, from large hat to pointed shoe he is trembling and I push past him into the dense and smoky air of the vestibule where congregants, advisors, women and children are gathered. As they see me their faces one by one register intent and then they are pleading, their voices inchoate but massed. Save us, Rabbi, they are saying, save us, and I do not know what is going on here, an awkward position for a Talmudic judge to occupy but I simply do not know; I push my way through the clinging throng pushing them aside, Oh my God, Rabbi, they are saying, oh my God, and I go through the outer doors, look down the street and see the massed armaments, see the troops eight abreast moving in great columns toward the building, behind them the great engines of destruction, and in the sky, noise, the holocaust, Rabbi, someone says, the holocaust has come, they will kill us, and I feel disbelief. How can this be happening. There was no purge in Bruck Linn to the best of my recollection; there have never been any great purges on this part of the continent. Nevertheless here they are and behind me I can hear the children screaming. It is all that I can do to spread my arms and, toward them, toward the massed congregants and advisors behind, cry, "Stay calm, this is not happening; it is an aspect of the imagination, some misdirection of the machinery." Surely it must be that, some flaws in the fabric of my perceptions being fed through the machines and creating history out of context, and yet the thunder and smell of the armies is great in the air and I realize that they are heading directly toward this place, that they have from the beginning, and that there is nothing I can do to stop them.

"Be calm, be calm," I cry, "you are imagining this, indeed you are all imagining," but the words do not help, and as I look at the people, as they look at me, as the sounds of Holocaust overwhelm, I seem to fall through the situation leaving them to a worse fate or perhaps it is a better, but it is only I who have exited, leaving the rest, these fragments of my imagination, to shore themselves against their ruins, and not a moment too soon, too soon.

□   □   □   □

Otherwise, life such as it is proceeds as always. I spend a portion of the time on the hypnotics and in the machinery, but there are commitments otherwise to eat, to sleep, to participate in the minimal but always bizarre social activities of the complex; even, on occasion to copulate, which I accomplish in methodical fashion. The construction, I have been reminded, is only a portion of my life; responsibilities do not cease on its account. I maintain my cubicle, convey the usual depositions from level to level, busy myself in the perpetuation of microcosm. Only at odd times do I find myself thinking of the nature of the hypnotic experiences I have had, and then I try to push these recollections away. They are extremely painful and this subtext, as it were, is difficult to integrate into the outer span of my life. In due course I am assured that the fusion will be made, but in the meantime there is no way to hasten it. "You have changed, Harold," Edna says to me. Edna is my current companion. She is not named Edna, nor I Harold, but these are the names that they have assigned for our contemporary interaction, and Harold is as good as any; it is a name by which I would as soon be known. Harold in Galilee. And I have spoken his name and it is Harold. She leans toward me confidentially. "You are not the same person that you were."

"That is a common illusion provided by the treatments," I say. "I am exactly the same person. Nothing is any different than it was."

"Yes it is," she murmurs. "You may not realize how withdrawn and distracted you have become." She is a rather pretty woman and there are times, during our more or less mechanical transactions, when I have felt real surges of feeling for her, but they have only been incidental to the main purpose. In truth I can have no feeling for anyone but myself; I was told this a long time ago. She puts a hand on me intensely. "What are they doing to you?"

"Nothing," I say quite truthfully. "They are merely providing a means. Everything that is done I am doing myself; this is the principle of the treatment."

"You are deluded," she says and loops an arm around me, drags me into stinging but pleasurable embrace. Forehead to forehead we lay nestled amidst the bedclothes; I feel the tentative touch of her fingers. "Now," she says, moving her hand against me. "Do it now."

I push against her embrace. "No. It is impossible."

"Why?"

"During the treatments?"

"Nonsense," she says, "you are avoiding me. You are avoiding yourself. The treatments are anaesthetic, don't you see that" They are forcing you to avoid the terms of your life and you cannot do that." Her grasp is more insistent, at the beginning of pain. "Come on," she says. Insistent woman. Against myself, I feel a slow gathering.

"No," I mutter against her cheekbone, "it is impossible. I will not do it now."

"Fool."

"The chemicals. I am awash in chemicals; I remain in a sustaining dose all the time. I would upset all of the delicate balances."

"You understand nothing," she says, but in an inversion of mood turns from me anyway, scurrying to a far point. "Have it as you will. Do you want me to leave?"

"Of course not."

"Of course not. You are so accommodating. Do you want me to entertain you then?"

"Whatever you will."

"You have changed utterly. You are not the same. These treatments have rendered you cataleptic. I had hopes for you, Harold, I want you to know that. I thought that there were elements of genuine perception, real thought. How was I to know that all of the time you merely wanted to escape into your fantasies?"

"What did you want me to do?" I say casually. "Overthrow the mentors?"

She shrugs. "Why not?" she says. "It would be something to keep us occupied."

"I'd rather overthrow myself."

"You know, Harold," she says and there is a clear, steady light of implication in her eye, "it is not impossible for me to like you; we could really come to understand one another, work together to deal with this crazy situation, but there is this one overwhelming problem, and do you know what that is?"

"Yes I do," I say wearily because this has happened before. "I surely do."

"Don't deprive me of the satisfaction," she says. "Harold, you are a fool."

"Well," I say shrugging, "in these perilous and difficult times, this madly technocratic age of 2219, when we have so become merely the machinery of our institutions, where any search for individuality must be accomplished by moving within rather than without, taking all of this into consideration and what with one thing being like every other thing in this increasingly homogenous world, tell me, aren't we all?"

"Not like you," she says. "Harold, even in these perilous and difficult times, not like you at all."

☐ ☐ ☐ ☐

On the great and empty desert he takes himself to see the form of Satan, manifest in the guise of an itinerant, wandering amidst the sands. Moving with an odd, off-center gait, rolling on limping leg, Satan seems eager for the encounter, and he is ready for it too, ready at last to wrestle the old, damned angel and be done with it, but Satan is taking his time the cunning of the creature and seems even reluctant to make the encounter. Perhaps he is merely being taunted. Once again he thinks of the odd discrepancy of persona; he is unable in this particular role to work within the first person but is instead a detached observer seeing all of it at a near and yet far remove, imprisoned within the perception, yet not able to effect it. An interesting phenomenon, perhaps he has some fear that to become the persona would be blasphemous. He must discuss this with the technicians sometime. Then again, maybe not. Maybe he will not discuss it with the technicians; it is none of their damned business, any of it, and besides, he has all that he can do to concentrate upon Satan, who in garb of bright hues and dull now comes upon him. "Are you prepared?" Satan says to him. "Are you prepared for the undertaking?"

He looks down at his sandals embedded in the dense and settled sands. "I am ready for the encounter," He says.

"Do you know the consequences?" Satan says. He has a curiously ingratiating voice, a warm and personal manner, an offhand ease which immediately grants a feeling of confidence, but then again this was to be expected. What belies the manner, however, is the face, the riven and broken features, the darting aspect of the eyes, the small crevices in which torment and desert sweat seem to lurk and which compel attention beyond the body which has been broken by the perpetration of many seeming injustices. Satan extends his arm. "Very well, then," Satan says, "let us wrestle."

"*Non-disputandum,*" he says. "I understood that first we were to talk and only after that to struggle."

"Latin is no protection here," Satan says firmly. "All tongues pay homage to me."

"*Mais non,*" he says in his abominable French, "*voulez-vous je me porte bien.*"

"Nor does humor exist in these dark spaces," Satan says. "From walking up and down upon the earth and to and fro I have learned the emptiness of present laughter. Come," he says, leaning forward, his arm extended, "let us wrestle now."

He reaches for that gnarled limb, then brings his hands back. The sun is pitiless overhead but like a painting; he does not feel the heat. His only physical sensation is of the dry and terrible odor seeping from his antagonist. "No," he says. "*Mais non, mon frere.* Not until we have had the opportunity to speak."

"There is nothing to speak about. There are no sophistries in this emptiness, merely contention."

Do not argue with Satan. He had been warned of this, had known it as his journey toward the darkness had begun, that there was no way in which the ancient and terrible enemy could be engaged with dialectic and yet, *non disputandum*, he has faded again. Not to do it. Not to try argument; it is time to wrestle and it might as well be done. He seizes the wrist and slowly he and the devil lock.

Coming to grips with that old antagonist it is to the man as if he has found not an enemy but only some long-removed aspect of himself, as if indeed, just as in sex or dreams, he is in the act of completing himself with this engagement. The stolidity of the form, the interlocking of limbs, gives him not a sense of horror, as he might have imagined, but rather comfort. It must have been this way. Their hands fit smoothly together. "Do you see?" Satan says winking and coming to close quarters. "You know that it must always have been meant this way. Touch me, my friend, touch me and find grace," and slowly, evenly, Satan begins to drag him forward.

He understands, he understands what is happening to him: Satan in another of his guises would seduce him with warmth when it is really a mask for evil. He should be fighting against the ancient and terrible enemy with renewed zeal for recognizing this, but it is hard, it is hard to do so when Satan is looking at him with such compassion, when the mesh of their bodies is so perfect. Never has he felt anyone has understood him this well; his secret and most terrible agonies seem to flutter, one by one, birdlike, across the features of the antagonist, and he could if he would sob out all of his agonies knowing that Satan could understand. Who ever would as well? It must have been the same for him. I do not believe, he wants to cry to the devil; I believe none of it; I am taken by strange, shrieking visions and messages in the night; I feel that I must take upon the host of Heaven, and yet these dreams which leave me empty and sick are, I know, madness. I hear the voice of God speaking unto me saying I am the Father, I am the incompleteness which you will fill and know that this must be madness, and yet I cannot deny that voice, can deny no aspect of it, which is what set me here upon the desert, but I am filled with fear, filled with loathing and trembling " he wants to cry all of this out to Satan, but he will not, he will not, and slowly he finds himself being drawn to the ground.

"Comfort," Satan says in the most confiding and compassionate of whispers, covering him now with his gnarled body so that the sun itself is obscured, all landscape dwindled to the small perception of shifting colors, "comfort: I understand, I am your dearest and closest friend. Who can ever understand you as I? Who would possibly know your anguish? Easy, be easeful," Satan says, and he begins to feel the pressure come across his chest. "So easy," Satan murmurs, "it will be so easy, for only I understand; we can dwell together," and breath begins to desert him. The devil is draining his respiration.

Understanding that, he understands much else: the nature of the engagement, the quality of deception, exactly what has been done to him. Just as Satan was the most beautiful and best loved of all the angels, so in turn he would be Satan's bride in the act of death. It is the kiss that will convey the darkness, and seeing this, he has a flickering moment of transcendence: he thinks he knows now how he might be able to deal with this. Knowing the devil's meaning will enable him to contest, and yet it would be so easy, "inevitable" is the word necessary to yield to his antagonist and let it be done, let the old, cold, bold intruder have his will, thy will be done, and Satan's too, and the yielding is so close to him now he can feel himself leaning against the network of his being, the empty space where desire might have rested, in the interstices the lunge toward annihilation ""*mais non*," he says, "*mais non, je renounce, I will not do it!*" and forces himself against the figure, understanding finally the nature of this contest, what it must accomplish, in what mood it must be done and wearily, wearily, carrying all of consequence upon him he begins the first and final of all his contests with the devil.

□   □   □   □

It is a madly technocratic age, a madly technocratic age, and yet it is not cruel; the devices of our existence, we have been assured, exist only in order to perpetrate our being. Take away the technology and the planet would kill us; take away the institutions and the technology would collapse. There is no way in which we can continue to be supported without the technology and the institutions, and furthermore they are essentially benign. They are essentially benign. This is not rationalization or an attempt to conceal from myself and others the dreadful aspects of our mortality, the engines of our condition grinding us slowly away … no, this is a fixed and rational judgment which comes from a true assessment of this life.

It is true that a hundred years ago, in the decades of the great slaughters and even beyond, the institutions were characterized by vengeance, pusillanimity, murder and fear, but no more. In 2160 the oligarchy was finally toppled, the reordering began, and by 2189, the very year in which I was born, the slaughter was already glimpsed within a historical context. I was nurtured by a reasonable state in a reasonable fashion; if I needed love, I found it; sustenance was there in more forms than the purely physical. I grew within the bounds of the state; indeed, I matured to a full and reasonable compassion. Aware of the limits which were imposed, I did not resent them nor find them stifling.

There was space; there has been space for a long time now. Standing on the high parapet of the dormer, looking out on Intervalley Six and the web of connecting arteries beneath the veil of dust, I can see the small lights of the many friendly cities nodding and winking in the darkness, the penetrating cast of light creating small spokes of fire moving upward in the night. Toward the west the great thrust of South Harvest rears its bulk and spires, lending geometry to a landscape which would otherwise be endless, and I find reassurance in that presence just as I find reassurance in the act of being on the parapet itself. There was a time, and it was not so terribly long ago, that they would not have allowed residents to stand out on the parapet alone; the threat of suicide was constant, but in the last years the statistics have become increasingly favorable, and it is now within the means of all of us if only we will to come out in the night for some air.

Edna is beside me. For once we are not talking; our relationship has become almost endlessly convoluted now, filled with despair, rationalization and dialogue, but in simple awe of the vision she too has stopped talking and it is comfortable, almost companionable standing with her thus, our hands touching lightly, smelling the strange little breezes of our technology. A long time ago people went out in pairs to places like this and had a kind of emotional connection by the solitude and the vision, but now emotions are resolved for more sensible arenas such as the hypnotics. Nevertheless, it is pleasant to stand with her thus. It would almost be possible for me at this moment to conceive some genuine attachment to her, except that I know better; it is not the union but its absence which tantalizes me at this moment, the knowledge that there is no connection which will ever mean as much to us as this landscape. The sensation is unbearably poignant although it does not match in poignance other moments I have had under the hypnotics. At length she turns toward me, her touch more tentative in the uneven light and says, "It hurts me too. It hurts all of us."

"I wasn't really thinking about pain."

"Nevertheless," she says. "Nevertheless. Pain is the constant for all of us. Some can bear it and others cannot. Some can face this on their own terms and others need artificial means of sustention. There is nothing to be done about this."

"I don't need artificial means," I say. "I have elected."

"Surely," she says. "Surely."

And they are not artificial, I want to add; the experiences under the hypnotics are as real, as personally viable, as much the blocks of personality formulation as anything which this confused and dim woman can offer, as anything which has passed between us. But that would only lead to another of our arguments and I feel empty of that need now. Deep below we can hear the uneven cries of the simulacrum animals let out at last for the nighttime zoo, the intermingled roars of tigers.

"Has it made any difference?" she says. "Any of it?"

"Any of what? I don't understand."

"The treatments. Your treatments."

Tantalizingly, I find myself on the verge of a comment which will anneal everything, but it slips away from me as if so often the case, and I say, "Of course they have made a difference."

"What have you gained?"

"*Pardonne? Pardonnez moi?*"

"Don't be obscure on me," she says. "That will get you nowhere. Tell me the truth."

I shrug. My habit of lapsing into weak French under stress is an old disability; nonetheless I find it difficult to handle. Most have been more understanding than Edna. "I don't know," I say. "I think so."

"I know. It's done nothing at all."

"Let's go inside now," I say. "It's beginning to chill here."

"You are exactly the same as you were. Only more withdrawn, more stupid. These treatments are supposed to heal?"

"No. Merely broaden. Healing comes from within."

"Broaden! You understand less than ever."

I put a hand to my face, feel the little webbing where years from now deep lines will be. "Let's go inside," I say again. "There's nothing more

"Why don't you face the truth" These treatments are not meant to help you; they are meant to make you more stupid so that you won't cause any trouble."

I move away from her. "It doesn't matter," I say. "None of it matters. It is of no substance whatsoever. Why do you care for it to be otherwise?"

There is nothing for her to do but to follow me into the funnel. She would argue in position but my withdrawal has offered the most devastating answer of all: I simply do not care. The attitude is not simulated: on the most basic level I refuse to interact.

"You are a fool," she says, crowding against me for the plunge. "You do not understand what they are doing to you. You" simply don't care."

"Quite right," I say. "Quite right. Absolutely. Not at all. That is the point now, isn't it?"

The light ceases and we plunge.

□ □ □ □

I am in an ashram surrounded by incense and the dull outlines of those who must be my followers. Clumped in the darkness they listen to me chant. It is a mantra which I appear to be singing in a high, cracked chant; it resembles the chanting of the Lubavitchers of Bruck Linn, although far more regularized in the vocal line, and limited in sound. *Om* or *ay* or *eeh*, the sounds are interchangeable and I am quite willing to accept the flow of it, not rationalize, not attempt to control those sounds but rather to let them issue according to my mood. It is peaceful and I am deeply locked within myself; the soft breathing of my followers lending resonance to the syllables which indeed seem to assume a more profound meaning, but at a certain point there is a commotion and the sound of doors crashing and then in the strophes of light I can see that the room has been invaded by what appear to be numerous members of the opposition. They are wearing their dull attack uniforms, even this if nothing else is perceptible in the light and from the glint of weaponry I can see that this is very serious. They move with an awful tread into the room, half a dozen of them, and then the portable incandescence is turned on and we are pinned there in frieze.

I know that it is going to be very bad; the acts of 2013 specifically proscribed exactly what is going on here and yet five years later the pogroms have dwindled to harassment, random isolated incursions. I did not think that in this abandoned church in the burned-out core of the devastated city they would ever move upon me, and yet it seems now that my luck has suddenly, convulsively run out, as I always knew that it would. Surely in some corner of the heart I must have known this; the *om* must have always been informed by doom; and yet it is one thing to consider demolition in a corner of the heart and another, quite another, to live it. *Ahbdul,* one of them says pointing, his finger enormous, dazzling, and as I lift my eyes to it I feel myself subsiding in the wickers of light, *Ahbdul, you are in violation of the codes and you have brought woe to all.*

In a moment, in one moment, they will plunge toward me. I know how it goes then, what will happen; they will strike at me with their weapons and bring me to a most painful position; they will obliterate consciousness and cause blood-stains; not of the least importance they will humiliate me before my small congregation, which has already witnessed enough humiliation, thank you very much, otherwise why would they have gathered here? And yet I can tolerate all of that, I suppose. I have dreamed worse, not to say suffered many privations and indignities before opening this small, illegal subunit. In fact, none of this concerns me; what does, I must admit, is the fear that I will show weakness before my congregation. To be humiliated is one thing, but to show fear, beg for mercy, is quite another; I would hardly be able to deal with it. A religious man must put up a stiff front. A religious man whose cult is based upon the regular, monotonic articulation of ancient chants to seek for inner serenity can hardly be seen quivering and shrieking in front of those who have come for tranquility. if tranquility is all that I have to offer, I cannot give them pain. Thinking this, I resolve to be brave and draw myself to full stature or what there is left of it after all these years of controlled diet and deliberate physical mutation. "You will not prevail," I say. "You cannot prevail against the force of the *om*," and with a signal I indicate to my congregation that I wish to resume the chant, humiliate them by my own transcendence, but they do not attend. Indeed they do not attend at all, so eager do so many of them appear to search out any means of exit open to them. A small alley has been left open by the massed opposition leading to one of the doors, and in their unseemly haste to clear the hall they ignore me. Religious disposition, it would seem, is a function of boredom: give people something really necessary to face in their lives and religion can be ignored, all except for the fanatics who consider religion itself important, of course; but they are disaster-ridden. Like flies these little insights buzz about, gnawing and striking small pieces of psychic flesh while the hall is emptied, the opposition standing there looking at me bleakly, but I find as usual that this insight does me no good whatsoever. It can, indeed, be said merely to magnify my sense of helplessness. "Gentlemen," I say, raising a hand, "this is a futile business. join me in a chant." I kneel, my forehead near the floor, and begin to mumble, hoping that the intensity of this commitment will strike shame within them, convince them that they are dealing with someone so dangerously self-absorbed that all of their attacks would be futile, but even as I commence the syllables I am pulled to my feet by a man in a uniform which I do not recognize, obviously a latecomer to the room. He stares at me from a puffy, heart-shaped face and then raises his hand, strikes me skillfully across first one check and then the other. The collision of flesh is enormous; I feel as if I am spattering within. "Fool," he says, "why have you done this?"

"Why do you care" Why are you asking?" He hits me again. No progression of the sacred blocks of personality; the levels of eminent reason have prepared me for this kind of pain. I realize that I am crying. "Give me a response," he says. "Don't withdraw, don't protest, don't argue; it will lead only to more blows and eventually the same results. Simply answer questions and it will go much easier for both of us. Knowing all of the penalties, knowing of the responsibilities for your acts and what would happen to you if you were discovered, why did you nonetheless persist? Didn't you understand? Didn't you know what danger you brought not only upon yourself but the fools you seduced? Now they too will have to pay."

He is choleric with rage, this man; his face seems to have inflated with blood and reason as he stands there and I begin to comprehend that he is suffering from more than situational stress. Looking at him I want to accentuate that sudden feeling of bonding, but there is every emotion but sympathy in that ruined face and suddenly he hits me again convulsively; this the most painful blow yet because it was not expected. I fall before him and begin to weep. It is not proper context for a martyr, but I never wanted it to be this way; I never imagined that there would be such blood in sacrifice. He puts one strong hand under an arm, drags me grunting to my feet, positions me in front of him as if I were a statue.

"Do you know what we're going to have to do now?" he says. "We're going to have to make an example of you, that's all, we're going to have to kill you. Why did you put us into this position?"

"I am not able to believe that you will do that," I say. I am struggling for tranquility. "You wouldn't kill me, not here in the temple?"

"This is not a temple. It is a dirty cluttered room and you are an old fool who imagines it to be a church."

"*Om*," I say. The word comes; I did not calculate. "*Om. Eeeh. Ay.*"

"You would fight the state regardless. If the state believed in *om* you would cry for freedom of choice. If the state were stateless you would wish to form institutions within. There is no hope for you people, none at all; you would be aberrants in any culture at any time and you cannot understand this. You want to be isolated, persecuted, to die. It has nothing to do with religion."

"*Eeh. Ay. Oooh. Alih. Om.*"

"Enough," he says, "enough of this," and signals to the others at the rear; they come forward slowly, reluctantly, but with gathering speed at the approach, perhaps catching a whiff of death which comes from the syllables. "You wish a public death, you wish a martyrdom; then you will have it. Reports will be issued to all of the provinces. Icons will be constructed. Dispatches will even glorify. You will achieve everything that you were unable in life. But this will do you no good whatsoever."

The fear is tightly controlled now. Truly, the syllables work. I would not have granted them such efficacy and yet what I have advised my congregants all of this time turns out to be true. They paste over the sickness with the sweet contaminations of courage, grant purchase upon terror, make it possible for the most ignorant and cowardly of men, which must be myself, to face annihilation with constant grace. "*Om*," I say. *Eeh.* If it were to be done, then it must be done quickly."

"Ali," he says, "it is impossible. Nothing will be gained from this and yet you still will not face the truth. It would be so much easier if at least you would give up your bankrupt purchase, if you would understand that you are dying for no reason whatsoever and that it could have been no other way; it would make matters so much easier?"

"Ah," I say. "Oh."

"Ali, shit," the man with the heart-shaped face says and gives a signal to one of the supporters, who closes upon me, a small man in uniform with a highly calibered weapon and puts its cold surfaces against my temple. His hand shakes, imperceptibly to the vision, but I can feel that quiver against the ridged veins. It is remarkable how I have gained in courage and detachment; just a few moments ago it would have seemed impossible. Yet here I am, apparently, prepared to face what I feared the most with implacable ardor. "Now," the man says. "Do it now." There is a pause. *Om* resonates through me; it will be that with which I will die, carrying me directly to the outermost curved part of the universe. I close my eyes, waiting for transport, but it does not come, and after a while I understand that it will not. Therefore I open my eyes, reasonable passage seeming to have been denied me. The positions are the same except that the leader has moved away some paces and the man carrying the gun has closed his eyes.

"Shoot him, you fool," the leader says. "Why haven't you shot him?"

"I am having difficulty."

"Kill him, you bastard."

There is another long pause. I flutter my eyes. *Om* has receded. "I can't," the man with the gun says at last. "I can't put him down, just like that. This isn't what I was prepared to do. You didn't say that it would be this way. You promised."

"Ah, shit," the heart-shaped man says again and comes toward us, breaks the connection with a swipe of his hand, knocking the gun arm down and the supporter goes scuttling away squealing. The leader looks at me with hatred, red-tinted veins alight. "You think you've proven something," he says. "Well, you've proven absolutely nothing. Weakness is weakness. I will have to do it myself."

I shrug. It is all that I can do to maintain my demeanor considering the exigencies but I have done it. Will; everything is will. "*Om*", I murmur.

"*Om*," he says, "*om* yourself," and goes to the supporter; the supporter hands him the gun silently; the leader takes it in his left hand, flexes fingers, then puts it against my temple."

"All right," he says, "it could have been easier but instead it will be more complex. That does not matter, all that matters is consummation."

"Consummate," I say. "*Om*."

"I don't want to do this," he says with the most immense kindness. "I hope you understand. It's nothing personal; I have little against you; it's just a matter of assignment, of social roles." Unlike the others he seems to need to prepare himself for assassination through a massive act of disconnection. "Nothing personal," he says mildly, "I really don't want to."

I shrug. "I don't wait to die, particularly," I say. "Still, I seem able to face it." And this is the absolute truth. Calm percolates from the center of the corpus to the very brain stem; I seem awash in dispassion. Perhaps it is the knowledge that this is all a figment, that it is a dream and I will not die but awake again only to sterile enclosure and the busy hands of technicians. "Do it," I say. "Do it." Is this the secret of all the martyrs? That at the end, past flesh and panic, they knew when they would awaken and to what? Probably. On the other hand, maybe not. Like everything else it is difficult and complex. Still, it can be met with a reasonable amount of dignity, which is all that we can ask.

"Indeed," he says sadly, "indeed," and fires the gun into my temple killing me instantly and precipitating in one jagged bolt the great religious riots and revivals of the early twenties. And not one moment too soon, Allah and the rest of them be praised.

□ □ □ □

Systematically I face examination in the cold room. It is a necessary part of the procedure. "The only hint of depersonalization other than at the end of the last segment," I say calmly, "has been during the Jesus episodes. I seem unable to occupy it within the first person but feel a profound disassociative reaction in which I am witnessing him as if from the outside, without controlling the actions."

The counselor nods. "Highly charged emotional material obviously," he says. "Disassociative reaction is common in such cases. At some point in your life you must have had a Jesus fixation."

"Not so," I say. "in fact I did not know who he was until I was introduced through the texts."

"Then it must have hit some responsive chord. I wouldn't be unduly concerned about this. As you integrate into the persona it will fall away and you will begin to actively participate."

"I feel no emotional reaction to the material at all. I mean, no more than to any of the others. It's inexplicable to me."

"I tell you," the counselor says with a touch of irritation, "that is of no concern. The process is self-reinforcing. What we are concerned about is your overall reactions, the gross medical signs, the question of organic balances. The psychic reactions will take care of themselves."

I look past him at the walls of the room which contain schematic portraits of the intervalley network. Interspersed are various documents certifying the authenticity of his observer's role. The absence of anything more abstract disturbs me; previously it never occurred to me how deprived our institutions seem to be of artistic effect, but now it does; the hypnotics must be working. There is a clear hunger within me for something more than a schematic response to our condition. "Are you listening to me?" he says. "Did you hear my question."

"I heard it."

"I am going to administer a gross verbal reaction test now, if you will pay attention."

"I assure you that is not necessary," I say. "I am in excellent contact."

"That is a judgment which we will make."

"Must you?"

"I'm afraid so," the counselor says. "We wish to guard against exactly that which you manifest, which strikes me as a rather hostile, detached response. We do not encourage this kind of side-effect, you see; we consider it a negative aspect of the treatment."

"I'm sorry to hear that."

"It is often necessary to terminate treatment in the face of such reactions, so I would take this very seriously."

"Why do you do this to us?" I say. I look at his bland, pleasant face, masked by the institutional sheen but nonetheless concealing, I am convinced, as passionate and confused a person as I might be, perhaps a little more passionate and confused since he has not had, after all, the benefit of the treatments. "Why can we simply not go through this on our own terms, take what we can take, miss the rest of it?

Why must we be monitored?"

"The procedures "

"Don't tell me of procedures," I say, leaning forward with a sudden intensity, aware that I am twitching at the joints and extremities in a new fashion, emotionally moved as rarely has been the case. Definitely the treatments are affecting me.

"The real reason is that you're afraid that unless we're controlled we might really be changed, that we might begin to react in fashions that you couldn't predict, that we wouldn't be studying religion and fanaticism any more but would actually become religious fanatics and what would you do with us then?"

"Confine you," my confessor says flatly, "for your own protection. Which is exactly what we want to avoid by the process of what you call monitoring, which is merely certifying that you are in condition to continue the treatments without damage to yourself."

"Or to the state."

"Of course to the state. I work for it, you live within it; why should we not have the interests of the state at heart? The state need not be perceived as the enemy by you people, you know."

"I never perceived?"

"You can't make the state the repository of all your difficulties, the rationalizing force for your inadequacies. The state is a positive force in all of your lives and you have more personal freedom than any citizenry at any time in the history of the world."

"I never said that it wasn't."

"In fact," the counselor says, rising, his face suffused now with what might be passion but then on the other hand might only be the consequence of improper diet, highly spiced intake, the slow closure of arteries, "we can get damned sick of you people and your attitudes. I'm no less human because I have a bureaucratic job, I want you to know; I have the same problems that you do. The only difference is that I'm trying to apply myself toward constructive purposes, whereas all you want to do is to tear things down." He wipes a hand across his streaming features, shrugs, sits again. "Sorry to overreact," he says. "It's just that a good deal of frustration builds up and it has to be expressed. This isn't easy for any of us, you know. We're not functionaries; we're people just as you are."

There seems nothing with which I can disagree. I consider certain religious virtues which would have to do with the absorption of provocation without malice and remain quietly in my chair, thinking of this and that and many other things having to do with the monitoring conducted by these institutions and what it might suggest about the nature of the interrelation, but thought more and more is repulsive to me; what I concentrate upon, what seems to matter is feeling, and it is feeling which I will cultivate. "Some questions," the counselor says in a more amiable tone. "Just a series of questions which I would like you to answer as briefly and straightforwardly as possible."

"Certainly," I say, echoing his calm. "*Tres bonne, merci. Maintenant et pourquoi.*"

"*Pourquoi?*" he says with a glint in his eye and asks me how often I masturbate.

He looks at the man who has come from the tomb. Little sign of his entrapment is upon him; he looks merely as one might who had been in deep sleep for a couple of days. He touches him once gently upon the cheek to assure the pulse of light, then backs away. The crowd murmurs with awe. This is no small feat; here he has clearly outdone the loaves and the fishes. They will hardly be able to dismiss this one; it will cause great difficulty when the reports hit Rome. "How are you?" he says to Lazarus. "Have you been merely sleeping or did you perceive the darkness" What brang you back from those regions?"

Documentary sources indicate no speech from the risen man, of course. But documentary sources are notoriously undependable, and, besides, this is a free reconstruction as he has been so often advised. Perhaps Lazarus will have something to say after all; his eyes bulge with reason and his tongue seems about to burst forward with the liquid syllables of discovery. But only an incoherent babble emerges; the man says nothing.

He moves in closer, still holding the grip. "Were you sleeping?" he says, "or did you perceive?"

"*Ah*," Lazarus says. "*Eeeh. Om.*"

He shrugs and dropping his hand moves away. If a miracle is to succeed, it must do so on its own terms; one must have a detached, almost airy attitude toward the miracles because at the slightest hint of uncertainty or effort they will dissipate. "Very well," he says, "be on your way. Return to your life."

The disciples surround him, all but Judas, of course, who as usual is somewhere in the city, probably making arrangements for betrayal. There is nothing to be done; he must suffer Judas exactly as Judas must suffer him; it is the condition of their pact. Peter puts a heavy hand on his shoulder. "What if the man cannot move, master?" he says, always practical. "What if he is unable to complete the journey from the grave."

"He will be able to."

Indeed Lazarus seems to have adopted a stiff gait which takes him slowly toward the crowd. The crowd is surprisingly sparse after all; it is not the throng indicated by scriptures, but instead might be only forty or fifty, many of whom are itinerants drawn to the scene in their wanderings. Scriptural sources were often only a foundation for the received knowledge, of course; the scribes had their own problems, their own needs to fill and retrospective falsification was part of their mission ... still, he thinks, it is often embarrassing to see how hollow that rock is upon which the church was built. Oh well. "I think we had better leave now," Peter says.

"Oh?"

"Indeed," this man of practicality says. "it will make more of an impression, I think; it will lend more of an air of mystery and have greater lasting effect than if you were to stay around. A certain detachment must be cultivated."

"We will surround you, Master," little Mark says, "and leave together hiding your aspect from the populace. In this way you will seem to be attended at all times by a shield." He beckons to Luke, John, the others. "Come," Peter says, "nothing can be served by staying here longer. It would be best to move on."

He does admire the practicality, the disciples simply acting within the situation to bring the maximum interest, and yet reluctance tugs at him. He is really interested in Lazarus. He would like to see what happens next: will the man leave the area of the tomb or will he simply return to it? The rock has merely been pulled aside, the dark opening gapes; Lazarus could simply return to that comfort if he desired, and perhaps he does. Or perhaps not; it is hard to evaluate the responses of an individual toward death. The man is now shielded from view by the crowd which seems to be touching him, checking for the more obvious aspects of mortality. "Let us wait a moment," he says. "This is very interesting. Let's see what is happening here."

"It would not serve, Master," Peter says.

"It is not a matter of serving, merely one of observation. I am responsible for this man, after all; it is only reasonable that I would take an interest in his condition."

"No," Luke says. He scuttles over, a thin man with bulging, curiously piercing eyes. No wonder he wrote the most elaborate of the gospels dictated, that is to say, all of the disciples being fundamentally illiterate. "That will not serve. It is important that we leave at once, Master."

"Why?"

"The mood of the crowd is uncertain; it could turn ugly at any time. There can be much contremps over miracles, and the superstitious are turned toward fear. The very hills are filled with great portents?"

"Enough," Peter says. "You have a tendency for hyperbole, Luke; there is no danger here. But it would be better, from many standpoints if we were to leave; an air of mystery would serve best."

"Oh, all right," I say. "*Je renounces.*" It is, after all, best to adopt a pose of dignity and to give in to the wishes of the disciples, all of whom at least intermittently take this matter more seriously than I … they are, after all, in a position of greater vulnerability. I cast one last look at Lazarus, who is now leaning back against the suspended door of the tomb, elbows balanced precariously on stones, trying to assume an easeful posture for the group almost obscuring him. How exactly is one to cultivate a *je ne sais quoi* about death? It is something to consider; of course I will have ample time to consider the issue myself, but Lazarus could hardly yield much information on the subject. The man is speechless, highly inarticulate; one would have hoped that for a miracle such as this that I could have aroused someone less stupid, but nothing to be done. All of existence is tied together in one tapestry, take it all or leave it, no parts. Surrounded by my muttering disciples I walk toward the west, kicking up little stones and puffs of dust with my sandals.

It is disappointing, quite a letdown really, and I would like to discuss this, but not a one of them would want to hear it. I know that they already have sufficient difficulties having given up their lives for the duration of this mission and it would be an embarrassment for them to hear that I too do not quite know what I am doing. Or perhaps I do. It is hard to tell. In the distance I hear a vague collision of stone. I would not be surprised if Lazarus had gone back into the tomb. Of the tapestry of existence *je ne sais pas.*

□ □ □ □

As I copulate with Edna, images of martyrdom tumble through my mind, a stricken figure on the cross, stigmata ripped like lightning through the exposed sky, and it is all that I can do under the circumstances to perform, but thy will be done, the will must transcend, and so I force myself into a smaller and smaller corner of her, squeezing out the images with little birdcalls and carrying her whimpers through me. She coils and uncoils like a springy steel object and at long last obtains sexual release; I do so myself by reflex and then fall from her grunting. It is quite mechanical, but in a highly technological culture sexual union could only be such; otherwise it would be quite threatening to the apparatus of the state, or so, at least, I have deduced. She lies beside me, her face closed to all feeling, her fingers clawed around my wrist. I groan deep in my throat and compose for sleep, but it is apparent then that there will be no sleep because suddenly she is moving against me and then sitting upright in the bed, staring. Hands clasped behind my head, elbows jutting at an angle of eighty-five degrees. I regard her bleakly. "I can't talk now," I say. "Please, if you must say something, let it be later. There's nothing right now."

"You mean you have to face your treatments in the morning and you need your rest so that you can be alert for the drugs. That's all you think about now, those treatments. Where are you living? Here or there? Come on, tell me …

"I don't want to talk, I told you."

"You've changed," she said. "They've destroyed you. You aren't what you used to be."

There comes a time in every relationship when one has approached terminus, when the expenditure of pain is not worth the pleasure input, where one can feel the raw edges of difference collide through the dissolved flesh of care. Looking at Edna I see that we have reached that point, that there is not much left, and that it will be impossible for me to see her again. This will be the end. After she leaves this time there will be no recurrence. It is this, more than anything else, which enables me to turn from her with equanimity, to confront the bold and staring face of the wall. "Goodnight," I say. "We won't talk about this any more."

"You can't avoid this. You can run from me but not from what has happened. You're not living here any more; you're living in the spaces of your own consciousness. Don't you realize that? You've turned inside; you've shut it out! These aren't experiences that you're having; they're dreams, and all of this is taking place inside you. I hate to see it happen; you're better than this; together we could have helped one another, worked to understand what our lives were, maybe even made progress."

Too late. I stand. "You'd better leave now, Edna."

Arms folded across her little breasts, she juts her chin at me. "That won't solve anything at all. Getting rid of me won't change it."

"The only truth is the truth we create within ourselves."

"I don't believe that. That's what they tell us, that's how you got started on these treatments, but it isn't so. There's an objective truth and it's outside of this and you're going to have to face it sooner or later. You're just going to have to realize." I look at her with enormous dispassion and my expression must be a blade which falls heavily across her rhetoric, chopping it, silencing her. At length, and when I know that she is ready to receive the necessary question, I pose it as calmly and flatly as I have ever done and its resonance fills the room, my heart, her eyes until there is nothing else but her flight, and at last that peace which I have promised myself.

"Why?" I say.

□ □ □ □

At Bruck Linn they do not start the pogrom after all, but instead seize me roughly and burl me into detention. It seems that it was only this in which they were interested; they entered in such massive numbers only to make sure that they could scour the area for me if I were not at my appointed place. In detention I am given spartan but pleasant quarters within what appears to be their headquarters, and a plate of condiments on which to nibble, as well as the five sacred books of the Pentauch, which, since they know I am a religious man, they have obviously given for the purposes of recreation. I look through them idly, munching on a piece of cake, but as always find the dead and sterile phrases insufficient on their own to provoke reaction, and it is almost with relief that I see them come into the room, obviously to explain themselves and advise what will happen next. It is high time. There are two of them, both splendidly uniformed, but one is apparently in the role of secretary; unspeaking, he sits in a corner with a recording device. The other has a blunt face and surprisingly expressive eyes. I would not have thought that they were permitted large wet blue eyes like this.

"You are giving us much difficulty," he says directly, sitting. "Too much and so we have had to arrange this rather dramatic interview. Our pardon for the melodrama but it could not, you see, be spared; we needed to seize and detain as quickly as possible, and we could not take a chance on riots."

"Certainly," I say rather grandly. "I am a world figure. My abduction would not be easy."

"It is not only that."

"But that in itself would be enough."

"No matter," he says. He looks at me intently. "We're going to have to abort the treatments," he says. "You are becoming obsessive."

"What?"

"It has leached out into your personal life and you are beginning to combine treatments and objective reality in a dangerous fashion. Therefore under the contract we are exercising our option to cut them off."

"I have no understanding of this," I say. "Treatments" I am the Lubavitcher Rabbi of Bruck Linn and I have been torn from the heart of my congregation in broad daylight by fascists who will tell me this? This is unspeakable. You speak madness."

"I am afraid," he says, and those expressive eyes are linked to mine, "that you are displaying precisely those symptoms which have made this necessary. You are not the Lubavitcher Rabbi, let alone of Brooklyn. You are Harold Thwaite of the twenty-third century; the Lubavitchers are a defunct, forgotten sect, and you are imagining all of this. You have reconceived your life; the partitions have broken; and we are therefore, for your own good, ceasing the treatments and placing you in temporary detention."

"This is an outrage," I say. "This is impossible. Pogrom? Pogroms I can understand, I can deal with them. But this madness is beyond me."

The uniformed man leans toward me and with the gentlest of fingers strokes my cheek. "It will go easier if you cooperate, Harold," he says. "I know how difficult this must be for you, the shock."

"My followers will not be easy to deal with. You will have to cut them down with rifle fire. I am sure that you can do this, but the cost in blood and bodies will be very high, and in the long run you will not win. You will find a terrible outcome. We are God's chosen; we and only the Lubavitchers carry forth his living presence in this century, and you cannot tamper with that presence lacking the most serious consequences."

And I see to my amazement and to my dismay that the interrogator, the one who has come to intimidate and defile, this man in the hard and terrible uniform of the state, appears to be weeping.

□ □ □ □

I part the Red Sea with a flourish of the cane but the fools nonetheless refuse to cross. "What is wrong with them?" I say to Aaron. "It's perfectly safe." I move further into the abyss between the waves and turn, but the throng remains on the shore staring with bleak expressions. Only Aaron is beside me. "I'm afraid they don't trust the evidence of sight," he says, "and also they don't trust you either; they feel that this is merely a scheme to lead them astray and as soon as they step over, the waters will close upon them."

"That is ridiculous," I say to him. "Would I take them this far, do so much, walk with the guidance of the Lord to betray the Children of Israel?"

Aaron shrugs, a bucolic sort. "What can I tell you?" he says. "There's no accounting for interpretation."

□ □ □ □

At the first great hammer to the temple it comes to me that they were all the time as serious as I. More serious, in fact. I was willing to trust the outcome of my rebellion to a higher power, whereas they, solid businessmen to the end, decided to make sure that the matter rested in their own hands.

Nevertheless, it hurts. I never knew that there was so much pain in it until they put me down at the mosque and oh my oh my oh my oh my no passion is worth any of the real blood streaming.

□ □ □ □

"You see now," the counselor says to me, "that you are clearly in need of help. There is no shame in it; there is precedent for this; it has all happened before. We know exactly how to treat the condition, so if you will merely lie quietly and cooperate, we should have you on your way before long. The fact that you are back in focus now, for instance, is a very promising sign. Just a few hours ago we despaired of this, but you are responding nicely."

I rear up on my elbows. "Let me out of here," I say. "I demand to be let out of here. You have no right to detain me in this fashion; I have a mission to perform, and I assure you that you will suffer greatly for what you have done. This is a serious business; it is not to be trifled with. Detention will not solve your problems; you are in grave difficulty."

"I urge you to be calm."

"I am perfectly calm." I note that I appear to be lashed to the table by several painless but well contrived restraints, which pass across my torso, digging in only when I flail. It is a painless but humiliating business and I subside, grumbling. "Very well," I said. "You will find what happens when you adopt such measures, and that judgment will sit upon you throughout eternity."

The counselor sighs. He murmurs something about many of them at the beginning not being reasonable, and I do not remind him that this is exactly as Joseph had warned.

□ □ □ □

Tormented by the anguish on the Magdalene's face, the tears which leak unbidden down her cheeks, he says, "It is all right. The past does not matter; All that matters is what happens in the timeless present, the eternal future." He lifts a hand, strokes her cheeks, feeling a strange and budding tenderness working which surprises him in its intensity; it is of a different sort from the more generalized tenderness he has felt through his earlier travels. "Come," he said. "You can join me."

She puts her hand against his. "You don't understand," she says. "This is not what I want."

"What?"

"Talk of paradise, of your father, of salvation; I don't understand any of it. I don't know what you think they want."

"I know what they want."

"You don't know anything," she says. "You are a kind man but of these people you know nothing." She smooths her garments with a free hand. "To them you are merely a diversion, an entertaining element in their lives, someone who amuses them, whereas you think in passionate terms. You will be deeply hurt."

"Of course."

"No," she says, "not in the way you think. Martyrdom will not hurt you; that is, after all, what you seek. It will be something else." Something else, he thinks. Something else, I think.

She is an attractive woman not without elements of sympathy, but staring at her I remember that she was, until very recently, a prostitute who committed perhaps even darker acts, and that it is an insolent thing which she, of all people, is doing in granting her Savior such rebuke. "Come," I say to her. I should note that, we have been having this dialogue by a river bank, the muddy waters of the river arching over the concealed stones, the little subterranean animals of the river whisking their way somewhere toward the north, the stunted trees of this time holding clumps of birds which eye us mournfully. "It is time to get back to the town."

"Why?"

"Because if we remain out here talking like this much longer some will misconceive. They will not understand why we have been gone so long."

"You are a strange, strange man."

"I am not a man. I am?"

"I would not take all of this so seriously," she says, and reaches toward me, a seductive impact in the brush of her band, seductive clatter in her breath, and oh my Father it is a strange feeling indeed to see what passes between us then, and with halt and stuttering breath I hurl myself upright, thrust her away, and run toward Galilee. Behind me, it cannot be the sound of her laughter which trails. It cannot, it cannot.

□ □ □ □

"Fools," I say, my fingers hurtling through the sacred, impenetrable text, looking for the proper citation. "Can't you understand that you are living at the end of time" The chronologies of the Book of Daniel clearly indicate that the seven beasts emerge from the seven gates in the year 2222, the numbers aligned; it is this generation which will see the gathering of the light." They stare at me with interest but without conviction. "You had better attend," I say. "You have little time, little enough time to repent, and it will go easier for you if you do at the outset."

One of the congregants raises his hand and steps toward me. "Rabbi," he says, "you are suffering from a terrible misapprehension?"

"So are you all," I say with finality, "but misapprehension can itself become a kind of knowledge."

"This is not Bruck Linn and the Book of Daniel has nothing to do with what is happening."

"Fool," I say, lunging against my restraining cords, "you may conceive of a pogrom, but that cannot alter the truth. All of your murders will not stop the progress of apocalypse for a single moment."

"There is no apocalypse, rabbi," the congregant says, "and you are not a rabbi."

I scream with rage, lunging against the restraints once again and they back away with terror on their solemn faces. I grip the Pentauch firmly and hurl it at them, the pages opening like a bird's wing in flight, but it misses, spatters against an opposing wall, falls in spatters of light. "I have my duties," I say, "my obligations. You had better let me go out and deliver the summons to the world; keeping me here will not keep back the truth. It cannot be masked, and I assure you that it will go better for you if you cooperate."

"You are sick, rabbi," he says very gently. "You are a sick man. Thankfully you are getting the treatment that you so desperately need and you will be better."

"The great snake," I point out, "the great snake which lies coiled in guard of the gates is slowly rising; he is shaking off the sleep of ten thousand years."

"To throw a holy book?"

"No books are holy. At the end of time, awaiting the pitiless and terrible judgment even the sacred texts fall away. All that is left is judgment, mercy, the high winds rising."

"If you will relax, rabbi?"

"I want to walk to and fro upon the earth and up and down upon it!" I scream. "From all of these wanderings I will come to a fuller knowledge, crouching then at the end of time with the old antagonist to cast lots over the vestments of the saved and the damned alike, bargaining for their garments out of a better world?"

"If you will only be quiet…"

"The snake is quiet too," I say, "quiet and waiting for the time of judgment, but let me tell you that the silence which you will demand is the silence of the void?"

And so on and so forth, *je ne sais pas*. It is wearying to recount all of those admonitions which continue to rave through the spaces of the room at this time. If there is one thing to say about a Talmudic authority in heat, it is that once launched upon a point he can hardly pause; pauses would form interstices where the golem itself might worm. And of the golem, of course, little more need be said.

□ □ □ □

"Will you yield?" Satan says to me, putting me into an untenable position upon the sands. His face looms near mine like a lover's; he might be about to implant the most sustained and ominous of kisses. "Yield and it will go easier with you."

"No," I say, "never. I will not yield." The French has fled, likewise the depersonalization, I feel at one with the persona, which is a very good sign, surely a sign that I am moving closer to the accomplishment of my great mission. "You may torture me; you may bring all of your strength to bear; it is possible that you will bend and break me, but you will never hear renunciation." I grab purchase with my ankles, manage to open up a little bit of space, which of course I do not share with my ancient antagonist, and then with a sly wrench drag him toward me, defy his sense of balance and send him tumbling beside. He gasps, the exhalation of breath full as dead flowers in my face, and it is possible for me now to hurl myself all the way over him, pressing him into the sands. Gasping, he attempts to fling me, but as I collapse on top of him my knee strikes his horned and shaven head, administering a stunning blow and from the opening I see leaching the delicate, discolored blood of Satan. His eyes flutter to attention and then astonishment as I close upon him and my strength is legion. "Do you see?" I say to him. "Do you see now what you have done? You cannot win against the force of light," and I prepare myself to deliver the blow of vanquishment. Open to all touch he lies beneath me; his mouth opens.

"Stop!" he says weakly, and to my surprise I do so. There is no hurry, after all; he is completely within my power. "That's better," he says. His respiration is florid. "Stop this nonsense at once. Help me arise."

"No," I say, "absolutely not."

"You don't understand, you fool. This dispute was supposed to be purely dialectical; there was no need to raise arms." Ali, the cunning of Satan! Defeated on his own terms he would Shift to others, but I have been warned against this too, I have been fully prepared for all the flounderings of the ancient enemy; there is nothing that he can do now to dissuade me, and so I laugh at him, secure in my own power and say, "Dialectical! No, it was a struggle unto the death; those were clearly the terms and you know that as well as I."

"No," he says, twitching his head. "No, absolutely not, you never saw this right. There was never the matter of murder; don't you realize that? We aren't antagonists at all! We are two aspects of the overwhelming one; our search was for fusion in these spaces, and that is what we are now prepared to do." His head sinks down; he is clearly exhausted. Still he continues muttering. "You fool," he says. "There is no way that one of us can vanquish the other. To kill either is to kill the self."

Sophistry! Sophistry! I am so sick of it; I intimate a life, a dark passageway through to the end lit only by the flickering and evil little candles of half-knowledge and witticism, casting ugly pictures on the stones, and the image enrages me; I cannot bear the thought of a life which I contain little more than small alterations of language or perception to make it bearable, reconsideration of a constant rather than changing the unbearable constant itself, but this is to what I have been condemned. Not only Satan, but I will have to live by rhetoric; there will be nothing else.

But at least, this first time on the desert, rhetoric will not have to prevail. Perhaps for the only time in my life I will have the opportunity to undertake the one purposive act, an act of circumstance rather than intellection.

And so, without wishing to withhold that moment any longer, I wheel fiercely upon Satan. "I've had enough of this shit," I say. "I've got to deal with it; I cannot go on like this forever; there has to be a time for confrontation." The words seem a bit confused, but my action is not; I plunge a foot into his face. It yields in a splatter of bone, and in that sudden rearrangement I look upon his truest form.

"Well," says Satan through flopping jaw. "Well, well." He puts a claw to a slipped cheekbone, "Well, I'll be damned."

"Oh, yes," I say, "but you don't have to take all of us with you."

His eyes, surprisingly mild, radiate, of all things, compassion. "You don't understand," he says. He falls to his knees like a great, stricken bird. "You don't understand anything at all."

"I do enough."

"I'm not here by choice," Satan murmurs. "I'm here because you want me. Do you think that this is easy" Being thrown out of Heaven and walking up and down the spaces of the earth, and to and fro upon it, and the plagues and the cattle and the boils? I've just been so busy, but it was you who brought me into being, or again?" Satan says, drawing up his knees to a less anguished posture, fluttering on the desert floor, "is this merely rationalization? I am very good at sophistry, you know, but this isn't easy; there's a great deal of genuine pain in it. I have feelings too."

I stand, considering him. What he is saying is very complex and doubtless I should attend to it more closely (I sense that it would save me the most atrocious difficulty later on if only I would) but there is a low sense of accomplishment in having dealt with this assignment so effectively, and I do not want to lose it so easily. It may be one of the least equivocal moments in a life riven, as we all know, with conflicts. "I'm dying," Satan says. "Won't you at least reach out a hand to comfort me?"

The appeal is grotesque and yet I am moved. He is, after all, a creature of circumstance no less than any of the rest of us. I kneel beside him, trying not to show my revulsion at the smell of leaking mortality from him. Satan extends a hand. "Hold me," he says. "Hold me; you owe me at least that. You called me into being; you have to take responsibility for my vanquishment. Or are you denying complicity?"

"No," I say, "I can hardly do that." I extend my hand. His claw, my fingers, interlock.

"You see," Satan says gratefully, "you know at least that you're implicated. There may be some hope in that for all of us and now if you will permit me, I believe that I am going to die."

Grey and greenish blood spills from his mouth, his nasal passages, eyes and ears. It vaults into the desert and as I stare fascinated, he dies with quick muffled little sighs not unlike the sounds of love. It is an enormous and dignified accomplishment not noted in all the Scripture, and I am held by the spectacle for more than a few moments.

But as his claw slips away, as touch is abandoned, I have a vision and in that vision I see what I should have known before going through all of this. I see what might have saved me all of this passage, which is to say that knowing he is dead there is a consequent wrench in my own corpus indicating an echoing, smaller death, and as I realize that he has told me the truth, that the divestment of Satan has resulted only in my own reduction, I stand in the desert stunned, knowing that none of this, and I am here to testify, gentlemen, I am here to testify!, is going to be as simple as I thought.

□　□　□　□

"Even the minor prophets have problems," I point out in the mosque. "The fact that I am not famous and that many of my judgments are vague does not mean that they are not deeply felt or that I will not suffer the fate of Isaiah; Jeremiah, Zephaniah, had their problems. Ezekiel had a limp and was tormented by self-hatred. Hosea had blood visions too."

They took at me bleakly, those fifteen. This is what my flock has dwindled into, and I should be grateful to have them, what with all of the efforts to discredit and those many threats of violence made toward those who would yet remain with me. They are quite stupid, the intelligent ones long since having responded to the pressure, but they are all I have, and I am grateful, I suppose, to have them. "Attend," I say. "The institutions cannot remain in this condition. Their oppression is already the source of its own decay; they panic, they can no longer control the uprising. The inheritors of these institutions are stupid; they do not know why they work or how, but just mechanically reiterate the processes for their own fulfillment, massacre to protect themselves, oppress because oppression is all they know of the machinery. But their time is limited; the wind is rising and the revolution will be heard," and so on and so forth, the usual rhetorical turns and flourishes done so skillfully that they occupy only the most fleeting part of my attention. Actually I am looking at the door. It is the door which I consider; from the left enter three men in the dress of the sect, but I have never seen them before and by some furtive, heightened expressions of their eyes I know that they have not come here on a merciful business.

They consult with one another against the wall and it is all that I can do to continue speaking. I must not show a lapse of rhetoric, I must not let them know that I suspect them, because all that I hold is the prospect of my inattention, but as my customary prose rolls and thunders I am already considering the way out of here. My alternatives are very limited. The windows are barred, the walls are blank behind me, there only exits are at the edge of the hall and what has happened to the guards? Did they not screen this group? Are they not supposed to protect me, or are they all part of the plot? "Be strong, be brave," I am telling my followers, but I do not feel strong or brave myself; I feel instead utterly perplexed and filled with a fear which is very close to self-loathing. Their conference concluded, the men scatter, one going for a seat in the center, the other two parting and sliding against the walls. They fumble inside their clothing; I am sure they have firearms.

I am sure that the assassins, on my trail for so very long, have at last stalked me to this point; but I am in a very unique and difficult position because, if I show any fear whatsoever, if I react to their presence, they will doubtless slay me in the mosque, causing the most unusual consternation to my followers assembled; but on the other hand, if I proceed through the speech and toward an orderly dismissal, all that will happen is that I will make the slaying more convenient and allow for less witnesses, to say nothing of giving them an easier escape. Anything I do, in short, is calculated to work against me, and yet I am a man who has always believed in dignity, the dignity of position, that is to say, taking a stand, following it through whatever the implications; and so I continue, my rhetoric perhaps a shade florid now, my sentences not as routinely parsed as I would wish but it is no go, no go at all; they have a different method, I see, as the seated one arises and moves briskly toward me. "This is not right," I say as he comes up to me, takes me by an elbow. "You could at least have let me finished; if I was willing to take this through, then you could have gone along with me." The congregants murmur.

"You'd better come with me, Harold," he says. "You need help."

"Take your hands off me."

"I'm afraid I'd best not do that," he says gently, gesturing toward the two in the back who begin to come toward me solemnly. "You see, what we have to do is to jolt you out of these little fugues, these essays in martyrdom, and it would be best if you cooperated; the more you cooperate, the quicker you see that it becomes evident that you are accepting reality, and therefore the more quickly you will be back to yourself. Come," he says, giving me a hearty little tug, "let's just bounce out of here now," and the others flank me fore and aft and quite forcefully I am propelled from the rostrum. To my surprise my congregants do not express dismay, nor are there scenes of riot or dislocation as I might have expected; on the contrary they look at me with bleak, passive interest, as I am shoved toward the door. It is almost, I think, as if they had expected me to come exactly to this state and they are glad that I am being taken off in this fashion.

"Can't you see," I say gesticulating to them, "can't you see what is happening here? They don't want you to know the truth, they don't want you to accept the truth of your lives; that's why they're taking me away from here, because I was helping you to face the truth."

"Come on, Harold," they murmur taking me away. "All of this has its place, but after a while it's just best to cooperate; just go along," and now they have me through the doors, not a single one of my congregants making the slightest attempt to fracture their progress. I shake a fist at them.

"For God's sake," I say, "don't any of you care, don't you know what's going on here?" and so on and so forth, the sounds of my rhetoric filling my ears, if hardly all of the world, and outside I am plunged repeatedly into the brackish waters of Galilee, which to no one's surprise at all (or at least not to mine) hardly lend absolution.

□   □   □   □

"You'd better destroy them," I say in a conversational tone, settling myself more comfortably underneath the gourd. "They're a rotten bunch of people as you all note. Not a one of them has but a thought of their own pleasure, to say nothing of the sexual perversity."

"I may not," he says reasonably. He is always reasonable, which is a good thing if one is engaged in highly internalized dialogues. What would I do if he were to lose patience and scream? I could hardly deal with it. "After all, it's pretty drastic, and besides that, without life there is no possibility of repentance."

"Don't start that again," I say. "You sent me all of these miles, through heat and water, fire and pain to warn them of doom, and you would put both of us in a pretty ridiculous position, wouldn't you, if you didn't follow through? They'd never take me seriously again."

"You let *me* decide that, Jonah," he says, and there is no arguing with him when he gets into one of these moods, no possibility of argument whatsoever when he becomes stubborn, and so I say, "We'll see about this in the morning," much as if I were controlling the situation rather than he, which is not quite true of course, and slip into a thick doze populated with the images of sea and flying fish, but at the bottom of the sleep is pain, and when I bolt from it it is with terrible pain through the base of being, my head in anguish, my head as if it were carved open, and looking upward I see that the gourd which he had so kindly spread for me has shriveled overnight, and I am now being assaulted by a monotonous eastern sun. "Art thou very angry?" he says companionably, lapsing into archaicism as is his wont.

"Of course I am very angry," I say, "You have allowed my gourd to die. And besides I want to know when you're going to get rid of these people. Looking down from this elevation I can see very distinctly that the city is still standing."

"Ah," he says as I scratch at my head, trying to clobber the sun away, "thou takest pity upon the gourd which was born in a night and died in a night; why should I not take pity upon forty thousand people who cannot discern their right hand from their left to say nothing of much cattle?"

"Sophistry," I say, "merely sophistry."

"Unfortunately," he says, "there is no room for your reply," and smites me wildly upon the head, causing me to stumble into the ground, Gomorrah still upright, and I am afflicted (and not for the first time I might add) with perception of the absolute perversity of this creature who dwelleth within me. At all times.

□ □ □ □

The thieves have died, but I am still alive to the pain of the sun when I feel the nails slide free and I plunge a hundred feet into the arms of the soldiers. They cushion my fall, lave my body with strong liquids, murmur to me until slowly I come over the sill of consciousness to stare at them. Leaning over me is a face which looks familiar. "Forgive them," I say weakly, "forgive them, they know not what they do."

"They know what they do."

"*Jamais*," I say and to clarify, "never."

"You have not been crucified," he says. "You'd better accept that."

"Then this must be hell," I say, "and I still in it." He slaps me across the face, a dull blow with much resonance.

"You're just not being reasonable," he says. "You are not a reasonable man."

"Help me up there, then," I say. "It is not sufficient. Help me up there and crucify me again."

"Harold?"

"*Jesu*," I say admonishingly and close my eyes waiting for ascent and the perfect striations of the nails through the wrist: vaulting, stigmata.

□ □ □ □

The face looking at me is Edna's, but this is strange because Edna will not be born for several centuries yet, and what is even stranger than that is the fact that despite this I recognize her. How can this be? Nevertheless, one must learn to cope with dislocations of this sort if one is to be a satisfactory martyr. "They asked me to come here and speak to you," she says. "I don't know why I'm here. I don't think it will be of any use whatsoever. But I will talk to you. You have got to stop this nonsense now, do you hear me?"

"You could help by getting me out of here," I say, plucking at my clothing. "My appearance is disgusting and it is hardly possible for me to do the work when I am confined to a place like this. Or at least you could have them hurry and order up the crucifixion. Get it over with. There's no reason to go on this way; it's absolutely futile."

"That's what they want me to talk to you about. They seem to think that this is something that can be reasoned with. I keep on telling them that this is ridiculous; you're too far gone but they say to try so I will. They're as stupid as you. All of you are stupid; you've let the process take over and you don't even understand it. Face reality, Harold, and get out of this or it is going to go very badly?"

"*Jesu*," I remind her.

"Do you see?" she says to someone in the distance. "It's absolutely hopeless. Nothing can come of this. I told you that it was a waste."

"Try," the voice says. "You have to try." She leans toward me. Her face is sharp, her eyes glow fluorescent in the intensity. "Listen, Harold," she says. "You are not jesu or anyone else any of your religious figures. This is 2219 and you have been undergoing an administered hypnotic procedure enabling you to live through certain of your religious obsessions, but as is very rarely the case with others you have failed to come back all of the way at one point, and now they say you're in blocked transition or something. They're quite able to help you and to reverse the chemotherapeutic process, but in order to begin you have to accept these facts, that we are telling you the truth, that they are trying to help you. That isn't too much, is it? I mean, that isn't too much of an admission for you to make; and in return look at the wonderful life you'll have. Everything will be just as it was before, and you can remember how you loved it that way."

"Let me out of here," I say. "Where are my robes? Where are my disciples? Where are the sacred scrolls and the voice of the Lord? You cannot take all of this away; you will be dealt with very harshly."

"There are no sacred scrolls or followers. All of those people died a long time ago. This is your last chance, Harold; you'd better take it. Who knows what the alternative might be? Who knows what these people might be capable of doing?"

"Magdalene," I say reasonably, "simply because you're a whore does not mean that you always speak the truth. That is a sentimental fallacy."

Her face congests and she spits. I leave it rest there. A celebration. A stigmata.

□　□　□　□

Conveyed rapidly toward Calvary I get a quick glimpse of the sun appearing in strobes of light as they drive me with heavy kicks toward the goal. The yoke is easy at this time and burdens light; it is a speedy journey that I have made from the court to this place and it will be an easier one yet that I will make to Heaven. A few strokes of the hammer, some pain at the outset: blood, unconsciousness, ascension. Nothing will be easier than this, I think; the getting to this condition has far outweighed in difficulty this final stage. Struggling with the sacred texts has been boring, the miracles sheer propaganda; now at last I will find some consummative task worthy of my talents.

"Faster," they shout, "faster!" and I trot to their urging. *Vite, vite, vite* to that great mountain where I will show them at last that passion has as legitimate a place in this world as any of their policies and procedures and will last; I will convince them as I have already convinced myself a hell of a lot longer. *Brava passione! Brava!*

□　□　□　□

So they yank me from the restraints and toss me into the center of the huge room to meet the actors. There they all are, there they are: congregants, disciples, Romans, pagans, troopers, all of the paraphernalia and armament of my mission. Edna and the Magdalene are somewhere, but concealed; I have to take their presence on faith. I have had to take everything on faith, and at the end it destroys me; this is my lesson.

"Enough of this!" they cry. Or at least one of them says this; it is very difficult to be sure. The shout must come from an individual but then again it would appear to be a collective shout; they all feel this way. "This is your last chance, your very last chance to cooperate before it becomes very difficult."

"I don't know."

"*Ne rien,*" they cry. A great clout strikes, knocking me to the floor. It hurts like hell. *Attende bien,* I could have expected nothing less; I have waited for it so very long. Still, one tries to go on. I scramble for purchase, hurl myself upright. My capacity to absorb pain, oh happy surprise, seems limitless after all.

"Listen!" they say, not without a certain sympathy, "Listen, this is very serious business; it cannot go on; the matter of the treatments themselves is at stake. The treatment process is complex and expensive and there are complications, great difficulties?"

I confront them reasonably. I am a reasonable man. I always have been. "I will see you with my Father in Heaven," I say. "That is where I will see you and not a bloody moment sooner."

"Don't you understand" Don't you realize what you are doing" The penalties can be enormous. This must stay controlled; otherwise?"

"Otherwise," I say. "Otherwise you will lose your world and it is well worth losing. I have considered this. I have given it a great deal of thought. Martyrdom is not a posture, not at all; martyrdom springs from the heart. I am absolutely serious; it did not begin that way but that is the way it has ended. I will not yield. I will not apologize. I will not be moved. Thy will be done, *pater noster,* and besides, once you get going you can't just turn it off, if you have any respect, if you have any respect at all."

There is a sound like that of engines. They close upon me. I know exactly what they have in mind but am nonetheless relieved.

It would have had to be this way. "I will not yield," I say to them quietly. "I will not apologize. I will not be moved. This isn't folklore, you know; this is real pain and history."

They tear me apart.

☐ ☐ ☐ ☐

I think of Satan now and am glad that we were able to have that little conversation in the desert the second time, to really get to know one another and to establish a relationship. He was quite right, of course, the old best loved angel, and I wish I'd had the grace to acknowledge it at the time. We wanted him; we called him into it. It was better to have him outside than in that split and riven part of the self. Oh how I would like to embrace him now.

☐ ☐ ☐ ☐

They leave me on the Cross for forty days and forty nights. On the forty-first the jackals from the south finally gnaw the wood to ash and it collapses. I am carried off, what is left of me, in their jaws and on to further adventures I cannot mention in bowels and partitions of the Earth.

The Men's Support Group

SO EVERY month we meet, second Monday, and bring our lives to the table. This night only Wilson the accountant and Chambers the imports guy joined me there. This is not uncommon — the low attendance — as one might think, because most of us have responsibilities and can be out of town a lot. This however was part of a long period at home for me, and getting to the Men's Support Group was not only an obligation but a splendid way to get me out of the house. I need to get out of the house more and more, and perhaps the middle years of a long marriage are dedicated to finding legitimate excuses. If a group of mutual support and brotherhood among professional men who live in this Northeastern suburb is not a legitimate excuse, then what is?

Let me tell you about my friend Fred, I said. I've been thinking about telling this for a long time, but the occasion has never been right. There's been this or that or someone's crisis to occupy us or my own misery. But Fred has been on my mind all this time and now I really want to talk about him.

You all know my situation, I said. I don't have to go into that again, right? A marriage is a marriage until it's not, and I constructed no alternative to this one, so here I am except that I travel a lot on business and play trumpet with the Sizzlers and take art education so I don't have to face it maybe three or four nights a week. It's pretty much the same as it's always been, I said, but that doesn't mean I can't take it. Adele has her own inner life and accommodation.

The rule is that we don't talk about what the women may feel. We just don't bring that into play. They feel plenty but that is for their own group and if they want to form one, that's all right with us. I want to talk about Fred, I said. I have for a long time. Fred is a paradigm. His is the most tragic, the most complex story I know: it is King Lear in Red Hook, Medusa or Electra in the Sisterhood, Medea in the PTA but who would know? Who would know? Fred owns a shoe repair store, he looks like a shoemaker, in fact he is a shoemaker by inclination. Dumpy, merry, mustache, little eyes, big forehead, his features four circles on his face. You look at Fred and want to pass on by. But he's Lear, I said. This is King Lear I am talking about. It is Jason in the amphitheatre looking at the bodies of his sons. It is Laertes standing by the dead Hamlet.

Listen, I said, listen to this.

Wilson and Chambers said nothing, sat with their arms folded on the table, looked at me quietly. These are the rules of the Men's Support Group: once one of us begins to speak the others are silent until the end. Then comment or pity may be offered as desired, or perhaps not offered at all. Then to the next statement, the next expostulation. One holds the floor as long as one needs to talk and is never pressed to hurry but once one has finished that is it, the speaker may never start again. So we have one chance to make our case, appeal for the squalor of our lives and then no more until our next turn which may not be for several months or not at all if we leave the group. This rule, worked out over our considerable history, worked out years before any of the present membership was there, was the most central and respected rule of them all and Wilson and Chambers honored it with silence and cold attention.

All right, I said, listen to Fred's story. A shoemaker, a shoe repair shop guy but more labor than capital, a simple, sad, sweet little guy, fifty-nine or sixty when this happened to him. He got married young like the rest of us, got married to the first woman with whom he had any suspicion or real apprehension of sex and of course as time grew the love died, then the sex, then perhaps the rest of it, all but the mechanics and reflex which we all know so well. Which got us to this place, I said. Fred married Frieda — we'll call her that, you get the idea — at twenty-two and he is married to her today, it is fifty years now, twelve or thirteen years past this thing I am going to tell you about and as far as I know they are still going on. He made money and worked hard and had children and slowly, inch by defined inch, bought substance and accommodation even as love shriveled and the tumble of the sheets became a tangle of spent dreams. The usual stuff, as I say. Do you know? We all know, right? If we know anything we know this. Everybody knows everything.

I stared at Wilson and Chambers until slowly, reflexively, they nodded, giving me that and no more. All right, I said. But there was one factor at the heart of this which changed both everything and nothing. Frieda had a sister Marilyn, three years younger. Fred knew Marilyn then as long as he had known his wife: Marilyn opened the door for their first date. Later, when Marilyn married — forget this part, the guy was named George but he is no factor — the sisters and brothers-in-law spent much time together, holidays, cousins and the like. Fred and Marilyn through all of this, from the week before Fred got married and for thirty years afterward were fucking each other. They did it without Frieda's knowledge and when George came along he didn't know either. They snuck into hotels, did it in Marilyn's office a couple of times when she had a clerical job and a key so that they could sneak in nights. They went to motels and once, excitedly, the Plaza in New York. It was an intensely exciting affair, Fred did things to and with Marilyn of which Frieda had no inkling. It informed his life. It granted him consequence. Do you understand? It changed everything. In front of the curtain Fred hammered shoes, bullshitted the customers, took Frieda and their two sons to the Adirondacks in the summer, spent Christmas with Marilyn and George and the cousins. He lay spiritlessly but necessarily with Frieda in their sheets all the nights of his life. He never spent a night apart from her except for childbirth (the night after, both times, Marilyn and Fred fucked in a motel). Behind that curtain Fred did unspeakable things to Marilyn, found his knowledge and her depth, those depths of expressivity which he could not otherwise have known. Oh it was powerful, powerful!

Now how did I know? Because I was his one confidant, his only true friend he told me. Fred told me everything. He said that someone other than Marilyn had to know or it would not be real; lying next to his wife in the night or trapped with her in public places it indeed seemed to be lost to him, utterly shut off. If he had one true friend who knew, though, it would seem real even when it was not. That is how Fred explained it to me.

I found it something of a mystery, of course. Marilyn and Frieda, sisters, three years apart, short soft-edged women, little definition in their faces, the same lagging and hanging bulges under their clothing, indistinguishable in a soft or perhaps a harsher light. But who is to tell? Really, gentleman, who is to know? Fred had pictures of Marilyn. They were — she had insisted upon this — cut off at the neck so that only her breasts and pudenda were visible, some of the poses quite graphic. Marilyn touching herself and so on. He hovered over the photographs as he lay them before me and snatched them quickly off the table. I want you to see, he said. I want you to know. But you cannot tell and you cannot look for long. Because it is a pure thing between us.

Do you understand that? he said. It is a pure thing.

That is all I have to tell of Fred and Marilyn and their affair. What can I know? What apprehension have we of desire, of secret knowledge, of the expenditure of limbs and sighs in the secret passages? I neither sought this information from Fred nor wanted detail. What he told me was already too much and yet how could I refuse him? I was his little aperture into some external reality, some aperture which took down the walls of his life. Do you think this is easy? Fred said to me once. It is tearing us up. But she is happily married and that is it. That is where it all must stay. Can you imagine what the word "happy" must have meant to Fred if he would use it in this context? A man who used the word in this way either had never been happy or he understood it all too well. But I cannot speculate, gentleman. The Men's Support Group is the place where we show our pain. Our thoughts or speculation are not revelations but masks for pain.

There is very little more, I said. Wilson and Chambers looked at me intently. It sounds as if the story is just beginning but it is close upon an end. Here is all the rest of it: after a long time George died, cancer, the liver, the usual kind of thing in his family. This was after thirty-five years. The cousins were grown, Marilyn had all the life insurance, the mortgage was paid. A tragedy but not all that much except perhaps for Frieda who took George's death surprisingly hard. Harder than any of the rest of them. Well, maybe George and Frieda had their own cross-conversation going, yes? That is not something that occurred to me before this moment, I said. That is a sudden and new insight. Of course it is plausible. That may well be the fact: that Frieda and George were also lovers. That is not the payoff of this story, however.

I said I was close to the end but not quite.

Marilyn met someone through the church and remarried. There was no question of anything else. Fred would not leave Frieda to marry Marilyn, it would have been a disaster. Marilyn might have been "free" if that is the word I am seeking but not in any meaningful, useful way. None of these people were free, I said. Not you or me or Fred or Frieda or Marilyn or George, no one was free and they knew it. That is why we have the Men's Support Group, right? Wilson and Chambers nodded. Well, of course I am right, I said.

Look at it this way, I went on, if we were free we would not be here, we would be living our desire elsewhere. Whatever those desires might be. Of course we may not know what they are, which is all part of the problem.

Marilyn remarried. Someone named Arthur, I think. Maybe Max, someone even less important to the story than George and George as you can see was not important at all. Through all of this too — the bereavement, the solitary period, dating the new guy — Fred and Marilyn kept on humping. The motels, the hotels, a risky couple of times in the empty house whose mortgage was paid. That would never change, Marilyn said. It had never occurred to Fred that he would even have had to ask. Of course it will never change, she assured him when she saw his surprise. What does this have to do with anything else? Arthur or George or anyone, it's always going to be us and the bed and the pictures, she said. I am getting old and fat Marilyn said so maybe not so much with the pictures any more.

Marilyn and Arthur went to the Grand Canyon for their honeymoon. This discomfited Fred a little: it was odd, the first time perhaps that he had ever felt anything resembling jealousy. Still, the situation was different: Marilyn had been at least nominally free and had been his love for all those decades and it was something of a shock to Fred when she and Arthur booked their two week honeymoon, then got married quickly at City Hall, only official witnesses, it wasn't seemly, Marilyn said, Arthur recently widowed too and this second time she preferred not to marry in front of Fred if it was all the same to him. Not that she had given him a choice.

They flew away, landed in Arizona, got the rental car, went off to the Canyon and the rest of the things New Yorkers do when they go on that kind of tour. Tijuana, a border run was somewhere on the triptych. I am almost finished now, I said, this is the end of it. The phone by Fred's bed rang at four in the morning one Wednesday, he yanked it in stupor, pulled from a dream of Marilyn's breasts. He did not dream of her often but he was this time. Then he heard the voice on the telephone and cried Marilyn's name with impunity because Marilyn was dead.

Marilyn and Arthur were in fact both dead. They had been hit head-on. The Interstate had dense fog and some big tanker had not seen the median line. They were killed instantly, the trooper said. We found your name and her sister's in the effects. What do you want to 40? You'll have to come out for the bodies, the trooper said. We can't release them without a relative present.

That's all, Fred said to me. He told me this a few weeks later. That's all. Can you imagine this? The first thing I have to do is tell my wife, then I have to control Frieda's hysterics, then I have to put water all over her body while she understands that her sister is dead.

I do not have, he said, the time to think that I have lost the love of my life-and that is what I call her in my heart for the first time, then, love of my life. In the first place Frieda needs me and there is no room for that and in the second place, Fred said, in the second place if I let myself go, if I tell my wife what I am feeling, if Frieda sees anything then I am doomed, I am lost forever. She will die and I will die too but not before knowing that I will be in hell for the end of time. The trooper calls back to say that they would like an estimated time of arrival because there is a lot of complicated paperwork and also the coroner would like permission for an autopsy. Can my wife give consent for the sister? Meanwhile they have turned up some name for Arthur in his wallet which it turns out was not consumed by the fire. They will go to that name for permission then. Nothing more, Fred said. Nothing more to say. Can you imagine this? Frieda is crazy, she is destroyed, she cannot move, she cannot travel; I call the children. They will come and stay with her. I do not even wait for them to show, I fly out there alone. I make arrangements alone. I view the bodies which is something else, I arrange for transport. Then I fly with the bodies in the plane, land, make all the calls from the airport, call a funeral home, turn it over to them, go for an interview, all of the time holding Marilyn's ghost and trying to hold Frieda together and telling myself nothing.

I will not speak to myself, do you understand? I know that if I let myself go into this wholly then I will die too and with me everyone will die. My wife, my love, my sister-in-law, my marriage, my children, my destiny. The photographs. The cry when she was about to come.

I am a shoemaker, Fred said. A cobbler, I have no gift for language, no taste for emotion, no real sense of the heart. Don't you know that? Don't you know this of a shoemaker? We have no interior, we have no sensibility. We carry photographs secretly and bullshit the customers.

Then we have the funeral. Frieda asks me if I will say a few words, someone should, she is too distraught. It should not be a stranger, though. I say a few words. I have lost more than a sister-in-law I say to the cousins and the children and the fifty or sixty friends who have come out of courtesy. I have lost a sister, I say. Marilyn, my sister. Frieda and I have lost our sister. Then we go to the cemetery. Then we come home.

Now, Fred said to me, I am living the rest of my life every day and cannot cry unless I am away from the house of course but I cannot do that either because if I cry there or anywhere I will not be able to stop. So I go on and on, Fred said, and that is all I have to tell you but I hope you will please forget about the photographs and never mention them to me. Frieda is not herself any more, Fred said. I understand now that it was the Marilyn who lived within her who made life at all bearable for her and made her bearable for me.

But that is another situation, Fred said. I have nothing more to report.

Nor do I, I said finishing it off, the little light on the wall refracting the dust. I have wanted to tell this for a while, I said, but I did not know the way to do it. And having done it, I said, having given this, I do not know what it means. Is it Lear in Red Hook? Or am I a fool? Or is Fred the fool and all this agony while Frieda was casually fucking George all these years and for all we know sharing her secrets with Marilyn who shared no secrets with Fred?

I thought I needed support for this, I said, but now I do not know. I don't know. That is all, I said. There is nothing else to say.

Wilson said I will tell you what I know about Fred's situation by telling you what I know of my own.

Three years ago, Wilson said, I had an affair with my daughter's roommate, a lovely young woman who Jan met through a listing service when she came to the city for her first job. The roommate, Elizabeth, was extraordinary. A Vassar graduate; 23, tall, thin, an assistant copy editor at an advertising agency working on automobile accounts: what do I know? What the hell do I know of any of that business? All of those firms and jobs are just names to me, I understand nothing. Profit and losses, auditors and dodging through the revenue service, that's all I know, Wilson said. But oh my, oh my, did Elizabeth and I have a time!

I met her when I came to help Jan get settled in the apartment and, what can I say: the first time, that look, it was explosive. I could feel the pain and need arc all the way through.

And she told me later that she could see that pain as it struck and was hers too, she just wanted to find and take it out inch by inch. That is the way she talked to me from the first time. I had never talked that way with anyone in my life. I guess I had been more like your Fred and Frieda than I had imagined. I was just another of those men you see on the bus with the papers and charts spread on their laps, half-nodding on the way to and from work and you ask this: are they alive or are they dead? Do they know the difference? I thought that I was the one asking the question but Elizabeth told me, taught me, showed me that it was the other way. I had been that man. But no more, no more when we came together in that room on her sudden afternoon off with Jan definitely in training at the hospital — we always called first — and with the police lock set from the inside.

We were very careful but we made mistakes. That was the agreement from the start. We could have this but we could not afford any mistake because just one would be like three. Like four, putting in my own stake in it too. Four lives destroyed and how much freedom for her after all of this, Elizabeth asked. I had no answer but I made no mistakes either. Oh, what I discovered rooting on that bed! Oh what I learned of myself and the darkness and light at the excruciating taper of my life. But of course you know all about this, don't you?

Well, don't you? That is why we are here in the Men's Support Group. We know, we know of the falling taper, don't we? That's why we come to this basement and spend these evenings together.

Chambers and I nodded. Wilson ran a hand over his face and was quiet for a while. We let that be. That is the arrangement. Finally, he looked up and said, Well it was extraordinary. I guess you can understand this kind of thing. Elizabeth was assaulted. Well, no, let me put it bluntly, we must escape the euphemisms which have so coiled and destroyed our lives. Elizabeth was raped. One night on the way back from the office.

I had worried about that, I had admonished her but she said that if we were to have the afternoons she would have to make up the time at night and what could I say? Someone dragged her into an empty subway car, he had a key, might have been an employee, and he raped her on the floor. It was brutal and quick and terrible. He was off at the next station. She bled a lot but got herself to go for help. She was in the hospital for almost a week, . there was a lot of bleeding and she had a clotting problem and they were afraid she was damaged inside. Children. That part, and then there were the AIDS tests and everything else.

The counseling. The sessions. They never got the guy of course. Oh, this was about two years ago, maybe they got him for something else that's often the case, but no one ever confessed to it and they couldn't put it on anyone. It was pretty bad. She was broken up inside about as badly as outside. She got through it but something went out of her forever. The light, the life, even her old darkness. And of course she could never be alone again. Jan stayed with her as much as she could but Jan was in medical training, she couldn't give it up to care for Elizabeth or she would have lost the year and all the money. And Elizabeth couldn't be alone. She moved into a residence for young women. Gave up the job because she was afraid to travel and after what happened she couldn't care what the copy chief said. Her parents wanted to help her any way they could so after a while she went back home to apply to a school of social work. She wanted to get into victim counseling or maybe therapy for brutalized children.

There was another long pause. Chambers and I let it go on. The rules are strict on this. Well, that's it, Wilson said. There's nothing else at all. The last time I was with Elizabeth alone was the day before the rape, we spent the afternoon together. It was profound and beautiful, I thought. Then we had hopes for Saturday if I could convince my wife that I had extra work in the city and if Jan's assignment in the 24-hour emergency room detail held. It would have been our longest time together but even if it didn't work we knew that would have other chances.

Wilson tried to say more, could not, shrugged and sat for a long time. We were never alone again, he said. I couldn't even reach out to her, couldn't tell her how awful it was for me, couldn't tell her anything at all. She could not be alone. Jane knew that. Jan hovered over us, my daughter. She was always in the room. Once I touched Elizabeth's hand and the sensation was terrible: I felt the quivering and then as if from inside her, that sheer stab of revulsion. I moved away quickly. I don't know if it was the exposure or the rapist. Was it the rapist she saw in my face as our hands connected? I could never ask her. I didn't know. I lost her twice, Wilson said. Something like your man, Fred, with Marilyn but maybe not quite the same. It's not clear. It is hard to tie all of this .in a unit, you know?

There's no postscript, Wilson said. Elizabeth moved away 18 months ago and I haven't seen her since. There's no correspondence and no excuse to correspond. Jan tells me that she hears from Elizabeth occasionally but Jan doesn't tell me much and why should she? How can I ask? What can I ask? She's just my daughter's friend, that's all.

Should I start again?

Should I tell you of the room, the shadows, the dark messages in the walls as slowly we came together for the first time, each time being the first? No, I don't think I have anything more to say. I want her to be all right, Wilson said. I love her, I want only her happiness. But at the same time in a way I am glad because I think this: I think that she will never fuck anyone again without that fear and horror at the bottom. I am the last person she will ever fuck for whom it was pleasure and perhaps love. That is all that I can take from this. That's horrible, I know, Wilson said, and it's not the worst with which I have to live either but that is all. Do you want anything more?

I want everything but there is nothing, he said.

Much quiet now and after a while it became clear to all of us, Wilson, too, that he was finished. I don't have anything to say, I said while they were looking at me. Well, Chambers said, moving around a little, there is this too. I do not know how to put this, but it is even simpler than the other parts and it has to do with me. Yours had to do with Fred, he said, and Wilson's had to do with Wilson. I will break the tie because mine is personal too. Maybe everything is personal, what do you think? So my best friend, doesn't matter what his name is, call him David, left his wife for another man after eight years and two kids. Left the wife, Dorothy, who was also a good friend of mine or maybe even a little more than that. She was devastated. It destroyed her — all the time he had been fucking her he had been imagining men, he told her when everything came out. Dreaming of cocks and pectorals to make himself get stiff and hard, to get himself to come.

You can imagine what this does to a woman. Dorothy and I had never had sex, I had never thought about it because I have this thing about my close friend's wives, they make me impotent because I am a gentleman and this was my best friend. At the time this happened I had known David for a quarter of a century. But when she called me, when we had lunch in the city and she told me everything it was as if I had been given cock and balls back. I could feel her looking for them under the table. So the rest of it you know, Chambers said.

You know it, right? There's really nothing I have to say here. We went straight to the Days Inn and we did it at day rates, after all those years I had known her I could at last have her as I had not imagined possible. It was remarkable. I have cheated a little over the years of my marriage like everyone else but there had never been anything like this for me. We heaved and rammed and squeaked and screamed all over the room and almost through the walls beyond. The wallpaper was patterned. I felt I was going to drive her right through that wallpaper and me on top of her and that was just the first time.

After that there were plenty of times. She said that David had made her feel that she wasn't a woman, he had taken the womanhood from her, but she was getting it back from me piece by piece. I don't have to tell you what I got from her.

Sometimes things just happen, you know? They happen and you understand that your whole life up to then had been a lie …but there is no way, just no way you can ever tell that to anyone or for a long time even to yourself. I called it doing therapy for Dorothy and joked to myself about that. I just didn't want to let myself know.

After a while though I came to admit what I already understood and stopped fighting the truth of the situation.

So that's really almost all of it, Chambers said after another long pause. We tend to pause a lot at Men's Support Group. It has to do with the highly charged nature of the material discussed. There is a little more, of course. David got AIDS, he told Dorothy that he had been positive for a long time and then the Kaposi's showed like a delayed houseguest. So Dorothy panicked and screamed and had the test and she turned out to be positive.

She told me all this after the fact, a week after the test. I'm positive, she said. You'd better get tested fast. You'd better take a look at the situation. It's never two in a bed anymore, she said, don't you know that now? It is three or four or maybe forty. He gave me AIDS, the son of a bitch, she said. I should have known but I didn't and I didn't want to face it. It's not AIDS, I said. It's just a positive.

She slapped me. Never had a woman do that, not ever. You son of a bitch, she said. Drop dead you bastard but first get the test and tell your wife if you have any heart at all. Then drop dead. Then she left me. This was in a large open-air restaurant, al fresco, they call it I guess, right? Left me flat as little kids say. A thirty-two dollar bill for two drinks each and one lousy order of guacamole and a positive diagnosis. And if you have anything to say don't say it to me, she said. It's done.

That's almost all of it, Chambers said. I should say that all through this I had kept up appearances with David, he was my best friend still after all and we had plenty to talk about, confessional stuff, although he had never told me about the Kaposi, or for that matter even the positive. Back end in is sometimes the only way. I was learning. I wasn't sure why Dorothy was so mad at me, I wasn't the guy who had given her the disease after all, who had lied to her for years and dreamed of men to keep it up, but there is no accounting for misdirection and the horror of choice, is there?

Anyway, he said, I had the test and that is the story.

We looked at him in the requisite silence for a while.

Well, that's it, Chambers said, you want an epilogue, is that it? You want more? Don't you understand that the axis of the story isn't: Does he have a positive? Did he give it to his wife? That isn't where the story is centered.

No, this is the point: everything has consequence, nothing is disconnected any more, we must pay and pay and there is a causality which makes no discrimination for possibility.

So, anyway, then, all right: I turned up positive and they did it again because false positives are common or at least that's what I wanted to believe. It was positive again. So that was that and I told my wife. Gloria, that's my wife. It wasn't easy but sometimes you just have to come out with something.

Gloria, I said, I am HIV positive, do you know what that means? I'm sorry but that is the situation. I had the test just as soon as I had reason to believe exposure and I am giving you the results immediately.

I mean, Chambers said, how do you tell someone something like this? It's not like saying you lost your job or they caught you embezzling. This is why I say that everything is connected now. Was that the way your guy Fred felt when he put down the phone with the death call and looked at his wife?

How do you say welcome to the abattoir? Gloria, that's it, I said. That's it and that's it and there's no way around this. You want ethos, I'll give you ethos and angst and betrayal and broken troths later on but right now I'm just telling you a situation. I am HIV positive. You may be. You have to get tested at once.

I've been tested, she said. I don't need a test.

Well, that got my attention I will tell you. There was a lot of staring, just as lush and round our eyes as you gentleman are giving me. You got tested? I said. What for? What does this mean?

It means exactly what you think, she said. Exactly that. And I am positive. I've been positive for over a year. Just as you've been giving it to Dorothy you see and I knew what that little trick was doing, I've been getting it on with David.

All right? she said. He seems to go both ways, so why are you so surprised? Two ways is two ways and we're all old friends here, aren't we? Sharing our lives.

I thought about telling you, she said. I thought about how we passed this thing back and forth like a beach ball. I thought about it but what would the difference have been? And then I thought: what if there is someone else, someone new in this, someone I don't know? What about her? Or what about him? Who knows? Who tells? Who cares?

Not me, stupid, she said, looking right my way. I don't care at all. For you, for myself, anybody. If you were screwing around on the side with someone out of the circle then he or she has got it too and I'm sorry but I still don't care. I certainly had better luck with him than with you, you lying, distracted son of a bitch. So that's why I decided not to tell. Not that I was getting plenty anyway.

We're all going to die, I said. Gloria, we're all going to die.

You fool, she said. We're already dead. We've been dead for years.

That's all, Chambers said. If there's any more I missed it. All right. This was two weeks ago. I haven't fucked a soul since, but I seem to still be living at home. Finances, you know.

We've been dead for years, Chambers said, but there's till the issue of money, beyond all epiphany, don't you think?

We sat there for a while and thought about it.

Still thinking.

Out from Ganymede

I

SETTLING INTO orbit around what he has decided to call the Mad Satellite (nothing personal but the mission itself is insane, so tough on Ganymede), Walker finds himself thinking of his estranged wife: unquestionably she was a terrific fuck. Often after he had emptied himself into her as the culmination of simply hours and hours of heaving, bucking, moaning perversity, she had fluttered her eyes underneath and invited him with a coy yank of her head, letting him know that, for everything he had done, the essential part of her lay untouched. How it had infuriated him! He thought that she had been subtly insulting his adequacy when all the time he failed to see the plea beneath the insouciance. The woman had been insatiable. He never should have left her. Still there were other things, other reasons; nothing is as simple as it seems and sexuality is only a metaphor. He comforts himself with this as he works on controls, does computations, juggles the ship into a tight circuit. Deprivation and tension turn the mind in strange ways; he has never really regretted leaving her. He concentrates on Ganymede, which hangs below him darkly, aspects of rock filtering through the cloud formation, the gas of Jupiter high behind him in the anterior port. It is really a great little moon, very Earthlike in its gravity and appearance, to say nothing of being the gateway to Jupiter.

Base, which has talked him into the orbit, asks Walker how he is coming along. Walker says that everything is fine, fine; he had merely been preoccupied for a few moments setting up the orbit on the computer and had dropped out of contact. "That's nonsense, kid," Base says, "everything is plotted right here, you know that. Don't let all that space get to you now. Keep organized."

"It isn't easy, you know," Walker points out. He does not have to address a microphone, the whole craft being wired for sound in such a way that even the sounds of his evacuation can be evaluated by medical personnel at Base. "I mean, it's difficult to carry on as if this was strictly routine. You could try a little understanding."

Base points out that it has cost billions of dollars to put Walker in orbit around Ganymede, that the security and importance of the project cannot be risked because of personal quirks and that nothing must get in the way of the successful completion of the mission. It advises Walker to shape up and reminds him that there is a broadcast due in some twenty minutes, audio and video. Therefore, Base adds rather petulantly, it would make sense to get the cabin in order and put all debris out of visual range. The question of the apogee can be left to the computer.

"The hell with that," Walker says but he says this subvocally and with his face turned toward the floor. Not that the floor does not have pickups also.

II

Walker has been selected for the Ganymede project since he is the fittest of the twenty astronauts left in the program. This says little for his competence — fifty years ago there were several hundred and Walker would have barely qualified for steward's duty — but the agency has been in decline for a long time and, relative to the present situation, Walker is about the best that they can get. He reminded them of this during the examinations, at the physical and at the final briefing but it hardly seems to have done him much good. There is a certain failure of respect. "You are but a piece in the machinery," they had warned him but he had been in no mood to accept that until he was on his way. Now the situation has changed; recently he has been feeling very much like an engine with a certain pistonlike creaking or hammering beneath the joints. Also his voice seems to have become somewhat metallic and his mind moves with the convulsions of slow gears. He does not *want* to be a machine, not particularly, but then again he understands the agency very well and is willing to agree that the alternatives might have been worse.

Walker has not had sex for several months and then in an inept performance with his estranged wife, who told him that she would do it once for the memories and then, limbs spread, regarded him with cold ferocity as he worked against her. Several times he has considered covert masturbation within the ship but even during the sleep periods they surely have ultraviolet light and would be able to detect everything that he was doing. Besides, there seems to be something ridiculous in the idea of a man carried past Mars twirling his genitals. Something mystical should happen to a man past the moon to drive him past need. Masturbation had never been part of the briefing process for reasons he now thinks he understands.

III

After he superficially cleans the cabin there is a five-or ten-minute dead space before the broadcast during which he has little to occupy him and he sits, looking at the walls of the cabin, admiring certain notations the agency has put up in bulletin forms, with absolutely no interest in turning rearward and looking at Ganymede. This way is much better; he can believe that he is only on another simulation. During this period, the aliens come to him. There are two of them, strange yellow bipeds with glowing eyes who wear archaic clothing. On their chests is stenciled *Ganymede Police* and they carry weapons in their appendages which look rather menacing. "Stay calm," one of them says to him, "we just want to talk."

"I'm perfectly calm," Walker says. They are the first living beings he has seen for twelve days and fourteen hours and, despite their dangerous appearance, he is rather glad to see them. Excellent training has long since made him matter-of-fact in relation to all challenge. "As you can see, I'm not too busy at the minute. I am due for a transmission soon, though, and I'm afraid that I'll have to make it."

"That's fine," the spokesman says. He shrugs and replaces his weapon inside his clothing. "I'll do the talking, the other one is just along verifying. The next time he'll do the talking. We work in shifts that way, it's much easier."

"I can understand that," Walker says. "But how did you get into the cabin?"

The alien shrugs again, this time with a rather coy tilt of his appendages which marks him instantly to Walker (who has been well trained) as a cunning article. "Dematerialization" he says. "Don't think about it too much. We want to take up with you this issue of invading our planet. Ganymede is sovereign territory, you know, and you just can't settle into orbit that way. Furthermore, you've got enough armament on this ship to sink a planet. Exactly what do you have in mind?"

"Oh," Walker says, "I knew that there would be trouble about that. The armament is just for show. There's no intention of using it." He blushes faintly. "I wouldn't even know how to make it work," he says. "I'm not sure that it *does* work. They don't bother me with things like that from the ground."

"Nevertheless," the alien says, "nevertheless, I'm afraid that you people simply didn't consider the situation. You're dealing with free territory here. You have absolutely no right in orbit and you must agree that if the situation were reversed you'd find it pretty frightening. You're going to have to leave."

"Well, how the hell did we know Ganymede was inhabited?" Walker says, trying to be reasonable. "There wasn't any sign at all. It's just a dead moon. How do I know that you people even are from Ganymede?"

"We're not people," the alien says, "nevertheless I . understand your terminology. I'm afraid that you're not being very reasonable about the matter. We're giving you two hours, your time, to turn around and go back to your planet, otherwise we will have to take retaliatory action. I don't want to be more specific than that."

"You don't understand," Walker says. "1 can't make any decisions like that. I can't even make promises. I'm just an engineer sent along for the ride. I have no authority."

"That," the alien says, "is your problem." He nods at his companion, his companion gives a brusque strained nod at Walker, they huddle together and at some prearranged signal vanish. Walker is left in the cabin sniffing a faint aroma of ozone which they seem to have left behind them. Base comes on and says that it is time for the transmission to begin. Walker asks them if they heard what just went on and Base says that they have had no time to monitor, they are very busy down there, does Walker really think the first transmission from Ganymede is routine business and they will replay the tapes at their leisure sometime when they get around to it. Everything going on inside the cabin is part of the perfectly preserved public record.

IV

Walker delivers a speech to the assembled peoples of Earth. He reads it slowly, precisely, off the prompter they have installed out of range of the camera, the words unreeling rather majestically. Someone in the higher echelons of the information division has a dash of eloquence although perhaps he is merely thinking of the top levels of the government; it is impossible to tell precisely who is guiding the mission. Walker reminds the people of Earth that in a time of torment and trouble mankind has historically looked toward the heavens from which heavens judgment and a sense of purpose have always come and that it is the spirit of the stars no less than that of the Earth which makes mankind human. By going to Ganymede as we have, by this rare act of disciplined courage on the part of thousands of dedicated people of whom he is only the most visible, Earth has been given a beacon, an instrument of its purpose. "We did not, after all, travel all this vast distance in the ether only to repeat the small banalities of our mistakes, we are refreshed and renewed by our glimpse of the void," Walker says, thinking vaguely about the machinery of the agency compound and how, at the checkpoints on the few occasions when he had had to leave the Base, he had seen thousands of people behind the barricades staring at him and mumbling. What the hell were they saying? Exactly what brought them there? Walker wonders as he goes on to recite some technical data; Ganymede is the largest satellite of the planet Jupiter, it was discovered by an Italian scientist in the seventeenth cenrury; of all the satellites of the planets it is the most Earthlike in appearance and atmosphere, more habitable than Venus, and may eventually be the only place in the solar system where men will be able to maintain a colony independent of the home planet. He turns the camera so that the audience, with him, can see the terrain five hundred miles beyond, swimming in gases, and then turns it back to the cabin, advising them that he will be transmitting three more times during his orbits of Ganymede and hopes that all men of faith and will can join him in the mission. The speech runs out but the transmission, judging from clicks and winks, apparently does not; he fills an embarrassed ten seconds with greetings to his wife and parents and then the light goes out and Base tells them that he has done very well, that everything is in excellent shape, that he should rest for the next cycle in preparation for his next broadcast.

"Yes," he says, "but are they listening?" "We have a full hookup, right through the satellites," Base says. "1 would think that four billion heard you just now."

"Ah yes," Walker says, "but did they *attend?*" He feels lightheaded, slightly disconnected. "And about those aliens; I want to tell you about the aliens."

"No time," Base says. "Rest cycle must begin now and you're slipping out of range."

"But look," Walker says, "you're not following me. Just before the transmission I was visited by these two aliens from Ganymede and they said — "

"No time," Base says, "we'll pick it all up on the monitors."

"But there's life — "

"No time, no time," Base says and slips out of contact; it is like the bodies sliding apart after intercourse, all evasion, all collapse to some central, detached part and, · clenching his fists, Walker finds himself alone in the cabin and nothing to do but sleep. Well, sleep then. He can deal with the situation later.

V

In his sleep Walker dreams and in the dream his wife is in the cabin talking to him. "It's all your fault," she says, "every bit of it is your fault, you never understood, you never cared, you never for one moment considered the implications of what you were doing." "Now wait a minute," Walker says to her (he seems to be in some kind of nightdress and his wife, wearing an opaque gown which he used to despise, is sitting cross-legged on his bunk, her chin in her hands, a complacent hostility severing her from him forever), "don't get started on that tack again, I'm just an employee. A functionary of the agency. In fact I'm only a technician so don't start pinning me with that guilt and culpability stuff again. It was only a job and I was in it long before you knew me and you took me on those terms so it's too late now." She says nothing for a moment, this being one of her most infuriating habits, and then, quite horridly, winks at him. "That won't go any more," she says. "You're forty years old. You know exactly what's going on and you've known for a long time now. You're a man. You're one of the oldest people in the project."

"But in very good physical condition. I'm in such good physical condition — "

"Three hundred years of death and dreams to put you on Ganymede," she says. "Three hundred years. Isn't the price a little too high?" And he leans forward to tell her for the first time what he truly thinks of her and what he has wanted to do to her on so many unspeakable nights but the bitch flicks out, just wanders out of there the way the Ganymedian police have, and there is nothing to confront.

"You bitch," he says, "you dirty bitch," but this is not too satisfactory either and so he only drifts into another dream, much vaguer and more sordid this time, having something to do with campaigning for national office after his triumphant return from Ganymede and finding himself at a party with fifty blondes and a fat national committeeman who fondles all of the women obscenely as he asks Walker to tell him, in twenty words or less, exactly why he thinks he is entitled to public office and what he will do for the national committeeman if he is granted the nomination.

VI

He is awakened by the aliens. They perch at the foot of his bed, shimmering in a kind of haze, and the spokesman reminds him that Walker has exceeded the two hours granted him to reverse the mission and return home. "You're leaving us little choice," the alien says. "We're going to have to take very serious action."

"I don't know what to tell you," Walker says. "I tried to talk to them about you but they cut me off. I really wanted to discuss this, I mean I wasn't sitting on it or anything like that."

"I'm afraid that's no excuse."

"And in the second place," Walker says, tearing himself from the bunk and starting to move around the cabin, trying to force some jauntiness into his bearing, no reason to let a couple of aliens get you down, "in the second place, I couldn't turn the mission around even if I wanted to. It's all remote control. It's all computer. All that I do is come along for the ride. Everything is triggered from the Base."

"That's very interesting," the alien says, "but I'm afraid has nothing to do with the situation. You really have to get out of here, you know; you're pushing us beyond our limits."

"Why don't both of you talk?" Walker says, slapping a bulkhead, dodging an overhang, reeling to his knees to reach the medicine cabinet and some simulated caffeine. "Wouldn't it be easier that way?"

"Policy and procedure," the spokesman says. The aliens exchange nods. "He's only assisting me on this tour."

"I'd really like to leave," Walker says. "I mean, don't get me wrong. The fact that Ganymede has life on it and so on makes your case a very strong one. I'm not a lawyer but I think that you have some very good arguments. But what can I do?" He shows them the palms of his hands. "I have no essential control."

The silent alien looks at him and says, "You have enough armament on this thing to destroy a planet."

"Yes," Walker says, "that's quite true, quite b·ue. I told that to you before and I admit that that happens to be the case. But we didn't intend to *use* it. It's just that the agency is essentially military in nature and we have to carry along war technology in order to make the financing. If you understand what I'm saying, it's very complicated the way they do things. Also, the armament is just for show so if we run into any aliens in space we can protect ourselves. Of course we've never met any aliens up until now and I wouldn't do anything at all to you. I mean, you can see that my position is hardly aggressive."

"Can you operate the armament?" the silent alien says. He seems to be genuinely engaged; unlike the other, once talking, he has a real interest in his work. Perhaps on Ganymede he is an ordnance expert.

"1 don't know," Walker says. "I've received a little instruction, just the basics and so on, but actually it's pretty sophisticated stuff and I don't think that anyone directly in the agency knows exactly how to operate it. I mean, I know a few things about it, yes."

"I mean, is it voluntary?"

"Oh. Is it voluntary? You mean, unlike the operation of the craft, could I actually use the weapons myself? Well, that's an interesting point," Walker says, "now that you bring it up. The answer is that I probably could, come to think of it. It isn't connected to the Base computer like everything else. Actually, it's kind of antiquated and hand-controlled, I believe."

"Well then," the chief alien says, "you certainly could destroy us if you elected to, now couldn't you?"

"But I wouldn't think of it," Walker says hastily. "I'm non-aggressive. Utterly. Really, I'm embarrassed about the whole thing, and I want to take it up with Base just as soon as possible. I'm sure that when they learn that Ganymede has inhabitants they'll be just as upset as I and cancel the mission. I'm *sure* they'll cancel the mission."

"1 don't know," the alien says. "The whole situation is very dangerous. Should we eliminate him?" "Let's give him a little while longer," the other alien says.

"After all, he's being honest with us. He has no authority."

"But I have good faith," Walker says. "1 can show good faith." He feels the shaping of an idea. "1 really could show you that I mean what I'm saying and that — "

"How about another two hours?" an alien says. "Two hours so that he can explain the situation."

"Give him three."

"Yes," Walker says, "I'll clear the thing up in three hours. That would be fine. And if I don't — "

"If you don't," the ordnance expert says, rubbing his appendage through the *P* on *Ganymede Police,* bringing it to something of a shine, "if you don't, we'll take measures."

"1 will," Walker says, "1 really will," and leans forward to tell them a lot more about the good faith he will show but they vanish; so much for *their* interest, and certain beeps from the transmitter indicate that Base thinks it is about time that he came out of rest period and did some useful tasks. "You dirty sons of bitches," Walker says to the receiver and then shudders with a thin sense of shock; he had never realized until this instant that he felt *that* way about them.

VII

He tries to bring up the matter of the aliens with Base but they are not hearing any of it at the moment; for reasons which are not made quite clear, he is to give another speech almost instantly. "Come on, come *on,"* Base nags him as he moves around the cabin setting up the equipment once again, "don't you understand there's no time to *waste?"* It seems to have something to do with riots and protests or perhaps Walker is merely working on a chain of inference. At any rate, the speech when he delivers it is full of soothing phrases and rather frantic reassurances which, because he has had no time to discuss it beforehand, make his delivery rather strained and awkward. "The project was rebuilt from the ground up for the sake of mankind," he finds himself saying and "Certain insignificant but noisy fractions of the populace are participating in a poison campaign" and "Ganymede, the jewel of the heavens, hangs before me now as a token forever of the ingenuity of mankind, his courage, his mission," and "The purpose of this expedition goes far beyond advantage to one party or persons" and when he has finished the speech the transmitters go into a glittering series of explosions, wires and circuits jetting a pure horrifying flame which he can only witness until they turn to smoke and ash. Base informs him that there is some minor problem, sabotaged circuits on the conveyors or whatever, and asks him to hold firm; they will be back to him in due course. "Another speech," Base says,

"you'll have to do another speech."

"Listen," Walker says, "about those aliens — "

"No time," Base says. "Certain adjustments have to be made here."

"But there are *aliens* — "

"I'm sorry," Base says. The tone is regretful, contained,
the sound of disconnection a crisp pop in the empty spaces of the cabin.

Walker squeezes himself through a hatchway or two and, blowing some dust off the armaments, looks it over. It seems comprehensible enough. He recalls vaguely reading an instruction booklet once.

VIII

"Children?" his wife had said. "Do you think I'm *crazy?*" and had looked at him with a mad, bleak expression; confronting her that way, in the jammed spaces of the bed, he had understood for the first time how far it had all gone and the depths of her estrangement. "Do you really think that I'd bring children into this situation? You don't understand me, do you?" she said, turning, her back fitting smoothly, coldly, against the palpitations of his chest, "you don't understand a Single thing that ever went on; I can see that now. I can see everything."

"It isn't that bad," he said, mumbling, futile, holding himself below in an in-stinctive gesture of loss, feeling the sag of his scrotal sac through spread fingers. (Could such devastation come from something that minute, that vulnerable?) "Things aren't what they should be but we're still going on; there's been a real leveling off of international tension and the race problems, well, we'll always have a race problem but some of the space pressure is easing and — "

"Oh, you damned fool," she said against him, her voice mingling into laughter, "you damned *fool,* do you think I'm talking about the world? The hell with the world! Do you really think I'd bring children to *us?*" And broke into laughter then, full harsh laughter, and Walker turned from her, back to back; like some sea beast, they had jammed against one another in the night, his mumbles and sighs against her whimpers, the conjoinment of their buttocks hard and yet somehow perfect under the cold damp of the sheets. And in the morning had fucked, simply and unspeakingly, he rising above her to such heights that he felt he could confront the walls.

Well, that had been a long time ago. No point in getting into any of that so late in the game.

He finds himself thinking that in many ways, in certain aspects, she had looked like the aliens.

IX

Base tells him that the mission must be aborted. They have no specific explanation but say that it has something to do with certain strains and stresses surrounding the project and also a vague issue of public safety. It has nothing to do with his conduct, which was exemplary but failed, somehow, to work. Perhaps later on they will be able to explain things to him in detail although there cannot be any guarantees; matters are somewhat confusing. Walker asks if there are any more transmissions for him to deliver and Base says no, thank you, not at *this* time, there is no point to it and in any event there is certain difficulty with the communica-tions. They will wheel him out of the next orbit and take him home. He asks them if they want him to do the planned probe and the leaving of the artifacts and Base says no, there really is no time for this and they can do it, perhaps, next time around. Walker gathers that the situation is somewhat obscure and perhaps they are Withholding certain information from him. "Trust us," Base says. "It's going to be a very difficult re-entry because of certain problems here but we'll talk you through without the automatics and everything will work out well. Trust us," Base says and leaves him alone for the time being. Walker busies himself dismantling the equipment for transmission and then lies on his bunk, arms behind his head, whistling absently through his teeth and trying to think of nothing at all. There really is little enough on his mind; the ship will be yanked out of orbit through remote control. The aliens return, looking dour. Walker raises a hand.

"I'm leaving," he says. "Don't worry about a thing. I'm leaving after the next orbit."

"Ab," the spokesman says, "that's fine. Nevertheless, you did not obey our instructions. More than three hours have elapsed since our final warning."

'I'm leaving anyway. What's the difference?"

"You defied us."

"Listen," Walker says, "you understand that there was no intent to intrude. We had no hostile intent. It was all a mistake."

"Nevertheless you were warned."

"I did what I could. Still, I'm leaving."

"Not sufficient," the alien says. He turns to the other. "Not sufficient," the other says. "It's a serious infraction."

"Listen to me," Walker says, sitting and coming over to crouch near the aliens (they are really quite short and at this height he can regard them level; see what truly attractive creatures they are). "I'll show good faith. I understand your position and I'm willing to show good faith. Just to point out to you that this was all a mistake."

"How can you? We can take very severe retaliatory action, you understand."

"Don't worry about it," Walker says. He leans forward, throws out an explicatory palm. Everything is very simple as long as you take it step by step. He explains.

The aliens listen quietly, look at one another, Finally nod. They agree that what Walker offers seems sufficient. Under the circumstances it is a fair and equitable offer.

Walker smiles and relaxes. For the last ten minutes of his stay in the orbit of Ganymede, he and the aliens talk intimately to one another, exchanging reminiscences, observations and, in Walker's case, some very frank details about sexual preferences of his wife which, unjustified as they were, Simply drove him mad.

X

Crouching over the armaments, suspended heavily against the wall, Walker finally sinks into a tension-induced doze, a sleep supported by sedatives and loss which carries him through five million miles of space. In this sleep he dreams that he is once again fifteen years old and present at the End of the World; staring through the window of the home in which he was born, he sees the sky turn into fire, the fire into streaks which encircle and enflame everything which he has always known. There goes the tree in the back yard, there goes the boot factory up on the hill, there goes the home of the girl whom he will, in some years, marry. She appears in the center of the flames, mournful, stricken, yearning, her mouth slowly opening to passion or torment at the center of the fire, and as the flames take her to agony she breaks into an expression more yielding than any he has ever known and, pressed as he is against his window, watching her through binoculars, he feels that he could reach and touch her, hold her in his arm, protect her against the devastation ... but this is impossible, she is dead beyond recovery, and he wakes screaming, screaming, against the cold web of the armaments which seem to snatch at him with gears come alive and he hangs on for all he is worth, waiting, waiting, only a few million miles more to Earth and he can bring upon them, upon her, a judgment more truthful than any they have ever known. "Because you deserve it, you sons of bitches," he says.

Behind him, the two aliens, along for the ride, chuckle wisely and make circles of approval at one another with their strange webbed appendages.

Kingfish

EVERY MAN a king, every king a saint, each and every one of us on our own piece of holy ground. That's what he said. That's what he said to the little guy in Berlin. I was there at the picture-taking after the private conferences, I could hear what Huey said to him over the sounds of the reporters, the hammer of the flashbulbs. Just look this way, boss. You and me and cousin Henry, Aunt Anna and Moses down the lane, there's a glory for each of us and it can be yours too. The little guy kind of jumped and twitched when Huey squeezed him on the shoulder. The interpreter was yammering away in that German of his, but somehow I think the little guy got the message already. He knew more English than he let on. He knew a lot more stuff than he let on about everything.

What do you say there, Adolf? Huey said, and gave an enormous wink. I could have dropped my teeth on the floor. You think we can get this rolling, just the two of us? Hey John, Huey said, motioning to me, don't stand there like a stupe on the sidelines, join the photo session. This here is my vice president, Huey said to the little guy.

The little guy said something in Huey's ear, up close. That's right, Huey said. That, too. He's everybody's vice president. He is the second in command, isn't that right? He gave me a Louisiana-sized wave, clasped my hand. Holding his hand that way, backing into the Fuhrer, I had the little guy boxed against Huey. We had him in perfect position, trapped. We could have stood and tossed him over the Reichstag. But we didn't, standing there frozen in the eye of the world, the press roaring, the sounds drifting around us and in that small abyss Huey squeezed my hand for attention and gave one perfect, focused wink. *Got him,* the wink said. *Got him, didn't I tell you?*

Got you too.

This was the meeting in the Bayou in November of 1935, the famous secret meeting. Never mind where. Huey's boys got to me and said be in Amarillo at midnight and leave the rest to us. We'll get you past the border and leave the delegation at home. It was easy to get away, I was back home for Christmas then. The President wouldn't even have known I had blown town. It had gotten harder and harder to get Roosevelt's attention; it wasn't even worth trying anymore. Now and then I had fantasies of sneaking behind his wheelchair during the State of the Union and pulling the podium away, showing his shrunken parts to the world. But I never would have done that. Damn near would never have done anything if Huey hadn't gotten in touch. Came into the parish humping my way in a big black car, it could have been Capone's chauffeur up there in front, the guys with me in the back Capone's party boys: But I wasn't scared. Who shoots the vice president? Easier to park him under a rug and let him die. I'm going to go for it, Huey said to me. This isn't to bullshit you, I'm coming straight out. I'm running for president.

That's no surprise, I said. It wasn't. The word had been out for years, this Senator wasn't running around Washington for the graft, filibustering for the sake of opening his yap. *Every man a king.* He wanted to be president, all right. If not Roosevelt, then why not him? But Roosevelt seemed to have the banged-out vote pretty well sewed up. I told Huey that. You can't run as the man of the people against this guy, I said, he knows the people too well. He's a sitting president. You'll just have to wait your turn.

I'm not waiting my turn, Huey said. Up close he was intense, even more so than on the radio. There was something in his eyes, something in the set of his body that made you not want to explore his depths. All of this was in a room one-on-one, he wanted no one in there with us. After I got shot at, Huey said, grabbing his arm, I got this insight. There's no sense waiting. You wait, you're just as likely to die. Two inches either way on the gun hand and the guy wouldn't have gotten me in the shoulder, he would have had me in the heart. I would have died there on the Capitol floor.

I know all about it, I said. I read the papers too.

You read a hell of a lot more than the papers, Huey said. You don't pull that dumb cowboy shit on me, John Nance Garner, you're the Vice President of the United States and no goddamned fool. I was calculating, let him have the two terms and run in 1940. But when I saw the blood spouting out of my arm, heard the screaming, saw that cocksucker lying dead on the floor instead of me, I said what the fuck is this? This is all bullshit. I'm making plans, biding my time, while the man on the plow is dying and I could have been dead. I'm going for it now.

That's your prerogative, I said. You've got a tough one ahead of you. But I can wish you well. I got no quarrel with you.

Maybe you should, Huey said. You Texans, you think we're all a bunch of savages and Cajun voodoo lovers here. Or grave robbers. But if you can take it, I can. I want you to run with me, he said. That's the only way. You run with me, we can split him away.

Run with you? I said. You're crazy. Bolt the party, give up the office?

Who said to give up? Huey said. You're Vice President. You're a constitutionally elected official, you're in as solid as him. He can't impeach you and it's only eleven months until the election anyway. Instead of running as a Democrat you run with me as an Independent. I don't want to go in the party anyway.

Never heard of anything like it, I said. I have to tell you, I was astounded. Ever since that thirty-hour stem-winder in the Senate when Huey had worked with applejack and a tin can strapped to his leg to stop the government cold while he argued the budget and the Book of Genesis and a hundred other things, I had known he was a man to reckon with, no one to underplay, but this was something entirely new. This went outside my experience. Shit, I said, you're crazy.

So I'm crazy, Huey said. You think I'm out of place here? It's all crazy. We got ourselves a country in collapse, we got ourselves a situation that won't quit. Got thirty million men wandering the roads of America, ready to kill for a slice of bread, got thirty million women who would hump for the price of an apple or some clothes for the baby. Think it's going to turn around? Think again. We're in critical times, boy. It's all falling apart on us. It's time for someone to take over who cares for the people.

Frank cares for the people, I said. In his way.

His way, Huey said. He gave me that smile, opened his mouth, showed me all the lovely white and open spaces. Just two guys on the Bayou talking sense, he said. Got all the doors closed. Want some whiskey? I got me a bottle of the finest here. He busted Prohibition, I'll give your guy that.

I don't care, I said. I never turned down any whiskey. Huey took a bottle from inside his coat, opened it, passed it to me. Here, he said. Got compunction? Want a glass?

Never heard of that, I said. I took a swig deep down — not bad stuff — and handed it over. You serious? I said. You really mean it?

Sure I mean it, he said. If you come over, I figure we got this election. It all falls into place. You've made a considered judgment, that's it. You're going with the real man of the people. Franklin will have a fit but what can he do? Maybe he can get Lehman to run with him. Two New York kikes, Huey said, and took a swig and giggled. Not that I got anything against kikes, he said. Kikes and shines and Micks and Polacks, hunkies and Cajuns and Injuns and all the rest of them, they're all the soul of the country. But I want this to be a done deal, I don't want to fool around. I want your commitment *now*, and then we'll go on from there.

And then what? I said. How do I go back to Washington and face the man?

You don't have to face him. You can stay on the ranch. You're constitutionally elected, remember? There's nothing he can do to you. We'll wait a couple of months, then we'll hold a joint press conference and announce.

Not Democrat, I said. You want to go third party.

Right, Huey said. He looked at the bottle, shrugged, took another sip. We could probably beat him in the party if we went out for it but we'd bust it wide open and then he'd probably go third party on *me* and split the thing.

No, we'll do it ourselves. The money is there. Don't worry about the money. Just have my ass there, I said, that's what you're telling me?

That's what I'm telling you, he said. Listen, you don't like this guy anyway.

That's no secret. And I'll tell you something, all right? He held the bottle out to me. I shook my head. (They have me down for a drunk but it is all part of their misunderstanding. No one goes as far as John Nance Garner has by being a simple drunk. Of course there are other factors.) Here it is, Huey said. I want to be a one-term president, that's all. I'll step aside in '40. You can have it then.

You got it all figured out, I said. What a generous offer.

I'm serious, he said. If I can't make this thing work in one term, I can't do anything in two. Besides, I don't want to be president all my life. I want to lie down here in the sun, run the dogs, know me another woman or two. But I got a few plans. In '40 I can put you over the top.

I didn't believe a word of it. Up to this point I had pretty well taken what Huey had said as he had presented it, but this part was not to be believed. It didn't bother me, of course. Long view or short, you cultivate the situation more or less as it is found and don't push for explanations. I'll think about it, I said. It's going to be ugly stuff. The Republicans want to be heard from.

Republicans! Huey said. Who they got? Hoover again? Charles Evans Hughes? Maybe Styles Bridges? I say the word *Hoover* three times a day until November, I don't have to say anything else. So much for the Republicans. Franklin will be tough but with his vice president jumping ship and every man a king, I think I got a chance. You think I have a chance, Big John?

Yes, I said, I think so. I want to think on this some.

Don't think on it too long, he said. You're getting first offer and best offer but you aren't the only one, you understand. There are a lot of people outside the parishes who see things the way I do, who would be happy to come along. The next person I ask is Rayburn. You think he'll turn it down?

I don't know, I said.

Well I do, Huey said. He turned it down. Conditional. He said I should ask you first, courtesy of the line of succession and all that. But if you don't want it, he said, I should ask him again. That good enough for you?

I'll have another sip of that whiskey, I said. I do declare that ain't bad whiskey, considering.

Yeah, Huey said. You know, I looked down at that blood on the floor of the Capitol and I said, it could have been *my* blood and no one would ever have known what I could have been. There are moments that change you, Big John. Maybe you've had a few.

I think I've had one just now, I said. I took the whiskey bottle from him and palmed it. It felt like a grenade in my hand. I ran the palm over it, up and down, down and up, then drank deep. I'm tired of this job, I said finally, this is a shitty job. Maybe you can give me somethirig to do besides hold a gavel and wait around for you to drop dead.

We'll have plenty for you to do, Huey said. We're gonna be a goddamned *team,* Big John. And in 1940, things work out the way I hope they will, you can have the whole goddamned thing. We'll probably be in a war by then anyway, ain't doing you no favors.

Landon was a clown. Huey was right, the Republicans had nothing, there was no way that they could campaign, nothing that they could say. That was the summer of the dust bowls, the failed crops, the riots in the Capitol. Roosevelt wanted me to step down when he got the word, and then he threatened to impeach me, and then he said he'd send me out to inspect the goddamned Navy in California for six months if I didn't shut up and get in line, but I just laughed at him. There was absolutely nothing that he could do. He was licked and he knew it. He had a sitting vice president who had shifted to an Independent ticket headed by a better man and there was no provision in the Constitution or in the articles of state that could touch me. He couldn't even say too loud that I was a piece of shit because, after all, he had picked me the first time around and I had enough friends in the party to embarrass him on the renomination. Anyway, the Governor of New Jersey ended up as the fool's candidate for vice president and Huey and I took to the road.

We stirred the pots in Metairie and prayed with the ministers in Dallas; we lit fires on a reservation in Albuquerque and then we went to a meeting with father Divine in Brooklyn. The father Divine stunt was a ripper, it looked for a couple of days that it would cost us everything, that we would blow the election on that, but then the East came roaring in with the editorials and Rayburn was able to hold Texas and the rest of the South in line just as I knew he would. father Coughlin went crazy and the Klan had some mighty doings in Florida and outside Atlanta, but father Divine stood up in Times Square and on 125th Street and then Independence Square and said, these are good men, these are men who understand, I take the curse of racism and hatred from these men because having come from the fires of Satan, the hardest place in the country, they know the truth that will set us free. The Governor of the State of New York — Franklin's state — met Huey in Grand Central Station and shook his hand. Out in the Midwest, crawling from stop to stop, we saw crowds like I had never seen in a hundred years in politics, and in California the farmers and the soldiers and the old soldiers came in a long line to Huey and shook his hand and wept. We know you got something for us, they said. We think you understand. Grandmas wiped his face with their handkerchiefs and now and then, seeing a hungry baby, Huey cried. Landon was flabbergasted, he gave it up in early October and went back to Kansas and just about sat on the front porch. Roosevelt fought and fought — no legs but enough courage, I had never denied that — but it all slipped away from him. As Vice President I slipped off to Washington now and then to preside over the Senate, get my face in the papers and pound the gavel and cloakroom a little.

We got 341 electoral votes. We got New York and Pennsylvania. We got California. We lost Ohio and Illinois and we almost lost Texas too, and we sure as hell lost Georgia and Florida, but we didn't lose too much else and in the early morning Wednesday when it was at last over, Huey turned to me and handed me a bottle, that same bottle I swear, and said, We did it, John. You did it and I swear I'll never forget. I want to do good, John, he said. You got to believe that, I've only wanted all my life for the working man to have a break — and the working man in this country, he's been screwed right out of his inheritance and his heart. We're going to set this country aright, John, you hear that? For the first time we're going to do it *his* way. I owe it all to you, John. Rayburn snuck in when it was all over, of course he couldn't do anything officially then or later, but he made his position clear. Huey went out the next day and had the press conference.

It was the goddamnedest thing I had ever seen. I had been Vice President of the United States and now I was going to be Vice President again and it was *still* the goddamnedest thing that I had ever seen. I guess I knew at the time that nothing could ever touch it again like that but I didn't care. There are only a few moments in life, as Huey himself said, and if you are lucky you know when they are there and you use them and you try to run with them all to — and maybe, if you are very smart and lucky past — the grave.

But it started to go badly, early on. By the time of the Olympics, even before the election, we knew that Adolf was no temporary phenomenon, that he was the real thing and that it was a bad situation. The worst. Adolf did things with crowds that even Huey couldn't do. We could see that in the clips. And the news drifting out was worse and worse.

We're in trouble, Huey said. This was in spring of '37, only the third time I had gotten in to see him since he had been triumphantly inaugurated. It hadn't taken long for him to turn me back into a vice president. This guy is murder, he said. I don't worry about Mussolini so much, he's an Eye-talian and he goes whichever way the wind goes, but Adolf is a killer. He's a killer boy, do you hear that? He is taking us to war.

So what can we do? I said. I fell into the role easily enough, feeding Huey lines, taking his whiskey — he always had a bottle now — and trying not to think about the times past. What the hell, it wasn't worth a pitcher of warm spit anyway, I had known that before. So I had just switched wives, that was all. It was the same bunch of crap and John Nance Gamer knew it. Besides, the only real populist is a dead man, I was smart enough to know that. What are we going to do, take Adolf out?

He's killing Jews and Gypsies, Huey said, and ugly looking types and enemies and a lot of good Germans too. He's killing everything that takes his fancy and he's dead serious about this. He is one out-of-control loon and he is putting us on a war footing, do you understand that?

I understand a lot of things.

I can't go nowhere, I can't do the kind of things that got to be done with one eye on that guy. We're going to go over there and try to reason with him. We're going to set up a run to Berlin.

I think not, I said. I think I'll preside over the Senate.

You too, Huey said. We'll take a slow boat, bring along some good whiskey and maybe a few friends. We'll have a nice cruise and we will try to reason with this gent. Maybe he can be persuaded to try reason. If not, we'll still get some good pictures out of it and they'll see that the President was willing to go a ways trying for peace.

I think this is a big mistake, I said. I think we ought to hunker down and wait this out. Wait what out?

Wait what out? Think he's going to stop? His country is leaking Jews. Soon as he's killed everyone he can there he's going to turn outward, want to go other places. This guy likes killing, you understand? We wait him out, he'll be in California.

What can I say? I said. I had another swallow of whiskey. I was always swallowing whiskey in those days. It's your play, I said. You always wanted it your way, Kingfish, so I'm not going to stop you. You want me to go over on an ocean liner with you, I'll go, I just hope it's not the *Titanic*. What the hell, I said, why don't we go all the way? Smuggle a thirty-eight caliber into a state meeting and shoot the fucker in the throat. You think that would solve the problem?

Huey gave me a long odd look. You think I haven't considered that? he said. I am ahead of all you Democrats. But it is not a wise plan. Not at this time.

You think he's a faster draw?

I think that we're at the Reichstag when we try it, that isn't too smart, Huey said. That's all I think. But it is something to be tabled for future reference.

I should have said something then. But vice presidents are not paid to say things other than *in accordance with the Constitution I cast the tie breaking vote in favor of this resolution*. Or, I *support our great President*. Or *it ain't worth a pitcher of warm spit*. Trust a vice president to know protocol.

After Berlin, Huey put the invitation right out. Come to Washington and we'll try to settle this thing. But Adolf had other plans, other stuff on his mind about then, and so for that matter did the Kingfish, things were getting cudgeled about in the provinces and Franklin, no quitter, was rallying the Democrats and talking about a people's coalition in 1940. The basic question, Franklin was saying, had to do with what Huey had *done* since the Inauguration and aside from going to Berlin to have his picture taken and making some good speeches against the Wall Street capitalists, Huey hadn't done much at all. These were powerful points and gave the Kingfish pause, or at least kept him preoccupied. So there were some lively times here and about when the food riots started to occur on a regular basis. Business was reviving a little and Hollywood was telling us that things were great but down on the Great White Way or the places where the Commies dwelt, there was a different cast to the situation. And the Commies were getting stronger; anyone, even the Vice President, could see how much real appeal they were finding in the cities.

But by that time it just didn't matter that much. There comes a time when your destiny confronts you and if you don't accept it, you don't begin to work in accord with that destiny, well then you're just a fool. I wasn't going to be president in 1940. I wasn't even going to be vice president by the end of that year; I had been sucked in and served my little purposes and now I was going to be frozen out. The Kingfish had gobbled me up, just a medium-sized fish in the tank. I would be dumped and Huey would run again, maybe win, maybe lose to Franklin this time, but that was going to be the end of it. And by 1940, it was going to be a changed situation anyway. I just didn't give a damn; I wanted to get back on the ranch, I wanted to see the old times out with as much dignity and as little whiskey as I could manage and the hell with the rest of it. So my accommodation was to simply hang on and go on my way. Huey was going to stay out of local statehouses and he had some pretty good protection. Even Capone or Legs Diamond would have had a hell of a time nailing the Kingfish by that time. No fortunate accidents were going to catapult me to any place that I hadn't already been.

But then, just when it seemed settled, it wasn't settled. After Munich, after he gobbled up the rest of Czechoslovakia, Adolf had Goring pass the word direct to Harry Hopkins. He wanted to take up Huey's invitation. He wanted to come over, explore a few things, do a little business.

Peace in our time, Huey said. He's looking for that now, right? Why should the son of a bitch take us up on this now? He's cleaning out the country, he's ready for war. What the hell does he have in mind?

Why are you asking me? I said. I haven't been in here twice in nine months, Huey, I got nothing to tell you.

Don't sulk, Big John, Huey said. I got you in mind all the time, it's just that I've been preoccupied. This is a big country, you know, and there are lots of problems. Maybe we'll get that redistribution working, maybe all of this stuff will come out in the long run, but it isn't going to be nearly as fast as I thought when I was a young man. Got to cultivate patience, that's all.

I have lots of patience, I said, I had it a long time ago. You were the one who was going to turn things around, make it all different by 1940, remember? I didn't say that it was going to happen.

Huey said, you're taking this too hard, John. You're taking it personally. Sit back and help me through this. I want you to meet the guy when he comes off the boat in New York, I want you to escort him around. The Statue of Liberty, maybe Liberty Square in Philadelphia on a day trip. Then you can bring him here and I'll meet him at the White House and we'll talk over things. But I need your support here, I don't want to go trotting out for him, it doesn't suit my purposes.

I'm not a messenger boy, I said. I'm the Vice President. You got to take the office seriously even if you got no use for me.

Ah, nonsense, John, the Kingfish said. You've said yourself what you think of this job and you were right, all the time. I got a crazy plan, John. I think we're going to save the world twenty years of agony and maybe a few million lives. I think we're going to arrange to plug this guy, if not at the dock then maybe when he's walking down Pennsylvania Avenue. We'll have an accident arranged for him.

That's crazy, I said. Our own lives won't be worth shit. A head of state killed in our protection? They'll go to war the next day.

Goring and Himmler? Goebbels? You think these guys want war? They just want what we have, John, they just want their part of it, that's all. They won't do a goddamned thing. They'll be relieved, they think this guy is crazy too. Every synagogue in the country will have the lights on all night the day he dies. Even Chamberlain will thank us. We'll be treated like heroes. I think the world will fall down and give us everything we want, we get the deed done. That's what I think and your own part is clear. You're going to help me, John, and that's the end of it.

And then what? I said. It's a crazy plan, Huey. And even if it works, can we deal with the consequences?

Well sure, Huey said. I've been dealing with consequences all my life. I love consequences, they're all we got. We don't know what causes, we only know what happens, you understand? I love these talks, I want you to know that. Just the two of us in a room with a bottle, beautiful, I don't know what I would have done if we hadn't had that. Have a drink, John, it's too late.

Too late for what?

Too late not to have a drink, the Kingfish said. So set them up.

So what was there to say? The rest seems very fast in memory although of course it was agonizingly slow in the development, waiting all through it in a suspended anguish, waiting for that heavy thud that would ejaculate us into the latter part of the century. Meeting the prancing, dancing little dictator and his company right off the boat, doing the ceremonial thing, then whirling them through Jimmy Walker's glittering, poisonous city. The Staten Island Ferry, Radio City Music Hall. Two Rockettes flanked Hitler, put their arms around him at my direction, mimed kissing his cheekbones. He glowed, seemed to expand. There was supposed to be a mistress but there was no woman in the party, no woman close to him. Just Himmler, Goring and the impossibly fat Streicher who always seemed to be confiding something to the Fuhrer. We had a private dinner at the Waldorf, talked through the interpreters of cattle and of conditions in Austria during the World War and of the shadows in Europe. Grover Whalen poured wine. I mentioned the Sudetenland, just to have it on record, but the interpreter frowned and I could see that there was no translation. Later, the dictator wanted to see Harlem at midnight. We drove there quickly in covered cars, then back to the Waldorf. At the corner where Father Divine had embraced the Kingfish, women looked at us indolently, poking knees through their skirts. The Fuhrer rumbled in the car but said nothing. We wheeled down Fifth Avenue until the lights glowed softly again, then back into the underground garage. I felt something like a blow at the back of my neck and the thought *Like the Statehouse*. These were the conditions. If it was going to happen, the place would be here. It would be now.

Seated next to the dictator I leaned over to whisper — what? What would he have understood? I had no German. Nor did I know what I would have said. Dead Jews, Gypsies, burning bodies in their graves, the awful aspects of war. I thought of this and leaned back. There was nothing to say. We stopped, the door came open. I got out first and then the guard in the jump seat and then Streicher from the front, panting in sweat, and then Hitler. Hitler came last of all, straightened, looked at me with those strange, focused eyes, that face like a claw. *Raus,* he said in a high voice, *raus —*

His head exploded. One eye seemed to expectorate, fall to the stones of the garage, then fragments of him were cast upward. In the heavy embrace of someone I could not see, I stumbled back. The grasp was enormous, absolutely enfolding, it felt like swaddling, like death, like ascension. The dictator was floating. The dictator, in pieces, was floating in the air.

Now we can begin the business of living, I thought I heard Huey say, his voice enormous in my head. Except of course, that there was no Huey there, only that stricken embrace, and then the broken screams in the garage, the sound of gabbled German, hysteria —

Hitler sifted over me in the sudden darkness.

Under the silt of Hitler, I fell.

The Kingfish sent shocked condolences and offered to accompany the body back to Berlin. But the party and their coffin were already on their way before the announcement at the press conference and then in the dawn, the first reports came of the attacks upon the Embassy. The declaration of war followed by noon.

Chamberlain was furious with us.

But the Kingfish was at the top of his mood, the happiest I had ever seen him. I always wanted to be a war president, he said. I guess that this was what I was aiming for from the start. We're going to save them, John, he said excitedly, we're going to get them out, we're going to stop the machine. We're going to save them all, Huey said. We're going to save *them all*.

Salvation from the parish.

Morning Light

SELL SHE-US: Dark my light and darker my desire. Roethke wrote that, I think. Theodore Roethke (1908-1963), mentor to a lot of slightly younger poets who did it to themselves by way of ovens, candlelight, bridges, walkways, or the more civilized spaces of furnished rooms and alcohol. For Ted it was a heart attack but who is to say, who is to calculate the etiology? But my desire is not dark, it is light, light as night, full as flight, plumes of breath drifting upward into the cold and preservative spaces as slowly, slowly I enter into the quiescent, embalmed spaces of my beloved. Live and learn. Look and listen.

At the heart's stubborn zero, on the bed where all connection is borne. Think of it, Frances, think what it could have been like, the two of us on those mild and quiescent shores of passage, the two of us locked and linked to the essentialities of the spirit. Of course, you had other ideas, Frances, which is what has led to these more difficult and sullen choices. Enraptured, enthralled, I nonetheless roll and roll toward that stubborn zero on these frozen sheets, looking for the still heart of desire. A generation of sunken poets would have approved. Desolate, those inner spaces of yours and yet, five miles from desolation in the Vegas desert is the dazzling sun of the Strip itself. One must counsel patience then in any direction.

Centigrade: "Excuse me," Randall Jarrell says. His eyes twinkle with introspection, with secrets which could stop a world were he only to divulge them. Some years later he will take that stroll down the highway and make fast calculations as headlights reach toward those secretladen eyes. "What do you think you're doing? Shouldn't you put on the heat? It's awful in this room, at least you should have a blanket. And look at your partner. She's absolutely blue."

"Blue is true," I agree. "She's cooperating now, though. There's something about real cold that brings them around, haven't you noticed?"

Randall Jarrell shrugs. Carrying original sin and the lost forests of childhood within him, considering this history (and the barren aspect of grown-up life) leaves him little room for dialogue, for the rigors of eschatology . "I wouldn't know," he says, "I wouldn't know what brings any of them around. " He removes his coat, tosses it. "Here," he says, "place it on the lady, if you won't protect yourself, at least be a gentleman. Even a bear cares. "

"Don't tell me what to do," I say. Nonetheless, I hold the cloak at arm's length, then toss it atop Frances. The folds conform to her limbs, she looks both smaller and more sufficient on the bed. A small arc of steam seems to come from beneath the coat, clouds the space above. "Well, thanks anyway," I say, "thanks a lot."

"Fifty-one American poets," Randall Jarrell says. He seems almost happy, now that Frances has been cloaked. "Fifty-two disasters. I am talking of a generation here. But don't let it bother you, it's not your destiny. It's the ball-turret gunner we must fear." He dematerializes, glides through a wall. "See you," he says, "in just a little while. Down the highways and byways of life." His stride is heavy, resonant in the new emptiness, I imagine that I can see his little bearded form speeding toward resolution. But that of course is surely not mine to say.

"We had plans, didn't we, Frances?" I say. "Big plans, large outcome." As usual, she says nothing. She has said nothing for a long time. Sometimes I feel culpability, other times sorrow, now and then the perverse need to enter her even in this diminished state and place the crystals of my being deep within her but more or less, more and more I try to control myself, keeping the example of my mentors and possessors before me.

Absolute Zero: Sylvia Plath is shivering. Upstairs her children sleep on and on, wrapped in their midday doze, unavailing, unrepresentative of her condition, but in the kitchen. Sylvia grasps herself, hugs herself, gasps. "I'll never get warm," she says. She bites her lips until little premonitory flecks of blood appear. "Oh Daddy," she says, "oh Daddy you bastard." Her gaze sweeps the room, she looks at me with interest. "It's not you," she says, "you're not Daddy."

"No I'm not."

"Who are you?"

"I'm an observer," I say, "a watcher in the glade of life. Fifty-one dead American poets keep me busy with their adumbrations. Are you very cold?"

"So cold unto death," Sylvia says. She looks longingly at the oven. "In there I can get warm," she says. "I'll just put it on, have a spot of tea. "

"You must consider this carefully," I say. "Absolute zero is no foundation, it is only a possibility. "

"Why fifty-one?" Sylvia says. She turns a switch, we listen to the ooze of released gases. "Why not forty-nine or fifty-four? Why are you so precise?"

"I was accused of that," I say. "Precision is all that stands between me and the void. You too. Most of us. Rigor, circumstance, ritualized versions of ourselves. You'll never get warm, not even there. Just a falling, a falling and then a cold you cannot conceive. I know."

"How do you know?"

"Don't ask," I say. I think of telling her about Frances, but it is a superfluity. Sylvia has enough on her mind; all of her compassion is reserved for herself. Not even the kiddies upstairs can distract her. She opens the grate of the oven, kneels. "I know it's different in there."

"Not necessarily."

"I'm looking for a way out," she says. She leans forward, puts her head inside, sniffs. "Yes," she says, "it's warm." She inhales deeply. "Aah," she says, "this is warmth." Her respiration levels, keens, I hear the sound of her panting. "Ariel," she says, "*a-real, a-real.* "

It is time to take my leave. Rounds are necessary, perhaps, call it a survey course, but they are also depressing. So much disaster! So many dead poets, damned poets, dying poets, self-loathing poets, self-mocking poets. So much copulation, fornication, inebriation, alcoholism, imbibition. So much adultery, fondle and putter in the small groves of academia, uptilted breasts like chalices, small groans as if from the vestry of self, distinguished heads leaning over the cusp of toilet bowls in their soon-enough remorse. It is more than one can bear, for penance or research.

Sylvia takes one shuddering breath and is still as I pad out of the English countryside, as deft and invisible at this moment as Jarrell. "Frances," I say, "it is unfortunate that you have driven me to this." I reach out, find myself on the accustomed bed, place her splendid and icy fingers on the back of my neck. Now at last the momentary soothing of embrace. I huddle with her under the blanket which Randall has so wisely suggested to us and ponder all of the circumstances of this difficult odyssey.

In the Ice House: Full fathom five Delmore Schwartz lies, crumpled in the corridor of the Times Square hotel where, so recently, he has incurred a fatal attack. His blood cools toward the risible, his eyes are already frozen in contemplation of that constancy he has for so long sought. "Genesis," I say, as if the sound of his own work will speed him toward a milder fate. "The world is a wedding of successful love." Delmore has no response to this; unlike the chatty Randall or the chilled Sylvia, he has taken a determined step toward the next phase of his career.

Considering him, considering the detritus within Delmore's room, the shambles of which I can clearly see through the open door, I think of the strange and shared fate of these postwar poets, some of whose work will even discuss the pity of their situation. If I were to look carefully enough, use the periscope of accommodation, I would — it seems to me — probably find underneath the orange rinds and incoherent handwritten manuscripts, the unreadable poems and the whiskey bottles heaped on the bed, the perfect and molded form of Frances, still hiding out in yet another poet's room, waiting for the line that will vault her into some kind of understanding of her life (and therefore mine) but I dare not look. Frances got around, Frances had a real understanding of modem poetry but only by proxy. In the sheets I would quote and sometimes lecture, promise her further insights but I would not escort her to the world. Humping toward the flower of her being, immersed in the cold and arching speech of the poets the century had bestowed upon me, I committed a rigorous and insistent research.

Falling to the Abscissa: On the high cliff, Berryman waves to me, measures himself for the leap. "What say, Henry?" he calls. "Are you ready for that great jump, are you ready for the dark? Soon there will be none of us, once there are two." He waves again. "It's cold in the river," he says, "and my bones are steaming. The river will put out the fire. "

"Don't do it!" I say. The intensity of this confrontation, so soon after the dialogue with Sylvia, the vision of Delmore, has quite undone me. "Always the eternal cold, past the fire. You'll never warm again, the river will sink your bones. "

"I hope so," Berryman says, "I've had enough, Henry, I've had enough." His grip is perilous, he sways, his glasses flash in the spectrum and tumble from his face. The arc of his lunge seems foreshadowed by desperate swaying. "Join me, Henry," he says, "we'll find the ice together."

"No!" I say. Unwillingly, desperately, I scramble on the rocks, reach out, assault the blank space of the wall with hopeless tread. "Suffer the warmth, stay with us, stay with us — "

"I think not," John Berryman says, "the late century condition is going to be even more hideous, the millennium is unattainable." So saying, he lets go, waves jauntily, falls like a shot tern into the river. There is nothing to be done, I scramble on the pebbles and watch him hit the stones, fall away. It is, as John undoubtedly planned, an unanswerable, in fact an insuperable, statement.

The Ice Age: "You see what I mean, then?" Robert Lowell says. He leans hugely over Frances and myself, his New England features rocklike and magnified by their accusation. "There's no way out, not at all." He touches my shoulder, that connection huge in the room, then withdraws. "Absolute silence is absolute darkness," he says, "but you'll have to find your own way in the canon."

There is much more to say, there seems to be much more to say, but clutching my absent beloved in the congealed spaces of that blanket, trying to avoid that gaze which freezes like that of John Procter, it is impossible to find the proper response. Perhaps there is no response. "Your problem," Robert Lowell says, adjusting his tie and coat for the walk to the flight to the taxi in which he will die, "is that you took modem poetry all too seriously. You confused anguish with answers. But then again, perhaps they are synonymous." And so on and so forth, he has a lot more to say and had I the patience I would record all of his magnificent if somewhat patronizing speech but Frances, insistent now in the absolute fury of dead zero, is drawing me in, drawing me in, taking me like a fragile candle flame into the center of her own necessity and nothing to do but follow. The snow rises and falls atop us. We become enormous, timeless, rigid in history, the snows of the century coming around us then to shelter us from the millenial fires. "Oh, Delmore," she seems to whisper in my ear, "oh Robert, oh Randall, oh John and Ted, oh rack and roc." But this must be illusory. I am, as the poet says, beyond words.

The Men Inside

In memory of Herbert Finney

I

COMPREHENDING HULM: In the night after his first Experiment, Hulm has a dream. In that dream, at last, the process has been perfected. Institutes bearing his name have opened all over the world, staffed by trained workers to speed relief to the millions, and now, as he hovers cloudlike over this agglomeration, all of the workers turn to him: to Hulm. Reduced by the process to seven six-hundredths of an inch, they mass, an army of elves speaking in chorus, their little lances poised deftly in tiny hands, and what they are saying is: YOU ARE A VAIN MAN, HULM, A VAIN AND STRICKEN MAN BECAUSE NONE OF IT TURNED OUT QUITE THE WAY YOU THOUGHT IT WOULD. NONE OF IT, NONE OF IT: CORRUPT, CORRUPT, and turn from him then to assault a phalanx of patients; patients are all around them now: they are lumps of flesh which heave under their little feet. The landscape of patients trembles under the thrusts of the lances and Hulm recoils.

"No," he says, rising, raising his fists, "no, it isn't that way; it wasn't my fault; it had to be a corporate entity to survive. I didn't want it but they made me!" Somehow it seems that he has gotten the whole gist of the argument from his tiny messengers, none of whom pay any attention to him as they dive toward pockets of metastasis. "Oh yes, you did," one of them calls back, the lone muted voice fluting in the dark, "yes, you did, indeed you loved it; you saw it all even then, the potential and the reward, and it was profit-making and it was the money more than anything else which drove you through your mad researches. Not to cure but to prosper, you old bastard. But the joke is on you, Hulm; it's on you, kid, because it's all been taken away, every single part of it, and only your name remains. You were a cripple; you had the greed of the entrepreneur, but none of the devices," and the Messengers march giggling away. Hulm screams, screams from his cloud, bellows himself to frenzy, but none of them are listening, no one, it seems, wants any part of him, and he says, "I wanted to do good, that's all I wanted; how did I know that it would have this effect on you?" and comes, awakening, to realize that he should have given it some thought, a lot more thought to the Messengers, because these were people who were going to make it work; better give some consideration to the psychic mechanisms of this thing but no time for that, no time ... stretched in ice, freezing in his bowels, Hulm has awakened dying to the dawn and before anything can be done for him it is late, far too late.

Only the Experiments and their notations can be saved. He had carried them to his bed, to sleep over them. Poor old bastard.

II

TELLING IT ALL TO THE PRIEST: So I killed him, which is true, but that was later on and an anticlimax. It means nothing, the killing. Soon you will come to see that. This is no apolOgia. The act is its own reward. I enjoyed it. I did it well.

The night I graduated from the Institute, I went to the Arena. Perhaps it was disillusionment; perhaps sheer perversity, but I got drunk then and destroyed a Priest while only trying to make my position clear. Later on, when all the factors coalesced, I discovered that things were almost that simple; I had not had to destroy in proof. By then, however, the Priest was done. So, for all I know, was my sensibility. The peace which passeth understanding, etc., comes after the fact.

Which is not to say that the job is good. The job is a disaster in every conceivable way. But it is bad in a fashion which I did not understand; good in ways which I could not have suspected. One learns. One cultivates perspective. One turns twenty-one and begins to see implications. By then, however, damage has been done. The night I ripped the Priest, I thought I was dying. Conventionally dying.

"Let's face it," I said to Smith, who had come with me that night, not because he was my friend (no Messenger has friends, ever) but because he was one of those off whom I could bounce the rhetoric without back talk, "and let us understand. We're menial laborers. Hod carriers. We swing our pick in the gut; all colors and flashes around. The lowest of the low in the post-technological age. In truth, we spent four years in the most dreadful training imaginable simply so that we could jive in mud. Disgusting. The whole thing is for a fast buck and it was dreamed that way. It's profitable and they've got fear working."

"Oh," he said, "oh, Leslie," and finished his drink one-handed, his dull eyes turning wide and large in the aftertaste, looking around helplessly for a servant, "Leslie, I can't argue with you, you're so much smarter than the rest of us, but do you think that this is so? The work is so important. And it's dedicated. Scientific."

(I should point this out: I am changing Smith's name for the purpose of making these notes publishable. Like most of the people from his Downside, he had a long unpronounceable ethnic name which sounded like a curse. Your correspondent, however, has given his true name and you will find him useful and creditable throughout, not a trace effeminate despite the misfortune of his name.)

"Pick and shovel," I said. "Move that caboose. That's all. They've trained us four years their way to make the optimum profit; now we're to breathe religion. On a five-year up."

The Arena, of course, is dedicated to the most practical pleasures but there is a small anteroom of a bar where serious drinking may be done and it was there that Smith and I had gone. I knew that it was only a matter of time until I left him for activities more situational ... but we were stupefied with drink and I had still to say what was on my mind. Whatever was left there. No Messenger can really handle liquor; we are not trained that way. The kind of mind which can be manipulated into a Messenger's would adapt poorly to drink.

"You're an orderly," I said. "Be realistic."

"Cancer. Cancer, Leslie! Just think of that instead. We're going to cure! Fifty years ago no one knew the answer and now people like you and me can make it. *We* are the answer. And think of the free education."

"They'll get it back tenfold. It's all calculated. Don't you understand the factor of turnover?"

"Education! It's all education and free; we've made something of ourselves. We're going to be people. They can't keep me down. The gut isn't afraid," Smith said and lurched, fell toward his feet. Alas, drinking Messengers! Alas, incoherency! He fell tablewards to land in a sighing heap.

"Stupid," I said. "They didn't have to hook you in; you were a sale when you were born."

Those fine Smithian hands that would soon cleave out colons twitched and he muttered, "*Leslie*," in a high guttural. I decided to leave him where he lay. In due time — there is always due time except in our business — he would come back to himself and deal with the situation and that would be enough. There were five years ahead of him. In the meantime he was entitled (or this was the way I really thought at the time) — to all the oblivion he could find. I could only envy his low threshold.

I left him.

I left the drinks too, went into the corridor and toward the fluorescence of the Arena. The attendant caught me at the rope and decided that I looked safe. She asked me what I wanted. She did not ask this graciously but then Smith and I were not in Clubhouse. Grandstand is the habitat for Messengers.

"I want a Priest," I said.

"A confession machine?"

"A Priest they call them, don't they? That's what I want."

She looked at me with some puzzlement on her fine, middle-aged face. (I could see a wart that would flower into metastasis in five or six years; one could see the intimation of filaments casting: burn it out fast and horrid with the deep knife.) "We don't get many requests for those now."

"People don't want to confess?"

"Not that way. Others."

"I want it that way."

"It's not working too well. It's an old model."

"I'll take my chances. Do I have that right?"

Something must have caught her or only, perhaps, the frenzied caper of my hands moving as if in bowels. She looked, shrugged, pressed a bell. "I'll have an attendant," she said. "You aren't just from the Institute, are you?"

"That's right. Graduation."

"I know about the graduation. I just wasn't sure for a minute, that's all. Most of them you tell right off."

"I'd get that wart looked at. I see desiccation."

"What's that?"

"Desiccation, death, intimations of waste. It could go rampant any time, break the seals. Get it checked," I said helpfully and went off with the attendant, a girl of twenty-four or -five who looked at me strangely and held me off as we eased down a corridor. From closed doors I could hear moaning. The attendant dragged me into an alcove halfway toward a door and, putting her hands on me, asked if I wanted some flesh.

"No," I said and laughed. "I'm neutered."

"Neutered? I don't understand that." She squeezed. I laughed some more, under this guise could feel the horrid pressure of her rising breasts under a layer of silk, whicker of lips deadly against the ear. "Come on," she said. "I can tell. Most of you can do it. We'll take it right on a table. Private rates."

"Don't touch me," I said, pushing, feeling her resilience cave to waste under pressure, all yielding, devastation, loss. "Don't touch me, I'm contaminated."

"Are you crazy?"

"I'm a Messenger."

"I know that. Oh well," she said with a shrug and took my hand wearily, "I can't give you confidence." "Nothing."

"Oh, it isn't all that bad," she said, her features congealing toward an asexual slant, perfect for celibates and lunatics. "It can be a great thing, Messengers. Besides, you should be proud. The contribution — "

"No contribution," I said, leading her down the corridor. "Give me to the Priest."

"It's in there," she said. "Don't talk any more. I can't stand this all of a sudden." She gave me a slight push into the room, closed the door.

I looked at the Priest for a while and then took a seat down front. It was an older model all right, no reclining chair, just stiff wood, no color. I put the machine on *receive,* waited until the green cleared, and said, "I have come to you, Father, for I have sinned."

"You have come unto me, for you have sinned," the machine said in a pleasant tenor, the voice only creaking a little.

"I wish for you to hear me; my sins are dark and grievous."

"Confess and be blessed," it said, rasped, came to an effeminate yowl on the *blessed.* Gears ground in the background. I inspected the small plate on the front which said 1993. A very old one. "Be blessed," it said again and clicked. "Confess and be known."

"I have just graduated from the Huhm Institute where I completed Messenger training."

"A fine undertaking. Messengers —"

"The Institute is a profit-making organization run under medical sanction as a monopoly. It exploits its one stroke of genius and the terror of its dependents for crude gain. It is destructive."

"Messengers feel this way in the beginning. Go on, relieve yourself."

"It is in the hands of greedy men who, having acquired the rights to the Huhn Projector, use fear as a means of maintaining power."

"How long have you felt this way?"

"Listen," I said, "listen to me. I have not come to this lightly; I have learned. I know the three causeways of metastasis, I know its lesser and greater pathways, its colors and symbiosis. I learned the seventeen manual and forty-five automatic means of incision, I learned of filaments, mitosis, and the scattering of cells. I saw demonstrations, I performed my own tasks. I learned of the history and implications, I —"

I went into the cadaver, the surfaces collapsing around me, and walked through the arches of death, toward the spot which had killed him; confronted it there, a dome a thousand feet high, and looked upon it in awe, then, bringing the fire from my lance, ground it to bits. They took me from the cadaver screaming, bits of cancer still dribbling from the lance. "Dont worry," they said. "It is always the worst the first time. That is why we give you poor dead ones to enter. They were doomed anyway."

"That all sounds very interesting. However, you have not yet detailed your problem. Speak loudly and clearly as you detail your problem."

"You're not even giving me a chance to finish."

"Confess and be blessed."

"I could have come here for anything, you know. Who needs confessors in a whorehouse? Show some consideration."

"Why personify?" the machine asked rather petulantly. "Why this compulsive need for iteration? The important thing is to come to terms — "

The new confessors have special circuitry. Even though demand for the machines is nil (who needs guilt any more if there is a cure for cancer?) connections are available which block the Priest at certain points so that you can finish a statement. (I have read much on Priests; I still believe in guilt.) There seemed no possibility of dialogue here. Also, the machine was hooked into a vintage Freudianism which is completely outmoded.

"Impossible," I said. "It's impossible."

"I beg your pardon?"

"Let me finish," I said. Rather desperately. One last time. There was no point in getting exercised about machinery: this is the basic understanding. "Let me conclude. I learned all the means of Reduction, to say nothing of the splendid history of the Hulm Projector, a beautiful piece of equipment whose commercial application began only after the sudden death of its inventor and the full details of whose functioning remain suppressed. I learned of Hulm himself, the poor old bastard: I learned about the vision which drove him in darkness toward a sense so enormous—"

"You are sweating. Your pulse is extremely rapid. Why do you react to this cold data with such excitement?"

"I don't want to be calm. Calm reasonable men got us into this."

"You cannot confess unless you are calm. You must suppress —"

"How do you know my mental state?"

"Why do you ask?"

"Why not?" I said. "I took the oath. I came from the Institute. I have been educated to all the greater and lesser evils into which the corrupted Messenger may stray and I have learned the ways of their avoidance. I received a drill and beam, I received a lance. An engraved diploma and memory book will be mailed me, the cost of which will be deducted from my first salary check. I will make thirty-nine thousand dollars a year before taxation and this is only the beginning; soon I will go to fifty if I keep my lance straight. I have all the advantages of which I would have otherwise been deprived in Downside."

"What do you think of this?"

"I think nothing of Downside. I had no future: the Institute nourished me. I had no possibilities, the Institute made them manifest. I had no hope, the Institute gave me a profession."

"So you must have gratitude."

"But this is not my question. You must listen to me now. All of this has been done for me, just as I have established it for you. If this is so, and it is indeed, why do I hate them?"

The Priest blinked. "Pardon me," it said, light wavering. "I am now on automatic. There is an overload in the circuitry. This is only a slight problem which can be swiftly corrected. An attendant will come."

I felt the walls were going to come in around me; I felt that I would perish in slick, dark flesh, an invisible mote struggling against entrapment, enveloped by decay, and I must have screamed then; rung my little alarm for assistance; they dragged me out on the attached string which is part of early training and falling through, past unconsciousness, I woke into a dream where I stood on a table top, expanding, now three feet high, and said, "I cannot stand this. I cannot possibly take this any more." "You will," they said. "You will."

"My circuitry is now overloaded," the machine said. "Please be patient. There is a small problem. An attendant will come; all will be corrected. Very little time will elapse until I am again functional."

"Listen to me," I said, pounding metal. "You dull son of a bitch — "

"Do not personify. Circuitry overloaded is. If you will — "

"I paid my money and this is my confession: I *want to kill*. Not to cure but to strike. All my life I have been maimed, burned, blasted, sullied, and turned off by deprivation, now they have taken me from those streets and told me of a future … but I do not want a future, I do not want the Hulm Projector or to clamber inside people like an itch to burn out cancer. I hate it. I will not —"

"I am not functional. My circuitry overloaded is. Patience and mendacity, lying quietly signals quietly and looking for an attendant soon will pass and then well again all must speak for now but it be coming now attendant overload is sing the circuit panel open dark —"

"And kill," I said. I rose to my full, delicate height, possessed of liquor and intent, five feet three inches of power (Messengers are treasured for this; one must not only be a Downside denizen but a *tiny* D.D.), and hurled myself against the metal, battered my tiny hands into the walls. Smashed my little feet against the damned iron couch and began to work on it in earnest application then, spinning controls, wrenching dials, moaning. "You too!" correspondent shouted. "You're just like the rest of them. All of it is machinery!"

Oh, correspondent! he was drunk indeed. Drunk so that I wished my hands were stone so that I could smash the Priest, smash while the whore-attendant returned and saw what I was doing, came to embrace me in a clutch as fierce and warm as death. "Don't worry," she said, "it's not so bad, you only think it is, but then you learn to live and live with it." And nuzzled me with lips like steel, this sweet machine of the Arena. Causing me to faint.

If you want Inside you can suffocate.

Correspondent paid for a battered Priest, vintage 1993. Eight hundred and sixteen dollars and forty-five cents, payable in ten percent salary deductions. The machine was a souvenir and here it sits, right here this moment before correspondent, right in his foul little room where he continues to transcribe these notes.

He has, at the present time, so little else to do that he might as well turn to writing. He could stroll through a window, of course, or phone the Protectors. This is useless speculation; correspondent has no plans, has come around to the belief that all energy is merely a cover for The Void; has bigger and better things on his mind as well he might. Circumstances will get better or maybe worse depending on one's point of view; the important thing is to maintain a caution and open-minded reserve.

Dwarflike but vigorous, correspondent sits in the highest room of the Clinic, behind barricades, and decides exactly what he will Make of His Life. No hammering in the corridors yet. I am glad he did it. He deserved to die. That is a constant.

III

REDUCTION: It hurts. It hurts, it burns, it is a feeling of compression and helplessness coming over in slow, thick waves of illness and impotence; from scalp to toes the body curls in upon itself, the flesh becoming desiccate and Sickly and then folding in a series of snaps like a ruler. Disproportionate it is, terribly so; the limbs are already gnomish when the shoulders and head have not yet begun to gather and the feeling is one of foreshortening: gloom and extended concentration then, the kind of emotions which, I understand, might be known in sexuality or gymnastics when the body, sighing, departs from its humors and takes a more ominous direction. And throughout ... throughout the pain, the pain which sears and rends, the helplessness of irreversibility. You cannot stop it, once it begins. The wish to supersede ... but nothing to be done.

My God, my God (but Messengers cannot pray), can they not understand? This is being done to people I At the tormented center, the fuse of a soul. (A Downside soul but nonetheless sacred for all that or so we are taught.)

Are the souls of patients larger because they contain us? At the core of my fuse, a light as wicked as death, as constant as night. It lights my lance.

IV

HOW THEY LIGHT THE DOWNSIDE: I think he screamed once as I killed him. Or perhaps it was my own scream in his chambers. Two screams then, melded to darkness. Did both of us die then? If so, why are they out to get only me? Better talk of Downside.

The way that they work it is this: flyers are pasted all through there, always vandalized of course, but repasted the same day … and you grow up with them. Grow with pictures of the Institute and songs of the Messengers and six times a year there is an enormous recruiting campaign, complete with festival and band. Politicians will venture in during these campaigns, enclosed in glass, to talk through megaphones of the virtues of dedication, the power of paraprofessionalism, and although there have been one or two really spectacular assassinations through the years, by and large the technique is effective. Obviously it is effective.

I love to this day, for instance, to meet celebrities, particularly politicians: it is the sense of *connection* they provide which is so exciting. Everyone from the Downside understands this right away. Ask them.

It seems that the bare facts of the case are enough. No invention in the recruiting campaigns has yet been noted. Since there is a certain paucity of returned Messengers anyway, the pitch proceeds without difficulty. Be a Messenger and Make Something of Yourself. Come to the lance, be a man. Enlist in the war against cancer. Fight a fighter; it takes one to know one.

My old man didn't know about the bonus. That is the best indication of the kind of seed from which I sprang.

Even without the question of a bonus, however, it appealed to him. For my eighteenth, as a coming-of-age present, he pulled me from a pocket Arena and took me to the enlistment office. There they told him of the bonus and their gratitude as well; he wept for humility, he took the bonus and attempted to hit the multimutuels for everything that they had taken from him in the forty-odd years intervening between Transfiguration and Death.

He did not succeed.

Were this my father's story rather than mine, I would now go into the particulars of his failure … but the hell with him, the hell with all of them; center stage to Leslie, please. Leslie overtakes all, even his father … because I learned through channels recently that the old bastard had applied for admission, as a subsistence patient, to Clinic #5 in Houston for the removal of his cancer. A subsistence patient! Charity! Of special value! He claimed relative privileges, of course. Somewhere in the recruiting bulletin this is promised and it had been read to him.

He found out, I am sure, the value of the Institute's promise.

But at this moment, even now, even writing these notes, I am convinced that that collection of angles and systems which he had accumulated through four decades — four! — stood him in good stead when confronted by the ninth race and that, even at the odds, he could have beaten the game. Do not bet fillies against colts. Never bet maidens in a mixed field. Watch for sudden drops in class. How painfully acquired, how preciously, he submitted these dicta to me! They were my only legacy.

This hardly matters. My tentative post-murder maturity assures me that ninety-nine percent of life is sheer abstraction and the remainder, all of it, can be handled as if it were. Nothing matters. None of it. All lies and small entrapment, manipulated cunning in the dark.

(A speculation for old time's sake: I see him lying on his bed somewhere in the last of the miserable, furnished apartments in Downside which have been his life. His eyes glint, his face sags, he looks through drugs at the ceiling. He is finally aware that he is dying and can even bring himself to say it—*the game is up, my laddie, the machines have now locked, it is now post time* — but inescapably, at some corner of consciousness, he is not sure of this. He wishes to think differently. Perhaps it is all a final elaborate hoax rigged by the Telegraphics to test his innocence.

(Three or four insects scuttle across the sheets. They chat with one another, wander on his palm. His eyes flutter, screams of children outside, the noise of Downside flooding the room in an expiring moan. *Watch for sudden drops of weights.* He gathers to absorb that sound, rises, gasps, air comes into his lungs. *Look out for lightly raced three-year-olds in allowances for threes and up.* Now he feels pain: pain in filaments and fragments, pain working through him at all levels, and he tries to hold it off. He shakes his head, mumbles, the noise rises, his breath sags. He falls. Watch the condition factor carefully. He expires, dreaming of four figures on the tote, rolling gracelessly from bed to floor then; exhibiting an acrobatic he has never shown previously.

(All reverence to this discovered grace of a father whose limbs insects now occupy. Insects and metastases. Cancer and apprentice jockeys.)

"Be a professional," he said to me in chronotime, "and make something of yourself. You're nothing now, you and me both, but you'll really be something if you're lucky enough to get into the Institute."

Lucky enough to get into the Institute! "You don't understand, Father," I said (I was only eighteen), "the Institute takes everyone. Everyone. Why do you think they push it all the time? Why the campaign?"

"Because that gives them the widest and finest selection of young men to choose among; that way they can sift for the cream of the crop."

"No. They'll take anyone."

"No sir, no sir," he said and fairly leaped for emphasis, "there you are wrong. They want you to feel that it is easy when it really isn't. The requirements are high, the processes, testing, and some of the very best do not make it. You'll be in by hundreds if we can get you in there."

I was not naïve, after all — a childhood in Downside, while no real preparation for Messengery, is an education against vulnerability of a different sort — but his intensity was alarming. "I don't know," I said. "I hear stories. I don't want to be a Messenger."

"What's that? Not a Messenger! Coward, you take me, the old man who has raised and nurtured you. I'm too old, too cold, got bold but slack in the limbs, got no potential any more. They wouldn't take me now. If they had had this thing when I was your age, it would have been the making of me. I'd enlist in two seconds. If only they had it when I was younger."

So I went down, we downed, through the corridors of Downside, holsters at ready, two steps behind my old man, into the main sector and right to the booth, which was hot and cramped and smelled of ozone. On the wall were posters showing Messengers twelve feet high advancing on a battlefield, lances at ready. The Messengers were clean and solemn, bright faces washed to vacancy by commitment, and in one of the posters a Minister was delivering a blessing under the line YOU'RE REALLY SOMETHING WHEN YOU'RE A MESSENGER. The booth was occupied by a fat man who breathed poorly; every time he exhaled, the papers on the walls and desk jumped. There was something about the aspect of the office which indicated that he had not had company for a while. Small marks of vandalism around the door hinted, however, that in its own way Downside kept him in mind.

"Take him, take my son!" my father said with a series of antique flourishes resembling those with which he encouraged horses by teletape. "Take this boy; he's just a young lad now with a streak of cruelty and bad manners but he's my own son and he has potential. I told him that you'll make something out of him, bring him to his purposes. It's all in the training; training is a wonderful thing when it works with the young animal. He wants to serve humanity, sir, he only needs a director."

"Of course," the recruiter said, "he looks like a very promising lad; indeed he does, and his height is good too. He has wonderful height."

"I told him, told him that smalls were tall," the old man said and winked. "It's grace, that's what it is, and entrance into small alleys, moving the good way."

"I have to ask a few questions, of course," the recruiter said. "It isn't automatic; we have a selection here. Firstly, to whom should the bonus be made payable?"

"Bonus? Bonus! You say there is a bonus?"

"It varies as to the conditions, the length of enlistment, qualifications and so on. You mean you weren't aware?"

The old man put his hand on my shoulder and I felt the grip move toward pain. Of Simpler stock than his son, he showed emotional reactions in blunt physical ways. "Of course I knew that," he said. "You're not meddling with an old fool and his tiny son; I just wanted to make sure that that came front."

"You mean you didn't know that?" I said. It occurred to me for the first time then that my father was insane. He had driven me toward the Institute not for money but for commitment's sake; this was inexplicable.

"I said I knew it, didn't I?" he asked sullenly and looked at his nails, uneven and green in the pastel light. "I know all that stuff."

"You don't think they'd get people into this for nothing, do you?"

The recruiter gave me a look, an expression strangely Far paralleling my father's, and I took the papers he handed me, began to sign them indiscriminately.

My insight had changed my life: I had not realized until that instant how badly I needed to get away from him. There is no future in being influenced by a man who believes that the Institute can get voluntary admissions.

"It should be several thousand dollars," I said. "Make sure of it. Large money in Downside."

"Several thousand dollars; that's just what I expected and one of the very reasons I brought my boy down this morning. He's a fine boy, brought up to be of high quality, and in these filthy circumstances that is not easy, of course. When do I get these thousands of dollars? It should be today, right?"

"Why should you get it?" I said. "Then, on the other hand, why shouldn't you? Let it be my gift to you."

"It's only a small return on my investment in you."

"We still have to get the questionnaire complete," the recruiter said, moving one palm against the other palm, "and we can talk out these arrangements a little later. If you'll just take a few inquiries now —"

"Just give me the dough," the old man said, having settled on the essential thread of the interview. "Just pass it over to me, for I'm entitled. It's all mine for raising him. The boy isn't of age anyway but there'll be some good investments for him too. I think of everything. I have plans."

The recruiter and I looked at one another in some horrid comity of understanding and then, perhaps, put all that to one side. "Your history," he said, "your biography, the details if you will. It's not necessary but a good option to tell the truth. Hold back on nothing; the Institute wants to know the best way to train any problems which might come up sooner or later."

So I filled out the forms. Filled them out in three minutes in their full complexity and meaning and was then rewarded with a moist Recruiter's Handshake, a winsome Recruiter's Wink and a deft Recruiter's Check, postdated. The check I turned over to my old man, the others I kept. He took the money.

What I am trying to make clear is that money did not interest me, then or now. My motives are never mercenary. Life in Downside is always the same, money or not, and the Institute is a way out. If he wanted money to color the question of his existence, my old man was entitled. This is the kind of thinking which one can entertain at eighteen. It lingers. I never did anything for money.

So I took my travel orders and went.

There's no waiting at the Institute, a new cycle begins every month, and in the meantime they give you a fine dormitory to lie within and interesting puzzles to perform. This is a Good Thing, at least from the point of view of the Institute, because one is provided a long waiver with lots of subclauses and qualifications and, thinking of this waiver, having time to consider it at home, might turn a speculative soul around. The waiver contains phrases like "irreversible reduction" and "accidental mortality" and "disclaim infective contamination" and even though faithful correspondent could not read or write well at this time (imagine that!) he took note of some of them with interest. "Don't worry," the recruiter had said, "it's purely routine, just a routine little waiver. No one ever gets injured on the job, not really. Nothing ever happens."

Recently, there were riots in Downside. Seventeen of the booths were bombed or burned out; one unfortunate recruiter happened to be working late when this occurred. (But, unfortunately, not mine.) Since then recruiting is allowed only at certain times of the year and in special circumstances: this means only that instead of being empty most of the time the booths, when they are opened, draw huge lines. Still, a few things have changed: a different quality of man was entering the Institute, a kind of Messenger who might be inclined to dance in the intestines. Consequences seem less final. Still, superficial change is still superficial: they will still not recruit women, Hulm's inheritors being a proper sort. Not that women have shown undue eagerness. They are still a minority of the patients.

Clatter of wood in the distance. Definitely they are on to me now. It is only a matter of time, but time enough to continue. They will not spare me. I will have to write it all down before this ends.

V

LIFE AT THE CLINIC: If only I had killed the first case, I would have been spared all of these convolutions. Confronted by simplicities, we do not act; we circumvent, we come back to it only much later and at a scuttle. The purity of the solutions before us is something we cannot grasp. Still, I am relatively content; I could have not done it at all.

Matters settled in at Clinic #4. Much of my revulsion was of the longer-term variety, not to be confused with apprehension. Clinic #4 of the Hulm Institute for Metastases, Easterly Division, deposit in full upon admission. Landscaped grounds: an aura of green for brief, recuperative walks. Private toilets for all patients. Erected in only 2019, it was a modern facility. Diamonds glittered in the lobby fixtures.

Correspondent was given a private full at the end of a corridor a mile long and half a mile high, a full plug into the music system. Correspondent was given full access to the employees' courtesy shop, the employees' lounge, the employees' cafeteria, the employees' recreational facilities. No possessives, of course. No mingling with the patients. Enough contact is enough. Correspondent was given a uniform with his house name stenciled thereupon in red, he was given with all due ceremony his own Projector. Mine to keep and treasure forever, liable to pay for the damages for the duration of my term as Messenger. My house name was Iones. I had requested but been denied a Hebraic. There is no sense of humor in the Institute. Imagine a tiny Goldstein in your gut!

I was given a tour of the facilities and an orientation lecture by Miss Greenwood, head of employee services, who made an obscene suggestion to me in an alcove. "I like Messengers," she said. It is impossible for even a Miss Greenwood to understand that Messengers are functionally neutered. If it is not congenital, it is nonetheless effective for all of that. Neutering is not, strictly speaking, a requirement of the job (and some Messengers have been known to flex their tiny limbs in copulation) but it usually works out that way. Sex too is a mystery and how many mysteries can we sustain?

(Perhaps the process is a metaphor for Entrance and that most basic of entries denies any other. Or it may only be a repressed homosexuality of which I am aware. The power of certain urges! The rage! The need! Messengers, even the least of them, are complex people: do not hasten to understand me.

(Also, I have a low threshold for exercise. Also I have never been able, during my few moments of sexual attempt, to avoid scatological images, clownish fantasies, dwarfs scampering in mire or seizures of deflation.)

The tour did not surprise me. I was not disconcerted, I was prepared for all of it. The only thing that I learned was that all of them — patients and doctors, nurses and attendants treated us like orderlies. Perhaps they thought we *were* orderlies. This they had not readied us for in the Institute. They spoke only of the unusual status of the Messenger and the special and privileged position he occupied in the War on Death.

The Institute prepared us for very little, outside of the technological questions. The rhetoric was poor: "Dedication is the first obligation of the Messenger, respect his reward, paraprofessionalism his outcome. Full professionals then work together in unified and sanctified accord under this benevolence of technology in an atmosphere of probity." The religion was puerile: "Purgation of the body and the blood, the holy lamb, the divine spirit. Cast your lance against doom like a prophet of old." The sanctions were dull: "Remember this, gentlemen, we are soldiers and must give no quarter. We are in the front line of the battle."

(I do not mean to down it entirely. Believe it or not, I came late to cynicism, despair in the early years being only the opposite coin of belief. The rhetoric was effective, they taught machinery well, the two came together and kept the Messengers in line. Whatever we expected of the job when we moved in, we knew this, for they had told us: we would be treated with a dignity upon which our skills were incumbent. They had their reasons. I can see them now.)

Nonetheless. Orderlies. We were treated like orderlies. In fact, at odd moments, it was possible for one to think that one *was* an orderly; a certain kind of grinning shamble seemed to overtake the walk, a certain vacancy around the eyes. The Downside stupor: seeing everything, registering everything, understanding nothing, rising only through small humiliations and grief to rage. One could well *have* been an orderly, of course, had it not been for the Institute. This was kept in mind.

Part of the patient problem was that we were introduced in exactly that way. Messengers and their function are not, after all, particularly appealing and it suits the public relations and policies of the Institute to make things as aseptic as possible. One does not go in (at the price they are paying) to have cancer burned out; one goes in for "a little job," something made you "a little tired," and one rejoins the world joyfully, having acceded to cosmetic change. This is the thrust of the Institute's public relations; a stay with the Institute is a *happy* stay; cancer is a happy disease. So, then, one met the patients very much out of role: *This is your helper, Mr. Jones, your personal-needs technician,* or whatever lie the effusive Miss Greenwood had in mind at that time. The fact that this grinning, genial, nicely miniaturized little helper would shortly go crawling inchwise into their guts was something to come by only peripherally, after the relationship had been established. Even then there was little interest: the thing about the patients was that they were perfectly willing to function as if the little job, the little problem, took care of itself and attending the Institute were essentially a *social* obligation ... like an obligatory party. (A certain dislike for patients seems to have filtered through. Let me make it clear then that I bear no grudge; the possession of money or status has never struck me as a basis for hatred of itself. The patients are manipulated; they come from the only group who can afford the Institute, they do the necessary for the Institute. One must look nearer or deeper to get into the matter of culpability.)

Reinforcement on the employee end to be sure. *Rule seven:* a Messenger may never divulge to a patient the nature of his responsibilities. A certain modesty of demeanor is recommended should there be inquiries. (Rarely are there inquiries: who cares?) A Messenger is technology's servant; it is not his right to call upon himself particular reverence. Humility is the source of strength.

Policy and procedure; procedure and policy. All of it carefully conditioned. Even now the manuals fall quickly into the mind's eye: regulation and ordnance, containment and meaning ruled neatly on the lined paper, the printing very large for the functional illiterates among us.

Little were we prepared, however, for being orderlies.

It was something else; the one thing, perhaps, that we (or at least faithful correspondent) allowed ourselves to believe and that was what we would be: benign priests of reduction, striding through the wards to the awed gasps of doctors and nurses, nurses and attendants, performing our green and terrible tasks in an oozing isolation of ease, under rich beams of fluorescence to occasional gasps and whimpers of applause. (Like a tennis match, perhaps.) It was the Hulm Projector which made us go; still, even the Projector's Tools were entitled to a little common respect. We had struggled years to learn to play our motions against the body's cave; we had practiced in a hundred corpses so that we could take on the husks of the World's Best; weren't we entitled to applause?

Gentlemen, the question is rhetorical: do not answer. Neither peer through the cracks in these doors in an attempt to see; Leslie has shrouded himself in smoke and haze, towels stuffed in all crevices. There is no way that you can get at me unless you break the door or I let you in and I am not ready, not quite for either, thank you very much. How my little fingers tremble on these notes! How my eyes bulge, my brow emits its antique and chiseled beadlets of sweat! Time, gentlemen, time! Everything will come to its conclusion.

I will even tell you why I came to kill. Presently, presently.

Correspondent's visions were incorrect. Things did not work out in that way. Disillusion is the condiment of the reflective life: nevertheless, I suffered. Bedpans were the lot of the tired Messenger, bedpans and strange prosthetic devices. This enamel was poor enough reward for four years of study but there were also changes of clothing to be made, rollings over and regurgitation, pattings in the night (postoperatives become nauseous from the recollected need to expel us), heave and retch, claw and moan, pat and wonder, the small activities of the postmetastatic patient being conducted in the smells and tightness of their rooms which for all the highly vaunted decor of the Institute still had a twentieth-century cast. Amorphousness and sleek panels of doom, overlaid on the emptiness. In the dark they would grasp at us to whisper horrid confidences. "I'm afraid," old or oldish people would whisper, bending their arms to crook's edge, staring from luminous eyes, the pall of cancer bringing strange knowledge to their faces, "terribly afraid, you see; I don't think that it can work out. I just don't see it."

"The process is infallible. Just relax. It's like a toothache, as antiquated as diabetes. Be reasonable. Be calm."

"But the pain," they would murmur, "still, the pain — " and I would not have the heart to advise them that the pain was mostly illusory, encouraged by the preoperative drugs administered by the Institute so that their gratitude at its vanquishment would be that much more profound, the process through which they had been that much more dolorous. Instead of telling them the truth (Messengers never tell the truth) I would assure them that it would work out, everything would work out; no problems at all. It was only a question of machinery and technique, calm and patience. The days had, I would say, already shaped themselves into a pattern that would see them strut from the ward, easy and freed ... but still the Institute counseled a certain amount of fear in lieu of credit agencies and while I could deal with the men, most of them, the women defied me. I could not deal with feminine emotions: no neuter can. And then there were younger ones too; even some children of the rich whom I found particularly trying, and then there were the semi-informed who had picked up knowledge on the side ... and these were the ones who suspected the true function of the Messengers, and they were apt to be the worst of all because when you came in the night (always the night) to do the Process, one might find them sitting at terrible ease, drugs discarded in a washbowl, peering through ominous eyes as the Projector was repaired. These were the ones the nurses had to condition with needles and it was difficult, difficult.

Illuminate if you will: a scene. A patient. A Process. "Boy," he said to me, "boy, I'm really sweating. You'd better clean this stuff up, I feel like I'm sitting somewhere in a pool." A middle-aged man, verging toward senility since his cancer is deep into the liver and lungs; I understand that he is the founder of the largest manufactory of masks in the nation. He provides masks for all rituals in the major Arenas. Still remaining then is the founder's Sense of Command.

"I've already done that," I say, reading. *(Journals of a Nihilist: A Romance.)* "I've cleaned you three times today. Already. You've got to rest now." I think I'll kill you tonight, I decide.

One transmits the full picture: the book is poised flapping in my hand, an unopened magazine for good measure on my little knee; I am sweating quietly myself in the strange heat of the room, neatly drenching my attendant's whites. Not five hours from now I am to go inside and remove it from him, a glowing filament which stretches from *here* to *there,* localized by X-ray, painted and gleaming for me. A nauseating operation: many capillaries to be by-passed. Preoperative and pained, he is restless. "I'm not comfortable," he says, "you've got to show some consideration and care. You're paid for that. Clean me up."

You will be the one I kill; I have waited too long, I think. "It's been done. Time and again. Why don't you try to rest now?" The request can only move him the wrong way, of course. A slight edginess wavers into my tone; I am entitled to apprehension. The Process is safe, very safe (the Projector has, after all, never lost a Messenger and it has had thousands of opportunities by now), but it is taxing, very much so. Hours after reduction, one still feels a sense of compression in the joints, liquid unease, a feeling of disassembly. Also, there is the question of archetypes to be posed: this is not respectful work we are doing. Perhaps the body needs to become cancerous and we have made it the other way; by preserving against devastation we make things more difficult in the Other World.

Still: one must stay with the patient through the end of the conventional shift, apprehensions or not. One is obliged to maintain the full responsibilities of the Messenger. This is policy. The patient must be soothed, relaxed, must have utter confidence in one. Only the Messenger may be the patient's attendant; only he can train him to his insights. (It also cuts the overhead.)

"You don't understand," I say. "I can't be in the service of your every whim. I'm tired."

"I don't care if you're tired, boy," the patient says as if he were ordering a consignment of greens, "you've got to make me comfortable. What am I paying for if not my care?"

Oh, how one would like to pity him now! He is after all a potential murderee. Pity has ravaged frame, pity his fear; one senses that in health he would again be wistful, gentle, attracted to picture books and small children, but the illness and its syndrome have made him cantankerous, have thrown upon him fully the aspect of the senile fool he would, due to prolonged life, become. It is hard to maintain tolerance in the face of this understanding; I could kill him now in the sheets for joy. "You're my orderly," he says, "and it's my right."

I stand. It is not easy and the book flaps uncomfortably floorward but nevertheless it is done. A pity in light of all this impressive effort that my height can hardly be calculated to close the gap. "Listen," I say, "you can't order me around like that. I'm not an orderly, I am a Messenger." (Knowing I will kill him should have been enough. Why I lost my temper I cannot say. Perhaps it is balancing action.)

He shrugs and says, "I know all about that part."

"In not five hours, maybe six, I am going to crawl inside, slither in your gut like a fish, and take the matter out. Can't you show a little respect? What do you think is going on here anyway?"

"That's disgusting," he says. "You made me sweat all over. You're never supposed to tell me what you're doing. What are you, anyway?"

"Come on now," I say, picking the magazine off the floor and tossing it toward a corner of the room. (It is one of our trade journals, full of glistening equipment and helpful hints to the voyager, written by advertising copywriters and largely involved with two-toning Projectors.) "I can't take this much longer. There are limits to everything. I can't clean you up; I can barely clean you out."

"You're frightening me," he says, rearing in bed, and I think of his little liver quivering, the cancer already knocking it down to one fifth of its normal size, the accretion of acids, the lava of amino; he is only making my job that much more difficult.

"Lie down, you ass," I scream, in another mood, "don't you understand that you'll make it impossible by infiltrating your gut that way?" I pummel pillows, slap sheets at his side, and begin to talk to him in a high-pitched but comforting tone, taking another line entirely. I have, after all, been a fool: isn't murder enough for me? I will make his alleyways impassable; I will never get the lance in. He must be calm, calm, for me to murder; I snatch alcohol from the bedstand and begin to rub, pummel, converse, his flesh like slate under my hands, his heart puffing and ticking in the distance.

"You frightened me," he says. "I didn't mean to say those things but you did frighten me."

"Forget it," I say, "the stakes are too large. Just be calm." An orderly's whine creeps into the assassin's tone: is it possible that one can become what they say?

I apologize, skulk to the relief room to urinate, light glittering before me, light shuddering and receding, the filaments of his gut weaving their way past my stricken consciousness and toward some deeper center. Push, pull, pummel, knead. And murder him that night. Why? Well, why not?

My father sent me one letter during training, the only letter I ever got from him, the only letter he ever wrote: THE SISTEM WURX, he said, ITS ALL QUESTION ENGLES IS ALL I SHOULD KNOWN IT A LONGA TIME AGO. I filed it a way. Three months later he contracted cancer. I should known it a longa time ago.

Now they are pounding at the door. Finally. Their voices rasp insistent in the hallway: it would be interesting to know what they are saying. I have toward this the kind of clinical interest that toward the very end I was able to sustain toward murder. But only toward the end.

Eventually they will become forceful, try metal and hooks, but long before that all of this will have been finished, all of it placed inside the drawer with the sock and I will await them with the dull, glazed assassin's smile, eyes narrowed, arms folded, a hint of arch in one brow, all quizzicality and compunction as they come to extract their due.

I have formulated what I will say to them; the first words, that is, before they begin to ask their foolish, hammering questions. "Gentlemen," I will say to them, "gentlemen, please listen to me and you will understand. I wanted to change lives. I wanted to change the way in which people regarded their situation. I wanted to prepare for large deeds, terrible shifts in circumstance, a different kind of person.

"And found only that it was all a lie and that ripeness, ripeness, gentlemen, is all."

THE PROCESS: "But," a voice says, somewhere in the distance, "but." (I think that I have externalized my father.) "But you still haven't made yourself clear. For one thing you haven't made it known what it's like, and secondly, the motives are still shrouded. Who can care about this?"

One hastens to answer. Correspondent hastens to answer. The point is elegant, meaningful, well taken, clear. A word then about the Process. A word about how it works. Keep on pounding, you sons of bitches, you'll never get me alive. I am going to finish this.

The Projector. You stand before the Projector. It is cold in the dark, cold and damp; one stands shuddering, wet in the crevices, wet to the bone of nakedness, only the huddle of the patient deep into anesthetic omnipotence hints the possibility of connection. Catalepsy moves from the trembling pores. In this night the noises of the hospital overwhelm. Tick of generator, wailing scream down the hall, patter of night nurses tossing scatology at one another. The singing of electricity, power in the coils. It is possible at this moment to conceive that one is no longer in a hospital at all, nor is this a patient. One is standing instead, perhaps, in one's own room; one is eight or nine years old, alert toward the dark and attuned to that very sense of possibility which seems to stream through the windows. The gasping of the patient is now only the sound of one's own dear parents fornicating in the hall, forcing fluid from one to the other in that slick dark transfer which we are told is love … and then one touches the Projector. The Projector, at least, is there, and it brings one back to some sense of origins, destiny, the fishlike twitches between.

One touches the Projector, the slick, deadly surfaces of Hulm's obsession, and comes to know then that it is a different quality of experience here. It is not the same as being eight or nine in the darkness. Here, one does not refract possibility but history. One had known this before, many times, of course. But each is a new onset. The Projector knows no history.

Hit the starting switch. (It must begin somewhere, although it really started so terribly long ago.) The batteries hum, pulse with energy; Hulm's madness seems to call upon the familiar of its inventor and issues his whine: a strange, characteristic clang. Lights flicker, the Projector is working. One hopes that it is working. One knows that there has never been an authenticated case of a machine breaking down in Process … but there are rumors, rumors which circulate through any population, and then too, there is always a first time. The thought of reduction continued or the thought of partial restoration within a capillary is enough to keep even the limited imagination of a Messenger hopping. Hop and hop; skip and connect. On schedule reduction begins. It is all automatic from the time of ignition.

It begins slowly, then accelerates. The Geometrical Progression of Diminution, it is called in the Institute, and they concede that they do not themselves know why it seems to work in this fashion … but it has long been graphed that, while it takes five minutes to lose the first foot, it takes merely another five to lose all but the necessary percentage of the rest. It is during this time then as during none other that the mind blanks, the corpuscles run free and there comes the slow, wild onslaught of epiphany. One sees things, one senses the dark. Reduction is narcotic, this being a theory I have, but it is based less on physiology than on the involved sense of anticipation.

Anticipation! One never knows, after all, what one might find inside there, what differences might be uncovered. am led to understand that less committed men obtain the same reaction from sex. (I know nothing of this.) One thinks of the Ultimate Metastases to be discovered in the blood, the biggest fish of all.

And talks. Something must be done, after all, to make the moments and exhilaration go by; to seal off the fear and the wonder, and besides, the patient is so deeply narcotized that for once almost anything can be said without it sounding strange. We have so few pleasures. Most of us have no vices and must take satisfaction where we may. One perches on the edge of the chair and finally the center, exposing the body to the rays of the Projector, and raves onward, a tiny voice in the still night. "You do not understand what you put me through, you stupid, rich son of a bitch, and you ought to show some appreciation, which is why I'm going to kill you," or one will lapse into neologism and rhyme such as "Hitch, twitch, litch, itch, rich to the body's bitch and ride the rising blood" or "Faster metastases" or, more simply, "I'm going to kill you because I hate too much and they couldn't burn that out of me the way I can burn out cancer."

And so on. And so forth. And in the meantime, reduction is working away; working away all the time so that the voice, even in the process of address, becomes gradually higher-pitched, moving from a fine, adult rumble to an adolescent whinny and then bottoms into a childish squeak, squeak from the Messenger, squeak for remorse, the voice finally taking up residence somewhere below the jaws and then at last —

At last one is something less than an inch tall, dancing angelic but upon the head of no pin and then preparing for entrance. One makes haste. One slinks into the body.

(How entrance is accomplished will be my only secret. I will not say, nor will any Messenger, no matter how great his disillusion. You will not find it either in any of the popularized essays, articles, or books on our splendid trade; you will see it in no procedural manual. It is expurgated, it is our one professional secret blocked by the oath. I cannot break the oath to reveal. Not even I, not even now.)

Into the bloodstream we stalk, little divers carrying our lances, the lance also reducible for crises. Now in the body's fever at last the noises have changed; sharpened, heightened, strange whines and sirens in the distance, a clanging and receding, Bicker and thud, as we stroll our way with surprising casualness up the alleys and toward the appointed spot.

The spot: ah yes, the spot; it has been localized for us, brushed red by radiation in the morning, turned orange by nightfall, nevertheless it does not show up clearly in that darkness, a thick, atmospheric haze descending like the soot of Downside, and illumination, cleverly provided by the tip of the lance (make of that what you will!), is necessary. In this cave, then, one can feel not only the humors but the instances themselves, the very seat of personality is here. Twitches of culpability, seizures of continence, revelations and platitudes, even a fanatic shriek here and there, and the corridors seem to curl in spots as if impaled. The siren rings faster, a bell knocks, we move upon the designed spot.

Oh, it is cold, cold! Temperatures are not adjusted through reduction and so one must shudder within one's little outer garb until reaching that designated spot. Stalk then, skitter, run, jump, sway, stagger, perch to a corpuscle and finally, finally, to the heart of the orange, now gleaming in the proximity. Doff the garments swiftly, hang them on some tissue.

Gloves, indicator, goggles: all gone. They flap on a filament in the chill, the strange intestinal wind moving them, and then the lance is carefully brought to fire through the old method, one droplet of heat applied. And burn, then, bum, burn I Mumble curses, eviscerate, quiver, until at last the burning, bright bulb of cancer emerges at the end of the lance.

One looks at it then in the light: one can see the whole of the lovely, lovely tumor, reduced to centimeters. It seems to have features; some of them mimic the faces of animals or men. Slash of mouth, wink of eye deep in the pocket, holding it then at little arm's length to avoid contamination, remove the tag from the lance and slap it in there. Don the goggles again, whisk the bag into the coat, and then off into the turbulence again. A boulevardier. A stroller out for his evening's pastime, the wind a bit damp, but what to make of it?

One shuffles much faster this time. Reduct exists only for a certain stated interval and after that one is known to enlarge, whether the patient can contain or not. Physics and Hulm cannot be embraced by simple willfulness. It would not necessarily kill the Messenger, enlargement within the patient, that is, but it would from the cosmetic and career standpoint do him little over-all good and, as far as the patient was concerned, it would be quite a pulpous mess, not to say a final one. Quicker and quicker on the boulevards, then, the metastases deep in the pocket of the coat, in the pocket, the metastases being carried like an awful little secret which the patient himself may never know; a high, penetrating hum over all of this which might only be one's nervous reaction. Although I believe differently. I believe it to be the song of the metastases, overtaking itself and making a carol of release. To the exit point (which I similarly dare not reveal) and into the light.

Perch on a table top.

Sing with the metastases.

One waits then. Sometimes one has exited too fast and there are terrible moments for this peculiar elf as he sits with legs dangling, wondering if this is the time that the Roof Falls In and then at last —

Ah, at last! There is a feeling of unfolding, flowering, heightening, and elevation as the reconstitution at last begins. To come right to the point, it feels *sexual,* not an erection merely of that quivering, useless organ, but of the axillae, the papillae, the deltoids, the jugular and so on, blood filling all the cavities as they rise to terrible authority, snapping like a slide rule, and finally, full height restored (it all takes only seven or eight seconds but how long is an orgasm?), one stands glinting from angry, mature eyes, toward the form lying on the bed of life.

For all that this form knows or cares it might as well be on the moon; it is beyond analysis, as insensate of what has been done to it as if it were roaming the blasted surfaces with power pack and nightmare, and one sighs, one packs up his equipment. It is all too much. Buttoning the little cancer securely into a flap, the figure trundles wearily through the hall to turn it in for analysis.

In the hall they look at you. They know. They always know when it has happened and what you have done and there is a rim of terror underneath the inquiry and the smile. For the way they look at you, you might as well have been fornicating with a sheep or committing self-abuse in a sterile washbasin, and yet I want to say to them, How can you look at me in this way? It is only a Messenger, a faithful Messenger, dedicated servant of man and enemy of cancer, moving wearily through these outer corridors; can you not understand that? Can you not understand that it is merely a process, a process more difficult than most but devoid of irony? Why do they look at us in this way?

I think I know the answer.

They see it, you understand, they see it and so do I, so say it and be damned, let it come then and no way around it. Knock down the door and kill me, take my notes and burn them, hang me before the Institute as warning to all who pass below, do that and more, and yet it must be said and in its purity and finality cannot be escaped.

Say it once and for all time, gentlemen: this intimation buried like the ant at the heart of the blooded rose, forty years age, deep in the gnarled gardens of Hulm's darkness. Say it, see it:

I LOVED MY WORK.

Standing Orders

THIS IS Luke Christmas, the President. The standing orders are in effect. President today, Secretary of Defense yesterday, Health and Welfare tomorrow. Then recycle and switch. Being President is the most fun of all, the day he looks forward to. With luck it happens twice a week unless they call off the Cabinet meetings on sudden notice and herd them all into the dayroom for extra Thorazine and career planning. Luke had been afraid that they would pull one of those switches today. They hadn't done it in a while, but here it is Wednesday and the Cabinet meeting seems to be going off without a hitch. Luke is having a good time, here in simulation therapy. That is what they call it in their charts and summaries. Luke has a better name for it, though. He calls it playing President. (Or playing Secretary of Defense, whatever.) It is about as good as it is likely to get for him. Luke knows that the future is nothing he can count on. Sometimes the drugs take hold and sometimes they do not. Sometimes he thinks he has the situation licked and other times he feels like an old loony in a ward somewhere, playacting power fantasies. Up and down, in and out. But today is a good day. Luke feels solid, all the way through and the Cabinet is listening to him with unusual intensity. They are paying attention and well they should. He is, after all, the President.

So here is Luke Christmas talking to the Secretary of Defense, the Secretary of State, the National Security Adviser, and so on and so forth. "We have to take a strong line," he says. "We are coming into a new game plan, a new universe altogether. A new millennium coming up. Everything is going to change in the two thousands, you know? Different times, different rules." He twirls the belt on his bathrobe, flaps it around, shows the three hundred and sixty degree angle which represents the Earth moving around the Sun. "Get it?" Luke says. "Everything is going into a different orbit. So what do you think down there? Is the Argentine situation under control?"

Argentina has been a son of a gun recently. Rebels, revolutionaries, struggles among the loyalists, a Presidential assassination, the succession of the widow to the unfilled term, a panic when flood relief *(flood relief in Argentina?)* went astray and slipped into Bolivia instead. Bolivia, Argentina, Nicaragua, Brazil: all of these people and places were in tumult and it was hard to sort them out. Still, you had to keep them separate in your mind, the President thought. That was part of the job. Every third day, anyway. "So what do you hear?" he says.

The National Security Adviser breaks the silence, looks over his shoulder, then stares at the President. "Borders," he says, "they're infiltrating borders. It has to do with the sheep."

"Sheep? Whose borders? What infiltration?"

"Well," the Adviser says, "we're working on this. We're trying to figure it out. It's not easy. We get conflicting reports."

Luke Christmas stared at his counselor, then looked up and down the table. "Hard to sort out," he said, "well, it's a confusing business. Are there any other comments?"

Carmen, the chairman of the Joint Chiefs of Staff today says, "We're having a little trouble with that situation in Montana. It looks like we're going to have to have a full mobilization there, try to control the situation." She shakes her head, looks toward the door. "I don't want to be too specific," she says. "You know what I mean."

Luke knows what she means. The reactor has been firing out of control for some weeks now. They cannot seem to control the chain reaction and the burn is moving inexorably through the earth, threatening to break free in Helena or some place like that. It is a situation with which he had to contend when he was Defense and he had no answers then; it certainly hasn't improved. "Well," Luke says, "if we have to call out the troops, we'll just do it, I guess. Keep it under control any way you can. I don't think there's much we can do."

The chairman nods vigorously. "I know," Carmen says, "Still, you have to try, right? We're all trying." There are little murmurs up and down the table. It is agreed that everyone is doing his or her best according to the parameters of the situation anyway, and no one should be unduly criticized. After a while the nods and mumbles subside and the Cabinet and sub-Cabinet officers look expectantly at Luke again. That is the problem with being President. It has its power and prerogatives, sure, but you have to *run* these things. But what If you don't feel like running them? What if you've had enough of this already and you have other things on your mind? It isn't all simulation therapy. Behind this masking, Luke knows that there are some real problems: the terrible family stuff and so on and the question of drug maintenance which is, when you think about it, delusory because how long can you use drugs to avoid a situation which just gets worse and worse if you didn't believe that you could deal with it. Things could just get worse and worse, and that was for sure.

Anyway. Luke felt the disinterest coming over him. Sometimes it happened just that way. You were at the center of things, simulating like a son of a bitch, and then you just wanted *out*. "Well," he said, "I guess that's all of it, if no one has anything to add. We'll proceed with the agenda in the usual way. Things should be much calmer by tonight, don't you think?"

They seem to think so. They look at him with rounded, glaring Keane eyes, the big eyes of drug induced accommodation and Luke supposes that he is looking back on them in the same way. They must be some bunch in this dayroom, sitting among the checkerboards and ping pong tables, doing simulation therapy, acting out power politics when most of them are so drugged, so filled with grief, that without the support of the situation they would probably be stretched out on the floor, twitching. "I think we'll adjourn now," Luke says. "Is that all right? What does everyone think? We have this busy day ahead, dealing with our own stuff, isn't that so?" Everyone seems to think that is so. Luke picks up the gavel which they gave him and pounds it once on the table. Sometimes it is fun to be formal even though he is sure that a gavel hasn't been used by any President other than he in all the years that simulation therapy has been going on here. Shrugging, gossiping, his Cabinet shuffles away, turning to give respectful nods, then leaving Luke standing alone in the dayroom. Dr. Williams waits until all of them are out, then comes through the side door and comes right up to Luke, dealing with him in that engaging, Williamesque way which Luke has always found so heartening and yet at the same time so irritating. "You did very well," Dr. Williams says. "We felt that you showed some real control, Luke."

"Well, thank you," Luke says. Really, what can he say? He is not sure he knows any way to deal with the shrink, even after all these months. You always have to be on guard with your doctor, but then again Williams is as engaging as a puppy, seems to want to be on informal terms. A strange reversal. Isn't it usually the shrink who is distant? "Well, sure," Luke says, vaguely, "sure thing. I'm doing the best I can."

"And a very neat job of it, too," Williams says. He is. a short, intense man with twinkling eyes — eyes very different from the dull-eyed, big-eyed bunch with whom he does most of his business — and a brisk manner, but Luke suspects that there is something very wrong with Williams inside, something deep and tragic, maybe something as troubling as whatever is inside Luke himself. "Well," Williams says, "what do you say we go back to the Oval Office now?"

"Well, sure," Luke says, humoring him. "Whatever you say, it's all right with me."

"We can layout some more of the day's events, you have a speech to the National Council of Churches at eleven, and then there's the Medal of Freedom ceremony in the Rose Garden at three. In between, you can have a really nice lunch. We're going to have sausages today, maybe some pastry, too. How does that sound?"

"Oh, good," Luke says. "It sounds good." Williams' hand is on his arm, guiding him. They move through the dayroom and into an empty anteroom, once an electroshock parlor Luke guesses, which serves as the Oval Office. "Now, Mr. President," Williams says, "why don't you just sit down and have a little rest while we get your schedule going. How will that be?"

"Fine," Luke says. "That will be fine." He is tired from that Cabinet meeting and no kidding. It may not seem like much on the outside, but there is a lot of responsibility there and one slip, a single slip could bring down the target bombs on your head. There is tension all through him. Sometimes it is very hard to remember that this is just a dayroom and he is in simulation therapy, damned if sometimes it doesn't feel real. *"Right* back," Williams says. He moves away, leaving

Luke alone in the Oval Office which is not, now that he looks around, really very big. They could do better than this even though if they took away that old electroshock machinery here, it probably would be a little bigger. Well, maybe a lot bigger.

Anyway, the Cabinet meeting is over and now there will be only ceremonial stuff and sausages and maybe pastry for lunch and the Rose Garden. The worst part of the day is behind him, Luke thinks, and tomorrow he can go back to Health and Welfare again which involves a lot less strain. Still, it would be nice if Williams did not cut out on him like this all the time and if Carmen had more of a definite plan instead of just talking about heavy mobilization. Signs of panic there.

Luke goes over to the window, looks down upon the grounds surrounding, listens to the sounds of the milling crowd in the distance. Certainly a lot of people in this place, more than you would think just looking at it. Doing simulation therapy of their own. Luke thinks about this and that, thinks of all the good and bad points about simulation therapy, waiting for Williams to come back. Where is Williams? He has promised to be back soon. But the gray-bearded, twinkly-eyed, undependable little fuck simply won't show and the sounds of the crowd in the distance are unpleasantly louder. It's the damndest thing. Luke has the intimation that in just a few minutes he'll be hearing gunfire. How about that, gunfire? It's remarkable the ends to which they'll sometimes take this kind of thing to provide realism. Luke waits and waits for Williams to come back, to tell him what the next thing to do will be, but there's no sign of him and after a time, Luke feels a sudden certainty that the guy isn't going to come back after all. What the hell is with him? What is going on in this place anyway? There are sounds in the dayroom, suddenly, which he does not like.

Here is Luke Christmas. He is President of the United States today. He wants to turn and tell them that this was not so yesterday and it will not be so tomorrow, simulation therapy will pass the baton to someone else, but as they come through the door, they do not seem inclined to listen. They do not seem to be interested in any aspect of Luke's intelligence. Here they are. "I think that I will skip lunch. I don't want to go to the Rose Garden. I think I need a lot more medicine now," Luke says very quietly in a bleak and mouselike little tone, barely audible to the hulking forms, some of them from Montana, who lay enormous hands on his wrists, seem to have enormous plans for him. Uncontrolled chain reaction, Luke Christmas thinks. There goes Luke now. He is gone. They are definitely taking him away and there is no Cabinet to help him out. There is *nothing* to help him out, as Luke in his secret heart has always feared.

Most Politely, Most Politely

D EAR COURTESY & Advisement Person:
  Have you ever felt that your clone was running your life rather than existing (as advertised) on a parallel plane?

Everything was working out beautifully, I was in a class 10 relationship and was taking an option to renew, my cyborg and I were tracking whole *levels* of intenification and on the professional level I was no longer suffering from Saturnian Dread as we moved closer to Titan in transit ... and then peculiar reports began filtering back from the extrinsic provinces. I had been seen dancing in Castor's Way Station. I was humping the asteroid belt in a most disheveled condition. Ecstatic and mysterious declarations of fertility 'were emerging from my communications path. All of the reports had credibility; some were accompanied by holographic recycling of the most specific sort. None of them was to be denied.

It was my clone, of course.

Nanotechnologically refined from my deepest impulses and sent sprinting into the system on Newday 2030, the initially complaisant but ultimately treacherous self-representation had been inadvertently programmed to enact some of the deepest and darkest insistences of my inner life and there was nothing to be done. Denials were fruitless, depositions of irresponsibility or separation were dismissed as legally inviolable under the various Cloning Acts of Origination. Soon enough, sooner in fact the debiting commenced along with various denunciations from advisers and my deceased father who warned me in his stubbornly unregenerated fashion that he had always known that cloning was up to no good;

that one life had been enough for him and for most of his generation and should serve for me. I must admit that I found his taunts most unseemly and overreacted, causing my cyborg to disconnect for several cycles, claiming the necessity to re-think every aspect of our class 10.

I am in short in a perilous situation. I need to have a stern confrontation with my clone of course and will do so at the earliest opportunity but that is all predict-able and I need no advisement on how firm and threatening to be. The question is: how can I convince my friends and advisers as well as the Titanian research squad on which I am so dependent that none of this can really be ascribed to me, that I am wholly victimized?

Raymond Q-Quasi Cyborg

Dear Raymond:

Courtesy & Advisement Person does not know where to begin; your com-munication is so wrongheaded, shows such delusions fancy and unfancy as to make Courtesy & Advisement Person despair. First things first, however: do *not* threaten or humiliate your clone in any way. Such tactics, such a breviary of emo-tion will lead to a dismal and watery end. (Or gaseous end I should have said since you are so associated with that perilous, misguided Titanian project.) Of *course* you are responsible; nanotechnics merely permit the amplification of desire just as the old megaphone amplified speech and your clone, created out of your own neces-sity, is doing that which clones are meant to do: enacting your underside. Become pedantic or threatening, ascribe blame to the hapless and doubtless victimized creature and you will bring terrible consequences to you both. The clone will, responding to your false repression, simply excavate more of your needs, attempt to hump not diminutive asteroids but perhaps the bleaker and more testing sur-faces of Ganymede and you will find yourself the target and specter of ever more evil gossip.

Speak as gently to your clone as you would to yourself.

Better yet, do not speak with your clone at all. Abandon pursuit. Cancel all appointments. Cultivate silence, exile, cunning through this difficult period. Greater repression and projection of denial upon your clone will lead to ever greater disgraces. Who, after all, is responsible for the nanotechnics in the first place? No one dragged you to the implantation crew or farced you to swaddle your germ tissue in blue liniment for a closer spermatazoic fix. Who do you think did this? Your dead father? (Whose lectures are, we suspect, imaginary; more of your experience is hallucinatory than you think.)

That leaves us with the question of your cyborg.

Class ten is running for safety; more perceptive to your neurosis than you have been, class ten cyborg is sending you a dread warning in the least provoca-tive fashion by putting a hold on the relationship and sliding into absence. You would best do everything within your power to placate your *cyborg* and let the clone fend as best as can be, something which nanotechnics if properly applied will make possible.

Actually, we think that you do not want your cyborg, you want your *father* regenerated and the clone's pitiful efforts to have a good time are all reactionformation of a most pathetic sort. But this leads Courtesy & Advisement Person into whole areas of commentary and analysis which fall outside the purview of this exchange and would probably lead you to *another* disastrous expedition to blue liniment and germ plasma; better to let it be.

Under certain circumstances, brutalized clones can become wistful, then violent, finally aggrieved out of all proportion to your ability at self-protection. After humping asteroids, not only does Ganymede seem possible but an original source of germ plasma looks easy. Now you have been warned.

Dear Courtesy & Advisement Person:

Feedback from the extradimensionality threshold informs me that in New Era 2046 one of my alternate selves apparently assassinated a head of state, thereby leading to uncontrollable effects in at least four other alternates. Militia with baleful expressions appear at the periphery of my rooms and consciousness and point weaponry at me and during sleep period, even under strong hypnotic, I encounter surges of panic and guilt.

As far as I know, this is the first time that an alternate self has ever had a misadventure and extradimensionality has been no problem to me up until now. Realizing that in *this* continuum I am no criminal and that there is no possibility ·of alternate bleed (I have asked some expert friends about this) of that murderous character, what am I to do? I want to take strong action, demand of the state that the militia be removed, but I understand that we are in a perilous state of adjustment and that confrontation might affect certain small paradoxical elements. Or am I full of information of the wrong side, clogged by stupidity? I didn't assassinate anyone. I have never had a murderous thought in my life. Now and then I see myself in a reflector however and there is a distinctly aggressive tilt to my head. *This* couldn't be alternate bleed, could it?

Boston 14

Dear Boston:

If you say that your friends (unidentified) deny alternate bleed, why do you ask me fifty words later if you're suffering from it? What precisely do you expect to gain from this situation? And if you have all the answers, why are you asking Courtesy & Advisement Person any questions?

There is a certain astonishing and not too subterranean aspect to your communication, in short.

But this is not really a courtesy & advisement question you are asking, is it? You do not seem to be seeking advice on conduct but rather justification for inaction. You say that you did not kill the state head yet in effect ask for *absolution* on the murder of that unfortunate figure. You say that your friends deny any kind of alternate bleed, yet ask me if you are suffering from it. You see militia "with baleful expressions" at the corner of your eye and want them removed but are concerned with "certain small paradoxical elements" which I suspect you find not so small at all. In short, you seem to be in a position of massive confusion and it is not courtesy & advisement you seek so much as it is some kind of encompassing answer.

I have no answer.

I have some suspicions and intimations, of course, but they fall outside the purview of this service. However, since you have taken the time and trouble to query I will, in similar spirit, respond. (After all, we are in the same reality and must do what we can to defend it, *n'est-ce pas?*) I intimate that alternate bleed (which has been well established as you know by certain pioneering studies) is operating here. I believe that you are the very gent who might have undone the head of state and have found yourself in this reality as alternate to your own. I think that those militia you see in the "corner" are in pursuit and trying to duplicate your own felicity with alternate bleed. I think that you are in a state of rigorous denial and are closer to being trapped, perhaps, than you might know. I think it is possible that you might be entrapped even before this communication reaches you. I recommend that you go quietly and that you cooperate with your blue-eyed militia. (I envision them somehow as having come from a world of blue uniforms, blue eyes, blue moods.)

So this *does* turn out to be a courtesy & advisement matter after all. I recommend that you show all the courtesy possible under the circumstances and in turn the paradoxical gulf between your old world and this will close and your captors, certainly grateful at the ease of this accomplishment, may be more merciful than otherwise.

Maybe the head of state needed assassinating. Cheer up, you haven't after all heard the reports. You may be a heroic figure. They may be coming to take you back to a grand reception. They may want to celebrate your accomplishment in a courtesy & advisement fashion.

Dear Courtesy & Advisement Person:

Perhaps you have heard of a problem like this and perhaps you have not. In my life I have set few precedents, hovering somewhere between median and mode, a kind of Maginot Line of circumstance, a demilitarized zone of possibility, but this is not duplicated, at least among my circle of friends. My implantation menu coil is seeking to have a relationship with me.

"No," my menu coil has been saying in early shift when I have ordered fritters & eggs, "this is bad for your protein levels and will clog your immortality circuits. Also, the fritters are particularly inferior right now. Try the meat & synthetic frogs, and you won't regret it." The menu coil, a sinister device, perches deep within my medulla oblongata and whispers such confidential possibilities and suggestions, ignoring my frantic shrugs and gestures of dismissal, continuing to wheedle, sometimes becoming threatening. "Fritters will destroy you," the menu coil has been known to say, "and eggs will drive you to a horrid and anonymous destiny. Stick with the meat." Of course I am giving you only random *exempla*, so to speak, sometimes it is the herbaceous which the coil recommends. Also it has been known to suggest that after mealtimes, on downshift, we spend some private time together, time not to be measured in heartbeats and brain waves. The suggestions seem to be ominously *sexual* although of course, common sense and the rhetoric of disjunction would suggest otherwise.

Under the Devices Liberation Act penultimately passed before the Year of Jubilation so recently concluded, I am aware that I have no *official* recourse, short of surgical removal, but this seems utterly drastic. It will curl my medulla from cell to cell for one thing and for another I have come to appreciate my coil's advice. The fritters are terrible more often than not and my pores seem to be cleansing. But I wish to make no plans for downshift activities; my time is fully booked by a non-cellular being.

All Soul's Day on Titan

Dear ASDT:

Courtesy & Advisement Person detects shades of reactionformation in your complaint. Are you *sure* that a cellular rendezvous does not inflame the blood, that the uncongealed and racing physique which your menu coil is conferring upon you does not seek forbidden outlet? To the very degree that so many of my correspondents express rejection, Courtesy & Advisement Person has noted, they seem to be signaling an unadmitted but powerful *need*. Just asking, of course.

In any event, ASDT (I assume that this is a pseudonomic which nonetheless can be tied to a perilous role undertaken in the Titanian Revolt of some cycles back, you might even be one of the Forbidden Generation, Courtesy & Advisement Person is not devoid of historical knowledge after all) the Devices Liberation Act, so recently and joyfully ratified by the full Congregation leaves you without a possibility of official suppression, legal devices are unavailable, your coil has as much a right to counsel against fritters, heckle your abominable taste for eggs as *I* do to applaud the good sense and goodwill of your medullian (medullic?) companion. Learn and live, ASDT, accept the equality of devices: cyborgs, clones, robots, and the Andromeda Group are as possessed of freedom, as certain of willful purpose as yourself. We live in an age of equality and you for one should be thankful for it. But even in an age of equality, fritters do not equal meat.

Dear Courtesy & Advisement Person:

In my new communal arrangement, a blessed septology, one of my wives — I have learned only a few moments ago and still reel from shock — is my ex-husband from a powerful and sonorous arrangement of my earlier years. *Quelle dommage!* as they once said on the streets of Laredo. What do I do now?

Masha

Dear Masha:

We live in the age of the Liberation of Devices, of transport and glee; we live in an age of the miraculous. Freeze down and enjoy it, Masha. I think it's London you have in mind, not Laredo.

Dear Courtesy & Advisement Person:

Vaguely heartened by the wisdom and good common sense of your responses to a whole heterogeneity of problems, ennobled by the possibility that practicality, humor, and goodwill still exist even in this technological trap which seems to have seized us, I ask only an abstract or perhaps it is a metaphysical question, as relevant now as it was all those unimaginable cycles past, knowing that if you cannot answer this, no one can. I have anguished over it to no particular outcome. Is life real? Is it earnest? Where are we slouching and what if anything will be born?

Poet

Dear Poet:

That is not one question, it is four. Or at least it is two if you factor in the question of quotation. All through professional life, from the very beginning, Courtesy & Advisement Person has been hounded (follow the reference) by those who in the guise of asking one question have actually posed four or six or eight and sometimes one hundred questions, all of them variants of what might be called the True Cosmic question which in this or any era is of such grandiose dimensions that it cannot be paraphrased or intimated but applies to issues of difference, inferiority, terror of mortality (even in the Regenerate Era), and so on.

Courtesy & Advisement Person must add you to this voluminous and ever-increasing list of jaunters, threateners, cranks, freeloaders and the like but does so without ill will or hostility of any sort, understanding as one does the question of cultural lag, astronomical in our time, and the fact that there are many billions such as yourself & clones who are trying to cope with the horrific and variegate present with the pathetic and clumsy tools of a long-departed and unavailable past. This can lead to terrible depression and sometimes consequence of the worst sort.

Read these queries for a while, if you don't already agree.

I bear you no malice, then, only concern and a *soupçon* of pity.

In any event, and to answer your four questions, forswearing any technicalities or quibbles over greed: life is no longer real but merely a matter of selection today. It is only as earnest as one or one's clone or successors wish it to be, a slouch is a habit of bad posture which must be discarded and *you* are in the process of being born, just as Courtesy & Advisement Person is born with every query and dies a little with every answer, but sinks like someone's lost clone only to be revivified again with the next.

Is that too technical?

Well, it is a technophiliac time. One does the best one can with what one has been given. Having been given nothing (as Courtesy & Advisement Person often complains and with every right) it therefore follows that anything divulged must be seen or granted as a gift. The last gift Courtesy & Advisement person was given was an alternate bleed several cycles ago, allowing a somewhat wiser person to take over these chronicles, so the goods given back must be pretty seedy as well.

But, then, ripeness is all, poet. All or nothing at all.

Moishe in Excelsis

MOISHE GOES for the deal.

How can he not? In the infinite spaces of purgatory, this is certainly better than sitting in antechambers waiting for the verdict or — worse yes, as rumor would have it — being pounding by imps with every large and small, deep and scant misfeasance of which the imps or angels could dream. So Moishe will play antagonist to the Boss's protagonist, rung the whole Job bit over and again, take sides, see if the matriarchs and patriarchs of legend are up to their reputation. Part of playing at Satan, of course, is to occupy an unsympathetic role; the antagonist has always had a bad press. The other part, of course, is to be engaged in utter reconstruction: one does not sit in purgatory, the deal has it, but allowed to replicate one's life as one chooses. Lose and burn in the fires for two millennia, win and find a ticket into the ambrosiacal dome of Heaven … this is the deal which the Boss has offered. It is remarkable how one goes through Satans in this business, the Boss says with a wink. He seems to be pretty affable old gent although, as Moishe does not need to be reminded, thee is a famous mean streak.

So on to the cliffs, the passages, the lower depths of 47th Street. Will Abraham, Isaac, and Jacob come through? Will Job maintain his solidarity with the Boss? It is up to Moishe to have them undone, but he knows the prospects are not good. His judgment has always been suspect. Is this why he ended in purgatory? His ambitions were so modest, so scattered; why such a bleak and tremendous fate?

Traveling around, keeping an eye on all the possibilities. Trapped on the cliff, the unpleasant signs and portents everywhere. Moishe watched as Abraham, once a shepherd, now a freelancer, poised over his beloved son Isaac, prepared to cleave the lad for human sacrifice. The patriarch's wrist trembled with indecision, but his eyes were firm, cast toward the heavens, syllables of Hebraic gibberish filling the dismal air. Crouched behind the thicket, the semipurgatorial Moishe Feyderman witnessed the scene so famous in all of the Biblical texts and commentaries, source of a thousand doubts and beseeching metaphors, observing that Isaac in this posture appeared almost comatose, the fear throttling his limbs, his posture making the rope unnecessary. A pathetic scene, Moishe thought; seedy father, needy son, both of them entrapped, embarked upon a ritual sacrifice which in a more enlightened time would have been truly recognized as lunacy. But there was none of that for Feyderman; this was the original, the Scriptural act itself, and as the highly aggrieved Moishe, wise to his disgrace, aligned to this Satanic rivalry, crouched in the thicket to obtain a closer perspective on the panorama of disgrace, he heard a sound of collision in the distance and then a high voice speaking behind the sky.

So here was the Boss, meddling again as he had meddled with situations throughout all of Book One, tilting the odds in his favor as he chose, leaving Moishe only with the hapless posture of witness. It was not fair; he should have protested immediately when the deal was being set, but who was he to argue with the Upper of Upper Management? The voice was uncontrolled, raving, bellowing. He brew polysyllables, not a one of which made any sense at all to the infuriated Feyderman, hammered to witness these unspeakable and confusing activities, hoping that Abraham would break the process this time. No such luck. Would never happen. Feyderman knew that it was the Boss's voice telling Abraham to cease, telling him that his hapless son could be spared. Feyderman grasped the branches, leaned forward, absorbed as much of this as he could before utterly losing hope. There was always the possibility of change: the point of faith was that it needed to be reaffirmed constantly, needed, as the Boss had pointed out, to be readjusted. You had to see it as a living and continued testament, not as aged data. So Abraham was nodding furiously, tears of assent and acceptance seemingly clawed from the old man's eyes, groans of enthusiasm or submission pouring from the Abrahamic throat. The eyes gleamed, were cast downward. Then Abraham strode toward the thicket, his steps determined, even frantic, and Feyderman prepared to deal with a confrontation he could barely comprehend.

No. He would not have to do that now. Abraham spared him, turned, strode pat without responding, and Feyderman could see at the end of the line of foliage the gigantic ram caught by the horns, twisted in the clutch of branches. The sources were certainly right on the ram, anyway. What a big son of a bitch this blown-up lamb was.

Isaac was weeping now, surfacing to an appalled consciousness, struggling in that emergent consciousness with the ropes while Abraham reached toward the ram, freeing it from the branches. The voice behind the sky raved on in Hebrew, but Feyderman, sunk in fury, gulping on his defeat and the Boss's mad primacy, could not find a word he understood and discarded a posture of attention. Abraham, a small and slightly deformed man, struggled with the beast in the bushes. Feyderman had never seen anything like it. The whole matter was clearly unduplicable. It was remarkable, as the Boss had tipped him, when you got to the story behind the story.

Another confirmation of Satanic suffering. Despite the appearance of equity, it had all been structured against him.

Morton Feyderman, nee Moishe, had been placed in this incarnation at the practical inside job in the diamond district which had been his years before the cancer had polished him off and put him into the dismal and purgatorial condition. He factored and reconciled the books for several independent jewelers so that they, patrician in their high hats and frocks, could walk the street with diamonds in their pockets and make the instant deals. Nonetheless, the Feyderman life, reconstructed or otherwise, was unraveling for reasons beyond Biblical rivalries or reconstruction. Twenty years ago when he had gone through this the first time, long before the AIDS crisis and the other horrors, there had been a small cathouse on the third floor of one of the buildings in the middle of the block; a factor or jeweler could go up there during lunch hour, take one of the five or six girls, get his ashes hauled. Simple procedure for the bearded and beardless, the yarmulked or peyussed dealers and factors of that simpler time.

Feyderman himself had indulged infrequently and never in ways which could have risked bringing home a disease to the clamorous, now departed Doris. (At least he did not have to suffer his wife during this tour of replication.) But even at the time of his greatest confusion so long ago, when sex, diamonds and possibility had collided in his frame of consciousness over and over again, not even then had Feyderman found himself as bedazzled and chaos-laden as he was now.

To have gone through this once was a challenge; twice, however, went beyond all possibility of indulgence. In moments of brief repose or micro-sleep, Moishe could now find himself reliving, even more intensely and often in Hebrew, some of the most intense books of Old Testament and New, half-recollected narratives which he thought had been put away with his official change of name (registered in the Bureau of Names and Licenses and everywhere else: Moishe Feigelenbaum, now Morton Feyderman) but which had emerged with horrific validity during what he could only take as moments of fugue or induced amnesic state, sometimes a witness, sometimes as with the Pharisees an actual participant in scenes of such squalor and intensity that he would never have been able to gauge the sheer dimension of his fanaticism. Reconstructed, reborn, the Satan-identifying Feigelenbaum, now Feyderman, stumbled through these dream states in a subterranean fashion, looking for some larger effect which they might have upon what he now mockingly called his "outside existence." As far as he could tell, there were no effects at all. He lived alone now as then, a barely assimilated Jew in a residential hotel, the room piled with pornography, familial scrapbooks and, recently, Scriptural sources and commentary. As before, he went from hotel to work, striding down 47th Street amongst the criers and chaos of the district, still took up his post in the morning, and performed acts of reconciliation.

Only the memory of the conversations with the Boss and the dreamlike Scriptural episodes seemed to have force. His life had otherwise shrunk to gray, shrunk to the swaddled dimensions which Doris had warned him so long ago were his true destiny.

"Because you are a weak man, Feigelenbaum," she had said to him during one of the last arguments, "and you would rather go along with what does not suit you because you are afraid of making a change." Well, Jonah had make a change and see where it had gotten him. The Testaments, both of them, were littered with characters of various sorts who had looked for big changes, and almost invariably they had come to bad ends, winding up blind or on roads toward revelation or scuffling with lions for the edification of brutes. What was wrong with trying to get along? But the simple right triangle of the resurrected Feyderman's old life, two straight lines leading toward the hypotenuse of resignation, had been scattered by this latest stuff, this dreaming business. Nothing met the standards of simple orderliness now; everything necessarily had slid from control in ways which bedazzled Feyderman, rendered stupefyingly irrelevant all of the easy and accepting postures of the Old Testament which he had thought in his pre-purgatorial existence had made any acceptance of the situation impossible. Becoming Satan had utterly bedazzled, not charmed, Feyderman; it was no real position for a man of even dark motives; it was a terrible circumstance for a man with a modicum of conscience and social responsibility.

But Feyderman was not religious, that was perhaps the reason he had been selected for this anti-textual posture and debate. He had long since emerged from his parochial background, found himself pointing out to Job (cunningly disguised as a Comforter and thus able to sneak around the edges of the situation) that Job was not handling the situation properly. This was one of those episodes in his own language. "Faith got you into this terrible condition, faith therefore cannot get you out," Feyderman said. "You can't put up with this kind of thing any more, you simply cannot."

"Nonetheless," Job said, 'one must try. One must hold on to constancy, yes?"

Once a famous cattleman, now a derelict reduced to scurvey and humiliation by the depredations of the playful and hitherto unchallenged Boss and by his own devices, Job sat sprawled in the courtyard, the mud in which he rested heavily covering his legs and giving him a distinctly earthy appearance. "Or don't you agree with that? Would you have me change?" Job said. "In what way could I change?"

The other comforters stared pointedly and with some triumph at Feyderman, who seemed to have been carrying the conversation, at least to this point. "You must show me some defiance," Feyderman said. "You can't allow these terrors to assault you without response." Oh, I could speak of resisting horrors. But I am here to put the best possible interpretation on events and hopefully to lead Job to action.

"Well," he said, "it was just a thought. Of course if you want to continue to submit, no one can stop you."

"Do you hear that?" Job's wife said, peering through the tent. From the situation as far as he could deduce, Feyderman saw her as something of a Doris type, something of a sexpot past her prime but still in the battle, doing the best she could with limited and fading equipment. But this version of Job's wife was nothing like that at all. She was a different kind of deal, one which eyes less Satanic and warped than his would clearly perceive as a remarkable woman, one of looks and valor. She was a transcendent comment upon and mockery of the denial of desire, Feyderman thought. "The man speaks truthfully. If I were you, I'd curse God and get out of this whole deal."

Now you're talking, lady, Feyderman thought. That's the way to take the situation, isn't it? Listen to the woman, Job. But the cattleman was an obdurate as the other comforters were mournful. None had anything to say. "Well, I've had enough of this," Job's wife said. "It is certainly enough for me."

She retreated from the tent. Job shook his head and said something which Feyderman could not quite hear. Not that he was too interested. He struggled aloft, swaying in the mud. The other comforters looked at him uncuriously; then their gaze swung toward the flap of the tent through which Mrs. Job had exited. She was a distraction all right. Feyderman struggled through the heavy canvas, stumbled through the mire, found himself in a sudden sliver of light, perceived Mrs. Job standing naked, her back to him, her gown open, exposing herself to the sun in a marvelous, pagan way. Well, Feyderman thought, well enough of this, and he stumbled toward her hoping that the constancy of the situation would last at least until he had a chance to get there; but in the wind was the voice of the Boss, enormous, quarreling, filled with reproof. Beyond that, he could hear the starving and diseased cattle in the distance. So much for Satanic practice. Mrs. Job raised a hand in reproof, the Boss screamed, the cattle groaned, and Moishe inferred the message all right. It was not going to be possible. Job would not relent, nor would Satan spring.

As per his usual devices, the Boss had some new mischief prepared.

In his old booth, it might as well have been the hall of purgatory, probably was in fact. Feyderman found himself seized at last by impatience. Perhaps it was sense of squalor greater than any he had ever known. "Listen." He said to the jeweler and to anyone else who might be listening. "I guess I just can't handle this any more, you understand? I'm a foil and I don't like it — a setup man, a straight man." He put down his pen for emphasis, faced the jeweler. "I've been doing the best I can here, in and out of scope." Feyderman said, "and I'm not getting anywhere at all; also I don't think I can put up with the Street anymore. I'm tired, I'm legally dead, I hear the sounds all of the time. It's just too much for me. I've given it everything possible and I think that's enough. Don't you think that's enough?"

The jeweler looked at him solemnly, somewhat reminiscent of Abraham in attack mode before the voice had begun shouting its Boss's Hebrew, but then again this was an illusion, a reconstruction, right? Right? Back to the District, that was part of the deal. Feyderman had all he could do to coordinate one time-scheme with the next, all that he could manage to attain was some crazed synchronicity. A synchronicity more allied to overlap, crazy synchronicity. The question of fusion was utterly beyond him. "I think I've got to get away from commerce of all kinds," Feyderman said hopelessly. "I think I need something more, well, open air if you follow." An open-air purgatory like a pretty graveyard, somewhere he could dance amidst flowers. Amidst flowers? Well, nothing that elaborate maybe, but it was a cause at which to aim. You had to have some kind of position, didn't you?

The jeweler was still impassive. An illusion, then, the Boss's temporal approximation of the District and its people, rather than actual tenants. The District was illusory, the real stuff was the deal Feyderman had made which more and more had been ripping at the hapless ersatz Satan's illusion of control. He waved hopelessly and scurried through the thin aisles, dodging this chassis here, a jewelry model there, a group of gangsters as he made his way through the squalling and desperate corridors to the Street. Maybe the deal was imaginary and the District real, Feyderman thought, looking up at what seemed to be a curiously insubstantial sky, but that is not the way to bet. That is not the deal I would take; the Boss has other plans. Transubstantial, transubstantiating transubstantiation: that seemed to be the word he was seeking. Standing outside the Gotham Book Mart, WISE MEN FISH HERE, the famous sign flapping and flapping in the wind, Feyderman nee Moishe Feigelenbaum, inmate of purgatory; DEAL-MAKER AND DEVIL TO THAT FIRST AND LEAST MERCIFUL OF GODS, *that* Feyderman found himself greatly transported in that sudden wind to a high and desperate place, the solid *thwack* of the wood coming into his arched and awkward posture. Circled by the cries of Jews, the glitter of diamonds, the echoes of an old cathouse and the glimmering of all his accords, Moishe took himself to be at the precipice of the most profound epiphany of all. The Boss spoke to him, manifest then in insubstantive guise.

You lose, the Boss said. You lose, Moishe. They'll always line up for me. I run the shop.

The Boss's pleased giggle filled all of the high and dense places. Moishe had been waiting all of his life, it seemed, to hear that giggle, to be overtaken, and there it was. There it was. You're just another loser, the Boss said, and Moishe was falling, falling from the peak of that most glittering of epiphanies. Satan falling to the bowels of the Earth, past exile toward disgrace. The Boss let loose childish howls of triumph. No room then for Moishe in excelsis. Falling thus, he will not soon rise, and that is a certainty along with Job's composure. Abraham's patience.

Call the roll, the Boss cries. Call the next contender.

And new Moishe — old Moishe, really, how many can there be? — comes forth.

Heliotrope Bouquet Murder Case

1917

SCOTT JOPLIN observes the rehearsals and opening night of his opera, STREEMONISHA. It is a disaster. The small audience there because they know of him are disappointed with the lack of ragtime; the critics are appalled by his ersatz European style, a sweetish and decadent mixture of Romberg and Friml, Lortzing and Sullivan; watching the one performance of the opera from the rear of the hired hall Joplin feels the shame pulsing through him, the slow and anguished shock of lost purpose, public exposure, horrendous limitation. A REAL SLOW DRAG, the finale, arouses the audience only to a dull and incidental applause; in that scattering of sound Joplin can feel the waves of illness pounding at him, the syphilis that will kill him shortly galloping through the shelves and spaces of the body, the merry and diminishing blood carrying the parasite to new angles of achievement. Failure stalks the crevices hollowed out by the illness: standing there, looking at the actors trapped in the frieze and sudden light, Joplin feels that he is peering through the roof of the century; staring down, the strobes or angle light of his vision carrying him to the bottom of all purpose and in that cluster of damaged and destroyed purpose, the shuddering of the instruments for which he has apparently written so badly, he thinks that he hears the throes of ragtime hammered out by steel and wire, the real slow drag, the looping run of his own indignity massed at the excavated plantation, mourning the extinguished sun.

1906

Joplin comes to the ward where Louis Chauvin lies dying of syphilis, the brain of the twenty-five years old pianist turned to jelly, decomposing through his eyes. Joplin sits by the man's bed, presses his hand. There is really nothing else to be done and in the rattle and drone of the twenty-five years old's ravaged breath Scott Joplin can hear intimations of his own doom, waiting for him he knows somewhere down the early decades of this century. He is 39 years old and he has already seen too much although then again perhaps he has seen nothing at all; perhaps the Ku Kluxers are right, perhaps it is the condition of the black man, torn from the righteous nature to his condition to be so quickly, so thoroughly done in: by syphilis, by music, by the ropes and wire of the avenging Klan. Chauvin turns to him, gripped by a sudden lucidity, some sanity slowly clearing his eyes and says: Scott, I have a tune. I have two tunes in my head. I was dreaming, I thought I was dreaming but when I awoke the music went on. They are tunes to make the devil dance, they are the dances of death itself, they are markers —

Rest, Joplin says. Louis, you must rest. Do not try to talk. Really, he should not be here. Why has he come here? His colleague he thought would not even recognize him and now there is this urgent and terrible confluence which is agitating Chauvin, causing his limbs to shake. The tunes, Chauvin whispers, you must listen to them. I do not have the strength to play them. I cannot write them down, I do not know how to write. You must listen, Chauvin says, you must do this for me, and slowly, slowly hauls himself to a half-seated position on the bed, the crook and cast of his skull awful in the sallow light of the charity ward, the cast light through the bars of the bed, the other beds, all of the pauper's bed, a weird and stricken jungle of vines at the foot of the bed. Chauvin, 80 pounds, a dead man, grips Joplin's wrist and pulls Joplin toward him with an awful and insistent strength. Here, he says, listen.

Joplin thinks: I came from whorehouses to this. From the back rooms of ill-repute and the shaking laugher of clowns to this terrible place. But he listens. He has always listened; to him the act of composition is one of taking dictation, the tunes come and he brings them home. Mozart, he had read somewhere, talked about composition in the same way, not that Scott Joplin is Mozart. Chauvin breathes notes into ear, major and minor thirds and Joplin can find the accidentals, knows just where the minor seconds would be placed to bring on the syncopation. There is syncopation in Chauvin's voice. The other one, Chauvin says, now it becomes a child, a child whistling. Joplin attends to this second theme which casts its way directly into the major, shuttling off the bargain the first tune had made between major and minor. Yes, he says, I hear that.

It's good, isn't it? Chauvin says. He seems energized, flushes in the spangled light. I heard them awake and I heard them asleep. I heard them alive and I heard them dead. So know that they are good, I know that these are the tunes I was given to hear. You must write them, Scott, a new ragtime.

Two tunes are not a tag for me, Joplin says. They are not long enough.

Then four, Chauvin says. His eyes, sunken, take on a terrible urgency. Make another two tunes for yourself and add them, make it a ragtime. It will be yours and mine together. But leave my tunes first, leave my devil dance. Chauvin gargles deep in his throat, falls back on the soiled sheets. Leave me this, he says, leave me at least that evidence, those markers. I have asked nothing of you in all these years, you know this, you know that I wanted nothing.

I will see, Joplin says. The tunes rattle in his head; he knows that they are embossed on his sensibility. There is no danger that they will be lost; he has always been able — always — to retain tunes when first heard. I will do what I can, he says, I can make no promises. I feel my own death, he does not say to Chauvin. What kills you will kill me too; is moving already. The tunes are high and distinct, a terrible clarity. Chauvin, stunned, lies back on the sheets, eyes closed, seems to diminish in passage, dwindles, becomes a child on the heaped and stinking bed. I can do no more, Joplin says, I can promise nothing else.

Chauvin says nothing. Conversation is over, everything is finished. Twenty-five years old, a boy when Joplin had first met him, an adoring boy at the edges of the piano listening, listening with eyes so lustrous, expression so fierce that it could have tenanted the world. This is what he has become but then again this is what Scott Joplin too has become. He stands, walks cautiously through the clumped bodies, the rattling chests, the little aperture between the beds leading him out of the ward. For now. In the hall he pauses, the orderlies looking at him without interest, without disdain, with nothing at all. Just like his public. The tunes are full in his consciousness and he feels rather than hears a third and fourth theme, antagonists but in accord, drop into place. This will write very quickly, very easily, he knows. MAPLE LEAF RAG and ENTERTAINER were like this at the beginning.

HELIOTROPE BOUQUET, Joplin thinks. He staggers into the clamorous night, the notes full before him. He knows that it will be done before dawn and he feels Chauvin impelling him into the night.

1914

Joplin conceives of his largest, his grandest, his most lucrative scheme, the scheme which he hopes will change his life. He will write a grand opera on themes of mythology and transcendence and open it in New York and Europe and it will make his reputation, it will change his life. As HELIOTROPE BOUQUET was his gift to Chauvin, so the tale of Treemonisha will be the world's gift to him. Earnest and seized with purpose even though he knows that long-accustomed doom will soon enough do him in Joplin embarks upon his task, the shackles of ragtime discarded as his fathers had stripped the shackles of their slavery. He hears the first act finals: the call to dinner. In the far reaches of the charity ward the curtains stir in the emptiness of the vacated bed and slowly wafts through the odor of flowers, sickly and stunted flowers, the flowers and tendrils of Joplin's history now destiny in the concatenation of all possibility.

The Lady Louisiana Toy

O F NEED then, and longing, and of the yearning which makes men bum in the night, men lacking any interior, what we once were taught to call "soul," men who plod and plod then way through the anguished and sterile routine of their circumstance... not reflecting upon that necessity or upon much else, men who were closed in early, taken in disarray from their own warm and living hearts and placed — well, placed where? It is not the nature of our metaphysics to consider this, now when the universe itself implodes so reluctantly and we are told, as if it were a declaration of truth, that this is the end of time.

Of those men, then, and of their uses, of what can be made of them from the sterile detritus of their necessity but first, because there is no understanding any of this without the background, without the helpless, mocking heart of the truth ... of the Lady Louisiana Toy first.

In the known places her name was a curse or prayer and m the myriad galaxies not yet discovered or in discovery of hers that presence still might have been a benison, a plainchant, but here, too, and in the huge arcs among the stars where the birds of time themselves swooped, men knelt to her spirit and flesh with imprecations and cries, prayers infused with scatology, joined to a scatology which lifted from the ruins of their hearts. It was a ruinous age, one of blank corruption and discontent, yet one not without a certain romantic necessity, the architecture of desire still present in the space drives, in the whispers of the trawlers of space. In this age there were icons, icons for all of the men without interior which rose unevenly in small arcs from the concavities of the stars, and the greatest of them was the Lady Louisiana Toy whose dreams and spirit passed through the network, amplified to proportion beyond imagining, crushed into the hearts of all who witnessed her. She inspired woe and death, lust and darkness, cries of desperation and climax under the axis of her powerful emoting, that image of herself — and all we might have loved — spread in huge discolored patches through all the devices of dissemination. The treasure of the galaxies, Lady Louisiana Toy, and when she was kidnapped by those we called the Possessors a sigh like all mourning rose from a billion trapped and riven witnesses. What she did was not to be explained, her kidnapping unspeakable and yet this is only the least part of the actress and focused modem known as Lady Louisiana Toy. It will have to do as so much else of this limited document will have to grant service because it is impossible in these final times — or perhaps before them — to convey what had gone on, what it meant, we can only approximate, some sum of an ideal, dim image of the cave, flicker of approximation against the absolute of the cave, that Paolo and Francesca of the galaxies drifting by in their terrible embrace the closest simulacrum we might find.

They remembered Dante in this era, too. It was, perhaps, that set of cantos, the last of what they remembered. Heavens, the spirit of transcendence, all of this collapses but the purgatorial ring is not to be limned by the laws of relativity or the great, groaning hyperspace drives which opened before finally closing to us the universe.

This is not the story of the Lady Louisiana Toy.

It concerns her and she is at the axis, but of her and her kidnapping there is to be apprehension only by indirection. If it is ultimately her story (we cannot know and It is hard to rule the approximation) that would be only because it deals with the man who stole her back from the Possessors and the planet of the doubled suns where she had been smuggled, plucked her back, still beautiful but irreparably damaged from that prison of unspeakable pain where they had made her — for their pleasure, their pleasure, O brothers! — to cry out her necessity in the tongues of her projection. It is, then, the story of that simple and doomed man, a man very much like ourselves except that he possessed no interior whatsoever, no framing consciousness, no newstape of commentary as he struggled through his own purgatory, who lifted the Lady Louisiana Toy from her imprisonment, took her (but only briefly, only briefly!) for his paralyzed satisfaction and in so doing elevated far beyond his apprehension by the sheer expression of that unspeakable need. How could the stalker Stanley Montana have known then that he was the source of this chronicle, that it was he who triggered its necessity, he who had thought of himself only as a minor character, a wretched ingredient, a tiny actor in the story of the Lady Louisiana Toy, in the earlier and grayly unfolding chronicle of his life? We do not know what he would have said, and this at least is unavailable to us although too much else has been expressed. There are parts of Stanley Montana which, like his very soul, remain swaddled, cannot be apprehended. How did he know, this man, that what he had done would be magnified through the millions of telepathic receptors of the Possessors? How would he know that nothing was performed in secret, that detection no less than yearning would be an expressed and public act? But he could not know, of course, there is no way in which he could have known. This man knew nothing.

There is no understanding this chronicle if it is not known that the man knew nothing.

So this is really the story of Stanley Montana and his undoing, the latter undoing which he brought upon us all. It is the story of Stanley Montana and then necessarily of the ravishing Lady Louisiana Toy, all of it legend, long spoken, then passed out in that savage, blinking instant of revelation when the Lady, magnificent in her captivity and pain, suffused with the pale gold light of her sufficiency, suffused with the knowledge that what the Possessors had done had destroyed her utterly and yet had left her at some other level intact ... in that knowledge she opened her arms and mind to receive his cry, took that strangled confession from Stanley Montana then and with it the shrieking inference which took us to this terrific and ongoing explosion, that explosion which has sealed our doom even as it has closed off our fate and sprung us from that ravaged and beautiful final age in which these events took place. That was the end of this chronicle as we knew it then, although of course it did not feel like an ending as it was witnessed but like a series of acts which, beautiful and terrible in their juxtaposition, seemed to point the way to — well, to where? We did not know that either; in the spaces among the suns we crawled through our scripts, no less fixated, no more thoughtful than Stanley Montana.

This, then, the chronicle. It is offered not in reasonable explanation, there is none, but in humility and hope even as the very act — like the investigations of Stanley Montana — turn in upon themselves.

Dragged from the bed of the Emperor by the savage telepathic Possessors who had stalked her for years, had made their plans well, knew at last what they would do with her, the Lady Louisiana Toy felt them pounce upon her unshielded and now ungifted consciousness and she screamed. She screamed both within and without herself, trying to magnify that scream toward salvation, but it could not be done. She was the treasure of the Possessors now and they had taken her. She had not one moment for farewell, for some righting of accounts long since imbalanced against her.

Taken from the Emperor's bed, the Lady Louisiana Toy was placed into the closed box of corporeal transport and taken through secret and powerful means whose technology is unavailable to us and which will defy any reasonable explanation to places not known to any of the conventional historians of the galaxies, and the damaged Stanley Montana must have felt — we theorize as best we can under the circumstances — that thrill of displacement in his own sensibility, felt that he knew of the abduction of the treasured Lady Louisiana Toy before the awful news had been publicly disseminated, and it was at that moment, no later, that his odyssey began. We must consider his reaction as a *feeling*, it was visceral woe (looking back upon it he theorized) deep in the gut, not thought as we know it, thought being unavailable to Montana, and it was thus without apprehension. He did not know then, might never have known that subsequent events would bring him into the presence of what we called the Possessors, those plundering and predatory aliens of which he had previously known so little, of which Montana had thought nothing at all. His skull was impenetrable, his thoughts limited to his own transparent capacity. *Had he but known,* that song of regret of the spheres. We will not deal with it. He could not have known anything, of course. Tropism was his response, small and grumbling resistance to the prank the cosmos had played upon him was limited to vagrant drinking and curses.

There were then, as long before and at sometime in the imponderable future as well, so many men like Montana. They suspire in the small bars and lounges, the restaurants and galleyways of all the planets, usually alone, sometimes in groups with their blasted eyes at moments of repose revealing everything. They sit hunched unto themselves, their expressions casting not so much mystery — come to them close in the guise of a sympathetic companion and sketch this out if you will — as entrapment. They are men of small devices and foolishness who hire out their wretched and painful selves not so much for the small compensation which is their excuse but because they are looking for annihilation. They are looking for something so terrible to happen that they will be freely able to abandon the struggle to have their lives make sense and go over the line into that death they have always sought. They can be inspected at our leisure, they will be there again as they have been in all of the annals of that blasted time, and the message will be one of such utter consistency. They have no secrets, their faces *are* their secret and beat truth to the world.

"That is not so," Stanley Montana would say, confronted with this assessment. "Leave annihilation to the stars out there, speak to me of thugs and mean streets and the blood that runs toward the blood of killers. This is my business. Essential solutions to old mysteries, drink up, stay out of a coffin, go home." Do not listen to any of this, regardless of the fervency of Montana's wink and nod. Observe only the facts of the case, consider the testimony of what the ages have taught us. The thinkers and prophets of this terrible age of which we write knew the truth and they passed it on, the detective (and that is Stan Montana's self-designation, he is a detective, he would put it on his forms and identifying statement, seeker of solutions, detective for hire) is exquisitely and finally the man who would seek to unravel the primal scene, and come close to the struggling bodies linked on that bed locked away behind the primal door, turn those bodies — *hip ho turn!* — to his humble and needful face and identify at last Mommy and Daddy as they go about the heavy and sad business of replicating Montana, reinfusing Montana. This is the business of the detective, to crawl up to the masks *hip ho!* and ripping them away discover the sad and necessitous faces of none other than old Dad and Mom. Believe this, believe that all the rest of it — the plodding, the compensation, the deductions, the small scrambling connections of their own saddened and diminished lives, the posturing and good old self-annihilation — all of it comes from the need of these brethren to conceal this necessity from themselves.

Oh, really? "Having none of it. Good-bye, then," Montana would say, raising his hands from the bar in a gesture of perfect and final dismissal, making his plan to move toward another place where inquiries would cease. But all of this is denial, a denial of which Lady Louisiana Toy would more than the rest of us be clearly aware.

Louisiana Toy!

The name itself arouses, even these eons after her kidnapping, her recovery and destruction, these long limping ages after she had spun through the infernal heart of the stars a crazed and incessant longing, a twitch not unlike Stan

Montana's twitch as — *hip ho!* — he jiggled his leg underneath the stanchion and with blasted eyes considered anachronistic possibility. Descriptions and holographs abound these centuries later of this lady of sorrows; she is one of the most famous of her or any time at all, and yet none of them can conjure but an approximation, so great the force which she could bring without even trying to bear. Capacious bosom, longing arms, lips and eyes reproduced on a billion transceivers, the image of lust and connection for all of us febrile doomed of the Republics and the lady herself, sad and witnessing, watching all of this at the secret heart of her own possibility, carrying her own difficult way through the annals of her life with the sad sustenance, the dignity and the self-knowledge of the truly possessed.

A treasure swept away by the Possessors, our lady, a descendant of a race of telepaths similar to them so that she could apprehend everything, the flood of our longing, the lustful and needful thoughts like tracer fire skidding across the consciousness which she gave to the visiphones. Her parents were unknown, the legends said. She had been found abandoned, adopted at birth by the nurturing institutions who sprung her telepathy from its locked-away place and made it bloom no less than the flowers and purchase of her being. This is what the holographs told us, what the advisers said; how much of this was true, whether Louisiana Toy, no less than the emotions and actions she placed over the visiphone, was "real" we cannot know, but ultimately it does not matter. If there has been one lesson to be absorbed from the fourteen centuries of guilt and abomination before at last the collapse of which we read it is this: that there is no difference between what exists and what we would have exist that cannot be patched over by technology, lies, the insistence of our dreams. Even the fourteen centuries themselves must come into dispute; there are those who will argue for fifteen, others saying that fourteen millennia would not truly apprehend the situation. So the arguments go on and on in their echoing and imprecise fashion, but of the lady's true torment and distress we can only speculate in this chronicle.

We can speculate, but the speculation itself is true; what we would have is what will exist, or so the Possessors told her during the disgusting months of her captivity and indoctrination. We can get no nearer her distress, that distress is part of a story which — were it cataloged would become appallingly sentimental and would then involve the necessity of discussing the seventeen hundred worlds, the politics of genocide which led only to the mild fracture of the Republics (genocide being only another arm of policy), the corruption of the lost judges, the nefarious and wretched spin of dispersion which had made the occupation and performance of the damaged Stan Montana and those in his trade essential to any realpolitick of that long surpassed century which we can consider only as paradigm. Image of an image, dusk of a night, there was the Lady Louisiana Toy, telepathic treasure, her bosom of lace and dreams hurled heavenward in a trillion reproductions to the storming gates of Montana's lust. Louisiana Toy, actress and saint, Mother of God and cruel partisan of the lost spirit, Mary and Medusa and Medea and Electra and a thousand other icons as well, taken from the very center of her being and laid out for us, just as the Possessors — that stem and damaged lupine race of telepaths and technophiliac monsters — took her then to the cold and distant heart of their own galaxy. It was only at that point that the practicalities commenced; the initial crime had been so audacious, so furious and — somehow beyond conception as to deny paraphrase. The demands were issued, of course, through telepathic beam and — for the rest of us who were not telepaths — the lesser systems of transports.

They were blackmail, of course, they were insouciant and outrageous. Even in what the inhabitants of this period thought of as "advanced times" the rockets yet crawled between the stars while in the bowels of those machines creatures whose pain and appearance were unspeakable and thus unknown to the passage hammered and stoked the slow fires of increase While trying not to be consumed by the FTL drives and trying to make of the universe a small, elegant, somehow comprehensible business. The messages crawled with the rockets then, the telepathic waves crackling only to the very few who could· understand them and who (by the prejudicial and murderous nature of this age) could not reveal their telepathic capacity.

For only at the cutting edge — this is an interpolation and it may be forgiven for its relevance ultimately will become clear — does one feel the rush of possibility, does the interface of history and condition, threat and desire, need and damage become somehow fused and resistible. The rest of us stagger in the dark of our desire like rockets crawling at slower than light speeds through the ridges of space. All of what we do is controlled by our ignorance; in the flickering instants of Lady Louisiana Toy's image we may feel that something different is possible, but it is not possible and that understanding bounds everything we do.

Had the Possessors had the true wherewithal or means which they threatened, had they, too, not been bound to the sublight speeds of the stokers, none of this would have happened, they would have been invulnerable. But their vulnerability was sealed by the fact that telepathy was not a universal gift, they had to proceed in the language of their inferiors or not function at all. Had the case been different, the likes of the hapless Stan Montana would never have been engaged. He would not have lived to function. But the Possessors. were trapped in the glue of their constancy, the very ether itself contained them.

Ultimately it was not their age after all. It was the age of Stan Montana.

For Montana lived, even at this sprawling and unspeakable time, at the margins of all possibility. Ungifted by an interior, deprived of coherent or reasonable thought, he scuffed into his clothing, made his arrangements with prostitutes, heaved and unloaded his discharge of semen or necessity, collaborated with any who would hire him, engaged on the most dubious and slimiest of deeds which at this or any time at all still comprises the text and sorrow of life. In the twenty-ninth century (where this does not take place) or the thirty-fifth, in the ninth or the unspeakable billionth millennium, the business with which Montana was engaged will go on. One will find him here and there, at this or any other point of the past, pounding his fist against tables, ordering his feet to move even when they would die on him, bribing the ships' porters or space jockeys in the holes of the rapt Beltegeuse system to yield small bits of information on adulterous pursuit. His whine of release maybe heard in the dives or alleyways of the millionth planet, his plans and formulations scrambled like Kilroy's upon walls so distant that we cannot imagine them.

For this, then: Stan Montana and no one else, not even the Lady herself, must be seen as the abcissa upon which the stars themselves turn, he is at the center of our condition now and forevermore, and it must be admitted that he was as stunned and distracted by the news of the Lady's abduction as any of us. Perhaps he was more shaken because in ways that he, too, could not have known he had secretly loved her, dreamed, of her body, confessed to her image, kept her holograph along with the ever ready but certainly unconscious primal scene close to him in the dark and inelegant pause of his nights. If Stan Montana did not then love Louisiana Toy, he came as close to that as any simulacrum of "love" could be known in the spaceyards and boneyards of this disastrous age which we are forced to remember as the last time when it was possible to come together through the transceiver, to find a kind of community, to understand anything. They had selected Stanley Montana to seek the Possessors and recover Louisiana Toy because, they said ("they" involving the massed governments and corporate entities of that time who interpreted the kidnapping as the most audacious infliction yet upon their perilous way of life, and so they were able for the duration of this crisis to work together in a kind of unity) he lacked subtlety, lacked understanding of any kind, lacked — as we have been pointing out from the earliest part of this recollection — any significant interior life. He obviously knew nothing and therefore he had a chance with the Posessors which heavier and more sophisticated help — with genuine technological knowledge. With something approxitimating an interior monologue — could not have possessed.

"You are stupid enough not to know that you must fail," was the way they explained matters to Stanley Montana when they put her holograph and last known whereabouts in his hands and sent him spinning clumsily on his journey to seek the Lady and somehow return her. "You have absolutely no conception of what is against you therefore you may succeed." is what they said and this was probably far more than was necessary, but they gave him this much at least as he was sent out. With him rode the fate of suns for Louisiana Toy, as the Possessors knew and those who defended her interest, were responsible for her condition, was at the secret heart of all purpose, she was no metaphor but a constancy; It was this constancy which granted her the power she held.

Her body was the primal vault of the galaxies themselves, at least as they had been rearranged, in her ovaries she carried the imploded hearts of suns and other galactic debris which need not be further evaluated in this context. A universal figure, a truly generating force, a metaphor gone so lucidly explosive that she had beep forced to become an entertainer simply as a means of controlling her visibility, if she was on the transceivers they knew at least where she was and could track her movement at all times. Of the dangers, the climactic risks, the sheer lunacy of allowing the Galactic Riddle to become a holograph for the billions we need not speak, it is of course this lunacy itself which gave the age its divination and truest madness and not to apprehend this is to miss the point; further explication is not necessary. They owed Montana no part of the truth and did not give it to him. What difference would the truth have made? By the same reasoning, the truth is a part of this narrative only when it is of a momentary sufficiency, it must be left to other sources to explain how the galactic riddle had been placed into such a position. Of the reckoning and madness of that age we can ourselves make no judgdment.

"Go, then, and find her," they said to Stanley Montana. "Recover her, find her for us, bridge the gate of telepaths, and return the Lady Louisiana Toy to the hearts of those now bereaved." They added little to this essential imprecation and sent him away, promising rich compensation but only if he were successful and giving proper impetus in the form of the holograph and the promise they whispered to him in parting, he promise that they knew would work if anything would.

"For you may have her," they whispered. "She can be yours at last. Find her, shield your thoughts and purpose from the Possessors who would otherwise apprehend them. Find where she has been hidden, bring her back to us and we will put her in a room with you. There you may close the door and you may enact upop her — shall we say this, do we dare? — anything you wish. Anything of your description, anything you can imagine, that and more and we will help you. She is love, she is loving, she is the one who has always been in search of a handsome operative like you. She lusts for your need even as you and a billion others have prayed to her."

What is there to say? What is there to be made of such mischief as this? They lied to him, of course, but they lied no less than that which had beep the modicum of social and sexual intercourse for all of the indefinable history and in the stacks of deceit from which had beep tossed the sprawling galaxies, the quarks and their boneyards, how awful is their lie! Looking at the tablelands we have found now, is this the worst of all the evils which life has perpetrated upon life? It was at least for a good purpose. Purpose was all. Sincerity was a counterfeit, simply a position. And this Stanley Montana himself must have known for he had whispered to himself that confidence in all of the silent places as he had plodded his way through the small interstices of his tiny necessities. "Mean streets, mean doings," he had confided to himself. "Someone must always solve a murder; unearth the truth, find the wrongdoer, relieve the damaged, give comfort to the sick. Just as an army must always search, destroy, and occupy, so a man must take on the burdens of his time.

"I am good I am good," Stanley Montana would praise himself in those last chants before sleep, "I am of a necessity I am here to save, I act bad but I do good." Of this and so many other small deceptions we must be accepting then, seek complaisance; he suffered for us after all, Stanley Montana lived and died — multiplied by the millions! — for those of us who have, however, equivocally survived and if there are no explanations for this — well, then, there are no possibilities as well. One must equate one must show mercy in order to gain advantage or so at least has been another of the difficult lessons which (forever unlearned by the rest of us) have been the contemptible and limited total of all the burnt suns, all the progression of disaster and pain up to the time of these events. Or beyond.

But this, too, begins to edge into the theology of the Possessors, a race whose telepathy had created as one could imagine a complex teleological basis not really to be equated with our own numbed worship of disbelief ... their group purposes, intense gestalt, cynicism and retrieval does not really fit into this chronicle any more than Stanley Montana's halting and stumbling efforts to find them. We must

— like the Possessors, but With a different ascription to the word "faith" — take all of those deductive efforts of Montana with a kind of faith. He plodded and plotted (not through thought, through tropism as we must often be reminded) through the corridors of the dark and hidden passageways between the stars to find the Lady Louisiana Toy. And this, the nature of this quest must be seen as the evil and secret genius of those who had assigned him (in despair, of course, but With a kind of cunning) to the task: his thoughts his ploddings and tropistic scuttle could not be read by the assiduous Possessors, eager as they might have been to understand him because Stan Montana had no thoughts. His processes could not be deduced because there were none, there was only that small core of purpose, the low, flickering flame of his desire to get behind the door and read the faces, this codified by dim possession. On and on he prowled, doing the best he could, doing what he must as the stars curled in their traces and the Possessors cackled with the slow realization of their desire, demanding ransom then and performing unspeakable acts which like so much else need not be summarized here.

No, of the nature of the Lady's captivity of those acts performed upon and inside her during that terrible period of her captivity, we will not speak. Such a report would only be distressing to Stanley Montana, his residue and descendants (we are all, of course, his descendants) and would play little role in what is, for all of its tortuous rhetoric and sly inference, quite a simple recapitulation. It is a recapitulation as simple as Stan Montana himself, because we are not dealing with complex figures here, we are doing with a man of no interior life, a lady who was an icon and a telepathic net but whose own interior had been gutted from her so that the wires could be placed and she could become a vehicle for the necessity of others. Understand that long before the Possessors had taken their toll there were others who had touched the child Louisiana Toy and played with her, jiggled her insides and known her outside, filled all of her tender and vulnerable being with disgusting thoughts, human and panicky needs, hints of desolation, desolate and lasting purposes: she was assigned early to her task of enacting for all of the galaxies what they most wanted. Pictures were drawn inside and outside her heart and on the walls of her cell, she had been in a cell long before the Possessors then and the effect of her imprisonment was most equivocal. She had seen it all before.

Still there was that need for her to be shown, for the demonstration to be made. From time to time then the Possessors would take Louisiana Toy to the arena they had constructed for just this purpose and there she was compelled before, a stunned audience of several billion, all that they could summon to this greatest of all links, to reenact aspects of her life and anticipated death for their edification and amusement. She was not an actress, what she did was something far beyond acting and in the sands cast before her Louisiana Toy did what they wanted, knowing that she was giving back to them what from the first had always been in the contract. She bad never expected any different. If Stan Montana had expected everything, the Lady had — by charm and essence his doubled opposite — expected nothing at all. So she went through what she must and it is generally conceded by those who witnessed the events and made transcription at that time that these were indeed the greatest, the most memorable and shocking of all her performances.

The ransom demands were of course subordinate. Did the Possessors ever expect them to be met? One must doubt this, all of it was posturing, an excuse for the abuse and the inch by inch shrieking extraction of Louisiana Toy's memory. Worlds were demanded, then more worlds, then the flaming captive hearts of undiscovered stars which yet more worlds insidiously circled, then at last in an act of sheer audacious loathing the Possessors demanded the great Troast Lock itself with its billion suns; flaming passions, untold worlds of slavery and treasure. They demanded not only the Lock but the complete submission of all who were to be heaped up in the heat of the stars as untainted treasure. It was impossible. From the very start now, it was clear, the Possessors had never had any intention but the final evisceration of Louisiana Toy and the rupturing of her link. How it had taken so long to ascertain their purposes was not known, but now there could be no doubt.

The disciples and creators of Louisiana Toy; her lovers, those who had not known her at all but themselves had somehow been touched, all of them, the totality of witness in the billions was left with nothing to say nothing to be done. Grasping at last the full audacity and cruelty of the Possessors, they had been shocked beyond response, moved beyond edification. Had they been telepathic in the fullest sense — but only the Possessors and their captive and a few sterile mutants in this narrative were, that must be understood, what we encompass here are the trillions of dumb, enclosed minds excluded from the cold Circle of communion — had they been telepathic then, they would have been struck insensate,cleaved from their very powers. The hopelessness was that absolute, the devastating intention of the Possessors that clear. But in the absence of telepathy, knowing only empathy then and witness to the sufferings of Louisiana Toy, those that could weep did so … and the others — but what is there to be said of the others? There are always such. At the moment of Crucifixion, the horse and rider carry on, sail out of the clear frame of the picture in the Beaux Arts Museums of our souls.

Stan Montana plodded on.

He plodded on, that is all. That is what the Montanas do. In the junkshops and the small arenas, in medieval or real time, they go on and on. Their living is a kind of dying to us, but what do they know? They do not grasp any of this. They think little of themselves less of their needs or destination, do not after a while even consider those who hire them, they know nothing either of that tropism which unfurls them like pennants wearily in the night. They pay that tropism as little regard as primal Mommy and Daddy did to the watcher beyond the window. In his insensibility, say it and be done, Stanley Montana was unconquerable. That is the burning heart of this chronicle. One cannot destroy that which was never born or (choose your vision of demolition) that which has been hammered to silt. How does one vanquish a nullity? This is a mathematical conundrum to puzzle Xeno. Like Caliban, another refugee who had learned speech and the only good of it to curse, Montana went here and there, flagged spaceships, curled into the engine rooms with the press gangs, knew captains and kings and the lower spaces, went around and about in the eternities of Louisiana Toy's imprisonment, plodded through and around and beyond purpose and at last — through means which we will elide the question of exposition — confronted the Possessors in that small jeweled cave at the furthest point of the finite, that cave which they had taken to be utterly secret, unapproachable.

How did he do it? How did he *not* do it? That is the essential mystery … for he had moved beyond paradox to that point where nullity and confrontation were the same. Some of this has to do with the curvature of space but more with the wretched anchorage of the heart.

Inside his garments, the holograph twinkled, then made sullen noises as Stan Montana entered the cave and confronted the astonished Possessors. Amazed, they leaped toward their weapons, but they were unprepared for consciousness and quickly they were cut down by the conventional weaponry of Stanley Montana, devoid of incantation or cleverness. They were, ultimately, that vulnerable. They fell away and Stanley Montana moved beyond their fallen bodies, looked behind the stones to see the lady herself waiting. She had been crouched there, apprehending it all, broadcasting this (as she had broadcast everything, the flickering transceivers picking up this astonishing moment. Oh, they had been hard with her.

The Possessors had been hard with Louisiana Toy but no harder than she with herself, trapped by remorse, blocked in her own passageway. She had laid down her lovely life and spirit again and again until at last that spirit, broken, had seemed to rush from her in a dying exhalation. But as Stan Montana could now see, that was only part of her spirit, the rest had remained, clinging to the walls of what looked at him in that cave and it was this spirit, now rebounding to her flesh, which seized Lady Louisiana Toy with awful force and turned her on Stan Montana, then past him to the Possessors who keyed to the awful confrontation in the cave had gathered, those that remained around and about her.

Now! she said, now! Her thoughts were projected as speech, speech had become codified only to a great desire and at last, come to some consciousness in this space Stanley Montana heard it. "Now!" he shouted, carrying forward, "now it is our time, our turn!" and the clumsy weapon which he had carried through all the passageways of his great and storming quest was in his hand, it was a revolver, and he fired this antique weapon — a point ninety-eight if you will, a Dramatii welded from the backs of the beasts of the Drunk Worlds — just as his predecessors in myths too old to be available to him had fired. The Dramatii trembled and flayed him and the stunned Possessors collapsed, all of them fell there in the view of the transceivers and the transmitting Louisiana Toy.

They collapsed, too sophisticated and smart by far to be able to deal with that which had no interior at all, too smart to know that dumb is the only way to get through the universe, they fell and fell and Stan Montana tossed the weapon high and away. Lady Louisiana Toy was upon him then, clung to Stan Montana tightly and because of her great gift, a gift which makes possible the emergence of this chronicle at the same time that it doomed the chronicle and all who witnessed it to the ages of descent which so quickly followed — the brief and flickering moments between them were opened to all of the tearful galaxies who had watched through all the millennia for the supraprojectivity of a moment like this. Cries like the origin of all cries came from Louisiana Toy, sounds came from Stan Montana which the detective could neither describe nor locate, and then the two of them held one another in terrible and clinging embrace under the merciless attention of the billion suns. "Oh. yes," Louisiana Toy murmured, "I knew that I would be spared, I knew that you would come, I waited and waited, but I always knew that you would be here."

"*Madre*," said Stanley Montana. "*Madre de Dios. Maman. Ah Pieta.*" The dead Possessors around them, the acres of the dead oozing and blinking in their appalled truncation caught them with blood, welded them ever tighter With the gouts of their extinguishing. "*Ala, Madre,*" Stanely Montana said. "Mommy." He held her then, ever more tightly, uncaring of the celestial breakup which then began.

The celestial breakup began. The collapse began. The implosion commenced at that moment. The slow and long-awaited dismantling of time and space previously intimated in so many sources but only known at this moment began … but of this we are not entitled to speak, not in these chronicles which are limited to the hard and crucial joining amplified through the billions of transceivers. "*Madre,*" Stanley Montana said. He grafted himself upon the lady. "*Ah, Maman.*"

Thus was the mystery Solved.

Thus was the spirit of our strange and tentative quest, the arc of our passage so tenderly and terrifically revealed. Of the implosion which followed and followed and followed and whose seizures are with us yet we need neither write nor speak, broadcast nor think. It goes on. It goes on and on. Louisiana Toy and Stanley Montana, drifting through the rings of that inferno, clasped to one another now and for the ages to come, drifting, and falling, falling like a dead body falls. Thus, then, the tale of the capture and the salvation of the Lady Louisiana Toy, the ascension of Stanley Montana, and the fate of all the suns. There is less on the record. There is little left on the record. The record is still being compiled. The time and the constancy are yet unrevealed; wait and watch as to morning, to morning.

Here, Paolo. There Francesca. Everywhere the ninth circle of light.

ACKNOWLEDGMENTS

"A Galaxy Called Rome," *The Magazine of Fantasy & Science Fiction*; July, 1975

"Agony Column," *Ellery Queen's Mystery Magazine*; December, 1971

"Final War," *The Magazine of Fantasy & Science Fiction*; April, 1968

"The Wooden Grenade," as "The Sense of the Fire" in *Escapade*; July, 1967

"Anderson," *Amazing Science Fiction Stories;* June, 1982

"As Between Generations," *Fantastic*; October, 1970

"Death to the Keeper," *The Magazine of Fantasy & Science Fiction*; August, 1968

"State of the Art," *Dimensions IV*, ed. Robert Silverberg, 1974

"The Only Thing You Learn," *Universe 3*, eds. Silverberg & Karen Haber, Bantam, 1992

"Leviticus: In the Ark," *Epoch*, ed. Robert Silverberg & Roger Elwood, Berkley, 1975

"Police Actions," *Full Spectrum 3*, eds. Aronica/Mitchell/McCarthy, Bantam, 1991

"Report to Headquarters," *New Dimensions V*, ed. Robert Silverberg, Doubleday, 1975

"The Shores of Suitability," *Omni*; June 1982

"Hop Skip Jump," *Omni*; November, 1988

"To Mark the Times We Had," *Omni*; April, 1984

"What I Did to Blunt the Alien Invasion," *Omni*; April, 1991

"Shiva," *Science Fiction Age*, May, 1999

"Rocket City," *Isaac Asimov's Science Fiction Magazine;* September, 1982

"Tap-Dancing Down the Highways and Byways of Life, etc.," *The Magazine of Fantasy & Science Fiction*; July, 1986

"Coursing," *Isaac Asimov's Science Fiction Magazine;* June, 1982

"Blair House," *The Magazine of Fantasy & Science Fiction*; March, 1982

"Quartermain," *Isaac Asimov's Science Fiction Magazine;* January, 1985

"Playback," *Universe 1*, eds. Robert Silverberg & Karen Haber, Doubleday, 1990

"Corridors," *Engines of the Night*, Doubleday, 1982

"Icons," *Omni*; March, 1981

"Something from the Seventies," *The Magazine of Fantasy & Science Fiction*; April, 1993

"Le Croix," *Their Immortal Hearts*, ed. Bruce McAllister, West Coast Poetry Review 1980

"The Men's Support Group," *Polyphony 3*, Wheatland Press, 2003

"Out from Ganymede," *New Dimensions II*, ed. Robert Silverberg, Doubleday, 1972

"Kingfish," *Alternate Presidents*, ed. Mike Resnick, Tor, 1992

"Morning Light," *Cold Shocks*, ed. Tim Sullivan, Avon, 1991

"The Men Inside," *New Dimensions II*, ed. Robert Silverberg, Doubleday, 1972

"Standing Orders," *Journeys to the Twilight Zone*, ed. Carol Serling, DAW, 1993

"Most Politely, Most Politely," *Universe 2*, eds. Silverberg & Karen Haber, Bantam, 1991

"Moishe in Excelsis," *Deals with the Devil*, eds. Resnick/ Estleman/Greenberg, DAW, 1994

"Heliotrope Bouquet Murder Case," *Nonstop Science Fiction Magazine*; vol. 1, #3, 1997

"Lady Louisiana Toy," *More Whatdunits*, ed. Mike Resnick, DAW, 1993

OTHER BOOKS FROM NONSTOP PRESS

Lord of Darkness by Robert Silverberg
Trade paper $17.95 (ISBN: 978-1-933065-43-4; *ebook available*)

"... gripping and compulsively readable." — George R.R. Martin

SET in the 17th century and based on a true-life historical figure, this novel is a tale of exotic lands, romance, and hair-raising adventures. Andrew Battell is a buccaneer on a British ship when he is taken prisoner by Portuguese pirates. Injured and ailing, Andrew is brought to the west coast of Africa where his only solace is Dona Teresa, a young woman who nurses him back to health. Andrew's sole hope to return home is to first serve his Portuguese masters, but it is a hope that dwindles as he is pulled further and further into the interior of the continent, into the land of the Jaqqa — the region's most fierce and feared cannibal tribe — overseen by the powerful Lord of Darkness. This story demonstrates the timelessness of any great adventure and the determination to persevere at any cost.

Meeting the Dog Girls, stories by Gay Partington Terry
Trade paper $14.95 (ISBN 978-1933065-20-5; *ebook available*)

"... nonpareil fantastika that will stay with you for a long time."
— *Asimov's Science Fiction Magazine*

A THIEF, languishing in prison for stealing moments, escapes and becomes a chronometric fugitive. Women wait in a long, endless line, night and day, without knowing what is at the beginning of the line. An otherworldly marble called the Ustek Cloudy passes through the hands of Ambrose Bierce, Amelia Earhart, and D. B. Cooper just before they each disappear off the face of the earth. Whether they are called fantasy, magical realism, science fiction, or brilliant parodies, the stories in this collection—the first from Gay Terry—blend the real and the fantastic in an imaginative and mischievous way. Written in the tradition of Ray Bradbury, Angela Carter, and Neil Gaiman, these contemporary fables present remarkable characters trapped in unusual situations.

The Collected Stories of Carol Emshwiller Vol. 1
$29.95 Hardcover (ISBN: 978-1-933065-22-9; *ebook available*)

"... offers not only hours of pleasure through its dozens of wonderful, magical stories, but also the rare joy of seeing a master's work develop over decades."
— *Strange Horizons*

A MASSIVE NEW COLLECTION of 88 stories. Carol Emshwiller's fiction cuts a straight path through the landscape of American literary genres: mystery, speculative fiction, magic realism, western, slipstream, fantasy and of course science fiction. Arranged chronologically, this landmark collection, the first of two volumes, allows the reader to see Emshwiller's development as a writer and easily recognize her as a major voice in the literary landscape.

Musings and Meditations: Essays and Thoughts by Robert Silverberg
Trade paper $18.95 (ISBN: 978-1-933065-20-5; *ebook available*)

"This delightful collection reflects Silverberg's wide-ranging interests, wit, and mastery of the craft." — *Publishers Weekly* (Starred Review)

A NEW COLLECTION of essays from one of contemporary science fiction's most imaginative and acclaimed wordsmiths shows that Robert Silverberg's nonfiction is as witty and original as his fiction. No cultural icon escapes his scrutiny, including fellow writers such as Robert Heinlein, Arthur C. Clarke, H. P. Lovecraft, and Isaac Asimov.

Why New Yorkers Smoke edited by Luis Ortiz

Trade paper $14.95 (ISBN: 978-1-933065-24-3; *ebook available*)

SUBTITLED; *New Yorkers Have Many Things to Fear: Real and Imagined.* This collection of original stories answers the question "What is there to fear in New York City?," with fiction from Paul di Filippo, Scott Edelman, Carol Emshwiller, Lawrence Greenberg, Gay Partington Terry, Don Webb, and Barry Malzberg, among others. The contributors represent a combination of New Yorkers, ex-New Yorkers, and wannabe New Yorkers, and their tales of fear all use New York City as an ominous backdrop. Blending the genres of fantasy, science fiction, and horror, the stories in this anthology showcase work from up-and-coming writers as well as veterans of fantastical fiction.

Steampunk Prime: A Vintage Steampunk Reader
Edited by Mike Ashley, with a foreword by Paul di Filippo, illustrated by Luis Ortiz.

Trade paper $15.95 (ISBN 978-1933065182; *ebook available*)

"These tales have the pulpy goodness steampunk fans adore...."
— *Publishers Weekly*

"Within this collection, readers will find romance, mystery, adventure, and, of course, the iconic steampunk airship." — *School Library Journal*

Science Fiction: The 101 Best Novels —1985-2010
by Damien Broderick and Paul Di Filippo.

Trade paper $14.99 (ISBN: 978-1-933065-39-7; *ebook available*)

"If you want to know the essential science-fiction books to read that were published in the last 25 years, this is your go-to guide." — *Kirkus*

INSPIRED by David Pringle's landmark volume, SCIENCE FICTION: THE 100 BEST NOVELS, which appeared in 1985, this volume will supplement the earlier selection with the authors' choice of the best SF novels issued in English during the past quarter-century. David Pringle provides a foreword.

The Nonstop Book of Fantastika Tattoo Designs

Trade paper $14.95 (ISBN: 978-1-933065-26-7; *ebook available*)

Edited by K.J. Cypret, with over 180 fantastic tattoo flash design inspirations. Artists include: Hannes Bok, Ed Emshwiller, Lee Brown Coye, Virgil Finlay, Jack Gaughan, Harry Clarke and other esteemed artists of 20th century fantastika.

. . . .

Nonstop Library of American Artists

Vol. 1: Arts Unknown: The Life & Art of Lee Brown Coye by Luis Ortiz; $39.95
Hardcover (ISBN: 978-1-933065-04-4) *Fully illustrated, color.*

"A must for lovers of the weird and fantastic." — *Publishers Weekly*

"A smashingly beautiful book ... reading this fine biography is like riding a train through the history of three-quarters of the 20th century, and seeing Coye's monsters through every window." — *Asimov's Science Fiction Magazine*

Vol. 2: Emshwiller: Infinity x Two
The Art & Life of Ed & Carol Emshwiller by Luis Ortiz; Hardcover, $39.95
(ISBN: 978-1-933065-08-3) *Fully illustrated, color*
A Hugo Award nominee and Locus Award finalist.

"... fascinating .... a must have for anyone interested in SF art, writing, and history."
— *LOCUS*

Vol. 3: Outermost: The Art + Life of Jack Gaughan by Luis Ortiz; $39.95 hardcover
(ISBN: 978-1-933065-16-8) *Fully illustrated, color*

FANTASTIC IMAGERY, explosive color, and occasionally creepy creations merge together in this elaborate collection of the work of genius artist, Jack Gaughan. Extremely prolific and popular from the 1960s through the 1980s, Gaughan is showcased in this chronicle that is the first to detail the art and life of this master of the science fiction and fantasy genre. Overflowing with samples of work from the artist's personal archives and exploring examples of his working method, this definitive guide provides an inside look into this four time Hugo Award winner.

. . . .

Cult Magazines: From A to Z, A Compendium of Culturally Obsessive & Curiously Expressive Publications
Edited by Earl Kemp & Luis Ortiz

"Contains a wealth of arcane information about many of the oddball magazines that once graced newsstands." — *New York Times Book Review*

Oversized trade paper, $34.95 (ISBN: 978-1-933065-14-4)

Featuring full-color reproductions of hundreds of distinctive cult magazine cover images, backgrounds, histories, and essays that offer a complete picture of a bygone era.
Fully illustrated in color.

Other Spaces, Other Times: A Life Spent in the Future
by Robert Silverberg; $29.95 Hardcover (ISBN: 978-1-933065-12-0)

"For all [science fiction] devotees and novelists in training who relished Stephen King's similarly autobiographical *On Writing*." — LibraryJournal.com

Capturing a behind-the-scenes glimpse into the world of science fiction, this unique autobiography by Robert Silverberg shows how famous stories in this genre were conceived and written. Chronicling his career as one of the most important American science fiction writers of the 20th century, this account reveals how he rose to prominence as the pulp era was ending—and the genre was beginning to take on a more sophisticated tone—to eventually be named a Grand Master by the Science Fiction Writers of America. Stating that this will be his only autobiographical work, Silverberg's book includes rare photos, ephemera from his own archives, and a complete bibliography of his science fiction, from novels and short story collections to nonfiction. *Fully illustrated, with color sections.*

The Monkey's Other Paw Edited by Luis Ortiz (available October 31, 2013)

ALL NEW, subtitled "Revived Classic Stories of Dread and the Dead". This anthology presents sequels, prequels, retellings, homages, and alternate POV takes on classic terror tales re-imagined by some of the best writers of horror, fantasy, and sci-fi working today including: Steve Rasnic Tem, Don Webb, Paul Di Filippo, Barry Malzberg, Damien Broderick, Alegría Luna Luz, and Artist Martos' graphic story showing what became of the Dorian Gray painting after the death of its subject.

BARRY N. MALZBERG is the author of more than 50 books and more than 250 short stories, won the first John W. Campbell Memorial Award for the Year's Best Science Fiction, two Locus Awards, and has been a nominee for both Hugo and Nebula Awards. He was born in Brooklyn and now lives across the Hudson River in Teaneck, New Jersey.

JOSEPH WRZOS, a retired educator, now a freelance writer/editor, has edited both *Amazing Stories* and *Fantastic* (in the 1960s); *The Best of Amazing* (Doubleday & Co., 1967); completed August Derleth's SF anthology, *New Horizons* (Arkham House, 1998); edited *In Lovecraft's Shadow : The Cthulhu Mythos Stories of August Derleth* (Mycroft & Moran, 1998); co-edited (with Peter Ruber) *Night Creatures*, a collection of Seabury Quinn's horror fiction (Ash-Tree Press, 2003); and, most recently, has edited *Hannes Bok : A Life in Illustration*, a sumptuous art volume issued by Centipede Press in 2012. Currently, he divides his leisure hours copy-editing for both Sanctum Books and Centipede Press.